the curse of crow hollow

BILLY COFFEY

THOMAS NELSON
Since 1798

NASHVILLE   MEXICO CITY   RIO DE JANEIRO

Published in Nashville, Tennessee, by Thomas Nelson. Thomas Nelson is a registered trademark of HarperCollins Christian Publishing, Inc.

Published in association with Books & Such Literary Management, 52 Mission Circle, Suite 122, PMB 170, Santa Rosa, California, 95409-5370, www. booksandsuch.com.

Thomas Nelson titles may be purchased in bulk for educational, business, fund-raising, or sales promotional use. For information, please e-mail SpecialMarkets@ThomasNelson.com.

Scripture quotations are taken from the King James Version.

Publisher's Note: This novel is a work of fiction. Names, characters, places, and incidents are either products of the author's imagination or used fictitiously. All characters are fictional, and any similarity to people living or dead is purely coincidental.

Library of Congress Cataloging-in-Publication Data

Coffey, Billy.
The curse of Crow Hollow / Billy Coffey.
    pages ; cm
ISBN 978-0-7180-2677-6 (softcover)
I. Title.
PS3603.O3165C87 2015
813'.6--dc23
2015006826

For Dad

Thou shalt not suffer a witch to live.

Exodus 22:18

I

Say there, friend!

Come on out that sun and tell me hello. Devilish out, ain't it? Hard to believe only a few months back, me an everybody else's pining for summer. Now here I sit, wishing the leaves'd hurry up and turn. Ain't that just how folk are? They want all but what they got.

Seen you driving up the road all slow, like you went and got yourself turned around. Don't nobody ever come up this way on purpose. Was a time folks would. They'd take these back roads up from Mattingly and Camden every Sunday after filling their souls and bellies, stop here long enough to realize both the Exxon and the grocery was closed for Sabbath. Preacher Ramsay used to call it an abomination to have business on the Lord's Day. He had a tight grip on this town back then, before the Trouble. The Reverend, I'm saying. Lord did, too, I suppose, though after the witch it was unsettled whether He did still. Some said God had gone out of this holler, never to return. Others say even in the blackest dark a light will burn, and there it will gather and build and drive that darkness away. You ask me which it is now, I can't say. All I'll tell you is this ain't no place to be lost in, friend. Not a year ago, but especially not now.

But hang on a minute, that don't mean you got to leave. A body like this one gets tired of seeing the same old faces and hearing the same old things. Be nice, having somebody new to visit with. We got this nice bench, got some shade. Come on and sit awhile, would you? Keep a tired old man company. Let me move my old cane out the way, clear you a spot. Won't nobody bother you so long as you're with me. Sides, ain't many around these days. Guess that makes me town greeter, don't it? All right, then:

Welcome to Crow Holler.

I know it ain't much. Right here where these two clayed roads meet's about the only things left. Got Foster's Grocery down the way a piece; you can see the sun off the front glass. Just opened up again awhile back. Old one, it burned.

Speaking of which, that charred mess on the corner from the church used to be Medric Johnston's funeral home. There's folk here who'd never want a black man to plow their fields or dig their wells, but they never minded old Medric burying their kin. Funeral home's gone now. Medric too, long with that cross the Circle put in his front yard. You can ask Joe Mitchell about that. He runs the Exxon, right down from the grocery there? You go over, though, make sure you mind yourself. Joe ain't been right since his old place got blown to heaven, same night as the grocery.

You see that little blue car over there by the council building? That's our sheriff's car. Man who once owned that? Bucky Vest. Bucky was constable hereabouts before his daughter, Cordelia, and her friends crossed the witch. You'd be hard-pressed to find a soul in the Holler who'd call Bucky nothing but a good man, even if a little simple in the mind. Most of that comes from how he once worked up to the dump. Wasn't nothing pleased him more than getting to work every morning and watching the sun peek up over a big heap of county trash, fire up that dozer, and settle in under the hum of all that machinery. Just him and open sky and the knowing that he'd spend his day moving, digging, and burying, part of his evening shooting rats to keep his gun-handling sharp, then some of the night keeping the Holler safe. You tell me there's a man in the world don't think that's a fine way to spend his days, I'll call you a liar. There's a peace in life that comes when you know your place in it, and that was Bucky Vest.

But then Alvaretta Graves come and the demon come with her, and that's when life in Crow Holler turned. Bucky ain't constable no more. What happened to him is something I'll get to in time. Until then, I'll ask you the question he once asked himself: Would you know evil if you looked it in the eyes? Would you truly?

I don't know how far I should get into things, you being from Away. But listen here, I got to tell somebody. I'm alone now, maybe we all are here, and loneliness is a hell all its own. So you take some pity on me, friend. Sit with me a spell, there's time yet. Here in the mountains, time's all there is. I'll tell you of Alvaretta Graves and the manner of her death, and what she couldn't keep hidden in her little two-room shack up on Campbell's Mountain.

I don't know the whole story, but I know more'n most, and what I don't know I can guess with a good degree of accuracy. That don't mean to say I know where things went so wrong, but I can tell you it all began when Cordelia Vest stole her momma's bracelet. A little thing, you could say. Nothing so different from what any other teenager might get a mind to do. And yet somehow that little thing grew into something so big that it would come to ruin many, even me.

This holler's home to me for as long as I'll have it, and I mean to have it for a good long while. Let the rest scurry away if they want. I tell myself ain't nothing gonna run me off, nosir. I say it every morning when the sun rises over these ridges and I say it again when the cold wind rolls down from the mountains at night, clawing at the windows and wanting me.

I say I won't leave, but I'll tell you this: I'm scared. I ain't got pride enough left to be wounded in saying that. I'm scared, friend. Scared because it ain't over. I thought it was, but it ain't. People ain't never who they say they are, you ever noticed that? You think they're one way and they turn out to be another, and that's what's happened here. And I'll tell you something else that's happening here too:

Something's coming. Something soon.

I can feel it.

I I

Stealing the bracelet. The party.
John David arrives. Like wood over stone.

-1-

Like I told you, that bracelet's where it started.

It was a Saturday, one a those pretty ones in the spring when summer's calling but winter's still refusing to let go, and all Cordelia Vest wanted was to make that day a good one for her friend. Bucky was pulling some golden time at the dump. That suited his wife, Angela Vest, just fine, as she had the whole day off from Foster's Grocery and a week's worth of stories saved on the TV.

Having Bucky gone suited Cordy too. It meant there'd be one less set of eyes to catch her sinning.

Cordy'd spent all that morning and most of the afternoon taking care of the washing and straightening up so her momma could settle down in the La-Z-Boy and lose herself in a world of depravity and betrayal. Soon Angela had the volume up so loud Cordy could hear the cross on the living room wall vibrating against the Sheetrock. Once she got to talking to the people on the screen like they was real, Cordy decided now was the only time.

She stepped out of her bedroom and snuck down the hallway of their little double-wide just as calm as could be, even if I'm sure that girl shook something fierce on the inside. Hearing her mother say *Get outta there, Nikki, you just get your little fanny out of there right now* as she hung a left into her parents' bedroom, feeling her belly as she did, wanting to know what was going on in there. Opening the wood jewelry box that sat by the mirror on the dresser, lifting the blue velvet divider that halved the dull earrings and necklaces that Angela wore most days from the fancier jewelry she liked to keep for special occasions. Angela saying *He's gonna kill her Cordy he's gonna kill Nikki oh Jesus and Mary get out* and Cordy not bothering to reply, because she knew her momma wouldn't hear her anyway. Lifting the diamond bracelet from its place in the box as Angela screamed *No*, slipping it into her pocket as Angela screamed *Stop*. Back down the hallway now, hugging the wall and running a finger along the plain wood molding that hung on by a few rusting nails.

The living room had gone quiet but for the sound of mournful music and the rattle of a Doritos bag. Cordy ducked into her bedroom and eased the door shut, leaned against it until she fell into a position almost like sitting. She brushed her black hair away from her eyes and held her belly like it was fluttering. Then she pushed herself up and walked over to where her phone lay atop the sleeping bag on her bed.

Cordy and her friends, they all had these smartphones with this thing called MeTime (and don't that sound like the perfect name for this younger generation? Sums them up nice, I think). What them kids do is record little movies of themselves on this MeTime, and then somehow it gets sent out in the air for all their friends to ogle over.

Cordy picked up the contraption and hit Record. She dug Angela's bracelet out her pocket and held it to the camera. The diamonds glinted off a shaft of light coming in the window.

"Hey, y'all," she said. "Getting ready to leave. Bringing you a little party favor, Scarlett." And then she smiled and added, "See everybody soon. Maybe."

Outside came the sound of tires over gravel. Cordy scooped

the bracelet back into her pocket and grabbed her phone and sleeping bag. She made it to the living room just as a horn beeped twice from the driveway.

On the big-screen TV that had cost Bucky a whole two months' pay, the dead face of Nikki Whoever-it-was stared out in a look of frozen horror matched only by the one on Angela's face. The fresh bag of Doritos she'd bought special sat half eaten on her wide lap. Yellow crumbs formed a trail from her lips to the lock of black hair she twirled. Was a time there weren't a prettier girl in this whole holler than Angela Vest, but then life got hold of her. Her face had filled in over the years, her skin grown pale and flecked. Once-long fingernails had been reduced to gnawed nubs.

She looked up and said, "She's gone, Cordy. I knew it would happen, I pulled the *Digest* off the rack the other day and read it and I knew it was coming. I just didn't think it'd hurt this much." She shook her head and sniffed. "Where you off to?"

"Scarlett's here," Cordy said. "Her party, remember?"

"Scarlett?" Angela hit Pause on the remote and kicked the footrest down. She stood, showering the carpet with corn chips. "That tonight? I thought maybe you'd sit awhile with me and watch this."

"I would, but it's her birthday and I don't want to be late. We have to be at Harper's Field before everyone else."

"The field?"

"Yes, ma'am."

"For the whole night?"

"Yes, ma'am. Daddy said I could."

Angela's eyebrows shot up the way I expect every momma's always do once their babies get grown, that expression of *Well your daddy's one thing, and I'm another.*

"Hays Foster be there?" she asked.

Outside, the horn beeped again.

"Yes'm, but it's not like we'll be alone. Lots of other people will be there. Everybody, really. Scarlett and Naomi, all the kids from school."

"Won't you stay?" Angela asked. "We could have a girls' night. I don't like you with that boy, Cordelia. I know you don't want me harping on it, but it puts me in an awful situation."

"I'm not with him," Cordy said, even if she couldn't look Angela in the eyes as she said it. Stealing was one thing. Now Cordelia Vest had added another sin to an already lengthy list—bearing false witness to her momma. Which, I don't know, maybe could count as two. You'll trust me when I say the girl had other secrets, ones a whole lot bigger. She bit her lip, probably hoping the pain would stanch the tears that had begun pooling in her eyes. "Please, Momma?"

"Your daddy's gonna want you at church in the morning."

"We'll be there. Promise."

"No drinking?"

"I'm not old enough." Answering, but not really.

Angela's thumb twitched over the Play button on the remote, no doubt torn between what she feared would happen should she let Cordelia go traipsing off with a boy like Hays Foster for the night and how to continue on with that Nikki-sized hole now in her own heart. I do believe Cordelia felt a pang worse than sadness, having to stand there and watch.

Couldn't be easy for a woman like her momma, working five and sometimes six days a week for the man she'd meant to marry, having to deal with the woman he'd married instead, and now knowing the boy the two of them had brought into the world was sweet on her own daughter. Running the register and stocking the shelves, filling in back at the meat department when Tully Wiseman was too drunk to come in. You think about all that, I guess it wasn't a wonder Angela pined so for her soaps.

"Okay," she said. "Since it's Scarlett and her birthday, and since you're promising me there'll be no skin slapping."

"That's gross."

"Promise me."

"I promise," Cordelia told her. "Love you, Momma."

"Love you back. You tell Scarlett me and your daddy wish her well."

They kissed cheeks, Cordelia tilting her hips away as she did, not wanting her momma to feel what she had in her pocket. Angela took her place in the recliner and fumbled with the remote as Cordelia bounded out the door and off the front porch, skirting the beds of rosebushes Angela kept (prize-winners those roses were, blue ribbons eight straight years at the county fair down in Mattingly). She held the sleeping bag tight against her chest. Inside the shiny new Volkswagen revving in the drive, Scarlett Bickford leaned over and pushed the passenger door open. A pale set of hands belonging to Naomi Ramsay reached from the backseat through the window, waving.

And there, friend, is where it all started. Right there in the Vests' drive. I can see Cordy right now with that diamond bracelet in her pocket, those three girls so happy and full of life, blind to the hell just ahead. Even now, I can see them smiling.

-2-

Scarlett Bickford's eighteenth birthday had been at the front of every teenaged mind round here on account of who she was. Every kid whose folks'd let them stay out past nine planned to be at Harper's Field that Saturday night, if only to be able to show up for school Monday morning and say they'd been. I guess that's the sort of fame only possible in a little place like this, where the fastest way to teenaged popularity is to come up with your daddy not only mayor, but pretty much the richest man in town. Had to be the reason everybody thought Scarlett been born of sweet dreams and magic, cause that girl was homely as a barn owl and twice as awkward. And there was that awful thing with Scarlett's arms, too.

She pulled her sleeves tight against the palms of her hands as Cordy flung herself into the brand-new Beetle the mayor had gifted her that same morning. Bright yellow with a black ragtop, looked like a giant bumblebee.

Scarlett threw the car into reverse and flashed a crooked smile as she raced for the road. "You get it?"

Cordy dug in her jeans. She pulled out her fist and opened it soft and careful like a secret, making Scarlett squeal.

"He's gonna love it, I know he is."

"He better," Cordy said. "I did so much sneaking around today, I'm afraid of my own shadow. Momma'll kill me if she decides to go looking." She handed the bracelet to Scarlett, who tucked it into the pocket of her shirt. "Hope that brings you luck."

"I need all the luck I can get. Ain't like I can fall back on my good looks."

"Shut up. That's not so."

Scarlett didn't bother arguing the point, knowing it was true. I believe some part of her suspected Cordy knew it as well. "How much you lie about tonight?"

"Didn't lie at all, if you got to know."

From the backseat came, "Then why you come busting out that door like your trailer's on fire?"

That'd be Naomi Ramsay. Now you may recognize her last name as that of our fair preacher. One of two children by David and Belle Ramsay, the other of which I'll get to soon enough. Naomi was—is—a kind enough girl, nearly as popular as Scarlett and just as pretty as Cordelia. Prettier, if you ask me. She kept her head down to her phone.

"Cordy's got forty-seven shout-outs on her MeTime post. Holy cow. Everybody's gonna be at the field tonight."

Scarlett smiled—just the way she'd planned things.

"What'd you bring?" Cordy asked.

Scarlett pointed behind them to the mound of supplies next to Naomi. "Black skirt, that red sweater you like, so much makeup it'd make a TV preacher's wife break the tenth commandment, and a sleeping bag big enough for two."

"Yeah, well, don't you—"

"Don't worry, got that covered too," Scarlett said. "Hays was good enough to buy some for me a couple days ago. He'll be waiting up there."

Cordy's eyes widened. "He didn't get them from the grocery, did he?"

"Yes, Cordelia, your teenaged boyfriend bought condoms from his daddy's store and got your momma to ring them up. Are you nuts?"

"Can we please stop talking about this?" Naomi said. She held her hands over her ears, feigning embarrassment. "You two realize who you're trying not to talk about and who's in the backseat, right?"

"Sorry," Scarlett said. She chuckled anyway.

Naomi shook her head and rummaged through the clothes Scarlett had brought for the night. "You're gonna freeze in these things," she said.

Scarlett chuckled again. "Doesn't matter. I won't be in them long."

"Stop it!" Naomi was screaming it now, making Scarlett double over, forcing the little car to veer toward the middle of the lane-and-a-half road.

When she got the Beetle back where it needed to be, Scarlett looked at Naomi in the rearview. "Seriously, is he coming?"

"Said he would," Naomi said. "He's just waiting for me to text him so he can sneak y'all's moonshine from Chessie."

"Y'all's?" Cordy asked.

Naomi smirked and studied her phone. "You remember prom? No way I'm drinking that stuff again. Couldn't control myself."

"You could stand to lose a little control," Scarlett said.

Naomi shook her head. "Don't you say that. It scared me. But you better be careful tonight. You know how my brother is now. You can get as dolled up as you want, Scarlett, it might not matter. John David ain't like he was."

"Tonight's the night. I can feel it. I'm a woman now." Scarlett leaned back in the seat and let the wind play with her hair through the window.

Cordy rolled her eyes. "Did Hays get the key?"

"Snuck it from Medric yesterday morning when he was helping get Henrietta Slaybaugh ready for burying. Which is gross, Cordy. I mean, you know that, right? Hays hangs out in Medric's basement more than he does at his daddy's grocery."

"Hays is complicated," Cordy said. "Says it's an honor, caring for the dead."

Scarlet mumbled under her breath, something about hoping Hays washed good before he got all handsy with Cordy that night, else he'd be smelling like Henrietta's dead old body. He might've gotten Scarlett what she hoped she would need that night, but it didn't change the fact she never had liked that boy. "Anyway, he's got the key. Said he'd meet us up there."

"What key?" Naomi asked.

And then silence. Scarlett gripped the steering wheel hard with both hands. She winced like her arms had gotten to itching.

"Hey? I said what key? Hays is up where right now? Y'all tell me what's going on."

Scarlett looked at Cordelia, who said, "You better tell her."

"Tell me what?"

"Party's not at the field," Scarlett said. "We're going to the mines."

That was, so far as I can tell, the only thing Naomi Ramsay could've heard that would make her drop her phone. It fell straight off her lap and thudded on the floor, and she never once reached down to pick it up.

"The *mines*? No way. No *way*, Scarlett. Nobody's supposed to go up there. Did you know about this, Cordelia?"

Cordy only said, "It's her birthday, Naomi."

"You think I'm going to spend my eighteenth with a bunch of underclassmen?" Scarlett asked. "No, thank you. Your brother don't want to hang around a bunch of kids either. We'll be alone up there, have the whole place to ourselves, and all the while everybody else'll be down in Harper's Field wondering what's going on. It'll be epic."

"Daddy'll kill me," Naomi said. "Your daddy'll kill *you*. And I don't even want to guess what Bucky will say, Cordelia. He's the town *constable*."

"Nobody will know," Scarlett said. "We'll go and we'll have fun and we'll be in church tomorrow morning and nobody'll know different. So relax, okay?"

But Naomi couldn't. And Cordy didn't look to be relaxing much either. I don't know what goes through the mind of a young person, friend; they are wholly different creatures from ourselves. It's that peculiar sense of invincibility that blossoms in a heart not yet tested, and an arrogance to believe the world they frolic in has already been tamed. How else can you explain why Scarlett Bickford decided to take her friends to a place as black as any you'll find in this world? Ain't a soul in these parts who don't know the mines at Campbell's Mountain is haunted. They belong to no man and no family. That mountain belongs only to the witch.

-3-

What we in Crow Holler call "the mines" ain't really mines at all. They're more five deep gashes cut out of the bottom of Campbell's Mountain in some forgotten time by some forgotten people for some forgotten reason. Scarlett's daddy based his entire political life on the idea it was his olden kin who first dug those holes, under the orders of President Washington himself, who held there was enough gold hereabouts to fund a new and God-ordained country. Believe that as you will. Others had their own stories.

Cordelia had been raised on her daddy's tales of how it was his people who'd first come to the Holler and found the Indians here using the mines to sacrifice their own to gods of stone and earth. All that come to an end when Cordy's kin showed them savages the love of the Lord by killing them all.

And then a course you had Naomi's version. To this day, Reverend Ramsay will use the mines in his sermons, telling folk they're a doorway to the underworld and how every soul alive is just a breath away from hell. That's the thing about them Christians, ain't it? They see the devil everywhere.

Everybody agrees on one thing though. At some point, an evil inside that mountain got loosed. Whether that's the truth or it was for some other reason, the mines got boarded up and the land around them fenced and gated sometime when Bucky Vest was a mere glimmer in his great-great-granddaddy's eyes. Not a soul lived near Campbell's Mountain for generations until Stu Graves come along in the fifties and claimed seventy acres of rock and trees a few miles east of the fence for farming. Not even Bucky drove up there on his constabling duties to check the padlocks. He didn't much have to. It was the legends that kept everyone away from that place. It was the fear and not the fence.

The sun had sunk behind the ridges by the time Scarlett arrived. Hays had left the gate open. Scarlett drove past big black signs with orange letters that spelled No TRESPASSING and DANGER and WARNING: NO ENTRY UPON PENALTY OF LAW. Cordy made a joke that nobody found funny about how her daddy would have to arrest them all.

Over a hill past the fence sits Number Four, the biggest of the holes in the mountain. Just past there rests a small meadow. That's where Hays Foster had parked his old Camaro, in a space of windless air where a bonfire burned. He kept his mop of black hair hidden under the hood of his sweatshirt and waved.

Scarlett stopped next to Hays's car and put the shifter into Park. None of the three girls moved. The world beyond lay covered in ancient oaks and spruces that sagged, either out of tiredness or the weight of where they'd been cursed to grow. Tangles of briars and weeds littered the area around the meadow, which itself looked more dead than alive.

No part a Crow Holler's ever been what you call picturesque. This town'll never show up on a postcard of the Blue Ridge. But those mines? They look more than ugly. They look . . . I don't know, friend . . . *taken*.

"I don't like this," Naomi said.

Scarlett turned around. "Stop. Please, Naomi? It's my birthday, and we're going to have fun. Okay? You know why we're doing this, right?"

Naomi looked at her phone again, turned it over. "Right," she whispered.

"Naomi? Why are we doing this?"

She couldn't say it, no matter how much Scarlett wanted to hear the words, and so Cordy said it for them both.

"Because there's an end coming," she said. "That's why it's just us tonight, Naomi. Me and you and Scarlett and Hays, because that's the way it's always been. Because graduation's coming and the fun times will be gone, and all that'll be left is to marry and grow old and hard. To be what our parents are now and what our kids will be after, because that's how it is here. Right?"

"Right," Naomi said.

Cordelia opened the door and grabbed her sleeping bag, smiling as Hays stepped away from the fire. He moved toward her and let his hood slip down, revealing a chin sharp enough to cut should you rub up against it. Their embrace was an awkward one, as if the two of them had not practiced it enough. He kissed her cheek. She took his hand.

Scarlett caught only a small glimpse of that meeting, though it looked more than enough to shine a bright light over the lonely place inside her. Well, John David would be there soon.

"Let me out," Naomi said. "I need to get by the fire."

"Don't be mad at me, Naomi. Please?"

"Too late. Let me out."

Scarlett sighed and opened the door, flipping up the seat as she stood from the car. Naomi gathered her own sleeping bag and walked past like Scarlett was a shadow. I can't blame her for acting so. Sure, it was Scarlett's birthday. And sure, she was the most popular girl in town. But that didn't excuse her from dragging her friends all the way up there just so she'd have a chance at Naomi's own brother.

"You'll still text him?" Scarlett asked.

Naomi kept walking, didn't turn around. Through Cordelia's laughter Scarlett heard, "I don't have a choice now. Only way I'm getting through a night up here's drunk out of my mind."

Scarlett reached into the backseat for her things and bundled them all in her arms as Naomi and Cordelia checked in on MeTime to see how many kids had already made it to Harper's Field. Hays had returned to his spot by the fire. Near enough to Cordelia but not *with* her, which pretty well sums up the way they'd always been, except for those five minutes in the back of Hays's Camaro two months before, which Scarlett knew was about to upend his life. Hadn't been a week since Scarlett and Cordy had been locked inside one of the stalls in the school bathroom, both of them kneeling over the toilet, a pregnancy test in Cordelia's trembling hands. Cordelia was crying. Scarlett, having nowhere else to turn, suggested prayer while they waited. And just as He had all the other prayers that ever come out of Crow Holler, the Lord answered with a single word—*Sorry.*

No one but Scarlett knew. Cordelia had promised she'd tell Hays soon, then her parents. If there was any consolation, she said, it was that Angela couldn't really say much. She'd gotten pregnant at seventeen too. Ain't only sins of the father that come to visit in these parts, friend. The sins of the mother will get you just the same.

Scarlett skirted the fire and said, "Hey there, Hays. What's up?"

He shrugged and waved the lighter in his hand. "Made the fire," he said, then tucked the lighter away. A knife lay on the ground beside him, along with a chunk of fallen pine he'd begun to whittle.

"It's a nice one. Really warm. You did great." *Great* meaning Scarlett had nothing else to say.

He pointed to the bundle in her arms. "Where you going?"

"Gotta go change. John David's coming. He's bringing some of Chessie's moonshine."

"Oh, right." He reached into his back pocket and tossed two condoms at Scarlett, who flinched as though they were diseased. She picked them up with her fingertips and hid them among the clothes in her arms. "There's a path back there to the mines," Hays said, and then waved over his shoulder. "Just don't get off it. These woods'll turn you around quick."

"I won't."

Scarlett stood there long enough to be socially acceptable. At the far edge of the fire by the cars, Cordelia and Naomi were making a video. Naomi laughed. That was good. Hays had picked up his knife again, sharpening the hunk of wood in his hand to a point.

"Okay," she said. "Well, I'll be back."

She'd stepped onto the path when Hays said, "Hey, Scarlett? Happy birthday."

"Thanks." Barely meaning it. "I'm glad you could come, Hays." Not meaning it at all.

He shrugged again. "Cordy wanted to. I didn't want her up here by herself. Without me, you know."

"Gotta keep the monsters away, right?"

Hays stopped carving. He turned and looked with a seriousness that melted Scarlett's expression. "That's right exactly."

"Hey," Naomi called. She waved her phone. "He's close."

Scarlett grinned and moved on, leaving Hays with his knife and lighter. She went far enough down the path that he wouldn't be tempted to sneak a peek. She didn't think he would. Hays had Cordelia, after all. Once you seen a body like that, you wouldn't care to see another.

Night pressed against her like cold fingers. She rushed as much as she could, pushing off her shoes and letting her jeans fall, snugging her plump thighs and wide hips—hips her momma had once said would someday be good for bearing grandchildren—into that tight little skirt. Even alone, she did not tarry in changing her shirt. Angela's bracelet went on atop the sleeve of her sweater, and then Scarlett felt a shudder when she heard the grumbling engine coming up the hill because that meant he was there, *John David* was there, and I'd wager that thought brought all manner of others to her mind. John David and that look of faraway places in his eyes; those tattoos on his chest and forearms, eagles and globes and anchors and the strange straight lines everybody talked about; the buzz cut he'd kept even though he'd been back in the Holler a good three months by then.

John David had left three years ago for war, against the Reverend's wishes, only to return hard and distant. People said he'd killed too many heathens and lost his way. That was the only reason they could think to explain why he'd spurned his family and taken up with Chessie and Briar Hodge, running their moonshine and dope. True or not, I don't know. But you better believe all that only added to Scarlett's infatuation. John David hurt. John David had suffered. And so John David might understand if he saw Scarlett's arms.

There'd been that Saturday night a few weeks before. Hays had thrown a party at Harper's Field and everybody had been there, and John David had spent most of that night drinking Chessie's moonshine and acting like he was blind and Scarlett was made out of Braille. The young being as they are, Scarlett had blown the whole thing into something akin to a marriage proposal. Cordelia had tried talking down her expectations. Even Naomi did, telling Scarlett the war had taken something from her brother that wasn't coming back. But all that convincing did nothing to halt Scarlett's pining neither then nor now, there at the edge of the mountain's darkness. She bent for her makeup and did the best she could without being able to see, trying to remember the rough feel of John David's hands and the softness that had been in his voice, asking Scarlett to go slow and stay close because he felt so cold. A drunken mumbling that could have been most anything, but that Scarlett had taken as love.

-4-

Now I doubt John David was thinking of Scarlett at all as he crawled the old Ford truck he'd bought off Briar Hodges up that hill past the gate, but I can near guarantee you this—he wanted to kill his sister. Was bad enough having to hear Naomi begging him for days to sneak some of Chessie's good shine. It was a far worse thing that he got a text saying she wasn't at Harper's Field like she was supposed to be. But this? Friend, this was about the worst that could happen.

He could see the glow on the other side and shook his head, probably thinking that was Hays's doing, that boy was always something of a firebug, and what better way to let everybody within two miles know you're in the one place you ain't supposed to be than build a huge blaze?

"Idiots," he said to the windshield. Nothing but a bunch of idiot kids stuck out here in God's wasteland, no idea what all was going on in the world. His eyes scanned the night to either side of the hill but could go no further than the thick black trees rising like tombstones to an empty sky. He reached for the volume on the radio, turned it down. No telling what might be out there. The way John David gripped the wheel hard with both hands and took a deep breath was enough to tell anybody weren't no monsters he was thinking on just then but how good a spot that side of the hill made for an ambush, and he had to stop doing that because these were different mountains and he was home now, back in the Holler.

His headlights crested the hill and came down on the other side, right where Hays and Scarlett had parked. John

David could see Hays and Cordelia huddled by the fire. Naomi stood farther away. Her feet were together and her hands were clasped in front like she was either cold or excited. She waved. No matter how mad he was, John David waved back.

He parked at an angle to the cars and left the engine running, making a safe perimeter around the fire to the edge of the meadow. Naomi ran and jumped, trusting he'd catch her. She squeezed her brother just as tight as she'd done the day he'd rolled off the back of a farmer's truck in his uniform, shocking everyone at his return because John David had told no one he was coming. Feeling his back and his face, like Naomi still had to convince herself he was really there. She hardly ever got to see her brother anymore. Reverend wouldn't allow it.

"Hey, you," she said.

"Hey, little sis."

She squeezed him harder. "Thanks for coming."

"Didn't have a choice, did I?" John David broke the embrace and held Naomi out at arm's length, looking down at her. "Somebody had to come up here and tell y'all how stupid this is."

He wouldn't leave Naomi there, not exposed in all that open, and so grabbed her hand and guided her to the fire. Stepping slow and light like he'd been taught in basic, trying to see through the wall of brush and rock.

"Hey, John David," Cordy said.

"What are y'all doing up here?" he asked. "You out of your minds? Your daddy catches you, Cordy, he'll skin you alive."

"Nice to see you too, John David," Hays said.

"Shut up. You steal the key to the gate from Medric? This your idea of a good time, bringing Cordy and my sister up here?"

"It wasn't Hays," Naomi said.

But Hays didn't care. He only grinned out from under that hood and pretended to whittle a bit more wood, flashing that Buck knife. "You bring our shine?" he asked.

"Sure, because stealing Chessie's shine and bringing it to a bunch of kids is a brilliant idea."

"It's Scarlett's birthday," Naomi said. "She wanted you to come."

John David looked at her, making his sister drop her eyes. "Only reason I come's to make sure y'all leave. It ain't safe here."

"Hays is here," Cordy said. "Ain't nothing gonna happen, John David."

"Hays?" John David asked, saying it like the name itself was a joke. "Come on, we're leaving."

He tugged at Naomi's hand again. This time she planted herself firm.

"I can't leave. It's Scarlett's *birthday*."

"I said we're leaving. I'm taking you home."

Naomi wrenched herself free and stepped closer to the fire.

Hays laid the block of wood down but kept the knife in his hand. "You think you can take off three years and come back being the big shot you were?"

"I don't want to be anything," John David said. "I just want to be left alone."

"So do we," Naomi said. "Just go on, John David. Or stay, I don't care. But I'm not leaving, and you can't make me."

"I can."

"What are you gonna do, tell Daddy? You'd have to *talk* to him first."

Hays snorted a laugh. Cordy tried to keep peace by telling Naomi that wasn't fair, knowing as well as anybody that people dealt with their own problems in their own ways. It didn't work. John David started yelling at Naomi and Naomi started yelling back, and there was nothing Cordelia could do about it because now another problem presented itself in the form of Scarlett, who must've decided this would be the perfect time to step out of the woods.

You'd have to be a fool not to feel how thick with strain the air around that campfire had grown since Scarlett had left to pretty herself up. And make no mistake, friend—that girl was plain, but she was no fool. She scratched at her arms and stepped into the brightness of the firelight near Naomi, flashing her chubby legs where that tight skirt ended and the curves under that sweater, trying on a smile as she gave a little wave to John David so he could see the sparkle off Angela's bracelet, but John David didn't so much as give her a glance.

"You can't make me leave," Naomi was saying. "You're not Daddy."

"It ain't right, being up here," he said.

"Hi, John David," Scarlett said. She waved again. "Been waiting for you."

Cordelia rolled her eyes, Scarlett trying to be coy and sexy but looking instead like she might as well have a bow on her head and a sign that read CONTENTS PERISHABLE, OPEN IMMEDIATELY hung around her neck.

"It ain't right?" Naomi asked. "You got a nerve telling me what's good and not, John David. When'd you grow a conscience? Chessie teach you?"

John David shot out a finger that ended near the tip of Naomi's nose. "You leave Chessie out of this. You want to call what she does sin, that's fine. But everybody knows it's Chessie's sin, not Daddy's sermons, that keeps the Holler alive."

He turned then, aiming for his truck, and finally saw Scarlett standing right there. He said to Hays, "Keep that fire bright. Somebody's gotta stay up all night, it's gonna be you. Something happens, boy? I'll kill you. And Scarlett, you must be out of your mind to come up in the mountains dressed like that. You're gonna freeze."

Cordy and Naomi lowered their heads. Hays tried swallowing a grin.

John David climbed into the truck and revved the engine, shouting through the window as he grated the gears. "Any of you got the sense God gave a rock, you'd leave right now. I mean it."

"John David," Naomi said, but he didn't hear. Didn't hear, or didn't want to.

Cordelia turned back to the fire, knowing what came next would be to try and talk Scarlett off whatever ledge John David had made her climb out on. But the place where Scarlett had stood was empty, and as the noise of John David's truck faded in the distance, the only sounds left were the fire cracking and Hays asking if anybody had seen where his knife had gone.

-5-

Scarlett didn't care where she ran so long as it was away.

She pushed through the trees and low branches in a darkness so thick it seemed a living thing, driven by the shame of how foolish she must've looked—all fancied up for a man who hadn't even seen her and who'd never be interested in her without half a jar of moonshine in his belly. She ran, beating back limbs that groped for her arms and rocks that snagged her feet, wiping her tears with one hand and clawing at her sweater and skirt with the other, wanting them *off*, and in all that thrashing and crying out, Scarlett never felt the diamond bracelet slip free of her wrist.

When her lungs and legs could take no more, she collapsed upon the path, where she sobbed and wailed at the night. Despair gave way to anger, anger to rage. Scarlett began hurling what bits of the mountain she could grasp. Dirt. Rocks. Twigs. Launching them into the dimness and gloom. Aiming, I suppose, for the picture she had carried in her mind of that party just after John David had returned, his strong arms and slender bones, the memory of him drunk and leaning on her, the way his lips had moved as he'd whispered in her ear.

But that's not near all I expect Scarlett railed at, covered in all that dirt and dust so far from her friends. I been in this world long enough to know how folk are and what they think, friend. That's how I can say that girl raged against what she *was* as well, against her very *name*. She was Mayor Wilson Bickford's Daughter and she was Her Daddy's Child and Her Dead Momma's Little Girl but she had never been merely Scarlett, and she had lived behind those high walls for so long that she believed her true self no longer existed and maybe never had. It is a pitiful thing, ain't it? Wanting so much to love and be loved for *who* you are instead of what. Wanting that so bad you will reach for even the slimmest of hopes, only to draw back a fist of hurt and wrath that you shake at the world.

Her last throw hit upon something hollow. Scarlett swiped at her face and rose to her knees, sobbing as she peered over the faint outline of a wide clump of shrubs to what lay behind it. A tiny yelp, barely heard, fell from her lips as she took in the mouth of Number Four's boarded entrance. I don't think it was the sight of the mountain's maw that frightened that poor girl so. I think what scared little Scarlett most was the knowing of just how far off she'd run, and the peculiar sense that she was no longer alone.

Now sure, Scarlett had no evidence of this. But you ain't ever been to Campbell's Mountain at nighttime, so you'll trust me when I say it's no place to be even in the day. I'm telling you, it's a *presence* there. And Scarlett didn't need to see it. She could feel it.

Behind her came the soft scrape of wood over stone. Quick, like something had stumbled.

Scarlett crept to her feet, never minding the dirt on her

bare knees and the stains on her skirt. She backed away from the stand of pines that hid whatever had made the sound, easing closer to the mine.

"Hello?" she managed.

A rustle.

"John David?"

And then the trees came alive. Branches flew and limbs cracked, a body shooting out from the moonlight. The words "Don't you wish?" piercing the air. Scarlett jumped, nearly falling into the scrub, as Cordelia shot forward and grabbed Scarlett's hands. "Where's it?" Cordy said.

Scarlett tried shrinking back. Cordelia wouldn't let her.

"I'm not kidding, Scarlett. Where *is* it?"

"What?"

"Hays's knife. Give it to me."

"I don't have it."

"Give it to me *now*."

"*I don't have it.*"

Cordy let go long enough to shove the sleeves of Scarlett's sweater up. Scarlett yanked herself away and shook her head no.

"I'm not kidding, Scarlett. You show me your arms, or I swear to God I'm gonna tell your daddy."

Scarlett had backed so close to the mine that she could feel the cold wind whistling through the gaps between the boards, as though the mountain itself was breathing.

"*Show me*," Cordelia said.

There was nowhere she could go, nothing Scarlett could do. She hung her head and, sobbing once more, raised her sleeves an inch at a time. The right first, then the left, revealing the jagged cuts that ran from just below her wrists to her bony elbows. All scarred and scabbed, but bloodless.

Cordelia's glower melted to revulsion and then to a pity

only love could bear. She stepped forward, ignoring Scarlett's flinches, and wrapped her friend in her arms.

"I'm sorry. You ran off. Hays couldn't find his knife. I thought—"

"It's okay," Scarlett said, and I believe it truly was despite her tears. Because the prettiest girl in Crow Holler had come looking for *her*, and I guess that made Scarlett feel . . . I don't know, *seen*. "I heard something in the woods. Just scared me."

"Just me, you big doofus. Traipsing all the way out here to make sure you're not doing something you swore to me you'd stop, all because of some redneck Rambo. Now come on. I don't like being here without Hays, and we have to figure out a way to have fun without any moonshine."

"I'm so sorry," Scarlett said.

"Save it for John David. He's the one's gonna be snoring in a bed all alone tonight."

They laughed then—laughed as much as the mountain allowed—and left hand in hand, working their way back to the bonfire and listening for the sound of something following. Neither heard more than a hoot owl and the wind through the trees.

I'd like to tell you more about Scarlett Bickford's eighteenth birthday, how her and her friends somehow managed to salvage things and have the night they'd all wanted. But I can't do that, friend, because that's not how it went. Cordy and Scarlett come back to find nothing but sullenness on the part of Naomi and Hays—Naomi because she'd managed to carve an even wider gulf between her and her brother, Hays because now there'd be nothing to do but listen to Cordelia until she fell asleep and then stare at the fire all night. He wouldn't sleep, not now. And they all knew the truth—John David had scared him.

Know what it's like, coming up in a town like this? Where everywhere you turn is mountains hemming you in, but you don't care because you know there's no use trying to get away? You grow up thinking the best you'll ever do's slide into a job with Hays's daddy and Cordy's momma down at the grocery, or at the dump like Cordy's daddy, or maybe take up with Chessie and Briar Hodge like John David done. That's all you got to choose from here, less you manage a way to suck off the government teat.

That's the future waiting for all those kids come June graduation. That's why they all wanted to party with some a Chessie Hodge's shine. For one night they could forget their troubles. But now all that hope lay in the half dozen mason jars John David had never brought, and with it went the promise of any fun at all.

Hays found his knife sometime between Scarlett running off and Cordelia running off after her. He sat with Cordy on top of her sleeping bag, flicking open that lighter he always carried, snapping it shut. He wanted to try out one of the condoms he'd bought for Scarlett. Cordy answered with a stiff no. Seemed a fine time for that boy to get all conscientious about what they'd been taught of male and female relations in school, now that it was too late.

Scarlett sat alone. Naomi got lost in her smartphone, letting the others know of the crowd still waiting down in Harper's Field. And in time their silence yielded to memories of the years that had already passed between them and years they hoped would pass between them still, all those long ones on the other side of high school. Naomi laughed. Cordy cried. Scarlett's arms itched. They trailed off one by one that night, even Hays, though he would find the satisfaction that his knife remained tight in his hand as he slept. No one saw what moved about them in the deep woods. No one heard the soft scrape of wood over stone.

III

The tracks. The cabin.
Alvaretta's curse.

-1-

What woke Cordelia the next morning wasn't the cold leaking into her sleeping bag but that the bag felt so empty. Sometime in the night Hays had left her to sleep alone, farther from the fire. He'd made a mat of pine boughs as long as he was tall and was now curled in a ball inside his own sleeping bag, snoring. Naomi poked her head out from her own bag. She fumbled with her phone to check the time.

"We gotta get, Cordy. Church starts in a few hours. Daddy'll kill me."

"Party's not over," Cordy said.

Hays rolled over and rubbed his back, looking up at the brightening sky. "Wasn't no party to begin with."

He struggled out of his bag as Naomi worked out what kinks the night had left in her muscles. Cordelia freed herself from her bed and stood, trying to stretch. She froze with her arms high over her head.

"Where's Scarlett?"

Naomi and Hays stopped what they were doing and looked to the far edge of the campsite. Scarlett's sleeping bag lay empty, her skirt and sweater from the night before strewn to either side. Naomi called out, then Hays and Cordelia. No answer came.

Hays took the knife and told them to stay there, he was

going to look. That's as far as his courage carried him, though. He hollered for Scarlett again and then said to Cordelia, "This was so stupid, coming up here."

A branch snapped close. Cordy flinched and ran to where Hays stood, the knife now shaking in his hand. Naomi's mouth hung open as though she'd forgotten how to breathe as something came walking down the path.

It was only when Scarlett stumbled into the clearing that Naomi seemed to remember again. Scarlett's clothes were a rumpled mess and her blond hair had been pulled back into something close to a ponytail, but that only made what makeup she hadn't cried off look worse.

"Something's happened," she said. "Y'all need to come."

"What happened?" Cordy asked.

Scarlett's voice cracked. "I woke up this morning and it was gone. Must've lost it last night. When I run off."

"What's gone?"

"Your momma's bracelet."

"*What?*" Cordy left Hays where he stood. "You lost Momma's *bracelet?*"

Scarlett fell into a full-on cry then, saying she'd spent since daybreak looking up at the mines and she couldn't find it anywhere and that wasn't even the problem, the bracelet going missing, the problem was something had taken it.

"Stop," Hays said. "What do you mean something took it?"

"Something," Scarlett told him. "Took it."

Naomi grew still. "How do you know that, Scarlett?"

"I'll show you," she said, then turned and disappeared into the trees.

They all went, picking their way through the trees and shadows until they reached the Number Four, which looks just as run-down and possessed in the early day as it does in the late of night. Scarlett led them to a bare spot midway between the mine and the clump of shrubs. She pointed at the ground.

"What is that?" Naomi asked.

No one answered. No one knew.

At their feet lay dozens of tracks shaped in a horseshoe, near the shape of a circle, leading in a straight line from the bushes to the forest beyond. Spaced as wide as Hays was tall, meaning what had left them carried a stride of near six feet. But there's more, friend. It was late April then, but the soil on that mountain was still hard as stone from the long winter. Hadn't been any rain in the Holler for weeks. But whatever had passed through there was heavy enough to press those tracks near an inch into the path. An *inch*.

Hays bent and brushed the hair from his eyes, tracing a finger along the length of one of the prints. He stood again and set his shoe against it. Naomi let out a gasp and covered her mouth, apologizing through her fingers for letting shock get the better of her.

"I'm a twelve," Hays said. "There's what? Another two inches left?" He turned his shoe sideways, gauging the length.

"Eighteen," Cordy guessed. "A foot and a half long and near that wide?" She paused. "I don't know nothing that big."

"Horse, maybe?" Naomi asked.

Hays shook his head. "You know a horse walks on two legs? Cause two's all I see."

Cordelia listened to Hays and Naomi and Scarlett go back and forth about what could've gotten so close to camp in the night, listened as Scarlett said maybe it was nothing and Naomi said John David had been right, they had no business being up there in the first place, but Cordy didn't care about any of that because the only thing that mattered was the bracelet.

She looked at Scarlett. "Momma's bracelet's *gone*, Scarlett.

She's gonna find out, and I need me and her to be good right now." She felt her belly, like she was trying to straighten her shirt.

Scarlett whispered, "I'm so sorry, Cordy."

"It's gotta be here somewhere," Hays said. He looked on, to where the tracks disappeared around a tall oak. "Come on."

"No," Naomi said. "No way. I'm sorry, Cordy, but I'm done. I want to leave. We should all just leave."

Hays swelled his chest. He could do that with somebody like Naomi. Not so much with somebody like John David. "That wasn't a question, Naomi. We stick together. Always have. Right, Scarlett?"

Scarlett nodded.

Hays pulled the Buck knife from his pocket and held it in his hands, just in case. He grinned at Naomi and said, "Don't worry, we'll be at church in plenty of time for Jesus and your daddy to wash our sins. Come on. Time's wasting."

It was just before seven in the morning when those three kids left the Number Four's shadow, aiming for that oak and the wide woods in the distance. By nine, they'd all be running for their lives. Funny how quick things can turn, ain't it?

-2-

I think all but Scarlett expected those tracks to keep right on through the woods a ways, or—and this would be much better— to simply vanish with as much mystery as they'd appeared, leaving the bracelet safe and sound in a soft pile of leaves. But what none a them could've imagined was those prints leaving the ground altogether, walking straight *up* one side of a tree and then straight *down* the other, like whatever'd left them had mocked gravity itself. Chuckle all you want, friend, I'm saying it's true. You go up there right now, get through the gate if you can. See them for yourself.

The trunk was wide enough for Scarlett and Cordelia to wrap their arms around it and still not touch, though neither had a mind to try. Hays fell to silence, trying to believe what his eyes said couldn't be. Naomi's lips moved slow. Her words came out soft, more for herself than any of the others. Cordelia was close enough to hear: "The Lord is my shepherd; I shall not want."

Hays reached out and traced a finger around the edge of the closest horseshoe-shaped hole carved into the wood. When he drew that finger away, it trembled.

"Burned," he said.

Cordy cocked her head. "What?"

"The . . . whatever they are," he said. "They're burned in. See the edges? All charred up."

Cordelia stepped to the other side of the tree. The prints there were upside down, marking a descent that led on into the woods.

"They lead this way," Hays said.

"Wait," Naomi said. "We're keeping *on?*"

Hays didn't answer. I don't think he heard. Out of all them kids, that boy understood that the stories they'd all been raised on about those mines and that mountain *could* be true, that maybe there really *could* be things up there waiting, hungry things that existed only in madness and nightmares. He'd never come out and say it, not to Naomi and Scarlett, not even to Cordelia, but Hays knew of the monsters in this world. He'd seen them.

Those tracks had done something to those kids, something powerful but so small they couldn't yet feel it. How else can you explain why Hays kept right on leading them and why Cordelia and Scarlett kept following, convinced everything was fine really, right as the rain? What other reason could there be that Naomi fell into prayer once more, begging them all to go back even as she herself pushed on?

They walked on in places few had ever trod with only Hays's rusted pocketknife to protect them. They followed when the prints ended at a deep pond hidden in the forest and reappeared on the opposite side, followed as the marks shrunk to disappear into the groundhog hole some distance on, followed still as those tracks emerged from another hole some dozen steps on and grew back to monstrous size. One mile and then two as nary a word passed between them, until they reached a boulder at the edge of a meadow fronting a sloped and barren ridge.

The rock was gray and large, wider than a car and just as tall, with a flattened top that sloped higher on one end. Drawn between patches of moss on the rock's front side was what looked like a slanted eye. Scattered inside the picture was a series of strange patterns: a long, flattened S; an X with hooked ends; crude pictures of hands and animals; a W; a 3. Many more, dozens of them that held no meaning to the kids at all, and all the while that eye was staring out at them.

"Indians," Cordelia guessed. "Daddy says there's stuff like that all over the mountains."

"Can't be," Hays said. "See?" He ran a finger over the W, smearing it on the rock. "It's new. Like somebody just drew it."

And here, whatever enchantment had settled over them fell away. It was different before, when what they followed amounted to little more than some queer footsteps. Now it was something with brain enough to write. And was the message it had left behind for them? Did it know they were following? Was it a warning?

"Please let's go back," Naomi said. "Please, Hays. I'm really scared now."

Hays had his lighter out, flicking the top open and closed, trying to think.

"Something's on that ridge," Scarlett said. She pointed with one hand and shielded her eyes against the sun with the other. "See it? Near the top, against that tree."

It was no monster waiting at the crest of that hill, but a dog, watching from the thin shadow of a dying maple, motionless but for its perking ears and a nose that swept the air. The footprints wound up the slope and over right near there, giving the animal the strange air of a watchman.

"That ain't the only thing up there," Cordy said. "See the smoke on the other side?" It wasn't easy to spot at first, but one by one each of her friends did—a single wisp of white rising up against the blue sky. "Bet you anything that's where it went."

"Then this is where we should turn around," Naomi said. "I'm not kidding, Scarlett. This don't feel right."

Hays would have none of that. "We've come this far."

"Let's just take a look," Scarlett told them. "Just to see. Won't hurt none to see, will it?"

Now a course all them kids knew deep down it could hurt plenty, but there really wasn't much else to say. Hays, Scarlett, and Cordy had found their nerve again. Naomi had no choice but to follow. She had a life back in town, after all, one that depended a great deal on how her friends thought of her. The dog bounded down the other side of the ridge and disappeared into a patch of forest as the four of them crested the top. All they could do then was stare.

The footprints led down the slope through trees older and taller than any they had seen that day. Heading toward where that single column of smoke rose into the clear spring sky, where they snaked around to the sagging front porch of a squalid cabin below.

-3-

Some places have a *feel* to them, like there's a heaviness to the air. You can't see it with your eyes but you know it in your gut, and what your gut says is those places are not made for humans at all, but for things best left alone. Every one a them kids had an idea whose cabin that had to be; you could tell the way their faces went slack and their bodies sank low to the ground to keep out of sight.

"That's the witch's place," Naomi whispered.

"Can't be," Hays said. "We're too close to the mines. Alvaretta lives farther than this."

"How do you know?" Naomi asked. "You ever been to Alvaretta's cabin?"

Hays didn't answer, didn't need to. Who else could it have been down there but Alvaretta, living all alone and so cut off from town? Their trail had led to the witch, plain enough. And as Hays and Scarlett and Naomi and Cordelia pressed their bodies even closer to the ground, groping for a hand to hold or a body to nudge against, you can bet your soul their minds recalled the stories of the witch that anyone who calls these hollers home was raised upon. We all know of Alvaretta Graves's past, friend. How she blamed every person in Crow Holler for her husband's death, and how she said Stu would never rest because the town refused to let her bury him on Campbell's Mountain. How she'd spent all the years since alone in the woods, communing with the devil. The droughts in the years that followed. The deaths.

Ain't no witches, you'll tell me, and I'll say that back then there was a few who'd say the same. But there wasn't a body in this town who'd dare speak Alvaretta's name aloud for fear she'd somehow hear it, and you always knew who'd driven by the narrow cut in the trees that led off the dirt road to her cabin by the three Xs they'd drawn on the windshield with their fingers as they'd passed.

"Could just be some old farmer," Scarlett said.

Cordy nudged her. "We gotta make sure."

"I'm not going down there," Naomi said.

Cordy reached for Hays's elbow, which he promptly shook away. The morning was cool but the walk had warmed him. A single bead of sweat ran from his hairline past his cheek, almost like a tear.

"Say that is Alvaretta down there," he said. "You want her holding something that belongs to Cordy's momma?"

And that, friend, was what convinced them all in the end. That's what made Scarlett, Hays, and Cordelia sidle around that little holler in the woods, keeping well inside the trees so they wouldn't be seen. Because it was bad enough Cordelia stole that bracelet. It was worse Scarlett lost it. But the thought of her momma's bracelet falling into the hands of the witch? That was too much for Cordelia to bear and too much for them all to risk.

Naomi stayed well back of the others at the start but then closed the distance, too afraid to be alone. They kept their eyes to the cabin and the single column of smoke rising up from the chimney. The dog that had watched them from the ridge appeared again, this time where the tree line met the dirt and grass of Alvaretta's yard. Dozens more dogs had joined it. Some sat, licking themselves. Others wound their way through the trees, watching with cold eyes and low growls. And the footprints, those hooves. Leading right down through the middle of them all, around to the front of the cabin and out of sight.

Cordelia led the way now, moving steady and trying not to dwell on the thirty or so pairs of eyes staring at her. Halfway to the side of the house, Hays found another rock bearing the same strange markings he'd found back in the field. Scarlett found two more not a ways on. They'd come to a spot in the woods where they could see the side of the cabin plain, where a large garden had been plowed. A single glass window stared back at them. The faded curtain inside was drawn closed, letting them believe they'd gone unnoticed.

Whatever shred of hope those children had that they'd come upon some old farmer's plot left soon as they made it around to the front of that cabin. Near twenty feet of trees lay between where the four of them stood and the open half acre or so that drew up to the cabin's porch. And on all those trees, on every branch low enough to reach, hung a dead crow. Hundreds of them, all strung up in nooses of thin rope to rot and twist in the breeze. A few held on to their feathers, a black so crisp and bright it hurt the eye. Most were little more than sagging bones. Some still had eyes that looked out into the woods, their beaks open like they was sounding a silent alarm. Others had only small holes where eyes had rotted. Scarlett vomited into the leaves. Hays and Cordelia stared on as Naomi fell to prayer once more.

On the opposite side of the cabin sat the broken-down Chevy truck that had been Stu Graves's when he was killed, back when the parents of Scarlett and Hays and Cordelia and Naomi had been teenagers themselves. The side was caved in where Stu had wrecked it. The windshield lay cracked and jagged in the sun.

"This really is the witch's place," Scarlett whispered.

Hays said, "Tracks lead to the porch."

They did. Right up to that rickety old porch and then on across, past the truck to a shed so old that the wood on it had gone gray and warped, leaving gaps between the boards. Cordelia slipped her hand into Hays's and squeezed. He squeezed hers back.

No words passed between them, but they'd seen the same thing. The sun had come alive over that little holler by then, lighting every shiny surface it touched. The cracked side mirror on Stu Graves's old truck, the front window to the left of Alvaretta's front door, the metal washbasin overturned in the front yard, all a them glowed like tiny suns themselves. But what sparkled brightest was the diamond bracelet that had been draped over the rusty doorknob of that leaning shed.

-4-

"We gotta get over there." Cordy turned to find Naomi and Scarlett had backed farther into the woods. Hays still had her hand, but he'd taken a step away as well. "Hays? We have to get over there. That's momma's bracelet, I know it is."

"No," he said. "No way, Cordy."

"It's just right there. We can sneak through the trees. Ain't nobody around."

He shook his head but didn't let go of her hand, like he meant to keep her there.

"John David said for me to keep y'all safe. I'm not going anywhere near that shed. I can't."

"What is wrong with you?"

"I just *can't*," Hays said, and there was a panic to his voice that looked to scare them all. "We come too far."

"Too *far?*" Cordy asked, and a little too loud, making the girls look around and at least one of the dogs somewhere in the trees bark. When she spoke again, it was nearer a whisper. "You were the one who said we should follow those tracks in the first place. You *brought* us here."

"I'll go," Scarlett said.

Cordy looked her way, to where Scarlett stood beside a trembling Naomi, who was now so scared she'd even given up her praying.

"I'll go with you, Cordy," Scarlett said again. "It's my fault. I lost your bracelet, and I know you have to get it back. You can't have problems with your folks now. So I'll go."

"No," Hays said.

"We have to. You stay here with Naomi and keep watch. Let us know if you see anything. Scream it, we'll run. The lane has to be around here somewhere. We'll all follow it to the road and then keep on running if we have to. Our cars'll just have to wait."

Cordelia nodded. "It's the only way, Hays."

"Then I'm going too."

Naomi let off to panicking, telling the rest no way was she going to get close to that cabin and no way was she going to stay in the woods alone, not with those dogs around and those crows hanging over their heads, watching with their dead eyes.

"You stay with Naomi," Cordy said. "We'll be fast."

Hays handed the knife over. "Use it," he said. "I'm not kidding. Something happens, Cordy, don't even think."

The two girls left Hays and Naomi there and made a wide arc through the trees, watching for Alvaretta's dogs and keeping both the cabin and the shed in sight. They met the lane not a hundred yards on, nothing more than a rutted path hidden in the trees. Feathers stuck to the bottoms of their shoes as they swung around and eased out of the woods between two dead crows, one hung upside down and another missing both legs. They saw none of the dogs that roamed the land around the cabin. Cordy unfolded the blade on Hays's knife, locking it open as she hugged the back of the shed. She peered around the corner, past the open space of dead weeds and dirt that made up the front yard to the trees beyond. Hays and Naomi couldn't be seen. Scarlett peered through a gap in the boards but saw nothing in the shed's darkness. Cordelia stepped around the side, motioning for her to follow.

A wisp of gray smoke rose from the cabin's chimney. Otherwise, the place looked dead and empty. Cordy peeked around to the front of the shed. The bracelet—her momma's bracelet—still hung on the knob, not ten feet away. Scarlett tapped her on the shoulder. She held up three fingers and pointed to Cordy first, then to the cabin's door, finally to herself and the shed. Cordelia nodded. A count of three, then. Three, and Scarlett would go. She'd turn the corner quick and snatch that bracelet, and then she and Cordy would run, run for the others and then run all the way home, and they'd never come to Campbell's Mountain again.

One.

A sound from the porch. Cordy shot her hand back, telling Scarlett to stay. She moved her hand away when she saw it had only been the breeze against the bear traps hanging from the pegs by the door.

Two.

Scarlett's body tensed. Cordy gripped the edge of the shed, no longer watching the porch but shutting her eyes in prayer.

Three.

Scarlett ran.

I told you it was maybe ten feet to the door and that's the truth, but I'd wager that distance felt like a mile to that poor girl. You know what it's like, friend, to be afraid? I'm not talking plain scared, like how Angela had sat all comfortable in her living room watching somebody get killed on the TV. I'm talking about terror. You get as scared as Scarlett Bickford was, your body starts turning against you. Parts don't move right, leaving you to feel like you're fighting the very air for purchase. You don't hear. You can't see. Time itself melts away. All that's left is a single moment you know will never end, and what you realize is you're as close to hell as you ever want to get.

You can bet that's what Scarlett thought as she ran toward

that door on two legs made of jelly. I can picture her fingers now, brushing against that shiny oval bit of gold and glass hanging from the knob, relishing that brief moment when she thought she saw a light at the end of the long dark hole they'd all found themselves in that morning. But just before Scarlett's hand could close upon the bracelet, the door of the shed flew open and all hope went with it, and all Scarlett could do was scream.

-5-

Scarlett stumbled backward, hand still outstretched, reaching for a bracelet Cordelia would never wear again. The witch charged from the shed's open door with a cry more animal than human and a rage that burst from the scrawny body that contained her. Her feet scuttled over the dirt, making tiny clouds gather about her black boots and the hem of her worn dress. She gripped a pitchfork in two bony hands, angling the tines upward. Scarlett would've fallen at the edge of that clearing (and would've died there too—the witch had murder on her mind, friend, I'll stretch that truth not at all) were it not that she fell against the front of Stu Graves's old truck. Her back met the edge of the hood, lifting Scarlett's head to expose her chubby white neck. That's where Alvaretta now aimed. She let out a final yell and pulled back on the handle, meaning to run the little trespasser through.

Hays and Naomi ran from the trees and across the yard, but they were too far to be of any help. Nor could Scarlett help herself. She was so frozen by Alvaretta's appearance that she could not even beg for mercy. Had Cordelia not screamed, I doubt none a them kids would've made it off the mountain that day. They'd all be dead, buried by Medric Johnston's hand and mourned over by their parents, or maybe hung up in the trees to rot like them crows, and there's where my story would end. Yet Cordy found courage enough in that last moment to call out *No* just as Alvaretta went to run Scarlett through and *Stop it* as the witch flinched and spun her head.

Cordelia raised her hands—to her eyes at first, not bearing the thought of meeting Alvaretta's stare, then high and out as if in surrender. No sound came from the witch's mouth other than a rough panting. Her bottom jaw hung free from the rest of her face, revealing stumps of brown teeth. Gray hair hung free down the middle of her back, held in place by tiny silver barrettes. Scarlett picked herself up as Hays and Naomi stopped in front of the cabin not twenty feet away. Naomi was crying. Alvaretta saw them and the knife at Cordy's feet and took a step toward the door.

"Get on." She stabbed the air with the pitchfork. "Go you. *Goway.*"

Cordelia dared not move. She kept her hands high and said, "We're sorry, ma'am. We didn't mean to trespass. We got lost is all."

The witch stepped inside the doorway. Her fingers had gone pale from gripping the handle so hard. She said again, "*GOWAY.*"

Scarlett chanced a look over her shoulder. Hays had moved closer in the last seconds, cutting the distance by half. He didn't see the mongrel dog easing around the corner of the house behind him.

"We were camping," she said, but the witch did not look. Her eyes were on Hays instead, and now Naomi. Scarlett took a step closer. "Up at the mines? I know we weren't supposed to and we won't do it again, but I lost my friend's bracelet and it's there on your door. You give us that back, we'll be on our way, and we'll never trouble you again. You got our word."

Alvaretta cackled through a grimace and spat on the ground, letting Scarlett know just how valuable her word was on the mountain. "*Mine.* I found it, I keep it."

Scarlett saw Hays's shadow creep next to her own. He stopped when Alvaretta leveled the pitchfork at him.

"Get on," she warned. The words came low and smooth, almost like a spell. "Leave us."

"Us?" Hays asked.

Scarlett eased along the front of the shed, meaning to flank the old woman and catch her by surprise. Her shoe landed on one of the footprints they'd followed from the mines. She cried out as though she'd stepped barefoot on a thistle. Alvaretta smiled as she turned, looking at Scarlett for the first time.

"I see the face behind your eyes, little one," she said. "I know it well."

Scarlett held her place. "What's that mean?"

"I see your pa grinnin out from the sour girl he's wrought." And then the witch licked her lips with a tongue that looked gray and dying, like she was savoring the bitterness in her next word. "Bickford."

Scarlett's face went slack. "How do you know me?"

That cackle again, low and soft, which only made the blood in Cordelia's face drain quicker. A brown dog with only one eye moved out of the trees to where Alvaretta stood. It leaned against the witch's spindly legs and growled.

"Yesss," she hissed. "Bickford. I see you well." She turned her head slow, studying Hays. "Foster," she spoke, and then to where Naomi cowered not a body's length from the other dog, Alvaretta screamed, "Ramsay," and spat once more. To Cordelia she said nothing.

The dog near Naomi raised its nose, no doubt smelling the fear coming off her. Her body had gone stiff but for her trembling hands. She stared at the witch with eyes that looked somehow brightened. "How do you know our names?"

"You ask me that? I know of you, but you don't know of me?"

"Give us the bracelet," Cordy said. "Give it to us and we'll go."

"'Twas given *me*."

Alvaretta stepped from the doorway and aimed the tines at Cordelia's stomach, as if she knew what grew there. Hays neither said nor did a thing. You put anybody in that situation, friend—you put yourself there—could you have done any different? I'd tell you no. He tried moving but was stuck in place, and then he heard something move inside the shed. One of the gaps in the boards had opened wide enough to let in a thin bar of sun through to the other side. It glowed and then winked out, like something inside had passed by.

"What's in there?" he asked.

Alvaretta whipped her head his way. Hays couldn't meet that awful stare and so dropped his eyes to the ground, where the long track of horseshoe marks led past the spot where Alvaretta stood.

"What's in there?" he asked again. "Let me see."

What came next happened quicker than you can blink. Mayhap it was a shadow of the rage that had burned in Scarlett Bickford ever since she was old enough to know her own name, a fury that had rumbled and built and finally blew right there in that dead part of Campbell's Mountain. Or it could have been plain fear. She shot forward in a spot where neither the witch nor her beast could see. Alvaretta saw the look of horror on Cordelia's face. She spun back, but not in time. Scarlett's fist slammed into the side of the witch's mouth with a wet, hollow sound that would haunt those kids forever.

The pitchfork went flying. Alvaretta staggered backward into the dog, which reared up and knocked her forward at

Scarlett's feet. Cordelia screamed as Hays and Naomi called out, and from inside the shed came a shriek that shook the very boards themselves. Dogs barked and howled, a chorus of them, calling out from either side of the cabin and behind. The one that had closed on Naomi and the one that had guarded the witch barreled away for the safety of the forest. *Run* was all those kids must've thought, *Run* and *Run far*, and yet as Scarlett lifted her foot, Alvaretta took hold of it like a vise. The Thing in the shed yowled in a language none of them had ever heard, guttural and olden. One of the boards broke free, like what was inside had kicked it. A hunk of it struck Hays in the knee, doubling him over. Scarlett struggled to free herself, but Alvaretta would not yield. The witch's hands went from Scarlett's feet to her legs and then her hips, her thick body like steps to lift Alvaretta off the ground. Hays had gone numb. His shoulders had moved inward, caving his chest, and he began shaking his head as what had lain hidden inside the shed now tried to emerge. Cordy tried moving away and tripped, nearly touching one of the hoofprints burned into the dirt. The knife lay beside her. Friend, I don't think she even saw it.

Scarlett tried tilting her head away. She felt the witch's arm squeezing her tighter and saw Alvaretta stand, so close that she could smell the stink on the old woman's breath. A trail of blood poured from the gash on the side of her lip. Scarlett shook her head *No* as the demon in the shed spoke again. Alvaretta shook her own head *Yes, yes*. With one arm she squeezed Scarlett tighter. The other came around front and produced a gnarled and swollen finger that gathered the blood from her own lip like a dark harvest. Alvaretta reached out and touched Scarlett's forehead, then made a straight line of crimson down the bridge of Scarlett's nose.

"Yesss," she whispered. "Curse ye."

Scarlett cried out. She wrenched herself from the witch's

grasp and took off, they all took off, not minding the crows watching them from their nooses nor the dogs chasing them nor the long hill to the top of the ridge, minding only the raging wail of what the witch had been hiding and the witch herself screaming *Curse ye* over and over, *Curse ye all for ye sins.* Oh yes, friend, they scampered. And know you would have scampered as well. You would have hastened to the ends of the world to be away from there, and what you'd find after your hastening was done would be just what those poor kids found: you could run from Alvaretta Graves, but you could not run from her words.

IV

The curse takes hold. At the hospital.
The prayer chain. Naomi makes a video.

-1-

I'd put it about seven that morning when Scarlett struck
Alvaretta Graves and so sealed the fates of us all. Let's call it
an hour later when the kids neared the mines again. Those are
guesses, a course. By then, Cordelia and the rest were too scared
and tired to worry about the time. Naomi never even bothered
to check her phone. But time was about the only thing on the
minds of everybody else back in the Holler. It was the Sabbath,
and that meant gathering down to the church.

Friend, I don't know where you come from or how the
people there handle matters of the soul, but round here religion is king. All the proof you need's to look yonder at that
sign. FIRST CROW HOLLOW CHURCH OF THE HOLY SPIRIT ON FIRE,
REVEREND DAVID RAMSAY PRESIDING. Mouthful, ain't it? Church
looks about as run-down now as everything else. But you have
to remember I'm talking about how things was then, and back
then, everybody come down to the Holy Fire. Every Sunday
morning and evening, then again for Wednesday Bible study.
And if you weren't there and Doc Sullivan ain't provided you a
reasonable enough excuse, you can bet people wondered. They
wondered plenty.

About the time Cordelia was getting her first eyeful of
dead crows at the edge of Alvaretta's wood, her folks was pulling out of the gravel drive a dozen miles off. Bucky had on his

best Sunday suit, having kept it hanging off the shower curtain in the bathroom since paying respects at Henrietta Slaybaugh's funeral two days before. Angela wore a pretty red dress and her hair down, which she thought made her face look less fat. They were late, having first waited for Cordelia and then given the roses a good watering. By the time they figured Scarlett could just as well drive Cordy and Naomi straight to church from Harper's Field, Bucky barely had time to grab his King James.

Angela asked him to keep the window down, it stunk in the car. Bucky turned the crank and promised he'd rode all the way home like that the day before, after his shift at the dump, which was true. Bucky was always conscious of the way his vocation made him smell. Still, Angela rode most the way to town with her fingers pinched against her nose. She tried prying the two kitchen sponges out from between the frame and window of her door. Bucky asked her to stop, telling her if that window fell there'd be no prying it up, and then what would they do?

"Maybe tomorrow I'll get down to Mattingly," he said. "Get one of those fresheners that hang off the mirror? Smell like pine trees."

"That'd be good."

Bucky moved his hand across the seat of the family's little car, an '88 Chevy Celebrity he'd bought off Raleigh Jennings two weeks after high school graduation and a week after Homer Pruitt had hired him on at the dump. He gave Angela's leg a squeeze that didn't look to improve her mood. She'd been sullen since Bucky got home from work the day before. The funeral, he'd thought at first, but then Angela had told him later that night about poor Nikki on her stories. From the car's only working speaker, Johnny Cash sang of a burning ring of fire. Bucky hummed a little and then told Angela everything would be okay, death must come to us all and even people like this girl Nikki, and who knew, maybe she'd come back. Anything's possible on the TV.

The wind fluttered the stack of flyers in the backseat— Bucky looking stern in a constable's jacket that had gone a few sizes too small over the years and a turtleneck that seemed to swell his face to the point of bursting, LET'S KEEP THE LAW IN ORDER— ELECT BUCKY VEST CONSTABLE printed across the top. The whole family had been hanging them up all over town in the last weeks, but I'll be honest and say Bucky never really had to bother. He'd been elected constable near as many times as Wilson Bickford had been named mayor, and for good reason. Everybody liked Bucky, even if he came off a little simple on occasion. Even Chessie and Briar Hodge would always get out near election time and drum up support, so long as the mayor agreed to make sure Bucky never got the notion to go after their moonshining.

The morning dawned a chilly one for April. Bucky flipped the heater switch to High and shivered at the cold air that rushed from the vents. Angela asked (not for the first time, but as nice as usual) if he'd take the Celebrity down to the Hodge farm one day the coming week, get Briar to look at it. Everybody took their stuff there, Angela said, and it was a whole lot cheaper than taking the car all the way to a real mechanic in Mattingly. Bucky drove with the wind in his face, reminding Angela (not for the first time, but as nice as usual) that he could not in good conscience ever set foot upon Hodge land unless it was in an official capacity, and it didn't matter how often Briar and Chessie sat in church or how much they helped the wanting in town, that family was villainous.

"Criminal or not," Angela said, "at least Chessie's got respect. That counts for something."

"She ain't got respect," Bucky told her. "She's feared."

"But she's known. Chessie's *somebody*. I'd rather be feared than just be another face."

"Whole world's full of other faces, Angela. Can't everybody be somebody, or else there'd be no common folk like us. We're the ones keep the world going."

"That's your laziness talking."

And so it happened that just as Cordelia was screaming her way back to the campsite, Bucky and Angela had their first fight of the morning. There were no voices raised or hard words exchanged, just the clipped sentences and sideways glances that had come to define their marriage these last hard years. Both of them shivering, his hand no longer on her leg. The two of them likely wishing it was all because their car didn't blow heat on a cold morning and knowing it was not.

-2-

Bucky pulled into the parking lot that circles the Holy Fire right ahead of Kayann and Landis Foster. They were in that fancy Mercedes, of course. And of course Kayann was driving. Both of them waved, though you could say Landis and Bucky seemed to mean it a little more. Angela, you could say she meant to wave at only one of them, and they all got out.

Kayann had on a black dress that flaunted both the flatness of her stomach and the bulge of her chest. She hit a button on her keychain that made the Fosters' car beep. Setting the alarm, even if near everybody in town would be inside that church and so disinclined to break and enter. Bucky rolled his eyes and tried not to let Landis see.

Kayann asked Angela if she'd heard anything from Cordelia, Hays hadn't bothered to call or text that morning. Bucky answered the same. Landis broke the silence that followed by making a joke that maybe Hays and Cordy had run off to get married and was met with more silence. Bucky said he was sure the kids would be there before the service started. Kayann said she hoped that was so, but a course it wasn't. Hays wasn't nowhere near church by then. He was tearing down the hill in his car from the Number Four, thinking the crow feather stuck to his collar and tickling the back of his neck was Alvaretta's reaching fingers.

Still, the four parents decided it best to maybe wait outside until Raleigh Jennings stepped out to ring the church bell, just in case the kids arrived. Townfolk came in a steady stream, men and women and children dressed in their finest, which round here meant the clothes least worn and faded. Briar Hodge arrived with Chessie. He parked his old truck near the front of the church and lumbered around to let her out, the two of them looking like lovebirds in the twilight of some gilded romance rather than the most wanted people in the county. Chessie puffed the bit of red hair in front of her eyes with her breath so she could see. She greeted the Fosters and Vests and told them to have a blessed day.

Medric Johnston had the shortest walk of anybody in the Holler from home to church, having only to step across the street from the funeral parlor next door. He said hello to the little group near the steps and tried to ignore the fact that Kayann didn't so much as lift her chin. Oh, I'm sure that coulda been on account of the way Hays had taken to spending so much of his time helping Medric with whatever poor soul had last fallen to death. Coulda also been that Medric Johnston belonged to a class and race that Kayann Foster considered well below her own. I'll let you decide. But I guess Medric was used to being treated that way, him being just about the only black man in the Holler. I like to believe he could stand there smiling under

Kayann's glare because he was thinking of how it'd be to one day lay that woman down on the gurney in the funeral home's basement and get her all prettied up to be put in the ground. Kayann'd probably make Landis buy the most expensive casket Medric had, which would be fine, and then Medric would dig the hole extra deep. That'd please him fine. Please Angela too.

Doc Sullivan and Maris (who was not only wife of the town physician, but also sister to Mayor Bickford and aunt to Scarlett) stopped to visit on their way inside. Bucky was saying how fine a send-off Medric and the preacher had given Henrietta Friday evening, and how good she'd looked. Landis agreed with that, and not just because the Reverend and Belle Ramsay had all but cleaned out every bit of the grocery's paper products and cake mix for the meal after. Whether you deal in goods or souls, ain't much in this world better than a good death.

Doc Sullivan said sometimes a person had to hang on until there was nothing left to grip, and after that comes the mourning. Medric took all in stride, telling Bucky and the doc that caring for a body's like caring for a house—when you go away for good, it's always best to make sure things is just so. Death was near as sacred to that man as life, maybe more, and he told Landis that was one of the things he was trying to teach his and Kayann's boy. I guess that's true. Course, Medric left out what he'd told Hays some weeks back, about how fickle a profession like tending to the dead can be. A man like Medric could pinch only so many pennies and stretch so many dollars before he'd get to pining for a few deaths to fill his pocketbook. Not many, a course, and not the young or those with mouths to feed, but maybe a few of the old and tired, eager for rest.

Bucky's attention turned to the wood double doors atop the church steps. Belle Ramsay had poked her head out, no doubt looking for Naomi. Behind her came the mayor, doing the same for his Scarlett. Both came down the steps, nodding and saying good morning to the worshipers flocking inside. The mayor asked Kayann if she'd heard anything of the party. There seemed no concern that nobody had. Belle said there wasn't much trouble anybody could get into down at Harper's Field.

Had Angela overheard that statement, she would've disagreed. As it was, she'd been pulled aside by Landis and looked to have lost all connection to the world. He wanted to make sure she'd done the grocery's ordering for the week. It's hard to believe how such a petty thing as that could flush a grown woman's cheeks, but it had. Yes, Angela told him, she'd done the ordering Wednesday, and she glanced at Bucky long enough to see him still talking to Medric and then said the truck should be there sometime in the next week. From then on, her eyes never left the man beside her. Landis ain't a handsome man by any stretch—lanky to the point of gaunt, with thinning hair parted to the side and those round professor glasses always on his face—but the sight of him was enough to send a warm shiver down Angela's leg that she'd long given up feeling guilty over.

Don't matter if they's the ugliest soul who ever drew a breath, the first one you fall for always remains beautiful to you in some way, and the memories you have of the time you spent together get colored over in soft shades as the years wear on. It was like that with Angela. She'd dated Landis almost their whole senior year of high school and was to be engaged before Kayann stole him away. The hole Landis left in her heart back then had needed filling before she found herself sucked down into it forever. Next thing Angela knew, there'd been her and Bucky and a sky full of stars out in Harper's Field one Friday night. It had been a fling, nothing more, some frantic way to get Landis jealous. Well, all that backfired when Angela come up great with child. She got a ring for graduation all right, just from a different boy and for a different reason. Landis's daddy, Henderson Foster, had been kind enough to hire Angela on at the grocery once Cordelia was born, and Landis had been kind enough to keep her on all the years after. At least there was that.

It was then that Raleigh Jennings carried his big frame outside the doors and pulled the rope on the tower bell. Bucky looked once more around the parking lot and then down the road for Scarlett's little car, then made his way inside with Medric. Kayann, Belle, and the mayor followed. Landis kept talking on about a sale he wanted to do on the produce and if maybe the next truck should come Thursday instead of Friday, and Angela kept on letting him. She'd clung to the faith that says all things worked together the way they was intended, and she loved her family dearly. But it was mornings like that one, when the church bells had set to ringing and her and her husband had come to feel more like strangers than partners, that Angela must have entertained the idea things hadn't worked out as intended at all. She paused at the top of the steps and looked down the long dirt road past the Exxon and the grocery. Watching for her daughter, who by then was in the front seat of that little Volkswagen bug, screaming that she couldn't get the witch's blood off Scarlett's face.

-3-

Most everybody in the Holler had their assigned duties come Sunday service. Raleigh Jennings was no different. His place was to ring the bell and then sit on the metal chair in the foyer until it was time for the plates to be passed. And that was fine with Raleigh, because that's about as close to the Lord as he could bear to get.

Fifty-seven years old, gray and balding. Gut out to here, friend, and I ain't kidding. Blood pressure high enough to be a constant reminder of his own mortality. Divorced near twenty years, his ex-wife, Eugenia, had fled to her hundred-dollar-an-hour therapist up in Stanley. Weren't the first time a married woman strayed with another man in these parts, don't get me wrong there. But to have that woman up and leave was rare, and to have that woman escape Crow Holler altogether was unheard of. Eugenia's leaving not only cost Raleigh a broken heart that would never heal and seven hundred dollars a month in alimony he didn't have, it very nearly cost him his job as principal of the high school and a place on the town council, too.

He set the stack of unused bulletins back in the holder nailed to the wall and watched as Reverend Ramsay came to the pulpit. Tall and fit with a full head of brown hair, trying to hold his smile at the empty place between Angela and Bucky and the other one between Landis and Kayann. That smile faded all the way when the Reverend looked at Belle, alone in the front row.

Raleigh could've told all a those watching parents that's how it would be. He saw enough young people go in and out at the high school to know kids had no respect these days—not for their parents, not for their town, certainly not for their God. They'd rather be out in the woods somewhere, fornicating with any and all and drinking up Chessie's moonshine. Sure, there was an agreement between the Hodges and both the mayor and the Reverend that Chessie would be left alone so long as she kept her poison outside the Holler and the town's pockets lined. But Raleigh'd heard enough talk in the school hallways to know that was a lie. He leaned his head forward and out the door, straining the chair beneath him. Scarlett and her horde weren't nowhere to be seen, but there was one person watching close.

Round the corner on the side of the street between the

church and the funeral home, Raleigh could see a sliver of the hood on John David's truck. The boy hadn't stepped foot in the Holy Fire since coming back to the Holler, had barely spoken to his momma and to his daddy not at all. People said all that fighting had changed John David and turned him a stranger to the town and himself. Raleigh leaned forward as much as he could without having to stand, thinking maybe he should have a little talk with John David soon. Take him out to the woods to meet the others, but first make sure the boy wouldn't go blabbing to that nosy Chessie Hodge. Maybe Raleigh'd do just that very thing. Maybe war had shown John David the truth of things.

The Reverend's last announcement was for the council meeting at the end of the week, and here Chessie turned her head—not out the door, but to Raleigh. She grinned that way she always did, like a cat that's cornered a mouse to play with. Raleigh could only smile back. What had saved his standing in town after the divorce hadn't been the Reverend's absolution or the mayor's blessing, it was the Hodges'. Chessie had put her foot down and said Eugenia Jennings had never been a good woman and everybody knew it, so Raleigh should keep right on serving Crow Holler as he always had.

When all was said and done, most everybody got what they wanted. Mayor Bickford didn't have to go through the hassle of another council election or help the county find another principal for a school that would get shut down in a few years anyway, Reverend Ramsay didn't have to go through the agony of kicking out the church's head deacon, and Chessie Hodge got her own mouthpiece on the town council. You could say everybody made out just fine except for old Raleigh.

Everybody stood for the opening hymn. Raleigh kept his seat and leaned out the open door, watching shadows ease up the steps.

It was like them kids had been waiting for just that time to come in, thinking no one would notice. They snuck around the corner of the church and up the steps past Raleigh in two clumps—Scarlett and Naomi first, then Cordy and Hays. They'd changed out their party clothes, thanks to some fast driving by Scarlett and Hays, but wasn't a thing them kids could cover of their blank faces and trembling hands. And if you looked close enough, you could see a faint streak of red down the center of Scarlett's nose. They branched off for their parents as Raleigh readied the offering plates. Cordelia snuck down the center aisle and sidled up to her daddy on the end. Bucky put an arm around her as Belle smiled at Naomi and the mayor slipped Scarlett a kiss on the cheek. Hays's parents barely registered his presence when he sat next to them in their regular place at the center aisle, near to the back.

Something was wrong with those kids. I think Raleigh knew that the second he laid eyes on them. Some a them parents knew it too. Surely the rest of the young people did, most of them having spent the night before up in Harper's Field waiting for a party that never started. And I'll tell you this: the way they'd seen Scarlett and the rest come into church—like they weren't trying to hide something as much as they were trying to push something *away*—only made them want to know more what had gone on.

Reverend Ramsay finished his welcome when the piano ended (smiling at his little Naomi as he did) and called for the offering. Three men stood and joined Raleigh in the back. He handed them each a silver plate and kept one for himself, then the group walked to the front and began casting for tithes.

The plates came back filled with more silver than paper, but it was the paper that Raleigh spied when he wasn't looking at Scarlett or Cordelia. He could pass the plate and say the prayer and offer two amens every Sunday, could dispense wisdom during council meetings and roam the halls of the high school as a person of moral authority. That's what everybody saw. What they didn't see was all the times Raleigh dipped into the offering when nobody was looking just so he could make Eugenia's blessed alimony payment. Or that all the shrewdness he spouted at the council meetings was just whatever Chessie Hodge whispered in his ear to say. Or how sometimes he stayed after school with Ruth Mitchell, the school's secretary, and how Ruth would leave sometime later with her dress wrinkled and her hair mussed and some extra grocery money to take home to Joe and their two brats. All that was hidden, you see. Just like all those times Raleigh sat alone in the darkness of his little house with a pistol in his hand, praying for the Lord to show mercy enough to pardon one final sin. Or the meetings Raleigh led deep in the woods with the Circle, talking on about the cleansing holy war that neared them all.

They collected the plates and brought them to the front. Raleigh turned at the altar and waited for the ushers to be seated, then he said, "Let's go to the Lord."

He got as far as *Our gracious heavenly Father* when Cordelia stood up. Bucky held out his hand like he was either trying to help or trying to sit her back down. Cordy brushed it aside and stepped into the aisle, lurching for the door.

Raleigh continued on—*We thank Ye for these blessings*—when Cordy stumbled.

A soft *Ooh* rose from the congregation. Reverend Ramsay opened his eyes.

And we ask that Ye bless these tithes and offerings was followed by Cordelia knocking herself into the pew where Hays sat with his family. Raleigh stopped his praying as Cordy's eyes grew huge. The left side of her face began to slacken as though the skin there was about to slough off. Her eyes melted to horror as she looked beside her and uttered one mangled word:

"Hayth?"

And then she fell hard to the wood floor.

A rumble came over the congregation that built like a summer storm, calm turning to swirl. Bucky and Angela rushed for their little girl. Landis Foster got to her first, shaking her and hollering her name.

Then Belle Ramsay hollered *Naomi* as her daughter began to seize. Naomi's arms and legs jerked, making her fall from the front pew and onto the floor. Foam crept from the corners of her mouth. Her eyes were nothing but whites.

Scarlett screamed and then seized her throat with her hands, acting as if she were choking. The mayor shot up from his pew and grabbed for her, panicking as blood began dripping from her nose.

They all started screaming then, friend, every man, woman, and child inside the Holy Fire. Doc Sullivan was bent over Cordelia, trying to wake her. His wife tried to stanch the bleeding from her niece's nose. Mayor Bickford was hollering at Scarlett, trying to get her to speak, to say *something*. Scarlett only stood there, bleeding and silent and holding her throat. And that was when all them young kids who'd missed Scarlett's party realized something horrible had happened, and when they all started getting jealous that it hadn't happened to them. Raleigh could only stand there with his hands still clasped in prayer, trying to take in all he saw and hearing nothing, not even the Reverend hollering. Telling Raleigh to call the ambulance, call everybody.

-4-

Took both Mattingly's ambulances to get them kids out the church and up to the hospital in Stanley, some thirty miles off. Both packed full, leaving the parents and those concerned to follow on their own. It was, so far as I know, the shortest Sunday service Crow Holler ever had.

The nurse behind the glass window inside the hospital's emergency room said the girls would have to be tended to alone for the time being. That left everybody with nothing to do but wait and pray. They all found an empty corner to settle themselves—Bucky and Angela, the Fosters (Landis, Kayann, and a shaken Hays), the mayor, the Reverend and Belle—away from the thirty or so others who'd found misfortune enough to be in such a place that morning. Chessie and Briar Hodge had made the trip, too, as had Medric, whose face had gone ashen by the time he arrived. He sat beside Angela, who said what was on everybody's mind when she asked the undertaker what had brought him there. Trolling for clients is what she guessed. Medric held his head in his hands and said that wasn't so, he'd come for Hays because Hays was his friend, all them kids were. I'd say that didn't sit too well with Landis and Kayann. Angela told Medric not to worry, things would be fine, then looked upset when Medric didn't say the same.

Doc Sullivan went back with the girls, leaving his wife to do what she did best—comfort. Maris was a Bickford before she became a Sullivan, and though she was the mayor's older sister by near twenty years and had spent much of her adult life outside the Holler, we still counted her as one of our own. She went from one family to the next, and by the time she reached the last, that whole area of the waiting room had gone silent from shock. You could almost hear their hearts and minds winding down to a slow hum.

Maris asked Hays if he was okay. He answered, "I didn't mean for it to happen."

Bucky sat up in his seat and leaned forward. "What'd you say, Hays?"

Hays would've had to either lie or face the consequences if John David hadn't walked through the doors just then. He come into that waiting room like a bull, eyes afire, thumping those heavy boots he always wore with every step. Bucky turned as the Reverend moved past him quick, heard him telling John David to get away, he wasn't wanted. Briar stood at attention in case Chessie needed him. Her eyes alone were enough to stop the Reverend, along with that big body of hers that blocked the way. Which was a good thing, friend, because no way was John David Ramsay gonna turn around and leave.

He moved past Chessie and his daddy both, aiming for the three chairs against the wall where the Fosters sat. Hays saw John David coming and pulled his skinny legs up to his chest, making himself into a ball. John David roared as he reached for the boy, pulling Hays off the chair with one hand and cocking a fist with the other. Kayann screamed out *No* as Landis, Medric, and the mayor tried to wrench her boy free of John David's grasp. Bucky went to stand. Angela grabbed his arm and held him in place. Only when Chessie nodded her permission to let Briar help did the two finally separate.

"Get out," the Reverend said. He laid hold of John David's arm and yanked his son backward, forcing their eyes to meet. "You hear me, boy?"

Chessie pushed herself between them and said, "I told John David to come, Reverend. Was *me*. I know that's you and Belle's little girl in there, but Naomi is John David's sister. He's got just as much right to be here as anybody. Now we ain't gonna have no trouble here, are we? Bucky?"

Bucky blinked at the sound of his name. He stood, sliding Angela's arm from his, and looked at the Reverend and John David both. "Chessie's right. Reverend, I know you're hurt because of your little girl. But John David's hurt just the same. You need to let him be here."

"It's the Christian thing," Chessie said.

I'd say Reverend David Ramsay's head near exploded then, what with the son who wanted nothing to do with him showing up and somebody like Chessie Hodge telling him what's Christian and what ain't. John David walked past his daddy with nary a glance and wrapped his arms around Belle. She held the back of her son's head and smiled through her tears. It was a tender moment in the midst of all that worry and fear, but one that ended when John David broke the embrace.

He looked at Hays. "I warned you, boy."

The mayor still had one hand to Hays's chest, like he was ready to push the boy away should John David charge again. He kept that hand there and asked, "You warned him of what, John David?"

John David shook his head. "You didn't tell them, did you?"

"Tell us what?" Belle asked.

"Where'd Naomi tell you she was going last night?"

"Harper's Field."

He looked at the others. "That what they told y'all too?"

Angela stood and looked at Hays. She shook a finger in his direction. "Where'd you take our little girl, Hays Foster?"

"It wasn't *me*," Hays said. "It was Scarlett's idea."

The mayor's hand went from open to closed on Hays's chest, pulling at the few hairs that grew beneath the boy's shirt until Hays winced. "Scarlett?" he asked.

"She's the one who said we had to go up to the mines."

Landis let out a little gasp from his spot on the other side of Kayann. He took two giant steps, then slapped his son across the mouth. The sound came like a firecracker. Hays buckled as the mayor let him go, and fell back into his seat. He looked up, eyes wide with rage. Landis pulled his arm back again.

"You look at me like that," he said. "Go on, boy. I dare you.

What business you got, going up to a place like that? You don't know *nothing*."

Kayann tried, "Landis, he didn't know—"

"Shut up," Landis told her, for maybe the first time ever. "Don't you understand what he's done?"

The mayor and the Reverend looked at each other, sharing the same horrible thought. Bucky missed it altogether. I don't think Chessie did. Angela was asking Hays what in the world would convince him that taking Cordy up to the mountain was a good idea and Kayann was telling her it was just as much Cordelia's fault as anyone's, and the whole room got so loud the nurse said she was calling for security. The only thing that kept her from doing it was Doc Sullivan coming through the automatic door that led deeper into the hospital. His church pants looked rumpled and his plain white shirt lay open at the collar, where a stethoscope hung limp. Half-moons of sweat stained the spots under his arms. He looked at them all and shook his head.

"I'm afraid I have some bad news."

-5-

Bucky pushed past the Fosters and the mayor and asked, "What's wrong with my girl, Danny?"

"They're all settling in," Doc said. "Resting and comfortable. So far as we can tell, there's no danger."

"What's that mean?" Belle asked. "'So far as we can tell'?"

The doctor measured his words. "It means no one, myself included, quite knows what's going on yet. The girls are being taken upstairs to be admitted so we can do more tests. You can all go on and see them." He held up his hands when Angela and the mayor tried to push past. "Wait, now. I need to tell you all something first. The last thing they need is to see the ones they love most just as scared as they are. So I'll ask you to swallow whatever it is you're feeling and act like the good people you are."

The mayor asked, "What do you mean about bad news, Danny? What's happened to them?"

"I'll have to address that to each set of parents, Wilson."

Briar Hodge eased Wilson aside and faced the doctor. I say faced, though Danny Sullivan had to crane his neck to even meet Briar's chest.

"Now listen here, Danny," Briar said, and he was speaking slow to keep a lid on the fire growing up inside him. "All us here might not always get along as we should, but it comes down to it, we're fambly. You can stand there thinking you're gonna talk to one person or t'other, but I'm telling you all us is going up there right *now*. So you best just say what you got to and move out our way."

It was, so far as I know, the most words Briar Hodge had ever strung together at one time in his life. And whether it was all those words or the wisdom in them (or that Doc Sullivan had caught a glimpse of the pearl handle tucked into the front of Briar's church jeans), the doctor decided Chessie Hodge's husband had spoken truth.

He looked at his brother-in-law first and said, "Mayor, we had to give Scarlett a sedative. She's resting, but she seems to have suffered some sort of paralysis to her vocal cords."

"Lord help us," the mayor whispered.

Doc shook his head and tried to smile. It came out looking tired and worried. "I believe it's temporary. We've given her a pad of paper and a pen, and she's able to communicate fine. But I need to see you before you go in. No protest either, Wilson. This is important, and it has to be kept private. I will not budge on that," he said, looking at Briar and Chessie, "no matter who tries to bully me."

He turned to the Ramsays next and said, "Reverend, Belle," before his eyes flickered at the man standing next to them. "John David, good to see you here despite the circumstances. Naomi is conscious and alert, though I'm afraid she's lost some muscle function. We're not sure what caused her seizure. As it is, she's developed a tic in her arms and mouth. She can't control it, doesn't even seem aware it's there."

Belle began to cry. The Reverend asked, "What caused this, Danny?"

"We're just not sure."

"Danny," Angela said, pushing her way toward the front. "What about Cordelia? What's happened?"

The doctor turned to the rest. "You all go on now, those girls are waiting. Wilson, you wait outside Scarlett's door for me. Understand? Hays, you can take your parents up to see Cordelia while I talk to Bucky and Angela. You all go on now. Let us talk."

Bucky nodded and said, "We'll be there directly," sending Chessie and Medric and the rest toward the nearest set of elevators. Maris showed them the way. Doc Sullivan took Angela by the arm and led her and Bucky off to the side.

"How long's it been since I last saw Cordelia in the clinic?" he asked.

"Been a year or so," Angela said. "We brought her in with the flu. Why?"

"Everything good at home?"

"Sure, Doc," Bucky said. Angela looked relieved he'd answered that. "What are you getting at?"

"She's awake," the doctor said. "Whatever she's fighting, it's caused paralysis to the left side of her face. Now such things have been known to happen, and for a variety of reasons. But she has no feeling there at all, and because of that her face looks fallen a bit. You need to know that going in."

Angela's hands went to her eyes.

"There's something else. We had to do a very preliminary exam to try and pinpoint whatever may be causing it. We found something else."

"Found what?" Bucky asked.

Doc Sullivan took a deep breath. This time he didn't bother trying to smile. "Cordelia's pregnant."

-6-

The elevator opened empty, and that was a good thing because Angela was crying. Bucky had never seen his wife do that. Not when Angela found she was pregnant herself. Not even back in '95 when Angela's momma caught cancer and her daddy had his stroke. She was saying, "How did this happen, Bucky?" and "Why didn't she come to me?" and "I can't let anything happen, I love her, I know I don't always show it but I do," and Bucky could only stand there watching the floors light on the display and think all those same things.

They reached the fourth floor and never turned their heads as they traveled the hallway. Never peeked in to see Naomi enveloped by her parents and brother, her arm fluttering like a bird's broken wing. Her left eye blinked like something had gotten in it, or she knew a secret she couldn't tell. Belle kept laying a hand to her daughter's elbow, trying to still it, but that arm just kept flopping on.

Nor did Bucky and Angela see the Hodges standing outside Scarlett's door just a few feet from where Doc Sullivan had appeared to tell Wilson how they'd found all the cuts on his daughter's arms. The mayor only stared at the floor as he was told Scarlett had been maiming herself for a long while.

Bucky and Angela didn't even see the Fosters and Medric,

waiting out of respect for them to visit Cordelia first. No, friend, all the Vests could do was keep their eyes to the last door at the end of the hall, number 412. As they neared it, Angela took her husband's hand in her own.

Bucky knocked and eased the door open to find Cordelia sitting up in bed. An empty box of tissues sat on a small table hovering over her lap. Its contents lay balled and spilled into three piles that made it look like Cordy floated on a cloud. An IV had been stuck into the back of her hand. Machines beeped and flashed. Bucky saw none of that, nor did he see the way one side of his daughter's face looked like a blown tire sagging on a rim of bone. What he saw was only his sweet baby girl. His joy. Their blessing.

Cordy broke into a silent cry at the sight of them. There were so many things that must have gone through that poor girl's mind just then, all the secrets she'd hidden that now would come to light, but despite all that she could only bunch her lips as a single tear fell from the corner of her one good eye and ask, "Am I thtill pwetty?"

They rushed in, friend, Bucky and Angela both, neither caring how maimed their daughter looked nor what grew inside her young womb, wanting only to hold their child and wet her head and face with their kisses. At that bedside, Bucky discovered that a man could mourn how small he felt against all the world's dangers and still call himself a man. He wailed as he held Cordelia and did not care who heard or if he acted like the good person Danny Sullivan had asked him to be. And when all the crying was done, Bucky laid his daughter back against her pillow and wiped his eyes.

He said, "You need to tell me what happened, Cordelia, and you can't hold back. Not a thing."

Angela scurried around to the other side of the bed, where she sat and took Cordy's hand. She looked into her daughter's eyes with a pain and fear that Cordelia could take only as love, and what could Cordy do then, friend? What could any of us do?

She started with stealing the bracelet.

-7-

It was Chessie who gathered them later that afternoon.

She and Briar went to check on Naomi first, knowing the Reverend and Belle's help would be needed to convince the others. It wouldn't be easy. Chessie and David Ramsay had never agreed on most things. He didn't approve of what Chessie did to make her money, she didn't like the way the Reverend could use God as a wedge to divide the town, but they'd managed to live somewhat peaceably over the years. Chessie counted on their shaky truce to last just a while longer. She didn't know how much if anything Naomi and Cordelia had told their parents of the past night and morning, but she guessed it was some. No child could keep such secrets for long, as evidenced by what Scarlett had written down for her daddy. And Scarlett had written it all. Much had come out in a mad rush of words strung together in sentences that never ended, scrawls on sheet after sheet of paper. But Chessie had understood enough. The horror on the mayor's face said he'd understood things too.

Turned out, the others had confessed much the same. What parts Naomi and Cordelia had left out got filled in by Hays, who'd confessed everything to Landis, Kayann, and both of the Hodges. David and Belle went along well enough with what Chessie wanted, but only after she promised it wouldn't take long. John David would stay with Naomi, who was jerking her head like it'd gotten tangled in an electric wire.

Chessie took them both along with Medric to check on

Cordelia. They found an empty bowl by the bed. Half of the chicken noodle soup had spilled down the dead side of Cordelia's face, leaving Angela in tears and Bucky nearly so.

The mayor came along last. He agreed a meeting was needed, but I think Wilson Bickford did that only because he knew that would be the only way for Scarlett to feel better. Her arms were under the covers now, hidden once more, and she had made the mayor swear never to tell a soul what he'd seen of them.

Maris remained behind to watch over Scarlett. Hays sat with Cordelia. The Reverend said the hospital's chapel would be best. And so that's where they gathered, inside that little room one floor down and beneath a shiny gold cross that hung from the front wall. They all held hands as the Reverend opened with a prayer no one felt much comforted by. After his amen was said and echoed, Chessie lifted her chin to speak.

"Kids shoulda never been to the mines. They know better. Mountain's fenced for a reason."

"No use dwelling on that now," Belle said. "Damage is done. What we need to focus on is getting our girls better."

Her voice cracked. No doubt Belle Ramsay was thinking about her daughter just then, twitching like a nervous Nellie for the rest of her days. Her faith said that wouldn't be so. But then again, Belle Ramsay's faith also said John David would one day turn from his wicked ways and run back to his momma's bosom. That hadn't worked out so well either.

Medric must've sensed the same, because he asked, "What if they don't? What if they all stay as they are?" And when they all glared, he whispered, "Just sayin'. Sure it won't come to that."

"If they don't," Angela said, "if my daughter looks like that for the rest of her life, it'll be square on your shoulders, Kayann Foster."

Landis took a step toward Angela. Kayann beat him there. "What did you just say to me?"

Bucky rubbed the front of his head, like he felt a headache coming on.

"Your son was supposed to be there watching Cordelia, watching them *all*. He talked Cordy and Naomi and Scarlett into following those tracks, and then he stood there and did *nothing*." She hit that last word hard, near shouted it, and then fell silent.

Landis shot back, "Our boy did the best he could. Hays would've never been out there if you woulda had the sense to keep Cordelia at home instead of letting her run around Campbell's Mountain."

"I didn't *know* she was going to Campbell's Mountain, Landis," Angela said. "None of us did."

"That's right," Kayann said. She turned to the mayor. "If it's anybody's fault, it's Scarlett's. She was the one who came up with the idea of going up there in the first place."

Wilson Bickford only stood there. He kept his voice low and even and said, "Landis, you better shut your wife up. Scarlett may've wanted to go up to the mines, that don't make no difference. She didn't have the key. Hays did." And now he turned to Medric. "My question is, how in the world did Hays get that key?"

"Must've snuck it," Medric said. "I didn't give it to him, Wilson. I'd never do such a thing."

"You wouldn't?" Kayann asked. "What exactly is it you and my son do shut up in that funeral parlor of yours, Medric?"

"Now what's that mean?" He looked at them all, saw their hard faces. "You blaming me for this? I never wanted them keys. It's the mayor's job to hold the keys to the gate and everybody knows it, but Wilson didn't want'm. Bucky didn't want'm. Said they're cursed like the mountain itself, and y'all think whoever holds the keys carries a stain on themselves. So you give'm to me. Say since the mountain means death, then the man who holds the keys should be the man who deals in it. Y'all think anyone should be stained round here, might as well be me. Well I have you know them keys stay locked tight. And Kayann Foster, I'll have you know your boy spoke of them something awful. He was drawn to the mountain long before he met me."

Kayann grit her teeth. "You are a vile creature, Medric Johnston."

Bucky said, "Shut up, Kayann."

Yessir, that's *exactly* what he said. And I guess he figured that since he'd gone on and said it, he might as well go on and say the rest.

"We can all stand around here laying blame till we're blue in the face, there's plenty to go around. Hays or Scarlett or Cordy or Medric, it don't matter. But wasn't none a them kids laid those footprints. Didn't none a them take that bracelet. It was Alvaretta. She made our girls sick. That's what we need to be talking about, and we need to be talking about how that woman knew your names just from looking on your kids. Wilson? David? Landis. Alvaretta knew your kids. She knew *you*. How is that?"

Friend, if you could've seen the way the Reverend and the mayor looked at each other just then, you'd have understood there was plenty they knew on how that was. But now wasn't the time to be getting into the past, not then and not after the two of them had taken such care to keep it all buried. I guess even then, they all thought there was still a way to keep their sins hidden. Fear sure can make you think some crazy things, can't it?

"She's a witch," Briar said. "That's how Alvaretta knew."

Medric shook his head. "Alvaretta ain't no witch. Just a lonely old woman is all. Only power she holds sits in her own broken mind."

"You say that, Medric?" Chessie asked. "That what you really think? You the one put Stu Graves in the ground all those years ago. You buried that man's body and you heard Alvaretta herself say a reckoning would come. You remember Wally Cork? How he hooked up Stu's old truck to his wrecker and took it back to Alvaretta? You remember what he said after?"

"Said he tried going in her house," Briar reminded them. "Said something come over him."

Chessie nodded. "Was Alvaretta's *grief* come over 'im. Alvaretta's *rage*. A woman's heartache can overcome a man. And when Wally tried to force hisself on Alvaretta and she beat him back, what happened? Found Wally dead a week after, that's what happened. Spread-eagled out in his backyard with the maggots eatin' what was left of his flesh. Or should we talk on the drought after? Huh? You remember that, Medric? Landis? You remember the fire at the grocery a day after your daddy said he'd give Alvaretta no credit on her supplies cause she didn't have no money?"

Landis couldn't help but shudder at that. He held that memory just as well as he did every other occurrence of the witch. That fire had nearly cost his daddy all he had in the world, and he made sure Alvaretta Graves had all the credit she needed after that, which turned out to be none at all. Alvaretta was seen in town no more, much to the relief of those in the Holler. She remained alone on the mountain, left to fend for herself. There was nothing the grocery could provide that the woods couldn't provide better, whether food or medicine or clothing. And what the mountain couldn't give her, the devil certainly could. Everything got quiet again.

After a while the Reverend said, "This world ain't all there is, Medric. You need to keep that in mind. There's a war we can't see being fought around us every day. There's light and there's the dark, and in that dark are things no man could bear knowing."

Briar snorted. "That's good, David. You gonna ask to pass a plate next? Bucky's right. We can stand here jawing or we can figure out what we gotta do. Ain't just that Alvaretta knows y'all's names, ain't even that the girls are sick. Them kids are being truthful, there's something loose from the mountain. Scarlett told us a demon's what leveled the curse, not Alvaretta. And Alvaretta's got it keeping her comp'ny."

Wilson fiddled with his mustache. He'd managed to keep things together in hisself so far—the Reverend too—which was a feat considering all that must've been going through his mind. I'm betting Stu Graves was hanging over both their heads like that big old cross hung up on the wall.

"What Alvaretta is or isn't giving shelter to ain't important right now," Wilson said. "We all been lied to, every single one of us. I don't even know what those kids say is truth and what's false. But I know if word gets out Alvaretta did this, we're gonna have a storm on our hands. We gotta keep this quiet. Let Crow Holler think it's a sickness what struck them girls. I'll call Raleigh and let him know it's a flu bug or something in the water. That's what you'll all say to anyone who asks. Nothing of what we know. Y'all understand?"

They each nodded one by one. And I think they all really did understand the danger of word getting out. At least for a little while.

-8-

Medric was first to leave that day, and he didn't take no time to do it. Never said a word to nobody, neither. Didn't tell Scarlett or Cordelia he hoped they'd be fine, didn't tell Wilson he'd be back in the morning. Now you can just imagine how worked up they all were, not only with what all had happened to the girls but how it had happened and by whose hand it had come. Oh friend, they was *all* worked up. But Medric? That man looked downright scared. You can bet Hays Foster made a note of it, no matter how much he liked Medric and appreciated all the time the two of them had spent together. That boy never missed much. The quiet ones seldom do.

The Fosters went home after dark. What with Angela still fuming over Hays and Hays acting like he was a million miles away, both Kayann and Landis felt it was time for them to go. Hays left without kissing either of Cordy's cheeks, the good one or the bad. She watched him close the door and laid her hands over her belly.

The Hodges left soon after visiting hours were called. John David went with them, having grown too weary of being so near his daddy. Chessie said there was a delivery out to Stanley. She acted like she felt bad, sending John David out while Naomi was laid up under Alvaretta's witchery. But business was business. Sooner John David learned that, the better off he'd be.

A nurse brought in a chair for Bucky. Angela took the one already by the bed. The two of them remained at Cordy's side until she fell asleep. Angela followed soon after. Bucky sat up for most of the night, staring out the window toward the mountains and wondering if Alvaretta and her demon were watching.

Belle and Naomi were near settling when David left the room. To pray is what he told them, and maybe the Reverend did do some of that before he called back here to the Holler, I don't know. Tell no one, the mayor had said, and David Ramsay had nodded along with all the rest. But sitting there watching Naomi struggle to keep her own body under control had changed the preacher's thinking on that. Wasn't no sickness, what had struck his child. Wasn't no flu. Wasn't anything in the godforsaken water.

It was the witch. And Alvaretta *knew* him.

How that could be—how it was even possible—David did not know. Maybe Briar had been right when he said it was Alvaretta's powers at work, but hearing Naomi wail in fear as she'd told him and Belle of Alvaretta calling out *Ramsay* and then spitting (as though the mere taste of that word was unbearable) had frightened David just as much as it had the mayor. Frightened him more, even.

He fished the phone out of his pocket and dialed a number, turned to see if anyone was watching. The line rang twice before Raleigh Jennings's voice came through.

"Naomi any better?"

"No," David said. "It's not good up here, Raleigh. Not good at all."

"Wilson called a little bit ago, filled me in."

"What'd he tell you?"

"Told me he thought it's either the flu or something in the water. I guess that's all he's got to go on, but that's what I've been telling the people who're calling. And plenty are, David. Folks is going nuts down here. You think it really is the water? Lord have mercy, I drink that water. Every—"

"It ain't the water, Raleigh."

The line went quiet.

"Raleigh?"

"Yeah, I'm here. What's going on, Reverend?"

"Raleigh, you do something for me? And before you say yes, you better know it could get us both in trouble. Lord knows I don't want it this way, but people need to know what's happening. I need you to make some calls. Start a prayer chain."

"Sure. What'm I supposed to say?"

The Reverend turned to take another look. Through the

small oval window, a nurse moved from the rack of desks in the center of the room toward Scarlett's door. She carried a clipboard in her hand. The door to Cordelia's room cracked open. Bucky walked out in search of a cup of coffee. I think it was the look on the constable's face that clinched it for David Ramsay just then, that expression of worry and fear that besets the utterly overwhelmed. That would be everybody soon, if what Naomi said was true.

"David?" Raleigh asked. "What should I say?"

He told Raleigh everything.

-9-

By the time David Ramsay was doing exactly what he shouldn't, Naomi sat in bed ready to do the same. She'd gone near twelve hours by then without talking to Cordy or Scarlett, having to rely on Hays for news of how they fared. Being cut off from her best friends like that was a source of anguish just as awful as the tremors and the memory of Alvaretta's demon shouting the language of hell. She had only feigned rest, knowing it would be the only way her momma and daddy would entertain the same. With no witnesses in the room, Naomi reached under her covers and pulled out her phone.

Belle had snuck it to her after supper, but made Naomi promise not to take it out around the nurses (and certainly not around her father). She knew it would be the one thing that might make her daughter feel better. Naomi brought it out now, scrolling through the dozens of texts from young folk wanting to know what had happened. She ignored them all and pressed the little picture that said MeTime. Her face twitched on the screen and wobbled in her shaky hands. She propped the phone against her knees and hit Record.

"Hey, y'all," she whispered. Belle rustled in the chair beside her. When she settled again, Naomi saw her momma's hands still clasped in prayer. "I'm so sorry. Scarlett wanted to go to the mines for her birthday. We shouldn't have done that. The witch got us, that's all I have time to say. I can't stop shaking. Scarlett can't talk. And Cordy . . ." She swallowed a sob. Lordy, it's hard to imagine a body could hold so many tears. "We're all sick. I think a lot more people are gonna get sick too. I'm so scared. Please pray for us. Pray for everybody."

Naomi wasn't awake to see her video sent out into that MeTime air. She began to drift soon after and barely summoned the energy to place her phone beneath the pillow. By the time the Reverend got back, his daughter was full asleep. Not five minutes more passed before thirty of the town's young gave her shout-outs. That number climbed north of a hundred within the hour.

Children they were, children all, from the lowliest eighth grader to the lowliest high school senior, all the ones who'd sat in church that morning and seen the whole thing. They may have thought themselves grown and mature in the calm and tedious days that was life in Crow Holler, where the world's always felt in shadow, but at least shrunken and predictable. But not a one knew the danger that lurked just beyond their sight. They knew not Reverend Ramsay's war between light and dark that raged unseen and unfelt around them.

They watched Naomi's message on their little phones and watched it again. Their parents paced worn living room floors or sat at chipped kitchen tables and felt a heavy silence of dread press in. Fathers stared from windows and ran calloused hands through hair that felt thinner and looked grayer than it had that morning. Mothers held their telephones tight against their ears, taking information and giving it back, sifting every word and speculation through the fearful notion that everything may well turn out all right but likely would not.

"Went to the mines, they did. Got the key from Medric."

"The Bickford one and the Vest one and even the Reverend's daughter."

"I heard they summoned a demon from the mountain."

"Footprints."

"The cloven hooves."

"Wild dogs, dozens of them, all in a rage."

"Spellbound."

"She knows our names."

"Demon."

"The witch cursed them girls."

"Cursed us all."

"Them girls' fault."

"The girls."

Ain't a much more reliable service to get out bad news than a prayer chain. This person calls that one, that one calls two more, and pretty soon what you got is a long set of fragile links made up of what-I-thinks and what-I-heards. By morning there wasn't a single person in town, young or old, who hadn't heard that something evil had befallen Naomi and her friends. There wasn't anyone who didn't know that evil was coming for us all.

-10-

She spent that whole day cleaning up, first herself and then the shed, patching the boards that had gotten kicked away as best she could with scraps from the pile in back. Weren't easy, carrying those boards in arms that had gone stiff and sore from being thrown to the ground. From being *molested*. Fastening the nails with hands swollen and arthritic. Feeling the beat of her heart in the cut on her lip. And yet now that chore was done, fueled by a rage that had long simmered in the black places of the witch's heart, wailing her curses as the hammer rained down, driving those nails more by the sheer force of her will than her own strength. Screaming at the body next to her, cursing that only a fool would do something so ill-considered as refuse to remain unseen and unheard by the four trespassers from town. And now they knew. She had let them leave and now they knew, now everyone would know, and what would become of Alvaretta Graves now? What would become of the thing she kept hidden?

Those questions had preyed upon her all that day, so much that Alvaretta had kept what she'd hidden even further from sight. She could hear the wailing even now, booming out from both the barred wooden door inside and the heavier one that led out onto the porch, where she stood staring at the flowering moon rising over the woods. Somewhere close, her children barked and bayed and stood guard should the trespassers return.

No matter. The curse would fell them, mayhap had felled them already. Alvaretta had seen the fear in the children's eyes, the chubby blond one especially. Bickford. Had nearly felt the very life drain from the little whore as she'd screamed at the bloodstained finger riding down the bridge of her plump little nose. Power. That was her weapon, and one Alvaretta wielded whether she herself was present or not. Her specter hung over all of Crow Holler, not just Campbell's Mountain. If the curse did not silence them, the fear would.

V

Chessie sells. At the doc's.
The girls come home. Trouble in town.

-1-

Wasn't nobody at Mitchell's Exxon when Raleigh Jennings came by the next morning. He eased his wheezing Cadillac off the dirt road and crossed the two strips in front of the pumps, setting off the bell somewhere inside, then stepped out and lifted his head to the blood-red sun.

There's a magic to spring in the Blue Ridge. Every other season will melt from one to the next, easing in and out so slow that you hardly even notice. But spring, friend? That one explodes. One day everything looks dead and gone. The next, all those bare branches and brown grass get colored in a green so deep you think it can't be real. The sky turns blue like the mountains. Flowers rise from the frozen ground like miracles, sprouting reds and yellows and violets, and with them come scents that take you to better times long past, back when the world held promise. You want to run a finger over it all, touch it like frosting on a cake. And all of that change, every bit, happens in the turn of a single day. I swear it's so.

Raleigh looked to be trying to feel that same magic then, his face all bent up toward that sun, trying to draw on its strength. In the end, all he looked to get was hot. He'd made the decision to rededicate both his work and his faith the night before. Like springtime in Appalachia, the change in Raleigh had come in an instant. Faster than that, even—I'd say just as long as it took the Reverend to say good-bye the night before and the line to go dead. Raleigh knelt beside his battered sofa and prayed maybe the hardest he'd ever done in his life, harder even than when Eugenia left. Because he understood what was coming to Crow Holler, now and finally. Ruin. He could see it galloping toward them all like the black rider of death, and that rider had come as a hate-filled and frightful old woman. Alvaretta Graves.

No one stirred from inside the small gas station, though someone had propped open the wood screen door with a case of Mountain Dew. Raleigh looked toward the back, where the Exxon's big propane tank sat. Nobody there either. He reached back into the car and laid on the horn twice.

"Joe?" he hollered. "You here?"

A voice echoed through the door—"Hang on." Raleigh waved no hurry to the air even though he didn't mean it. Hurry would be the order of the day.

The road through town lay quiet that morning. The grocery was open. (Raleigh had seen Landis out front when he'd drove by, sweeping the lot.) No buses, as both the Holler's schools had been closed by order of the mayor. Not for the proper reason, though. That's what brought Raleigh out to the Exxon.

Joe Mitchell walked into the morning light and wiped the sweat from his face with a red bandanna he pulled from the back pocket of his jeans and tried to smile. He rubbed a patchy beard that held more boy than man.

"Sorry you had to wait, Raleigh. Ruth was on the phone."

He paused here, like he was testing the words in his head first to make sure saying them wouldn't crack his voice. Raleigh held in a grin. *Family trouble, I bet* he thought. *Well, that's what Joe Mitchell got for letting his wife stray as she had.*

But his grin got swallowed when Joe said, "Chelsea's got the sickness, Raleigh. Woke us up last night with it. Thought it was just her muscles jumping at first. But we can't stop it, no matter what we do. Ruth's getting her to Doc's. I'm fixing to close up and meet'm there."

Chelsea Mitchell. Tenth grade, Mrs. Heishman's homeroom. A pretty little thing just like her momma, and well-mannered.

Raleigh rubbed his eyes. "Then it's starting. Little Joe got it?"

Joseph Mitchell Jr. was four years younger than his sister and still at Crow Holler Elementary.

"He's fine so far," Joe said, "but me and Ruth are keeping him away from Chelsea. Case it spreads by touchin or whatnot. You think that's how it's getting round, Raleigh?"

"No. No, I don't think it's that at all."

Joe shook his head. "Well, want me to fill'r up?"

"Don't need gas this morning, Joe."

"This business, then?"

"It is."

Joe's weary grin faded.

"You heard through the prayer chain?" Raleigh asked.

"Tully Wiseman called me. Said he got it straight from you."

"And I got it from the Reverend hisself," Raleigh said, "so you know it's true. All of it."

"I don't know, Raleigh. Alvaretta's a strange one, but a demon?" He rubbed his beard again. "Stretches things, don't it?"

Raleigh put a hand to Joe's shoulder. "I thought the same at first, but listen. Mayor called me just before the preacher did. He told me how the young'uns were doing and then told me to shut down the school next few days. Wanted me to test the water down to the reservoir. Like I even knew what to look for."

"The water?"

"Told me it was either that or a flu. Ebola, maybe. You believe that? Didn't utter a word of Alvaretta. Never said nothing about them kids being up to the mines or no footprints. Never mentioned nothing of a curse on the town."

"So somebody's lying, then," Joe said. "Reverend or the mayor."

"That's my thought, and I think it's the mayor. Ain't nothing wrong with the water, Joe. That was the case, a lot more'd be sick. Same for any flu bug. David was torn last night when he called me. Said telling me to start the chain would probably get us both in trouble. I'm principal, Joe. I'm on the council. Wilson told anybody the truth, it should've been me. Makes me wonder what else he's been hiding all these years."

Joe Mitchell shook his head slow. "Preacher woulda never called to start the chain, ain't none of us would even know what's going on. This something we should be keeping an eye on, Raleigh?"

That sun, so warm. Raleigh bent his face to it again. Just down the road, he saw Medric's car leaving the funeral home. Heading to the hospital, no doubt. Mr. Medric Johnston, Crow Holler's keeper of both the dead and the mines.

"I think so, Joey. I think that's just the thing. Too early in the day to get everyone together, so why don't you make some calls. Homer and Tully, all you can get hold of. What I been telling you all these years? Ruination's coming. Starts with letting somebody like Medric gain a place in this town, then he poisons Hays Foster and Hays poisons all his friends. Now they gone and poked the witch, and we'll all suffer for it. Time for us to stand up, Joey. Cut the head off the snake." Raleigh smiled. "Yessir, let's show Medric and them kids how appreciative we are for all they done to us."

-2-

Joe and Ruth Mitchell weren't the only ones who'd spent a restless night pondering the witch. All them who stayed up at the hospital did, too, tossing and turning and dreaming of Alvaretta Graves.

Naomi twitched and shook even in the thin sleep afforded to her. Cordelia woke often in the night, not because of pain but because she kept turning her good cheek where the bad one had been and settling into a cold puddle of drool. Twice after that, she'd sat up in bed and pinched the dead side of her face, digging her fingernails into the skin like she was trying to jump-start feeling. You can imagine what went through Bucky's and Angela's minds that morning when they woke to find their daughter's face streaked with drying blood. Took the nurses nearly half an hour to convince Angela that Alvaretta's demon hadn't snuck in during the night to hurt Cordy all over again.

Mock that all you want, friend. You weren't there. You didn't see the way Naomi trembled like it was something else altogether controlling her. You didn't see Scarlett straining with all her might to force even a whisper past her lips, only to collapse in silence. You didn't see Cordelia's poor, tortured face, and the way she stared toward a far-off place that existed only in her mind.

You weren't there before, neither, back years ago when Stu Graves lost control of his truck along the Ridge Road. You didn't see Alvaretta alone in the cemetery three days following, shrouded in a veil so long and black that to look upon her was to feel like you were looking upon the angel of death. You weren't there when she said Stu'd never had a drink in his life, it was the town that killed him and not the moonshine found with his body, and that a pall would be cast upon all of Crow Holler until those responsible came forward to judgment. So mock, friend, if that's your mind. Cackle and shake your head like the enlightened person you are. Call us rednecks and hillbillies and mourn our ignorance, and then look around at this town. Look at what's left, and hear me well: there is light in this world and there is dark, and in that dark lie things no man can bear knowing.

Whatever hope the Vests and Ramsays and Bickfords had

that the next day would bring healing was gone by the time Raleigh pulled into Mitchell's Exxon. The girls was all awake by then, and they was all just as shaking and staring and slobbering and silent as they'd been the day before. Reverend excused himself just before breakfast. What he told Belle was he needed to go back to the chapel to call on the Lord, but I think he just couldn't bear the pain of watching Naomi try to eat again. He paused in the hallway just outside Scarlett's door and stood there like he was pondering whether to go on and tell Wilson about the prayer chain. He kept right on walking instead.

I'll let you make up your own mind on Reverend David Ramsay, but I'll say that man truly did what he thought was right in getting Raleigh to spread the word. It was a war we was in, you remember. People needed to know the fight had come to Crow Holler, and it was time for every soul to choose a side. Here's another thing too: it wasn't lost on David that it had been Naomi and Scarlett that Alvaretta's demon had hurt the most. David couldn't tell Raleigh that (much less Belle), nor had he yet found the nerve to speak on it with the mayor. But that would have to come, and soon.

Alvaretta must have known the kids would be up on the mountain that Saturday night. Maybe she'd even called forth the demon from the mines just to steal Cordelia's bracelet, knowing the poor girl was so scared of Angela's wrath that she'd convince her friends to go off chasing it. Weren't enough for Alvaretta to mark David and Wilson. Alvaretta wanted Crow Holler to pain as much as she'd been pained.

She wanted the children.

-3-

I wouldn't say Angela Vest was embarrassed to have a husband handle trash for a living. It was, after all, a proper means to earn a wage, which spoke better of Bucky than many a man hereabouts. But just because Angela wasn't embarrassed didn't mean she was proud. Bucky didn't have the business sense of Landis or a gifted tongue like Reverend Ramsay. He weren't nowhere near smart enough to be a doctor like Danny Sullivan, nor did he come from old money like Mayor Bickford. Shoot, Bucky would be the first to say he never even had skill enough to do what Medric Johnston did, though he would often hold Medric up as an example to Angela of how things could be worse—he could be coming home every night stinking of moldy death instead of moldy trash. Angela would always answer that was true enough. Sometimes, if whatever discussion they were having had drifted into the realm of argument, she would add that at least there was enough money in stuffing bodies to get the heater fixed on the car.

Didn't none a them parents at the hospital have a harder time with everything that had happened than old Bucky. You take a couple like David and Belle Ramsay, them two could bear up under the weight of an ailing child. They had their faith, sure, though my experience has been faith is something that blossoms and wilts in a life as easy as the corn in these fields. But the Ramsays had each other more, and that's the thing. It's always easier to bear up under your misery when the person beside you's as crushed as you are.

Same could be said for Landis and Kayann Foster, who had never truly been amorous but complemented each other well enough. And even though Wilson Bickford had been a widower for going on ten years by then, he had close enough friends in the Holler to never truly feel alone.

But Bucky? He didn't really have nobody like that, sad to say. In the back of his mind, I suspect he'd known all along the only reason Angela even agreed to marry him was she'd had no choice in the matter. Pretty girl like that, young and in the prime of her life, settling down with a chubby little backward boy like him? Shoot, everybody in the Holler knew what that was all about even before Angela's belly had started to swell: it was either become Angela Vest or Angela the Whore, and while both paths had looked to her to lead to the same unhappy end, only one of them lay paved with shame.

I won't say Bucky ever minded that was the reason he got himself a wife—and a beautiful one at that, if only for a while. He loved Angela and promised she'd learn to love him back in time. He'd work hard and take care of her and their unborn child, and one day she would come to see that whatever earthly things a man like Landis Foster could buy would pale against the things that truly mattered. Things like family and joy and a good home.

And Angela tried, friend, hard and to her own credit—but I don't think that notion ever truly took root. Some part of that woman was always going to pine for Landis Foster. Angela had come to find peace in that and I think so had Bucky, both of them believing it wasn't a sin so long as those feelings were kept unsaid and penned in the heart. The baby was born the following January. Bucky suggested *Cordelia* after Angela's cherished grandmother, hoping the name would spark a love she had yet to feel for their child.

It was a hard time. Bucky got his job at the dump and was gone all day and some of the night, stumbling back after dark stinking and tired and griping of how hard Homer Pruitt pushed him. As a favor to his friend, Wilson had convinced his father that Bucky could be a fair constable. Even that paltry bit of money helped. Angela clipped coupons and stayed up all night with a colicky Cordy, squeezing the baby hard and then harder as she walked from the living room to the dining room and back, feeling like a hot poker had been jabbed into her ear, crying and wanting away from the life she'd been handed as she fought the horrible thought of how easy it would be to just cover that barking mouth and snot-filled nose with a pillow and watch her baby go to sleep forever.

Time passed. David Ramsay had returned from his time at preaching school and brought both John David and a pregnant Belle with him to take over the church. Naomi was born soon after. Wilson became a father and lost his own in the span of two months and took over the mayorship. Angela got her job at the grocery. Bucky didn't much like that. Things were peaceable but rarely happy, and that's okay. Peaceable is a good enough thing when that's all you can get. You spend time enough on this earth, you realize it ain't about getting ahead, it's about getting by.

All those thoughts must've gone through Bucky's mind that night and morning. It must've seemed to him this was where everything had led—right back to a hospital room with their baby.

The orderly wheeled in breakfast. Angela decided sitting beside Cordelia wasn't good enough and took up residence beside her on the bed. Bucky watched from the chair like he was witnessing some kind of astronomical alignment that promised either the end of the world or a new dawn of prosperity. Angela brushed Cordelia's hair. Angela smoothed Cordelia's blankets. Angela got the food ready and wiped the sagging side of Cordelia's face and asked if she'd been feeling any morning sickness yet, and Bucky just marveled at it all. He teared up some, too, knowing it'd taken their daughter getting cursed by the witch to part the thick bank of resentment that had hung over Angela's world for good.

She was feeding Cordelia scrambled eggs when the phone vibrated in Bucky's pocket. He reached into his suit jacket and pulled it out, saw the number there.

"It's Doc," he told them. "Probably wanting to check up. I'll step out and leave y'all some time."

Bucky made for the door, flipped open the phone, and raised it partway to his ear when he saw David Ramsay standing there. He waved. The preacher turned and walked toward the elevators like he never even seen Bucky at all.

"Hello?" the voice over the phone said.

Bucky held the phone to his ear. "Hey, Doc."

"It's actually Maris, Bucky. I'm afraid Danny can't come to the phone right now."

Bucky stuck a finger in his other ear and bent his head low, trying to better hear. It wasn't the noise in the hospital that was getting in the way, it was the racket on the other end.

"Everything okay there, Maris?"

"Bucky, we need you down here."

"What's going on?"

The voice in the background was a woman's, though it came through so frantic and high-pitched that was all Bucky could tell. What came over the line was, "Maris, I don't see anybody soon, I'm gonna start tearing stuff up."

It was like the world split in half when Bucky heard that, a sharp rent of the thin line between present and past. A bit of that old fear in him let loose, not at the voice that had shouted those words but the words themselves, tumbling over and over in Bucky's mind—*I'm gonna start tearing stuff up, I'm gonna start tearing stuff up, I'm gonna start tearing stuff up woman if you don't give me what I want*—turning Bucky from the man he'd become to the scared little boy he'd once been, the one who'd hidden behind the sofa the time the bad man got into the house.

"Maris?" He gripped the phone harder. "What's going on? Who is that?"

Maris didn't bother telling him. She shouted back, "Ruth, you sit down and shut up and wait your turn or so help me God I'll brain you."

"Ruth?" Bucky asked. "Maris, is that Ruth Mitchell?"

"Get over here now, Bucky," Maris said. "There's trouble. And don't tell Wilson. Hear me? You keep the mayor away from here. People are riled. It ain't safe."

-4-

Not everybody in Crow Holler had it so bad that morning. Things was going as smooth as ever down at the Hodge farm.

Now I say *farm* in the loosest sense. Briar Hodge's place has land enough to be called that—hundred acres or so, suited for both crop and cattle. And it's true he and Chessie keep a milking cow and some laying chickens, along with a few hogs to butcher. But the fact is Briar did no more farming than it took to till the garden every spring, and the only crop that come out those hundred acres was the moonshine he brewed and the weed he growed.

He had quite the operation down there along the Ridge Road, though Briar'd be first to say most of it had been handed down by his daddy and prospered by Chessie. Let me tell you, friend, Chessie's mind is a sharp one. Got a knack for managing things. It's almost like that woman can see what's gonna happen before it does, and in that's a danger. Things was different, I've no doubt Chessie could be running some company in the big city and getting her picture taken for the papers. As it was, Lord seen fit to sink her in Crow Holler and pair her with a man whose family had drifted from the straight and narrow sometime around the Dark Ages.

Briar was on the front porch of their little wooden ranch that morning, rocking in the chair as the sun eased its way over the trees. He'd gone through three pipes already. Some puffing and a little chewing on the stem of his meerschaum was usually enough to work out any problem. Briar knew as much as any-one Alvaretta Graves was not a woman to be crossed, and he'd been here long enough to know her power lay in something beyond fists and iron.

You could hear Chessie talking on the phone inside. It'd rung all that morning—people wanting some bit of news and to ask if what they'd heard from the prayer chain about hoofprints and a demon was true. Chessie wouldn't say one way or the other and told them everything would be fine.

Briar packed another pipe and struck a match. John David was already at work in the barn, feeding fire to the still and packing up crates for the next delivery. Good thing having that Ramsay boy around, he'd told Chessie. Knows how to handle hisself. Too bad what happened in the war.

The screen door creaked open. Chessie shuffled out and let out a weary breath as she settled into the nearest rocker.

"That was Wilson," she said.

"Scarlett better?"

"The same. All 'em. Said Bucky got a call from Maris. Left in a hurry."

"What's Maris need with the constable?" Briar asked.

"Mayor didn't know. Only reason he knew where Bucky'd gone at all was Angela told him."

Briar puffed and rocked. "What's this mean?"

"Means I don't know," Chessie said. "Somebody done run their mouth, and I'd lay money Reverend's the one. Always been a prideful man, looking down his nose at us and holding out his hand at the same time. I knew that man'd talk. Knew it even as he sat there nodding when Wilson said all this had to be kept close."

"John David showed me his phone this morning," Briar said. "Had a video on there Naomi made. Girl's telling ever'body Alvaretta's coming."

Chessie shook her head slow and cursed. "Kids'll be the ruination of us all."

Down the lane came the sound of a car slowing to turn. John David walked out from the barn, wiping his hands with a dirty rag. The three of them watched a battered old Ford wind its way down the lane. Briar rocked back and held there, his hand on the butt of the pistol tucked into his jeans. Weren't really a reason for him to do that—not a soul in Crow Holler dared such a stupid thing as threaten a Hodge, then or now— but such was Briar's way. Sides, up to a couple days before, weren't a soul in the Holler who'd dare such a stupid thing as crossing the witch, neither.

"Tully," John David said.

Briar went back to his pipe.

The car stopped at a respectful distance. Tully Wiseman stepped out with his head near bowed. In a moment of sheer humility that made Briar chuckle, the drunk lifted his hands in surrender.

"Ain't no need for that, Tully Wiseman," Chessie called. "Put your hands down and act like the man your momma raised. Come on up here and see us."

Tully smiled and approached. He wasn't yet fifty and already missing most of his teeth, which made him look nearer a hundred.

"Ain't you supposed to be cuttin' meat down to the grocery by now?" Chessie asked.

"I'll be there directly, Miss Chessie. Landis said to come on when I could." He chanced a step closer. "Our Daisy's fallen ill by the witch's hand. Woke up this morning mute. Cain't speak a'tall. Me and Lorraine took her to see the doc."

Another step. Tully lifted the cap from his head. His hand trembled so bad you'd wonder if Alvaretta's demon hadn't gotten him too.

Chessie stopped rocking. "Sick, you say?"

"Yes'm. Other'n too."

Briar cocked his head. "It bad at the clinic, Tully?"

"Oh, it's a mess, Mr. Briar. Whole place is full up. Everybody getting it now."

"Guess we know why Maris called up to Bucky," Chessie said. "Word of Alvaretta's out. You have our sympathies, Tully. I fear we're in for a dark time."

"Amen," Tully said. "Don't want to intrude, Chessie. Briar. I don't come with my hand out, neither. Can't make it to Mattingly for my groceries, not with Daisy being so bad. I wouldn't even go to work if the money weren't so sorely needed. Gotta swallow my pride as it is, knowing my pay's coming from a man whose boy helped bring this on. Hays and that Scarlett. I hear going to the mines was all on her."

"You heard right," Chessie said. "You come up here because you got a thirst. That the groceries you need?"

Tully bowed his head for an answer.

"Don't sell to Crow Holler," Briar told him. "It's been agreed. You know that, Tully."

"I do, Mr. Briar, I know. But like you said, Chessie, it's a dark time. I'm in pain for my little one."

Briar looked to his wife. She studied Tully with a gaze that made him shrink himself smaller than he was. You could see the rage burning just behind her eyes, the kind that begins as pity to the helpless before turning to rage against the weak.

"Jar'll last you no more'n a day," she said. "Then what? You'll be back, and you'll bring along every man and woman inside a dozen miles who spend their days figuring how and when they's gonna get buggered next. Reverend's apt to haul us to give an account in front of the church. You want that, Tully?"

"I won't speak of it. Swear on the Book, Chessie."

Tully raised his empty eyes and met Chessie's own, and I believe her heart cracked at that sight—a father stricken and wounded, knowing the girl he'd once bucked on his knee and still called Flower had fallen to the witch.

"You leave the money with John David. He'll get you a jar."

Tully bowed again. Looked like a peasant, he did, thankful for crumbs from the queen's table. He smiled through his tears.

John David did as directed, then watched in silence as Tully left, drinking as he went, swerving his car as he got back on the road. Briar said nothing, only sucked on his pipe. The sweet smell of cherry filled the air. A worried look crept across Chessie's face. She rocked forward in her chair and opened her mouth, like she was meaning to tell John David to get out to the end of the lane and get that jar back. But she didn't, friend. Chessie only leaned back in her chair again, and that choice would come back to haunt her. I said it was like that woman could see what was going to happen before it did. That's true, but not that time. Nosir, not that time.

-5-

About the fourth time Bucky's phone rang, he decided he couldn't ignore the mayor anymore. Angela must've told where Bucky'd run off to. That woman couldn't keep a secret if her life depended on it.

Wilson Bickford was screaming in midsentence when Bucky answered, wanting to know why in the world Maris would call Bucky Vest instead of her own brother, wanting to know a dozen other things, and Bucky could only answer that he guessed it was because Maris didn't want to get yelled at. He did the best he could to remember exactly what Maris had said, which wasn't much in the way of detail.

"And she didn't say anything else?" Wilson asked, and as that was the third time he'd done so, Bucky chose not to answer at all. "She probably thought she was calling me the whole time, Bucky. I had my phone on. Maris can't see to dial the numbers right. She's my sister and I love her, but that woman's blind as a bat."

"All I know's Maris wants me down there straightaway. Sounded none too calm about it, neither. Why don't you just call Maris and ask her yourself?"

"I *tried*," the mayor said. "Ain't nobody answering."

Bucky pressed on the gas, willing the Celebrity to go faster. Thirty miles to Crow Holler from the hospital in Stanley. More than an hour, given the back roads. He weaved in and out as he pressed the phone to his ear, doing his best to dodge the morning traffic, long haulers and minivans mostly, everybody going on as usual without a care of what was going on in the lonely corners of the world.

"Alvaretta," the mayor said. "You believe that, Bucky? What'd our kids get us all into?"

"I don't know, Wilson."

"We gotta try and stay ahead of this. The council. Landis is already involved, but we'll have to bring Raleigh Jennings in at some point too. The Reverend. Shoot, we'll have to get Chessie and Briar involved, even if I don't want to. You're with me, Bucky. Ain't you? No matter what comes of this."

Not a question. Bucky would back whatever play Wilson had to do next. He'd been following Wilson around ever since they were coming up, and for some reason Wilson never minded it. Them two played on the same Little League teams in the summer and the same Peewee football teams in the fall, and once high school come along and Bucky had to admit he couldn't play with the big boys, Wilson made sure he became the team manager for both. Wilson made sure Bucky was accepted, because he knew that's what Bucky needed. Aside from his constabling, that's maybe what Bucky had always needed most.

"Remember our senior year, Bucky? The game against Lexington? Everybody said we didn't stand a chance, bunch of hicks against those guys. But what happened?"

Bucky smiled at the windshield. You wouldn't think it possible, given what he'd gone through the past day, but it was true. It was a grin full of memory for a time when his life was brighter and clearer than it'd been before or since. My, that had been a grand time in Bucky's life. In everybody's life, really. The only dark spot was that Stu Graves had killed himself only a week before, and what people who weren't talking about Wilson Bickford's golden arm were talking about Alvaretta's revenge.

"Beat 'em," Bucky said.

"You got that right. We won state. Crow Holler's one and only time."

Bucky smiled. "Don't remember a 'we' there, Wilson. You won. Ain't nobody played a game like you did that night. It was like you was playing for your life."

"I was." And in a small waiting room all the way back in Stanley, Wilson Bickford grinned. Was a pain in that smile, though. You'd've seen the mayor right then, you'd know he was scared to death, and with good reason. Alvaretta knew him. And if Alvaretta knew him, she knew what he'd done.

"Well, all I did was carry the jockstraps."

"We were a team, Buck. Don't you let me hear you say otherwise."

You can still see that trophy, hanging there in the foyer of Crow Holler Secondary. It's gone tarnished a bit over the years, but if you look close at the faded photograph above, you can still see the young faces of Wilson Bickford and Bucky Vest looking at the camera, Wilson in his uniform and Bucky in a pair of tan pants and a white shirt.

"Now you get up there," the mayor said, "you call me. Let me know what's going on."

"I will," Bucky said.

He pushed the Celebrity to sixty.

-6-

Back then, the Crow Hollow Health and Wellness Center's where everybody went when they come down with something either prayer or folklore couldn't chase. That little building was Doc Sullivan's pride and joy. It ain't there no more, sad to say. Got boarded up along with the school after the Trouble. Anybody in the Holler gets sick now, they got to make the drive to Doc March down in Mattingly. Shame it's gotta be that way. But like I told you, whole lotta people are gone from here now that the demons is loose. Danny Sullivan, he might be missed most of all. People liked that man, even if they mostly thought him heathen.

He'd brought Maris home to Crow Holler some twenty years before, right about the time Wilson was scrambling up and down the field in the Big Game and seeing Stu Graves's face on every Lexington player that came after him. The clinic was no more'n a few hundred square feet, just enough for a waiting room, an office, and a room for Danny to look over the sick. Not a big crowd, usually. Maris used to say if the doc seen fifty people in a week, it was rare.

Wasn't no fifty people Bucky saw waiting there that morning. It was more a hundred. Mommas and daddies and grandparents, all standing in the hot sun with their young ones in tow. Maris moved down the line with a little clipboard, writing things down and patting people's shoulders. If Bucky'd been close to scared on that drive back to the Holler, he was near petrified now. Alvaretta hadn't just come for his daughter—she'd come for his town too.

He had to park a ways off and walk the road back, taking a hard left into all those angry-looking faces.

"What's all this, now?" he asked.

Nobody said a word back, not even Maris. Maybe it was the stupidity of the question that stumped them all. Even to Bucky, it was plain what all that was. All he had to do was look beside him at Ruth Mitchell, whose daughter, Chelsea, was jerking her head and feet like she was listening to music only she could hear. Tears stained her green eyes.

"You tell us, Constable," Ruth said. "Chelsea woke me an Joe up like this last night, and we ain't been able to get her settled down since."

"Well, I'm sorry to hear that, Ruth," Bucky said. "You tell me what I can do to help."

"You done enough," someone shouted.

Maris grabbed Bucky's arm and yanked him toward the clinic door, through a valley of rage so hot he couldn't bring himself to look at the people's faces. She shoved him into the little office off from the waiting area and slammed the door.

"You crazy, Buck?" she asked. "Waltzing up in here like nothing's happened?"

"Well maybe I wouldn't have if I knew what was going on," Bucky said. "You didn't tell me anything."

"You see all those people out there? Think I had time to explain things? Now sit here and keep quiet until Danny comes in."

"I can't do that, Maris. You need to let me try to calm things down."

"You go out there right now, those people will tear you apart." She took a breath and straightened herself, adjusted the collar around her wrinkled neck. "Please, Bucky. They *know*."

"Know what?" Bucky asked.

"They know what your kids did."

She let that hang in the air and backed out through the door to a room full of hollering people, leaving Bucky to ponder who had betrayed the mayor. He never did come up with an answer. He was too busy worrying about the other thing Maris had just told him, and how she'd put it.

Not that everybody knew what *Alvaretta* had done.

No, *what your kids did*.

-7-

Right about the time the doctors told Angela they were letting Cordy go, Danny Sullivan snuck into his office looking every bit of his sixty-two years.

"I'm sorry about Maris," he said to Bucky. "Once her stress reaches a certain point, she becomes someone else. I can't blame her today, though. I've never seen such a thing. A dozen already."

"Girls," Bucky said. "Right, Danny? All the sick ones are girls?"

"Very perceptive, Constable. You're right. Not a sick male among them."

"What's that mean?"

The doctor picked up the stack of files on the corner of the desk and waved them into a thick fan. "I've had four patients so far suffering from various tremors and spasms, just like Naomi. Another four are reporting the same lack of speech function that's affected Scarlett. Three have lost feeling in various parts of their bodies. That sound familiar, Buck? And I have one—I can't divulge her name, so don't bother asking—who swears Alvaretta came to her in the night to say we're all going to die."

"Lord have mercy," Bucky said.

"The Lord doesn't have anything to do with it, Constable. And neither does Alvaretta Graves."

"What you trying to say, Danny?"

The doctor sighed. "Bucky, I have to be careful here. I wasn't raised in Crow Hollow. In spite of Maris, I'm still seen as an outsider. And I'm okay with that because frankly, most of you people are certifiably nuts. I'm not supposed to say that, but it's just me and you here. And you know Wilson and I have had our troubles. He still blames me for not catching Tonya's cancer in time, and—"

"Doc?" Bucky asked. "Just tell me."

"Fine." Danny sat on the edge of the desk and folded his hands. "I don't think there's anything in the world wrong with the girls I've seen so far this morning. Just like I don't think anything's wrong with Naomi, Scarlett, or Cordelia."

Bucky blinked twice, like the doctor's words had smacked him. The more he looked to think on it, the angrier he got. Wasn't right, what Danny had said. Wasn't right everybody knows *what your kids did*. What happened had been the witch's fault, Alvaretta's alone.

"Now I don't mean there's nothing emotionally wrong, Bucky. There certainly is." Doc shut his eyes, whispered, "Scarlett's poor arms." Then, louder and more to Bucky, "But physically? I simply don't see it."

"What about Scarlett's arms?"

"Nothing. Look, all I'm trying to say is this can't be what everybody thinks it is. I don't doubt those kids stumbled across Alvaretta. I'm even willing to say they followed something they thought to be footprints to her cabin. But a curse? That stretches things beyond rationality, don't you think?"

"No," Bucky said. "I don't think it does. It's like you said, Doc. You didn't come up here. In the Holler we know there's more to the world than what you can find in books."

And that was true. But I'll say this too: Bucky also knew if Danny was right, it meant Alvaretta might not have a grip on them girls at all and Cordelia could be fixed. Come down to it, Bucky was smart enough to take crazy over cursed any day.

He asked, "If it ain't a curse, Danny, what is it?"

"My guess? A delusion. Not a mass one, at least not yet. It's been known to happen. Happened in New York State a few years ago. And for reasons unclear, young women seem most susceptible."

"Alvaretta Graves ain't no delusion," Bucky said, "and neither is what she can do. Now I appreciate all you've done for Cordelia and the others, Danny, and I thank you for taking care of all them sick folk waiting outside, so I'm going to give you a nickel's worth of free advice: You best keep your opinions quiet. It gets out this is what you think's happening, nothing good will come of it."

"But Bucky—"

"Nothing good. I mean it. I know these people, Danny. You say something like that, it'll sound more like witchcraft than anything Alvaretta can say. And speaking of which, I got to ask you something. Maris said all them out there know what Cordy and her friends did Sunday morning. You tell them?"

"No."

"You need to tell me the truth, Doc," Bucky said.

"I swear, Constable. Wasn't me."

"Then who was it?"

"I did."

Bucky turned in his chair to see Raleigh Jennings coming through the door like he'd been listening on the other side the whole time. His jaw was set and his chest puffed out.

Bucky stood up and said, "You tell me that ain't right, Raleigh."

"Something in the water, Buck? That what all y'all decided?" Raleigh came on into the office.

Maris tried shooing away the few who'd tried following Raleigh in, first with kindness and then with harsh words.

"Those are lies. Wilson shoulda been straight with me. I'm on the dad-blamed *council.*"

"Wilson's trying to protect the town," Bucky said.

"Wilson's trying to protect his *own.*"

Danny put himself between the two men, trying to get things calm.

Bucky would have none of it. "Who told you, Raleigh? Who told you it was the witch?"

"Was on the prayer chain, if you got to know. I was the first person the Reverend called. He trusts me, not like you. Preacher told me everything."

"And you told everybody else."

Raleigh sighed and spread his arms wide, like he was surrendering. "It's a prayer chain, Bucky. That's how it works."

Doc shook his head. "So now everybody in town knows Scarlett and her friends were up at the mines and had a run-in with Alvaretta Graves? That some . . . demon . . . cursed them and the town both? And now everybody's girl is coming down sick and everybody in Crow Holler is blaming them, and you're okay with that because it was a *prayer chain*? They ain't safe now, Raleigh."

"The girls." Bucky looked at the doctor first, then Raleigh. "They're headed this way. They're coming home from the hospital."

He fumbled for his phone and flipped it open. You ever pushed the buttons on one a them things? Tiny, especially for a big man who's just realized his wife and daughter might be driving into danger. Bucky hit a 2 when it should've been a 3, a

4 and a 5 instead of just the 5, cussing as he did. Danny slid the phone off his desk over and dialed the number himself, handing Bucky the receiver.

It was too late. Angela never answered.

-8-

"No."

The mayor took a hand off the wheel and placed it over what Scarlett had taken from her purse.

"No, just . . . let's leave that alone for now. Okay? Please?"

Scarlett barely gave her daddy a glance before easing his hand away and turning the phone upside down on her knee.

"Mine's off too," Wilson said. "In my jacket pocket right here, and here's where I mean to leave it." He tapped at his chest and tried to smile. I know that was a hard thing for that man to do, shutting that phone off without knowing what Bucky had found down at the clinic. If Wilson had taken just a moment to reach for his phone and flip it on, he'd've found plenty of messages waiting for him—Chessie and Raleigh and Ruth Mitchell, along with four texts from Bucky begging the mayor not to go home just yet. "I just thought . . . you know, long ride and all, we could . . ."

Talk. That was supposed to be Wilson's next word. But then Scarlett couldn't do that now, could she? No, all the talking she could do was chained to the pen and pad sitting on her other knee, a tongue made of cheap plastic and lips of thin paper with *Stanley Medical Center, Where the Patient Comes First!* written acrost the top. That was how Scarlett would talk for now and maybe forever, thanks to Alvaretta Graves.

". . . we could just be together for a while," he finished. "You know, just us. We don't do that near often enough, Scarlett."

We don't do that ever, Scarlett's eyes said. She tugged her sleeves down, like that would do any good at all now.

"I'm so glad you're okay, pumpkin."

He winced before the words were out, but too late to pull them back. Why's it so hard to talk to your kids sometimes? *Pick up your room* or *Take out the trash* or *Cut the grass* can roll off a parent's tongue, but anything deeper comes out like trying to describe color to a blind man.

"You're not," Wilson said. "Okay, I mean. You're not okay. I mean, you are, but there's still a ways to go."

Wincing again. And now Scarlett winced too.

"I'm sorry, Scarlett. I just can't say anything."

He took his eyes off the road. It was the interstate and those slow hours just after the morning rush. Traffic wasn't bad. Scarlett tried smiling and gave a little shrug—*I can't say anything either.*

"Why'd you do that, Scarlett? Not go up to the mines, though I've always told you to keep far away from that place. But why take off through the woods like that? Why keep going when you and the rest said how things got so weird? You should've turned and run soon as you *knew* that was Alvaretta's place down there. That was just so *stupid.*"

The words came so fast that the sun caught the little drops of spit flying from Wilson's mouth, forming a shiny rain. Scarlett reached for her pen. She wrote two words and held the page where Wilson could see it:

I'm sorry

Wilson bit the inside of his lip, blinking away tears that made everything look foggy. A rig blew past them, washing the inside of the car with diesel and exhaust.

"No," he said. "I'm the one who's sorry. This is all because of me." He looked at Scarlett's arms, covered with the long sleeves of the denim shirt she'd left the house wearing the day before.

"Do you do that because of me? I need to know, Scarlett. I promise I won't get mad."

He kept staring at that pad of paper, wanting so much for the pen to start moving and for those words to come. Words to prove Wilson's innocence, some far-fetched explanation of why his daughter would ever think such a thing as maiming herself would be necessary, would think it *good*. It would be school or friends or the godforsaken hole in the mountains where they'd all been fated to spend their lives. Anything but himself. Please, don't let it be himself.

Scarlett shook her head. Not her daddy. She ran a finger over her shirt, down by her wrist where the newest scar was healing (*new* meaning months old; Scarlett had promised Cordelia she would stop and she'd meant it). For the first time, she looked to wonder just how close to something important that cut had gone. Were there arteries in that place, right above her forearm? Were there veins or tendons?

"You sure?" her daddy asked.

She nodded and held the pen over the page, unsure what to write. And you know what, friend? I don't blame her. Not a bit. Because it would've taken more pens and paper pads than Scarlett could ever get hold of to explain the real reason she cut herself, and even then I doubt she thought it would all come out right. How can you explain such a thing? How can you attach to something like that any sort of rational meaning?

How could Scarlett ever tell her daddy that the reason she'd taken a blade to her own skin was to get the bad out?

-9-

Wilson and Scarlett Bickford weren't the only ones knee-deep in silence just then. Six miles up ahead on that same stretch of

Interstate 64, Angela and Cordelia were mired in an awkward conversation of a different sort, one that had grown quiet after miles upon miles of screaming. Cordy had known they couldn't put off forever talking about the baby growing inside her, had known Angela would ask exactly where and why it had been that her daughter had opened her legs for Hays Foster.

For her part, Angela weren't exactly looking forward to that conversation herself. But she had fired the first salvo, a sharp *How could you?* that made the healthy side of Cordelia's face slump to match the sick one. It didn't help when Cordy responded there really wasn't much her momma could say, people in glass houses shouldn't throw stones. Or, as it had come out of Cordy's numbed face, "Peefle in gass howfes fuldn't fow phones."

Angela had looked to be ready for that, saying times were different back when her and Bucky had been in high school. And even if times weren't, Cordy had no idea how hard it had been for the two of them, how many dreams had to be put on hold or die altogether, and couldn't she see that? Couldn't Cordelia see what a mistake that had all been?

"Tho I'm a mithtake?" Cordy had said. "Wow. Fanks."

So sure, friend. It had all gone downhill from there. Miles of silence after that, until the same rig that had blown by the mayor and Scarlett now blew by Angela and Cordelia, washing enough diesel smell through the open window to mask the stench of trash caught in the upholstery.

"You're keeping this baby," Angela now said.

Cordy looked at her in horror, as though any alternative had never been considered.

"We're keeping it, even if it's part Foster," her momma said. "We'll make this right, even if it's all so terribly wrong. I don't know how I'll face them. Does Hays know?"

"No."

"Then you won't tell him. Not yet. Not until your father and I can wrap our heads around this. Do you understand me?"

"I wu—*l . . . uhve* him," Cordelia said, even as I imagine she remembered the way Hays had looked at her the day before, the frantic look of fear in church that withered along with the side of her face to a look of near disgust; the way he'd leaned his body away as Doc Sullivan had bent over her; how Hays's mouth had hung open and his tongue had pushed against his teeth when he'd visited Cordelia's hospital bed that morning. You can't blame that boy, acting as such. Was a horrible sight to look upon Cordelia and see what the witch had done.

"You don't know what love is," Angela said. "And you didn't answer my question. Do you *understand*?"

"Yethum."

Angela reached under her sunglasses to wipe her eyes. "Why did you go up there, Cordelia? Why did you have to spend the night at the mines? Spreading your legs for a boy like Hays Foster is one thing—a *stupid* thing, and one you'll spend the rest of your life regretting—but crossing Alvaretta Graves? That's even worse."

"I had to get your bwacelet back."

And so that was it. That was when Angela understood that none of what had happened was the fault of Alvaretta Graves. Wasn't some curse. It was Angela herself. It was the way she'd thought of her daughter all those years, like Cordelia was less a light for Angela's future than she was a broken and tilted signpost in Angela's past, forever marking the spot where her life had gone astray. Cordelia had grown up, learned to crawl and then stumble and finally walk, sprouting the dark hair of the Vests and that perfect face that had once been her mother's. A quiet child, always in need of touching and holding hands, always so scared to be alone. Like she had been born into the world knowing how thin the bond between her and her momma was, and that it was up to her to make it stronger.

And all that while, Angela had believed those thoughts were locked away and hidden. They were buried in a suffering part of her that had been kept covered over by smiles and I love yous, and she was either unable or unwilling to see that all of our secrets are bound to leak out through the cracks in the walls we build to hide them. She could blame her daughter for what had happened with Hays, but what had happened with the witch could be placed only upon Angela's shoulders. Because in the end, Cordelia had decided that facing the witch was a better choice than facing her own mother's wrath.

Angela stared through the windshield and set her sunglasses closer to her face, not wanting Cordelia to see her hurt. A car passed in the next lane. Husband and wife in front, three kids in the back. All of them smiling and, it looked, singing.

They passed the Celebrity and snuck into Angela's lane. The wife had her left hand to the back of her husband's head, rubbing his hair in soft, tiny circles; the kids laughing and playing, parents smiling and touching, a family content, happy in the company they kept, joyful because they were going in the same direction and going together, and I do believe for the first time Angela Vest looked upon that sight and thought not What Could Have Been in another life with Landis Foster, but What Could Be in her own life now.

"I love you," she said. "I've always loved you, Cordelia. How could I not? You're smart and beautiful and so many things I thought I could be but found I couldn't. I know sometimes I haven't been a good mother. I haven't been a good wife. I try. But sometimes it's like I've spent my whole life trying to dig a hole deep enough to put all my troubles in and instead I keep throwing my own self into it. I know that's hard for you to understand."

Angela looked at her daughter and didn't look away until the right tires skirted the rumble strip on the side of the road. She corrected. The husband in the car ahead stared through his rearview mirror.

"I . . . *l-ove* you," Cordelia said.

And so Angela promised it would all be okay now, things would be different. No more silent meals at the supper table and awkward meetings in the hallway, even no more TV stories. ("Unless you want to watch with me," Angela said, and that coaxed a smile.) The Vests would make a new start, fix what had been broken for so long, and I don't doubt Angela and Cordelia both wondered why it'd taken something like the witch to make it happen.

They would go home, tell Bucky everything. Schedule appointments with baby doctors. And there was a psychologist in Mattingly. Norcross was his name. Yes. Cordelia could go see him. All of them could go.

It was a fine plan the two of them had worked out by the time Angela reached Crow Holler. And like all good plans, this one fell apart as soon as it met up with reality. Because people were scared, friend, because word of what the witch had done had gotten out.

And though everybody might've known deep down it was all Alvaretta's doing—her and her demon, playing with those kids like they was toys to toss away once the shine wore off— they also knew the danger of lashing out at her. But those kids? That was different. They were people we went to church with, people we saw every day. Scarlett and Cordy and Naomi and Hays weren't scary. They were just stupid.

And maybe it would've been okay had it ended there, with three girls in the hospital. But now the curse had spread to the Holler itself, and what started as a stupid decision by four kids had turned to danger for us all. All it took for Angela to understand that was one turn up the driveway to the double-wide, one glance at the sight of Bucky standing in the flower beds.

His hands were full of rosebush stems and thick roots that looked like tiny upside-down trees. His mouth was stuck in a wide O.

Every plant was uprooted and smashed. Dug up and thrown into the yard and onto the porch and against the trailer's front deck. Others had been mashed flat, run over by whoever had left the tire tracks through the beds and down the yard to the road.

Years of work, gone. Angela's hands went to her chest. It was like she herself had been violated.

"I tried to call you," Bucky said. "They're after us, Angie. Whole town's after us."

-10-

It's a boy

That's what Scarlett finally wrote, and only because that was the only way her daddy would feel better and because *a boy* was partly true. She didn't say who, and Wilson didn't press. He was happy enough to know Scarlett wasn't thinking of him whenever she stuck a knife under her skin.

A boy was why Scarlett had asked Cordelia to take her momma's bracelet that night. That's the reason she'd worn those skimpy clothes—to impress some "him" and make sure she was seen. Wilson took it all in with a bunch of slow nods and Poor Dears and pats to Scarlett's hand. Boy trouble. In the grand scheme of things, that was no trouble at all.

Nosir, the real trouble for Wilson and Scarlett lay back in town, once they got home and he decided it was okay to turn his phone back on. He started out standing by the front door as he listened to Chessie say kids were getting sick; Raleigh wanting to know why Wilson had lied about the flu or the water; then Bucky, telling him not to bring Scarlett home just yet. By the time he'd listened to Bucky again (this time describing the horrible scene in Angela's flower beds), Wilson was closer to the sofa. When he got the message from a frantic Landis, saying Kayann and Hays had come home from seeing Cordelia off at the hospital that morning to find a cinderblock through Hays's bedroom window, Wilson collapsed onto the cushion.

But the worst of it had come to Medric Johnston when he arrived back at the funeral parlor. His message to Wilson had been the longest, told in a voice far too calm to have really been truly calm. Telling the mayor of the thick stench of rotting meat that had greeted him first, and then the buzzing sound of all those flies. Telling of the long-dead raccoon nailed to his back door.

Hit by a truck, was Medric's guess, found and then scooped up from somewhere along the road. The sign underneath had been scrawled in an illegible hand, but the sentiment was clear enough. *Die . . .* well, I won't say what that last word was, friend. You look smart enough to figure it out.

By the time Wilson finished listening to all the people who'd called since that morning, he realized two things: his town was falling apart, and the only person who hadn't seemed to have suffered any trouble at all was the Reverend. And to that, I say why not? Weren't nobody gonna strike the family of the one man who'd been brave enough to speak out on exactly what was going on.

Wilson had no choice then but to leave and try to put out as many a those fires he could. He was our mayor, after all, and he'd been brought up holding fast to the idea that Crow Holler might've been a town full of people, but it all belonged to the

Bickfords and no one else. He couldn't take Scarlett with him and place her in danger, nor did he want to leave her there alone. Couldn't take her to Bucky's or Landis's; they had troubles of their own. I do believe for a brief moment Wilson considered the possibility of calling Chessie and asking a favor, but that notion quickly faded. No direness in the world warranted being in debt to a Hodge. Such was what Wilson believed, though not for much longer.

In the end he had no choice but to tell Scarlett he had to go out for a bit, see to some things, and then ask that she shut the blinds and the doors and not let anybody in. To make sure you get your rest is what he said. Scarlett, she was simple enough to believe.

She watched him go through the edge of the curtain drawn over the living room window. A single tear fell from her eye as her daddy backed out and sped off without even a glance back. Scarlett let the tear fall free. No one was there to see anyway.

She'd walked from the window and made it halfway to the kitchen when the knock came. Scarlett turned, thinking her daddy had changed his mind. All the warnings Wilson had given about keeping the house shut up tight left her thinking, and she flung the front door open with a smile that faded when she saw Tully Wiseman standing there about as drunk as a man could be and still remain upright. He wobbled on the small wooden porch, grabbing the rail to steady himself, then wiped his mouth with a hand that held Chessie's jar.

"Knew you's here," he said. "Watched you from acrost the way till your daddy gone. How you feelin, Scarlett?"

She stepped back (already knowing, I guess, that this visit wasn't the social kind) and nodded.

"What's matter? Cat got your tongue?"

Scarlett reached into her back pocket for the pad and pen the doctors had given her. She scribbled something and held it up. Took Tully a few minutes to read it all. Not because that man was filled to the gills, but because he was so stupid.

"Know it?" he snorted. "Course I *know* it. Whole dad-blamed *town* knows it, girl. Witch got y'all. You tempted her and she got you and now she's got us all. Now you step on back and let me in."

Scarlett shook her head. I expect right about then was when she figured out exactly why Wilson had told her to keep the door shut.

Tully sipped at his jar. "You know my Daisy, don't you? My Flower?"

She nodded.

"She's sick. Brought on by Alvaretta. By *you*. Let me in."

No.

"Let me in that house, Scarlett. Let me talk to you up close."

Tully threw the jar before Scarlett could shake her head once more. It bounced off the screen and landed with a thud on the porch, spraying her eyes with moonshine. She fell backward, clawing for a hold on the doorjamb and the drywall, blind now as well as mute. Tully tore the screen away and walked inside. He grabbed the back of Scarlett's hair. Her mouth hung open in a silent scream as Tully bent her head back, smacking her with open hands that turned to fists, yelling, "How bout I roon you altogether, girl?" as his fists rained down. Screaming, "Roon you like you rooned my *daughter*, like you rooned us *all*. Make you all the *way* ugly," and all Scarlett could do was suffer it in silence.

-11-

It took Bucky most of the evening to decide a fortified position would be best. He went out before sunset and moved the

Celebrity closer to the porch steps, so anybody who wanted to break in would either have to climb over the car or go through it. And just in case they did decide to go through, Bucky went on and locked the car doors too. Angela told Cordelia she saw so many holes in Bucky's grand design that she couldn't decide which one to start with, and so said nothing. It would work, Bucky promised. Ain't nobody gonna come up in here.

I don't reckon Angela thought anybody would. She'd spent more of her life around the people of Crow Holler than even Bucky had, first going to school with them and now ringing up their groceries down at Foster's. She knew who was sick by the medicine they bought and who was coming up on a birthday by the cards and frozen cakes. Don't nothing tell folk who you are more'n what you spend on, especially if it's at the grocery. Especially if that grocery's all there is in town.

Yessir, Angela Vest might've been a failed woman in the eyes of some hereabouts, but she kept her finger on the heartbeat of this town, however faint that pulse had grown. And what Angela knew was this: weren't nobody gonna come after them that night. She'd said the same over the phone when Chessie called to check on things, this after the best, most peaceable, most loving family supper the Vests had enjoyed in years. Oh sure, Angela still smarted over her roses and Bucky still hurt over the way the Reverend had gone back on his word. Cordy still had to eat with one hand holding a fork and the other moving the dead muscles on one side of her jaw. But it was hot food under a sturdy roof with the ones that mattered most circled together, and really, is there more warmth than that to be found in this cold life?

Once the plates were washed and put away, they all went outside to clean up the yard. Angela treated it as a kind of burial. She picked up each broken stem with gloved hands and stared like she was trying to remember when she'd set them in the ground and what the weather was, and how whatever day that had been was likely a better one than this. Cordelia helped. Her face looked dead but her strength remained. She threw her hands to work and sank them into the soft dirt, kneading the soil through her fingers. I think the labor made her feel some better.

Bucky paced the front porch through it all, and Angela had the good sense to let him. The old her would've asked for her husband's help to bag her most prized possessions before taking them to work and throwing them under the dozer the next day. But this was the new Angela, one born from the calamitous realization of her own selfish ways, and she knew Bucky wasn't loafing. He was up there pacing on the porch with a pistol so big the kick would break your shoulder. Looking out toward the empty road, praying it'd stay that way.

It took seven bags. Bucky jumped down from his lookout long enough to stuff them all in the trunk before ushering his two girls back inside. All the porch lights went on for the night.

Belle Ramsay called to check on everyone. She said she'd just got off the phone with Kayann and everything there was quiet, though Kayann was scared because Hays's bedroom window was now a Glad trash bag Landis had brought home from work. Naomi still had the tremors. Scarlett had been attacked but wouldn't write down who'd done it, and Wilson had vowed vengeance on whoever it had been. The thing with Scarlett was the worst, Belle and Angela both agreed on that, though the sordidness of what had greeted Medric when he got home came in a close second.

"David feels awful," Belle said.

"He should," Angela told her.

When the phone rang again an hour later, Cordelia had crawled into bed with her momma. Bucky picked up and heard Wilson's voice on the other end. He was staying up all night, too, watching over Scarlett.

"Heard what happened," Bucky said. "I'm sorry, Wilson."

"Scarlett wrote she was blindsided. Never even seen who hit her. I don't know how that can be, but I'd rather believe that than have to wonder why she'd like to protect the one who beat on her. But I'm trying to set that aside for now. Danny called me with the day's numbers. Sixteen girls sick, Bucky. And that's just today. No telling what tomorrow's gonna bring, so you stay sharp. Hear me?"

Bucky nodded into the phone and hung up. He pulled a chair from the kitchen table and sat it in front of the living room window. There he sat all night, surrounded by the darkness, with his daddy's old .44 on his lap, thinking of the bad man that had busted into his childhood home, remembering what that man had done to his momma and what he himself had not done at all.

Would be an awful thing, facing a night like that. Feeling that heavy night pressing down, knowing the waxing moon couldn't show you everything moving in the shadows. But Bucky remained straight-backed and steady without fear—not welcoming danger, but maybe expecting it. In the next room, Cordelia rolled over in her sleep and backed herself into the warmth of her momma's body. Angela drew her child in closer. And they were all happy, friend. Truly so. I'd say that night held every bit of peace and purpose the three of them had always wanted.

V I

Bucky loses his job. Chessie and Scarlett.
Medric has a secret. Bucky to the mines.

-1-

Bucky toasted dawn with a fresh cup of coffee. It was the first
time all night he'd left his post, and he winced at the knots in
his back and legs. His hand had gotten stuck in a claw around
the grip of his pistol. Not a cap gun, that firearm. Not as fancy
as the pearl-handled piece Briar kept tucked beneath his roll
of belly fat, but bigger. A lot bigger. Looked like one a them
you'd see Clint Eastwood carrying around in the movies. Dirty
Bucky, that was him.

There'd been no problems in the night. Twice Bucky had
shot forward in his chair, thinking something had moved in the
dark. One of those times, he'd decided it'd been his tired mind
playing tricks. But that other time something really had been
out there, inching its way up from the road to a place near the
porch. Too little to be a man. Coulda been a dog. Don't you
think that particular thought didn't cross Bucky's mind—it was
a dog, one of Alvaretta's—and don't you bother wondering if
he'd been close to going out on the porch and killing whatever
it was, because he nearly did.

He never heard a peep from Cordelia. Angela had gotten up
once, roused from a restless sleep by her aging bladder. When
she peeked around the corner into the living room and found
him wide-eyed and watchful, she'd smiled and said to Bucky

that he was a good man. Hearing that had been enough to get him through the rest of the night.

But now it was morning, and with it came the very sense of nervous hope that had greeted Raleigh Jennings the day before. There had been no trouble at the Vest place, and as the phone had yet to ring, Bucky and Angela allowed themselves to believe none of the other families had met misfortune in the night either. And in fact they hadn't. Wilson Bickford had spent the night in his own chair in front of his own window and witnessed nothing more than a few passing trucks that slowed before moving on. Scarlett sat up with him, unable or unwilling to sleep. They shared more in those hours than they had in all the long years since Tonya Bickford passed. Wilson paid attention as his daughter went on and on about school and the future. There was a sorrow to his eyes as Scarlett gently rocked in the recliner, offering up all those parts of herself she'd kept hidden. I expect Wilson considered it another part of Alvaretta's curse—Scarlett was finally talking to him, and yet he couldn't hear it and had to read it instead.

Medric had sat up with his shotgun at the ready. Landis too. They stood guard over their properties and kept hope that nothing would happen because, deep down, each worried he wasn't man enough to pull a trigger should things come to it. David Ramsay was the only one a them girls' fathers who'd gone on to bed, yet even he found no sleep. He spent the night with Belle snoring softly beside him, staring up at a dark ceiling and wondering what his God was trying to tell him. Come day, he still had no idea. Had any in Crow Holler taken the time to gaze upon the gathering clouds that morning and seen how bloodshot they looked coming up over the mountain, maybe they woulda paused to consider the old saying of sailors taking warning from a red sky. Because a storm was coming, and as it happened the Vests got the first dose.

They was all up, Cordelia too, and sitting for breakfast when the phone finally rang. Bucky jerked the receiver up before he knew what he did. Angela hunched her shoulders. Cordy drooped her head. Bucky just looked at them as a slow dawning spread across his face that what waited on the other end might well be the end of their peaceful morning.

He smiled and said "Hello?" as if it were nothing more than a normal day stacked in front of all the ones come before.

"Constable? It's Homer."

"Hey there, Homer." Bucky mouthed that same word—Homer—across the table, putting his family to ease, because the only news from Homer Pruitt would be the day's duties at the dump. "I's just sitting down to breakfast, getting ready to leave. Everything okay?"

"Everything ain't okay," Homer said. "You know ain't everything okay, Buck."

Bucky kept his smile. "Yeah," he said, "I know it. So what's going on?" Rolling his eyes, making Angela giggle.

"What's going on is me an Helen are taking our Maddie down to the doc's, Buck. That's what's going on. What's going on is our little girl woke up and can't talk no more."

And now Bucky's smile vanished. "That so?"

"It is. Called Maris a bit ago and she tole me rest and stayin' away from other folk's what's best. Like my little girl's got the chicken pox or something. But I'm taking my girl in anyway, because we both know ain't the chicken pox. Don't we, Buck? We both know where this comes from and who it was brought it to town."

Bucky looked down at his plate and pushed his eggs with his fork. "Uh-huh. Well, yeah, Homer. But things will come out. They always have."

"Does Cordy know what she's done, Bucky? What she's wrought?"

Cordelia stopped eating her breakfast. A drip of milk oozed down the side of her face, unfelt and unnoticed.

"No doubt about it," Bucky said. "But we can cover all that when I come in, Homer."

"No we can't, Buck. I can't keep you on knowing my girl's gone dumb on account of your daughter being fool enough to cross Alvaretta Graves. I won't have it."

"You . . ." Bucky cleared his throat. Wasn't his eggs that got stuck there, but his fear. "What you telling me, Homer?"

"I'm saying you're fired, Bucky. You been a good worker, and I 'preciate it. But your kid's put us all in danger now, and having you work for me might put me in worse than I already am. And right now, I just don't think I can look at you."

"Homer—"

"I'll clean your locker out, have somebody bring your stuff by. I'll be praying for you."

The line cracked and then clicked off. Bucky sat there like Homer was still talking, nodding his head and trying to smile. But by then Angela and Cordy knew something horrible had happened, because by then Bucky looked ready to cry.

-2-

The plan that morning had been for Angela to stay home with Cordy, but that was all shot now. Weren't no choice but to take her shift at the grocery. Somebody in the family had to be bringing money in.

Course it wouldn't do for Bucky to spend all that day at home neither. Sulking is what he would've done, and that wouldn't be good for him or Cordelia neither. That poor girl took news of her daddy's job harder than any of them. Bucky'd left off the part about it all being because of her, said it was a slow time and Homer had to cut back or some such, but Cordy knew. Didn't nobody get laid off from the dump. Hard times or not, everybody's got trash to get rid of.

A man's whole self is tied to his work. You take that work away, you cast him off with neither wind nor current and there he remains adrift, purposeless. So when Bucky told Angela he had to get to town, Angela knew why. And maybe he really did have it in his mind to go scare up more work. But maybe the real reason was that Bucky couldn't bring himself to spend all those hours alone with a daughter he'd just found was pregnant, and whose poor judgment the day before had now come to cost him near everything.

There was nothing for Angela to do but call Kayann and ask if Cordy could spend the day with Hays. The three of them piled into the Celebrity just before seven that morning. Bucky kept looking through the rearview at that bulging trunk full of dead rosebushes he'd never get to bury with his bulldozer, unsure now what to do with them. He tried saying the car might not stink so much no more, so maybe it was all for the best. Angela let him have his moment by chuckling and tapping him on the arm.

She kissed him hard when he dropped her at the grocery. "Don't you worry none, Bucky Vest," Angela said. "We're a family. We been knocked down before, and we'll stand again." She turned around in the seat and pulled her daughter close, nuzzling the bad side of Cordelia's face. "Now listen to me, little lady. You're gonna go to Hays's and you're gonna make sure Kayann locks that front door. Don't nobody get in and don't y'all go out. If there's trouble, the first call you make is to your daddy. The next one is to me. Okay?"

"Yethum."

"And you will not worry about any of this, no matter what. Hard times is a fact of life. We been through plenty before, and we'll get through this one here. We'll do it together. And there ain't nothing brightens a dark world like the light of new life."

Angela only turned back when Cordelia offered a tiny smile. She said, "I love you, Cordelia," and then, "I love you, Buck," and climbed from the car. She stood as regal as a person could be while wearing an ugly-colored smock from a two-bit store in a two-bit town. Back straight, chest out, eyes bright and determined.

Bucky looked at her as he backed away and said to Cordelia, "You just look at that woman. You ever seen a prettier thing?"

Angela offered a final wave as Bucky pulled from the lot onto the road, bound for the Fosters' home. Only then did she let that hand fall limp at her side. She walked away from the front doors to the side of the store where no one could see and pulled a tissue from her purse. There against a Dumpster full of trash, Angela shook and mourned and cursed her Lord, because she knew her life was done.

-3-

Landis was waiting once Angela had collected herself enough to clock in. She cried all over again after she said Bucky had lost his job. Landis stood there awkward, looking like he wanted to hug her, and don't you think Angela wouldn't have let him if he tried. People don't change much, that's my experience.

"I'm so sorry about this, Angela," he told her. "Bucky was never much, but all I've heard is he did his job well. Maybe Wilson can talk to Homer."

Angela sniffled and tried to throw out a brave smile. "I expect that's where Bucky's gonna head first. Him and Wilson's always been close. But all the talking in the world isn't gonna make a difference, Landis, even if it's the mayor doing it. Homer meant it. His Maddie's come down with the curse, and he's put that burden straight on Cordelia. Maybe if all this passes and the girls get better . . ." She shrugged, shook her head.

"I wish I could do something," Landis said.

"I know."

She moved to the register as she did every day, taking out the rag to wipe everything down. It was always a weight for Angela to have to work, not just at the grocery but anywhere. She'd always fancied herself whiling the days by lunching with the likes of Belle Ramsay and shopping at the mall down in Stanley, where the stores smelled new and the clothes were sold off wooden hangers. Places where Kayann shopped. I tell you, friend, it wasn't fair. Wasn't none of it ever *fair*.

"You have trouble last night?" he asked.

"Bucky stayed up to watch over things," Angela said. She turned and saw the grin Landis tried to hide. Them two had sometimes made a game of that over the years when the bills were past due and tempers got short, Landis poking fun at Bucky and Angela pitching in to do her share, but I think time for that was gone now.

"I stayed up," Landis said. "Guess everybody decided what they did yesterday afternoon was enough for one day. Least nothing happened here."

Angela turned around and went back to wiping the counter. "Anyone heard from Wilson or David?"

"Wilson called this morning. Said he had to go into work. Scarlett was going to Chessie's house."

"Chessie's?" Angela asked. "He'd have to swallow his pride to do something like that."

"Pride or not, anybody who's got it out for Scarlett wouldn't go to the Hodge place to do it. Don't you worry about Cordelia, though. She's with Hays."

"Hays," Angela said. The back of her head shook. Landis

couldn't see the sneer she made. Thinking, maybe, of Cordy in back of Hays's car, those windows all steamed. Thinking of what Hays had done to her little girl.

"She'll be fine," Landis said.

"Like she was fine Sunday morning?"

She kept right on wiping down the counter. I don't even know if Angela realized those words had passed her lips until she turned around to see Landis's face had gone red. But she had to lash out at somebody, you understand? She couldn't blame Bucky, not the way he was now, all broken over his job. And she could no more scream her hurts and frustrations at her daughter than watch the whole of Cordelia's face slump again.

"Don't you stand there glaring at me. I know you are. It's the truth, and you know it. Hays left them girls to fend for themselves. Cordy told me he even ran off first without a care for anyone's skin but his own."

"Angela," Landis said. He straightened his glasses. "That's not fair."

"Not fair? You're one to tell me what's fair. My husband's out of a job, Landis. We got nothing but fifty dollars in our savings, and that won't last a week. I ain't like your wife just like Bucky ain't like you. I can't go to him and complain until he shoves a handful of money at me."

"You'll watch your mouth, Angela." Landis was shaking, he was so mad. Looked like Naomi in a way. "Kayann and Hays are my *family*."

"Oh, and how proud you must be," she mocked. "Half a man's what you got for a son, and that's on a good day."

"We are not your concern here."

"It's *all* my concern, Landis. It's all *Bucky's* concern. The whole town's breathing down our necks now, and none of this would've happened if Hays had just *taken them girls back home*."

Landis said, "Hays is a good boy."

"Hays isn't *sick*."

That last word bounced off the shelves and walls as Angela screamed it, and she said it again in a whisper that sounded just as damning. "He isn't sick, Landis. You thought on that? My child is *sick*. Wilson's. David and Belle's. Their kids are cursed just the same, but not Hays. Hays is fine. You want to tell me how that is?"

Landis tried to swallow the lump in his throat. "That doesn't mean anything," he said. "What's that prove? Maybe it just hasn't taken hold of him yet"—saying it like he wanted his boy cursed, so Hays could fit in for once—"or maybe Alvaretta spared him."

Angela jumped on that. "And why would the witch spare your boy, Landis?" And what took off from there was hollering and screaming the likes of which you've never heard from grown folk. It was a row, friend, one so fiery that none of them heard Tully Wiseman dragging himself in half sopped for his morning shift in the meat section. His apron hung in his hand. He stood there, watching and smiling.

"Ain't thissa sight," he said. "What we got here, trouble in paradise? Measurin' your sins to see who's the longest? Well then, let me help y'all out." He pointed a shaking finger at Landis first, then to Angela. "It's the whole lot of ya. Alvaretta Graves got her hand round the necks of us all, and it's all on you. You and your sorry kids."

Tully waited for someone to speak. No one did.

"I hope to see you all in hell." He said it with all the sincerity he could muster, which was quite a bit. Nobody never took much of what Tully Wiseman said as anything near to truth, but in that statement, truth's all there was. "I hope the Lord grants me grace to watch y'all burn. I want to see you writhe. I'll hear your screams as song, and I'll be thinking of my Daisy as I listen."

He lumbered off then, stumbling toward the back as he tried to remember how to put on his apron, and the only thing Angela and Landis could do was stare.

-4-

I'll say this about Landis Foster—that man may have uttered some truly questionable things in his life, but it had been nothing but the truth when he'd said Scarlett Bickford was in safe hands that day. Chessie and Briar's house was a port in the storm and the mayor knew it, which was why he'd gotten in debt and sent his little girl there.

Chessie sent Briar to fetch her in that tall white Ford of his—the truck everybody in town knew was his, so nobody'd even consider trying something awful—with orders that Briar show Scarlett all the charm and courtesy she deserved. He showed up on the front porch with his hat in his hand and a smile on his face, even offered to carry Scarlett's pen and pad to the truck. I wouldn't say that girl particularly wanted to go, other than she knew she'd come across John David at some point. I guess that's why she spent much of that morning slathering makeup on her face to cover up where Tully'd wailed on her. Love's a crazy thing, is it not? One day you're throwing rocks you're so mad, the next you're pining once more for the very thing that riled you.

Wilson watched his daughter leave and made Briar promise nothing would happen and Scarlett promise she was okay with it all. He said he'd be back from work early as he could, right soon as he had a little talk with some people. Mayor went on to work after that, right about the time Briar went to work on Scarlett. All smiles and kind words was that man, putting the girl at ease, telling her of the old days when the witch knew her place. By the time they got out at the Hodge farm, Scarlett looked to be thinking Briar Hodge was just about the kindest, sweetest man she'd ever known.

Chessie waited at a table set up on the screened back porch next to a kerosene heater that glowed a soft red. Breakfast covered the table—milk, juice, a plate of sausage and eggs. She herself opted for coffee alone. Briar pushed in both their seats as she told Scarlett, "Always break my fast out here if weather allows. Cool air does you good. That and my coffee's only things get this old body moving. You're still a young filly, but you'll find that out soon enough, girl."

She smiled and then Scarlett smiled, and Briar excused himself for the morning's work. Scarlett watched him go, off toward where the barn stood, waiting to see who else might be there.

"John David's gone," Chessie said, and when Scarlett looked at her, the woman smiled. "Way I figger things, that's the only reason you'd try so hard to cover up your face. You crushing on him, girl?" She laughed when Scarlett bent her head and blushed. It was a hard chuckle, deep like a man's and full of feeling. "I don't miss much round here, Miss Scarlett. Nosir, not much at all. You be careful of John David, now. That's the only warning I'll give you, because I know warning's something the heart won't heed. He said he had an errand, so I sent him on his way. He sends his regards, though. John David took it hard, what happened to y'all. Thinks some of it's his own fault, and maybe it is. I took things plenty hard myself."

Scarlett looked at her full plate and the pad and pen beside it. She picked up the pen and wrote:

You didn't do anything

Chessie bent over the table and squinted her eyes, letting the morning breeze play in a shock of her red hair. "No," she said. "No, I didn't. But that don't mean I'm innocent here,

Scarlett, nor Briar. All darkness needs to spread is for a bunch of people to stand around and do nothing. You know that. Go on, eat. Fixed it special."

I don't know if it was the food or the fear, but something made Scarlett pick up that fork. Once she did, there weren't no putting it down. Chessie sipped at her coffee and glanced behind her to the barn. Briar stood in the loft, looking out the narrow window.

"I hear from your daddy you won't say who beat on you."

Scarlett stopped chewing. She didn't lay her fork down and trade it for her pen, only shook her head in a slow *No*.

"You tell me why that is?" Chessie asked. "You got my number, Scarlett. Coulda texted me soon as your daddy left, I'd've come right over myself to sit with you. Coulda avoided this whole mess. Don't make no sense you didn't." Her eyebrows scrunched. She leaned forward and in a quiet voice asked, "Weren't your daddy, was it? Punishing you for crossing the witch?"

No.

"Wilson ever beat on you before?"

This time Scarlett wouldn't answer.

Chessie leaned back in her chair. A cloud seemed to pass over her face. "Let me tell you something, girl. Ain't no woman deserves that. Ain't no*body*. You think Briar'd raise a hand to me?" She chuckled. "Man's got a temper like a hungry bear, but he knows he'd wake in the night with a blade in his throat if he ever touched me. You don't believe me, you ask him."

Scarlett didn't have to ask, friend. She knew.

"So it was somebody else this time? Somebody from town?"

A nod.

"You knew this man? Because I'd have to think it was a man. They the ones who got violence in their bones."

Another nod.

"I'd have you tell me who it was, Scarlett. And I'd have you say why you're protecting him."

Scarlett picked up the pen again. She wrote as the wind played with the edges of the paper, fluttering it and the clothes that hung from the line behind them, Chessie's big dresses and Briar's bib-alls, John David's jeans and shirts and underwear.

His daughter is sick because of me

Chessie leaned forward again. When she was done reading, she said, "That what you think?"

Scarlett nodded.

"People say you and your friends brought all this on, let'm. There's no changing a mind once it's been made up. But that don't mean you got to suffer more'n you do. You screwed up going to the mines, I won't sit here and tell you different, but you were looking out for Cordelia in going after that bracelet."

That thing stole her bracelet. Her demon

"It was a demon, then?" Chessie asked. "You sure?"

Scarlett bobbed her chin.

"I'd have the truth here, Scarlett."

Another bob.

Chessie looked over her shoulder toward the barn. "Then it's worse than we all know. Whatever the witch cast on you's come home with you, girl, and here it'll spread like stink on the wind. This town's had to live with Alvaretta Graves ever since the Lord struck down her husband. And don't you think it was anybody else, Scarlett. Wasn't. Lord Hisself took Stu Graves from this world, laying judgment on the crone he bedded. You'll hear your daddy say it wasn't till Stu's death that Alvaretta found the evil in the mountain, but I'll tell you that ain't so. She's always that way. You're lucky to get away from her alive."

Scarlett's hand shook—*But it's my fault*

"Don't you say—" Chessie started, but Scarlett was already

shaking her head no, scribbling out what she'd written before to write *I hit her.*

"You did what?"

Scarlett underlined that. And then she wrote *She was going to hurt us so I had to and then she cursed us*

Chessie didn't know what to say to that; she'd never heard of such a thing as anybody crossing the witch, much less laying a hand to her. "Don't you speak a word of that to anyone else, Scarlett. You hear me?"

Scarlett nodded before Chessie could finish talking.

"Might mean more then, the four of you making it outta there. You remember that. You faced down the witch, girl, and you come out on the other end of it. You stood *up*. Not like that worthless pansy Hays Foster. You got a fight in you. I like that." She sipped from her cup. "Your daddy didn't care for you coming down here for the day, did he?"

Scarlett shook her head.

"Your daddy and the Hodges ain't never seen eye to eye, Scarlett, just like us and the Reverend. You know that. Everybody in the Holler does. You'll hear it's because what me and Briar do up here. How we earn our wage. But that ain't the reason. Goes deeper. Guess you could say it goes to the heart of everything. There's a darkness to the Holler, Scarlett. You come up here long enough, you know it's there. Stalks you. You understand?"

Scarlett did.

"This a hard place to spend your days, stuck between these mountains. We get along best we can because that's what we always done, but there's a suffering to life here. An evil just under the surface, beating like a black heart. It was here long before Alvaretta Graves. Maybe it'll be here long after she's gone. We all take up stakes and move? Well, that darkness will only follow. We're as much a part of this holler as the trees and hills. It is who we *are*. No, Scarlett. We got to deal with it here, because this here's our home.

"Now you take a man like your daddy. He buries his head in the sand and just ignores it, says ain't no such a thing as that darkness at all. Naomi's daddy? He says the evil here's no different than all the evil in all the world, and it's here because we let it in and gave it aid. Constable?" She chuckled. "Well, old Bucky's a good enough man, but you think good enough will get us through what's coming now? You think Bucky Vest will stand in the end?"

Scarlett wanted to say yes, friend. Shoot, everybody did. Like I told you, Bucky Vest was long loved in the Holler despite his lack of aspirations. But she said no such thing, nor was such a thing written on her pad. That girl only looked.

"That's right," Chessie said. "People here? They'll like a Vest and a Bickford and a Ramsay. Shoot, they'll maybe even love'm. But they'll *fear* a Hodge. And do you know why that is, Scarlett? They fear us because they know we got a power. We the ones who call the evil here for what it is. And we say that evil must be fought with hardness. With *strength*. Devil comes up here wanting my heart, I'll spit on him as I take his head. That's the way it should be." She smiled. "You want to know how you face this world and come out with your head held high? Ain't with love. It's with anger.

"There's coming a dark time now, Scarlett. People in town won't see things as you and I do. They got to lay blame for their troubles on somebody besides the witch, and might as well be you. There's some in town—ones who scurry about in the dark where no one can see—who'll get it in their minds to turn this to their own gain. The Circle, they call themselves. Keep themselves hidden-like, and even I don't know who all they are. But I think one a them's who hurt you, and I won't abide by it.

It's bad for business. You heard what Hays and Cordelia found when they got home yest'day?"

Scarlett nodded.

"And Medric?"

She nodded again.

"I never minded Cordelia Vest. I like her and I respect Bucky for what he does. Angela I could take or leave. I could say the same for Landis, though Kayann Foster has a sour heart and their boy is badness in the making. And I'll say I've always seen Medric Johnston as a man of secrets. I guess dealing with the dead'll do that, but I don't trust him. But that's how the days are now, Scarlett, and that's how things will remain until somebody stands up and does something to put things right. I think that somebody should be you."

Scarlett wrote *How?*

"I knew your momma. Tonya Bickford was a good woman, and it's a sin what happened to her. A tragedy, because she never got to tell you the things every girl should hear. So I'll tell you one a those things in her stead: This here's a man's world. Always has been. They think's they got the power. They talk big and lie and cheat, then they come home and toss you in the bed to get their jollies. They call that love, and maybe that's all the love they're built to know.

"But listen to me—that's all a lie. Men can prance and preen, but there ain't a beauty to this world a woman ain't had a hand in. It's we who got the power, you an me, but we got to take it. We got to make it ours. My momma did. Her daddy laid a hand to her until she couldn't take no more, and then she near beat him to death in his sleep. I took hold of Briar's business and supported not only us but this town, and one day this business will be gone because that's my aim. No more moonshine, no more weed. I'm gonna be bona fide, and do you know why, girl? Because I choose my future. And you can choose yours too."

Chessie sat back. She drained the last of her cup as a robin called out and watched Scarlett write.

What can I do?

"You can start by giving me a name. Show this town you cross Scarlett Bickford, hell's gonna follow. You claim your life or someone else will, and on that I give my guarantee. That'll make folk respect you." And then Chessie stroked the short hairs sprouting from her chin and added, "You ain't even gotta be pretty to do it."

-5-

I expect it was the hardest thing Bucky Vest ever had to do in his life, having to get out his car and walk into the mayor's office that morning. I wouldn't put it down to either courage or strength, though. Bucky just didn't have no choice.

He walked into that council building and took a right down that long hallway until he reached Wilson's office at the end. Bucky didn't knock, just walked in and sat in one of the two chairs in front of the mayor's desk. Wilson had his back to the door, looking out the window toward the church and the funeral home. Had a picture of his dead wife in his hand.

"Thought you'd be up at the dump by now, Buck," he said.

"Thought you'd be out trying to calm everybody down."

"I did. Went up to the doc's this morning, talked to the parents who's bringing in all their sick kids. Had a dozen of them, I'd say. Some can't talk, some can't walk. Some jerking around like the Spirit's got'm. You find out yet who hurt my little girl?"

"Thought I'd look around some today," Bucky said. "I got the time."

Wilson turned his chair around. His hair hadn't been combed and his tie hung limp off his neck—a red one that matched the color of his eyes. "You wanna tell me what's going on?"

Bucky rubbed the back of his head and let out a heavy sigh that put a ripple through his double chin. It was bad enough he had to keep things together in front of Angela all the way to town. Worse on the drive to the Foster home, listening to Cordelia ask if they were going to be okay and saying it was all her fault, Bucky answering yes to the one and no to the other, over and over.

"Took Angela to work," he said. "Cordy's staying with Hays today. I told him to watch her and call me if anything happened."

"More like Cordelia's got to watch Hays," Wilson said. "Scarlett don't like that boy at all. I won't lie, Buck. I don't like him either. He's a strange one. You should consider getting your daughter away from him."

"Little late for that, I guess," Bucky said. He didn't explain more.

"Wish I'd thought of that, letting Scarlett stay with Cordy. As it was, I sent her to Chessie's for the day. I couldn't stay home, and she wouldn't come here—"

"Homer let me go, Wilson."

Wilson leaned back in his chair, making the springs squeak. "What you mean Homer let you go? He fired you?"

Bucky could only move his head yes. To speak would invite more tears. Crying in front of your family is bad enough for a man. Crying in front of your best friend is to be no man at all.

Wilson squeezed his eyes shut. "He say why?"

"Maddie's sick. Homer blames it on Cordy. I need help, Wilson. I need you to help me find work. Give me a lead, point me somewhere. Anything."

"Sure, I'll ask around, Buck. You know I will. But things are tight. Lots of people looking. And now there's this mess with Alvaretta."

"I know that."

"I could call Homer, try to lean on him."

"Homer'll tell you the same thing he told me. Only difference is he'll use Scarlett's name instead of Cordy's. Maybe when this is all done . . ."

"I been thinking on that," Wilson said. "We gotta find a way to get a handle on this before it all goes to pot. People are scared and their kids are sick, and that's what we gotta deal with. Doc thinks ain't nothing we can do about the sick part. I agree. None of this goes away until Alvaretta wills it. But the fear? I think that's something we can work on, Constable. I believe deep down these people will still bend to reason. I just don't know how we make that happen."

"What 'we'?" Bucky asked. He threw his hands up, waved them around the room like he was counting all the invisible people Wilson must've been seeing. "I can't do nothing, Wilson. I got no authority in town, you know that. I gotta take care of my own now."

"You got savings?"

Bucky snorted.

"Ain't the time for any of us to be going it alone, Buck. Now I know your pain, I do. And I know you're a proud man." He slid open the right-hand drawer of his desk and leafed through the files and papers on top, then pulled out a wad of cash. It had been folded once and tied with a thick red rubber band. The mayor slid it across the desk. "This should last you a week."

"I ain't gonna take a handout, Wilson. That's not why I come."

"I know it. Take it anyway. Consider it a bonus for your constabling, because that's what I need you to attend to right now."

Bucky reached out and picked through the stack. No hundreds or fifties, but enough twenties to see them through a while.

"Pay your bills and gas your car," Wilson said. "I'll make sure Landis gives Angela enough credit at the grocery to keep y'all fed. Take it, Bucky. Take it so you won't have to worry about that for a few days. We got a whole other mess to worry about." He turned his chair back around slow, pointing it at the window. "We friends, ain't we, Buck?"

Bucky was still looking at that money in his hands. Wondering, maybe, what it'd be like to have cash enough to shove inside a drawer.

"Sure, Wilson. We come up together."

"You stick with me through this? No matter what?"

"You know I will."

"Even if I told you all that's happened ain't Cordelia's fault? Or Scarlett's? Or none a them kids'?" He paused there and added, "Even if I told you it wasn't Alvaretta herself did this?"

"What you talking about?"

For a long while the mayor didn't say. Then came a soft, "Reverend, he started this. Told the town it was Alvaretta when the town didn't need to know. Them other kids only started getting sick after, you notice that? Everybody just kept their traps shut, none of this would be happening."

"Wilson, I—"

"But I don't blame him, and you know why I can't, Bucky? Because Reverend's scared. He's about as scared right now as a man can be, and I know that because I'm scared too. I pray to the dear Lord in heaven this is all it comes to, just a bunch a sick kids. Even my own. I can live with that. Shoot, Holler's lived with worse over the years. But fear can make people do some awful things, and that's what I'm scared of right now. Not Alvaretta. Us."

"This is all gonna be fine," Bucky said, though in a way that left him shaky in his belief.

"Not till the witch gets what she wants."

"What's she want, Wilson?"

"You should get on, Buck. Go back up to the mines and get that blasted key to the gate. Probably still in the lock where Hays left it. You lock things up tight, and then you bring that key to me. Should've been one of us holding those keys all along. Medric was right, we was too plain scared to keep them. So the decision was made to give them to Medric for safekeeping, and he didn't say no." He shook his head. "And you take that money, hear me? Least I can do for all you done for me over the years. You're a good man. Holler's blessed to have you." And when Bucky didn't move, he added, "Go on now. Leave me be. I gotta think."

Bucky nodded and went on his way. Walked back down that lonely hallway that once upon a time held all sorts of folk, secretaries and businesspeople and this and that, but now held only the mayor. He left the mayor's money at the end of the desk.

Wilson watched Bucky through the window, saw him get in that old creaky Celebrity. Then he leaned back in his office chair and picked up his dearly departed's picture.

"I'm glad you ain't here, Tonya," he whispered. "Never thought I'd say that. But I'm glad."

-6-

Now I guess what Bucky felt he should do next was either go up to the dump and beg Homer for his job back, or do what the mayor said and fetch the key from the gate around the mines. But some other part of him said he had to do something else, and that's the part he listened to. What Wilson said about the Reverend being scared stuck in his head and wouldn't jar loose. That's why Bucky got back in the car and drove over to the church instead. I don't guess he was any different than anybody else in the Holler then. What he needed was answers.

The Reverend and Belle Ramsay were already there, having parked their Jeep by the steps that led to two church doors ready to welcome any and all. None but the Ramsays had stepped foot inside the Holy Fire since the quick end of Sunday service, but they would soon. That's what people did when the world went from the gray it usually was to the black it could always become. Bucky's grandma once told him the locks on the church were taken off for good after Pearl Harbor. Everybody in the Holler had gathered there that December day to call upon the Lord. They gathered there again when Kennedy was shot, and then the other Kennedy, and then Reagan. Don't matter if you're a Democrat or Republican, Crow Holler's gonna pray for you whether you like it or not. On 9/11, those pews were full to bursting. David Ramsay was preacher by then. All the days since, those doors have been kept open. You can go over there now if you like, turn that knob yourself. David says the Lord's still in there waiting and maybe He is, I don't bother going in to see.

Bucky went on inside and wiped his feet beside the chair where Raleigh Jennings always sat, then stepped to the sanctuary. Belle was bent over in one of the pews in the middle, straightening up hymnals and capturing wayward bulletins from the Sunday before. Down at the altar, David and Naomi had fallen to prayer. The Reverend had his arms wrapped tight around his daughter so he could share every jerk and pull of her shoulders and head. Holding his eyes shut tight as his face lifted to the ceiling. His words came low and soft, mixing with Naomi's whispers into a mournful song.

Belle paused to watch and let a curl of her long brown hair dangle over her eyes. Reverend had prayed over his children before. Bucky had been there along with everybody else the night before John David had gone off to war against the heathens. Ain't it funny how we're always the righteous when it comes to killing, and it's everybody else who's the devil? I don't think the Reverend or Belle ever stopped to ponder such things. But there at the edge of the sanctuary, I believe Bucky did. Just as I think he pondered what depth of evil one had to plumb to curse innocent children.

He didn't see Belle come up next to him, and jumped when she touched his arm. "Morning, Bucky," she said.

"Belle. Sorry. I'm not interrupting anything, am I?"

"No, of course not. Church is always open. David's just going to the Lord for Naomi."

She turned back. Naomi still shook (and shook and shook), but David's countenance had changed from struggle to peace. His cheeks were flushed. The cords of his neck were taut, as if the battle he fought against the witch's hold was both pitched and ceaseless, and yet his mouth held a smile as his lips mouthed yes at the victory promised. To Bucky it was a beautiful thing, and also horrible.

"I need a word with David, Belle."

"About what? Is Cordelia okay? I'm sorry, I didn't even ask."

"She's the same. I'm just trying to figure why David told the town about Alvaretta. We agreed it'd be best to keep things quiet."

"David did what he thought was right, Constable."

"That's what I hear. Didn't really turn out to be right though, did it?"

In a statement that would've made Chessie Hodge spit her coffee, Belle said, "I have to support my husband, Bucky. Doesn't matter what I think."

I figure the Reverend had to know all this was going on, praying or not, because he said his amen and brought Naomi up the aisle. Poor thing could barely walk. She had to hold on to her daddy with one hand and the ends of the pews with the other just to keep herself steady. All the beauty had gone from her eyes, replaced by weariness that struck the very depths of what she could endure. Bucky could barely bring himself to look at her.

"Morning, Constable," the Reverend said. "Come to pray?"

"Afraid I'm all prayed out for now, Reverend. I would like a word, though. In private, if Belle and Naomi don't mind."

The Reverend's smile drifted for a moment and then regained its past glow. "Belle, why don't you take Naomi in back. Fix her some lunch? I'll be in directly."

Belle smiled and then so did Bucky—smiles all around, friend, and my, that was a happy-looking bunch—and then she took Naomi to the little door by the pulpit. Whole way down the aisle, Belle kept whispering it would be okay, all of it would, as if wishing would make it so.

Only when they were gone did David ask, "This is about yesterday, ain't it?"

"You talking about letting out word of the witch?" Bucky asked. "Or you talking about Angela's roses getting tore up? Hays getting a cinderblock through his bedroom window, maybe? Scarlett getting *beat*? Or maybe Medric coming home to find a dead animal nailed on his door? Which one do you think this is about, David? Because I'm thinking it's about all of them."

"I didn't have any of that in mind, Constable. I promise that."

Bucky moved past the preacher and sat at the end of the back pew and closed his eyes. The wood squeaked as his weight settled.

"Don't matter what you had in mind, Reverend. It's what *is*. That's what we all got to worry about now. My girl's sick. Cordelia's hurting, just like Naomi. Lots of kids hurting now. Shoot, just about everybody's daughter old enough to know what's happening has something wrong with them. Homer called me this morning. Cut me from my job."

"Homer let you go?"

"Thought I might go out today, try to scare up some work. Let people know I'm available, you know? If anything comes up." He looked at the preacher. "Maybe you can put it on a prayer chain. Everybody'd know then."

David flashed a bit of anger that turned to embarrassment when he saw the look in Bucky's eyes. It was a pleading there, nothing more. I don't think Bucky even realized what he'd said, much less how it could have been taken in an unkind way.

"I told Raleigh it was all Alvaretta's doing," he said. "And I made sure he knew that. People had to know. You understand that, don't you? We couldn't keep something like that a secret, Bucky. Town had a right. I had no idea it'd get turned around on the kids."

"I don't know about the town having a right. All I know's Wilson was trying to protect them."

"And so am I," the preacher said. "This is more than the witch we're dealing with here. There's what we've done to let the witch continue on free and unfettered, too."

"I wouldn't call being holed up on Campbell's Mountain being free, David."

"She's free enough to lay a curse on the town."

"Maybe," Bucky told him. "*Maybe*, Reverend. But I was up to the doc's yesterday, and he says Alvaretta's done nothing to the kids at all. Calls it some kinda insanity. But I don't even think that matters, because you got this whole town ready to string up our daughters. You got everybody thinking Alvaretta

Graves is gonna ride through here any minute and lay waste, and that's the thing we was all trying to avoid."

"Doc Sullivan ain't even from around here. He don't know. Things is different in the Holler. You think it's insanity? You really think that, Bucky? You tell me: Cordy crazy? Huh? Naomi? Scarlett? Hays? Or was it Alvaretta drew them there instead, meaning to hurt us all?"

Bucky wouldn't answer. I'd say that was answer enough, at least for the preacher.

"I know what I promised up at the hospital, Bucky. But I answer to a higher authority, and God told me otherwise. Alvaretta's *marked* us. We thought it'd be okay if she kept to her holler and we kept to town, but it wasn't enough. Light and dark can't mix, Constable. Sooner or later, one of them must yield to the other. We let it go when Wally Cork turned up dead. Didn't do anything when the crops failed. We did the same when all the work dried up and left. But this is our *children*, and the only reason it's gotten this far is because we've lapsed. In our faith, and in our deeds. I know you want to keep the town safe. I want the same. Only difference is you and Wilson think keeping everybody safe means shadowing them with ignorance, and I know it's the truth that'll set us free. Only that."

"What's that mean?" Bucky asked. "The truth?"

On that, the preacher fell quiet.

"I was over at Wilson's a bit ago," Bucky said. "He's all fired up over what you did, but he said he can't blame you. Said something about fear making people do things they wouldn't normally." He paused, considering his next words. "Almost like he was saying you knew a little more about all this than you're letting on, Reverend."

"Know?" the Reverend asked. "I *helped*, Bucky. God help me I did, then and now. I keep my mouth shut on the vile things Chessie does because of the agreement the mayor talked me into making. For every warning I utter from the pulpit over Wilson's handling of this town, I hold my peace for two. But I ache in my memories for what we did."

"Who's 'we'?" Bucky asked. "You and Wilson?"

"I tell myself the man I was is dead. Dead and raised again. We built this town, Wilson and me. Poured our sweat and tears into it. And then I see my Naomi and the way she is now, and I think it's all gonna get taken away." He was blubbering now, and not ashamed of it. "Alvaretta took my *boy*, Bucky. Something happened to John David. Everybody thinks it was the war, but sometimes I wonder. You ever think Wally Cork wasn't the only person Alvaretta got? Not just the crops and the jobs and him, but others? Like my boy? Ask the mayor if he ever thinks on that." And what the Reverend said last was the thing that chilled Bucky like a wind:

"You ask if he ever wonders where Tonya's cancer came from."

-7-

It's hard to say what all was on Bucky's mind when he finally left the church. The Reverend walked him out, saying how sorry he was for showing such emotion. The pressure, he kept telling Bucky. Just so much going on and so many people hurting, and sometimes even men and women of the Lord had to break down and have themselves a good cry. Bucky said that was okay, he'd shed more than a few tears these last days himself.

What was plain as he watched those church doors close (after promising the Reverend what all had been said would remain between the two of them) was job hunting would have to wait. Mayor had been right—there was a lot for Bucky to do now. Constabling was never hard work in a place like this, friend. You get your occasional vandals and every once in a while a farmer'd call saying somebody'd stolen some cows, but that's about it. People here relied on their own selves to settle any differences. Sometimes that meant words and other times that meant fists, but that's how it'd always been. Wasn't no need for any serious lawman, which was why the closest thing we allowed was a part-time constable. But Bucky? Part-time or not, he was on to something.

He stood there a minute, pondering things. Bucky could see all of Crow Holler from that spot atop the church steps, or at least what parts mattered. Mitchell's Exxon was nothing more than a pile of rust and rot jutting up from the dusty ground. No CLOSED sign had been hooked on the door, but neither had Joe propped open the entrance. Wilson's T-bird and Bucky's Celebrity were the only cars other than the Ramsays' anywhere near the church or council building. Wasn't nobody down to the grocery, either. The only movement he saw at all came from just across the way, so that's where he headed. He'd woke up intending to see Medric, and now seemed a good enough time.

He took the steps down and covered the lot, paused to look both ways before crossing the deserted road. Medric was in back. Bucky could hear him but saw only glimpses through the bushes that grew along the property's edge—a flash of Medric's thick black arms and a bit of his shirt, the brim of the straw hat he wore when he meant to be out in the sun for long. Something metallic shuffled. Bucky cleared his throat and went on around.

It was paint cans he'd heard. Dozen of them, in various states—white for the fence, brown for the doors, a light gray for the parlor's wood siding. Medric looked up and flinched.

Bucky lifted his hands and blushed. "Sorry. Didn't mean to scare you, Medric."

"What you doing sneaking around here, Buck?"

"Wasn't sneaking. I was over to the church, heard you out here. Fixing to do a little sprucing up?"

"Getting ready," Medric said, though not for what.

"Uh-huh. Well, I wanted to come by. Ask you about what happened yesterday? I'd like to investigate things. Might be able to turn something up."

Medric stacked another can of paint and pointed into the small backyard where a shed stood. "There it is," he said. "Go have yourself a look if you want."

Bucky took a few steps and stopped when he met the smell, rancid flesh and rotting fur. The raccoon's innards had dried and shriveled, leaving it nearly flat. Its jaws were wedged open in a look of rage at whatever run it over. Ants marched in and out a the hole where the nail had gone through and into the door.

"You should bury that, Medric. Or I can take it, if you want."

"Why you want it? You gonna dust fingerprints?" Medric smiled a little, but it was a sad one. "Run it through some contraption like they do on the NCIS?"

"No. I ain't got anything like that."

"Then let it rot. I want the whole town to get a good whiff. Carry the stench in their noses so they can smell it in their dreams."

"You keep the note?"

"Nope." He piddled around a little and said, "Guess you'll want to talk about that key."

"Guess so, while I'm here. You know folks'll ask, way you and Hays got a friendship. You give him the key to the mines?"

"I gotta answer that, Buck? You so in doubt you got to hear me say it outright?" Medric chuckled. "Something bad happens, it's the black man always gets it first."

"Gets what?"

"Blame."

"It ain't like that. Blame's shared, Medric. We all got vandalized."

"Not the preacher."

That was true enough. But, "Least you didn't get beat on like Scarlett did."

"And I mean to make sure that don't happen," Medric said. "It'll come though, Buck. You mark it. They'll try. Wilson don't get a hold on things, there'll be blood."

"Won't come to that."

"Won't?" Medric laughed. He set his stick aside and brought out an old brush from his pocket. In the tall elm that draped over the parlor's backyard, a crow called. "Let me ask you this, Bucky. Mayor told you yet to get on up to Campbell's Mountain and get the key to the mines? He tell you what to do with it after?"

Bucky didn't answer.

"Course he did. I get robbed—I get a *crime* committed against me—I'm the one turns up guilty." Medric shook his head. "I'm fifty-eight come fall, Buck. Been in this town my whole life, buried more dead'n I know. I go out my way to be left alone, I get a coon nailed to my door and a sign underneath for my trouble. You know what that sign said? Know what they called me?"

"I heard," Bucky said.

"You ask me bout all this? I say people here's finally getting as they've always given. Been a long time coming, and I'm just gonna sit back and watch it. I hope Alvaretta and her demon gets them all."

"Don't you say such a thing, Medric. We're a town. These are your neighbors."

"Like Alvaretta's your neighbor?" He laughed. "People here's no different than they are anywhere else. Only neighbors in this town's the ones who look and act the same as the rest. Leaves me and Alvaretta out, don't it?"

He stared at Bucky, daring him to say more. I guess Bucky didn't see that glare for what it was.

"You said at the hospital Alvaretta ain't no witch. Now you're telling me she is? Which is it, Medric? You know something I don't?"

I'll let you in on something, friend—very likely that answer was yes, quite a bit. But Medric just stuck his brush down into the can and turned his back, slathering paint on that door. Weren't no raccoon guts there or anything, just a swirl where Medric had scrubbed and a spackled hole where the nail had gone.

"Best you get on, Buck. I got work."

Bucky stood there a minute and then decided their conversation was done. At the gate he turned and asked, "You buried Stu Graves, didn't you?"

"I did."

"Spend much time with Alvaretta? You know, planning the burial and all that?"

"Spend time with all my customers."

"Sad thing, something like that. Woman left all alone. Might have occasion to open up to somebody. I'm just thinking out loud, Medric. Trying to figure things. But you know, seems like close to everybody in the Holler's had a tough time of it since then. Some would say all but maybe you."

Medric stilled his brush. "People always dyin'," he said. "Fosters and Bickfords seem to do all right. Or you not see that? Or maybe reason I'm okay's cause the Lord's black."

Bucky didn't answer that, making Medric chuckle.

"I'll see you, Buck," he said, then went back to the door.

-8-

In a lot of ways, the Foster home was every bit what the Vest home wasn't. Big and roomy with bricked walls instead of faded old siding, and when the wind blew there was no risk of the whole thing flopping over on its side. But there were other differences too. Like the way everything inside there always sounded so quiet and lifeless, or Cordelia always ended up walking around there with her arms folded across her chest, as though there were a constant draft soft enough to chill her but that she never really felt.

She was on the edge of Hays's bed that morning, arms crossed as usual, staring at the hole in his window. He'd taken down the trash bag Landis had put up the afternoon before to show her what remained. The last ten minutes had been him trying to explain how the form staring back at them was like a puzzle in reverse—a picture not of pieces put together but pieces taken away. Those jagged lines of glass, the wide pieces left at the sides and the slivers at the top and bottom, had created the clear face of a monster's hungry smile.

"I dun't fee it," Cordelia said. "It'f . . . *j*—ust a hole."

But Hays only shook his head. He stared out the window, past that grinning monster to the woods across the street. Only one other house stood in view on that stretch of road, and that was Joe and Ruth Mitchell's little ranch on down the way. Wasn't a soul there now. Both Joe's truck and Ruth's car were gone from the driveway. Which was strange because something was moving around in their backyard.

"Vut are you doing?" Cordy asked.

Somewhere in the kitchen, Kayann rattled dishes. She'd vowed to stay with the kids that day, keep watch in case someone else decided to come along with another cinderblock (or worse). Hays told Cordelia that wouldn't last. The grocery was always a busy place when a blow was on its way, and a curse is no different than a storm when you get right down to it. Once things got busy, Landis would be calling for reinforcements.

"Come thit down," Cordy said. She patted the bed. "I need to tawk."

"Something's across the road."

Cordy got up. "Vut?"

"I don't know what it is," Hays said. He pointed, not wanting to touch the sharp glass. "Right there by the Mitchells' shed."

Cordy leaned left and then right, squinting.

"Don't feek me out."

"I'm not. There's something back there, Cordy. I swear there is. Saw it last night too. I don't know. Like a . . . *thing*. Something's watching me. I think something followed me from Alvaretta's."

"Thould I call Daddy?" She reached into her pocket for her phone.

"No. Never mind. It's gone now," he said, though he didn't move from the window. Almost like he was willing whatever it was to return.

"Hayth," Cordy said. "Vut's wong wif you?"

He kept his eyes out to the yard (I think he just couldn't bring himself to look at Cordelia now, looking as she did) and said, "I ain't sick."

"Vut?"

"I ain't sick, Cordy. Everybody else is sick. You, Scarlett, Naomi. Not me." And as Cordelia looked at him, his back seemed to shudder. "Why ain't I sick?"

She put a hand to his waist, rubbing him there. But that had never calmed Hays before, and it didn't look to calm him then.

"Do you know what she did, Cordelia? The witch? She didn't just curse us. I mean, you know that, right?" He turned around now. His eyes were red and swollen. "What's Naomi always going on about? Staying so pure and disciplined and whatever other garbage the preacher's put in her head over the years. Staying in control of herself, right? She got drunk at my party, and all she's talked about since is how she can't do that anymore. Not because she didn't like it, but because she lost *control*. Now look at her. She can't even get hold of herself long enough to tie her own shoes and eat her own food."

Cordy wrinkled her brow like she hadn't thought of that.

"How many times has Scarlett said everybody but you and Naomi ignore her so much she feels invisible? Well, what's worse than being unseen?" He didn't wait for her to answer. "Being *unheard*. And then there's you."

Hays reached out and touched Cordelia's chin, like he was going to nudge it up to kiss her. Instead, he moved his thumb to the good side of her face, and then across to what had gone spoiled. "How many times have you said you always worried that you wouldn't have any friends at all if you didn't have a pretty smile?"

Cordy's chin trembled. "You're thow mean."

"I'm telling you the truth," Hays said. "She didn't curse us, she gave us the things we fear the most. That's what she did, Cordy. That's Alvaretta's curse."

He turned again, ignoring Cordelia's sobs as he stared at that gash in his window. And you can't blame him for that, friend. Hays didn't know no better. I don't think that boy ever cared what Cordy looked like, to be honest. Not before, and certainly not right then. Right then, he was too busy thinking on what he'd just said about the witch.

Thinking of that thing he most feared.

-9-

Bucky got out of the car and winced at the crick in his back, moving his eyes down one side of the fence and the next. He reached for the lock hanging off the gate's chain like touching it would bring a shock. The key was stuck. He wrenched it free and shook his head, then looked on up that little hill past the trees.

The gate had been left open. I don't guess Bucky could blame the kids for that. He sighed a little and went to swing the gate back when he noticed how the grass looked on the hill's slope. Mashed down, the way it'd be if a car had gone through there. And sure, a car had. Three of them, as you'll remember—Scarlett's bug and Hays's Camaro and then John David's truck. But Bucky saw a fourth set of tire tracks, and these looked fresh.

Bucky's gun (and by that I mean the hand cannon handed down when his daddy died in the war cradling a hand grenade) lay in a shoe box high on the shelf in the closet at home. Only time he took it out was when Homer Pruitt wanted him to cull the rat population at the dump. But Bucky wanted that pistol right then. Somebody was up at the mines.

Wasn't a choice what to do next. Bucky got back in the car and eased through the gate, following the tracks already made. The Celebrity sputtered and lurched as it took the hill, bald tires spinning in the grass. Bucky shifted to low and gritted his teeth. No way Scarlett's fancy new car and Hays's hot rod could make it all the way up here and not him. That climb had become a matter of pride.

I don't know who it was Bucky expected to find on the other side of that hill, but I guarantee you it wasn't John David Ramsay. His rusty truck sat in the same place he'd parked it that past Saturday night, only this time he'd turned off the engine.

Bucky brought the Celebrity to a stop. He'd gotten mostly out when John David stepped out from the trees.

"Guess locks and fences and signs ain't enough no more," Bucky hollered. "Maybe I should tell the mayor to go ahead and rip it all down, turn the mines into a spot for family picnics."

John David grinned and kept coming forward. "Wouldn't say that's a good idea, Constable."

"What you doing here, John David?"

"Trying to figure what in the world happened up here."

Bucky pursed his lips and nodded. But it was a slow sort of nod, one you might associate with a measure of embarrassment, like he'd just discovered that was something he should be doing too.

"You were up here Saturday night?"

"I was. Naomi wanted some shine for Scarlett's party."

"You didn't bring any, did you?"

John David raised an eyebrow, as though telling Bucky he should know better. Problem was, Bucky knew no such thing. The man standing in front of him wasn't John David anymore, or at least not the version of him everybody had known.

"You didn't see anything up here?"

"No. It was dark. Everybody seemed okay, though. I told them to leave, Constable. Give you my word on that. But Naomi, she's stubborn. Said there was nothing I could do about it."

"Maybe there weren't," Bucky said.

"How's Cordelia?"

"Same. Me and Angela's just trying to understand how this could happen. How Cordy could lie as she did." About being here, sure, but also about what she'd let Hays do to her.

"Well, I don't know if this'll help or not," John David said, "but she didn't lie about what they found up here. Found those tracks."

"That right?"

"Down near the Number Four. Horseshoed kinda, just like they said. And big. I can show you. Ain't never seen nothing like it. They lead on to that oak, straight up it and straight down. Then on I guess to Alvaretta's."

"You didn't go that far, then?" Bucky smirked. "Ain't afraid, are you?"

"No. Been afraid worse."

Bucky's smile kind of faded there. Guess he supposed John David was right about that.

"Fear's the world's way of reminding you of what you have," John David said. "Less you got to lose, less scared you have to get. I didn't follow those tracks because we always left Alvaretta alone. Nothing more. We leave her be, she does the same for us."

"An agreement, then. Like the one the mayor's got with Chessie?"

John David shook his head. "I don't want to talk about Chessie, Constable."

"No, didn't figure you would. Been up to Doc's this morning. Lotta girls getting sick. People getting worked up. I think this will all get worse before it gets better. You might not be afraid, but that's enough to put a scare into me."

John David cocked his head. "Because that means Cordy might get worse, or because you think you're the one folk'll turn to?"

Bucky didn't really answer that. Instead, he said, "Folk'll turn to the ones they always have in hard times. Mayor. Your daddy. Sure, maybe me. Maybe you too."

"Ain't nobody gonna turn to me."

"Sure they will. Don't matter how you act or what you say you are now, John David. You're a Ramsay. People look up to that name."

"Not interested."

"Yeah." Bucky kicked at the dirt. Thought about asking it, didn't, then thought again. "What happened to you over there, John David?"

"Same thing that happens to us all. See too much hurting in the world, Bucky, you just don't want to see no more. Don't want to *do* no more. I seen enough hardship and bad. Come down like a rain over there. Now I'm just looking for the sun."

"My momma? Used to say too much sun'll only leave you with a desert."

"I liked your momma, but she weren't right. There's things worse than a desert."

Bucky kicked the dirt again, harder this time. His cheeks flushed. John David could go on all he wanted about the horror of war. Bucky would let him because he didn't know nothing about it himself. But when it came to hurt, that boy had nothing on Bucky's momma. I know that for a fact, friend. And I think Bucky would've maybe even told him the story of the Bad Man right there on that little hilltop, told it for the first time ever, but he didn't because John David spoke again.

"Done my serving, Constable. I just want to be left alone now."

As if to tack a little irony onto the end of that statement, John David's cell phone chirped just then. He fished it from his pocket (flashing those dozen tattooed slashes on his right forearm as he did) and read the text.

"That Chessie?" Bucky asked.

"Best be going. Lock that gate back, Bucky. Do it tight. Then you throw away that key."

"Kind of like shutting the barn door after the horse got out, ain't it?"

"Yep," John David said. "Just like that."

VII

Tully learns a lesson. The panic.
Run on the grocery. The Holler has a sheriff.

-1-

The morning started like something out of a nightmare for
Landis Foster. It would become the stuff of his dreams by noon
before turning to the worst hours of his life by closing. I guess
that's how that day ended up for a lot of folk here—two book-
ends of worry and fear with a spot of ease in the middle. Sort of
day makes you wonder why you bother living at all.

It was bad enough Landis had sat up all the night before,
pacing the living room and fighting the nagging thought he
should be protecting the grocery instead of his home. It was a
look of elation on his face when he come in early that morning
to find no windows broken and everything still on the shelves.
But as dawn crept toward noon another fear came across Landis,
one far worse than the thought of vandals: nobody would ever
set foot in his store again.

But all it took was one townsperson to stop in, a single
brave soul to blaze the trail so everybody else could say at least
they hadn't been first to come crawling to Landis for what they
needed that morning. Ruth Mitchell had no care for such idiocy.
She'd long set aside any of those peculiar small-town predilec-
tions of pride and self-reliance. All you'd need for proof of that
was to ask her what she'd had to do with Raleigh to get grocery
money in her pocket. She come in bearing a long list of supplies
and a firm resolve not to speak to Angela or Landis no matter

what, not after what their kids had wrought on Ruth's precious little Chelsea. Only fourteen Chelsea was, yet she'd been trembling like an old woman for two days. To make matters worse, Doc Sullivan said all Chelsea had to do was go to bed. And so when Angela helloed, Ruth only lifted her chin in defiance. That didn't seem to bother Landis. He looked happy enough just to have a customer roaming the aisles.

Ruth showing up brought in a steady stream of others, all of whom looked to be in her same state of mind. They grabbed their buggies and gathered their fruits and vegetables and the meat Tully had finally started putting out, grabbed the medicine especially, pills for pain and pills for nausea and pills for sleep, because Doc Sullivan had told them all there was nothing he could do and Reverend Ramsay was already saying it would take healing of a different sort to drive Alvaretta away, but a parent will grasp at near anything to render a broken child whole again. They picked through the store and kept their voices to themselves, wanting none of the grocery's employees to hear. And yet as neighbor met neighbor and burdens were shared, those whispers rose to the comfortable rumble of community.

Angela spent the next hour running people's groceries down the little conveyor belt beside her, ringing them up and bagging what they had and trying to tell them to have a nice day. At first, no one much wanted to return her favor. But as the morning wore on and more townfolk arrived, Angela was reminded once again of a peculiar human trait she'd been well acquainted with for years: people would set aside almost any feelings of ill will if it meant obtaining a bit of gossip.

They'd prodded Landis plenty, wandering over to the day-old section in front of his office, feigning interest in the stiff breads and moldering rolls to casually ask what Hays had seen at Alvaretta's. If it was true about the wild cats the witch had enchanted and the dead crows that hung from her trees. As they wrote their checks to Angela or slid their credit cards through the machine, they wondered aloud if Cordelia had seen the demon and just how big the hoofprints she'd followed through the woods were.

Angela had always been one who sought both attention and favor, and she'd never much cared who it was from or how it was gotten. Didn't take her long to figure nobody would sneer and throw their money at her if she told them of the witch.

Like how it wasn't cats Alvaretta had but dogs, and Cordy had told them plenty out of her poor ruined mouth about how horrible those dogs had looked, how calculating, but that weren't nearly as awful as all those murdered birds. Telling them Cordy hadn't seen the demon but had heard it, all the kids had, and it had spoken its curse in a dark tongue that would make angels cower. Sharing with all those who wheeled their groceries into her aisle how it had not been easy for her and Bucky, that maybe they even had it worse than most, because not only did they have to suffer through a child gone disfigured, they had to deal with the heartbreak of knowing it had all started with their poor precious Cordelia. Swaying them, turning the crowd once against her to one that felt something close to sympathy.

That all worked fine until Ruth Mitchell finished a lengthy chat with Tully at the meat department and wheeled her buggy to the front. And when she'd had enough of Angela's talk, she shouted past the customers in front and said, "Pour all the syrup you want over your words, Angela Vest, that won't change what your girl's done."

Angela had just run a loaf of butter bread over the scanner. Her hand stopped midway between the counter and the bag, leaving the loaf to dangle in the air. She turned to Ruth. "What did you say?"

"You heard me plain. Only reason those kids come across

the witch was Cordy wanted to get your fancy bracelet back. We all know it." Ruth straightened up and tilted her head toward the ceiling, talking louder in case any inside the store hadn't heard. "Something took that bauble of yours, Cordelia had no choice but to follow. Because of you, Angela. Because your daughter's more afraid of you than she is of the witch."

"That ain't true," Angela said.

"Maybe you'd've been a better momma to your little girl, none a this would've happened."

Angela shot away from her register. "You hold your tongue, Ruth Mitchell."

Inside his little office, Landis picked up the phone to call the mayor. He told Wilson to get down there now. Trouble was brewing.

Ruth ignored what Angela said. "Tully told me everything," she said, and the crowd pressed in more. "Said he came in here this morning to find Angela and Landis arguing over whose kid was to blame for all this. I say they're all to blame, and their parents too."

A few murmurs in the throng. Angela saw all the goodwill she'd spent the better part of her morning building begin to fade.

"I say these two right here are gonna be the death of us all," Ruth said.

Landis had already gotten out of his chair. He ran down the steps, tie flying back, cheeks flushed, pushing his glasses against his skinny nose.

Angela was shaking now. She still had that loaf of bread in her hand. It was jerking like some darkness possessed it. "How dare you say such a thing. You come in here for your goods and speak ill of we who provide. This town'd be nothing without Landis opening his store every day and me standing on sore feet to take your money. You sit there all righteous and pronounce your judgment. Well, you cast a stone at me, Ruthie Mitchell. You go on, and maybe what'll happen is Landis'll bar these doors and let you starve."

"Angela," Landis said. He came up from behind her smiling and nodding like nothing was wrong. Chuckling, like all of what Angela said had been a joke no one but him could understand. "Why don't you go in the back and take a break."

"That true, Landis?" Ruth asked.

More murmurs now. Landis tried, "We're all upset here, Ruth."

"Why not?" Angela asked. "Serve you right, Ruth."

Landis all but shoved her aside. He pried the bread from Angela's hand and took her spot at the register, leaving her with nothing to do but storm off. She heard him telling Ruth everything was just fine, but by then things had gone too far for comforting. People were starting to shout, wanting to know the truth of what Landis had in mind. He couldn't answer them all and so ignored them, which only made the shouting grow.

Ruth took her receipt and ran for the lot. She sat in her car, body shaking. She fumbled for her cell phone and called Raleigh. Raleigh would know what to do. He picked up on the first ring and told Ruth to slow down. She tried, but the words were coming too fast. Telling Raleigh things in town were about to get worse. That Landis was closing the grocery.

-2-

John David read the text again, not wanting to believe what Chessie had typed even as a part of him likely knew all along. Given the unusual circumstances, Chessie or Briar both might not have seen any harm in selling a bit of their shine to town. But I believe John David had, and now that deed had bore its awful fruit.

THE GIRL GAVE TULLY'S NAME. MEET US AT THE GROCERY.

John David tossed the phone onto the passenger's seat and crossed the gate leading away from Campbell's Mountain. His left foot got to twitching and his knee bouncing up and down, the same as it'd always done before a mission. Nerves, I guess, or adrenaline taking hold. Either way, that was something John David couldn't turn off all the way on the other side of the world no better than he could back home in the Holler. Nothing good could come of this. Everybody would be at Foster's that day, gathering their supplies and getting their news as they always did. And here in the midst of it all would come Chessie Hodge, wanting to settle things. Wanting to prove her point and set right her bent sense of honor to a drunk like Tully.

He pulled into the grocery on past lunchtime and saw Briar and Chessie getting out of Briar's big truck. The lot hummed with people coming in and out. Rushing, like being near each other risked spreading Alvaretta's curse. John David got out of his truck flexing his hands. His eyes were wide and searching.

Chessie's orders were simple: "We got to get everybody out."

"These people need their supplies, Chessie. You chase them off, you'll only scare them more."

She bent her eyes to the sun and looked square into John David's face. Briar straightened up enough to let the handle of his pistol poke out from the roll of fat hanging over his jeans.

"I'm doing this for the town, John David. So they *won't* be scared. Tully didn't do this alone. It's all connected somehow, just as it always is, and I'm gonna nip this in the bud right here. Now you either come help us or tuck your tail and go home."

John David helped, though not because he was scared. Everybody from the Holler might've given the Hodges a wide berth, but that boy didn't really consider himself from Crow

Holler no more. He just wanted to make sure bad didn't go to worse.

Chessie and Briar busted into the grocery like a storm. Didn't matter how raucous things had gotten inside the store in the five hours Landis had been opened, it all went silent as soon as everybody saw them two. Angela had calmed down enough to resume her place behind the register. The mayor had come up from the council building, first to assure everyone that all was well and then to help Angela bag groceries.

Landis came running up the first aisle, trying to keep his tie straight and a look off his face that wondered what fresh hell had just presented itself. "Morning, Chessie," he called. "Anything I can help you find today?"

Her reply was short and to the point: "I know what I'm lookin for, Landis, and I know where it's kep."

John David looked at the dozen or so people in line. He took a spot at the end of the register, cutting off the only route inside the store or out. "Y'all need to get what you have to. Grocery's closing for a bit. Chessie's got business."

"Business?" the mayor asked.

"That's what we're calling it," Briar said.

Landis kept coming forward. "Chessie, you can't do this."

Chessie never broke her stride. "Can and will, Landis, now you move out my way. And you keep your trap shut too, Wilson."

She turned as people began shouting and nodded to Briar. He reached into the front of his pants and drew that pearl handle. John David reached for Angela and the mayor both, pulling them down as Briar shot three bullets into the ceiling.

"You hear me?" Chessie shouted. "I said *everybody out.*"

What people hadn't been chased by Chessie's presence ran screaming now, dropping their goods where they stood. John David let go of Angela and the mayor and did his best to make

sure nobody got hurt making their escape. The grocery emptied in seconds. John David turned the sign on the doors from
OPEN to CLOSED.

"Sorry to do that, Landis," Chessie said. She and Briar
turned again, heading for the back. "Won't be but a minute:
Just need a word with your butcher."

-3-

John David watched as Chessie and Briar disappeared behind
the door to the cutting room. Angela turned to him and asked,
"What's going on? You tell us now."

"I don't know," he said.

The mayor tried next: "John David?"

"She didn't tell me, Wilson. Never does. So y'all just stand
here with me. Landis?" he called, stopping the man in his
tracks. He'd made it halfway down the aisle and now looked
back. "You come back up here, okay? Like she said, it'll only
be a bit."

And it was. Just a few minutes is all, enough time for
Chessie to maim Tully Wiseman for the rest of his life and for a
few dozen people to drive up to the grocery to find the CLOSED
sign turned out. Raleigh Jennings was among them. He banged
on those doors and then pulled, yelling at Landis to open up,
but Landis wouldn't. Him and Angela and the mayor and John
David only looked. That's when the rumors started taking off,
friend. People saying Ruth Mitchell had been right. Everybody
knew the Fosters had always been in league with the Bickfords
and the Ramsays and the Vests. Every town has its own upper
crust; the Holler's no different. So they saw the closed sign on
the grocery and heard there was business going on inside, and
they all put two and two together—Landis had decided along

with the mayor and whoever else that if their kids got hurt by
the town, the parents would hurt the town right back and shut
the grocery for good.

Now I know that sounds like a stretch. Most times, it would
be. But these weren't normal times in the Holler. These were
the days of the witch.

John David turned back around and said, "Don't you worry
none, Landis. Chessie's doing this as much for y'all as she is
herself."

The mayor asked, "Who's 'y'all,' John David?"

"The town."

His face had taken on a steely sort of calm that comforted
Angela in a way Bucky never could. He was not as thick as
Briar, nor as muscular, and yet John David was more intimi-
dating in a way hard to put to words. His arms were inked in
tattoos he usually kept hidden much like Scarlett hid her scars.
The mayor glimpsed a bit of them, saw what looked to be a
snake eating its own tail on one forearm and the words CARRY
THE FALLEN on the other. He saw the twelve marks drawn on
the inside of the right wrist that some said were a tally of those
John David had killed.

It was a silent strength that boy possessed, one that needed
neither threats nor strong words to convey. His shoulders were
continually square, his back never bent, his chin (his father's
chin, let there be no doubt) forever high and confident. But
where his eyes had once carried a bright spark of life, they were
now two hollow pools where light would not dwell. Angela
would tell Bucky later that John David looked dead on the
inside that morning. I think that's about the best way anybody
could say it.

"I'm sorry for what happened to your kids," he said. "Cordy
and Scarlett. They're nice girls." He looked at Landis, saying
nothing of Hays. "I have to say I feel partly to blame. I'd've

known all that would happen, I would have stayed to keep watch."

"You were there," the mayor said. His eyes flew wide. "You were *there*, weren't you? At the mines? You told us at the hospital."

"Yessir."

The mayor stepped back. His mouth stretched into a kind of grin, not believing it. "It was you. Cordy took Angela's bracelet so Scarlett could impress a boy. Scarlett told me as much. Only boy there was Hays, and he's spoken for. It was you."

John David blinked twice, no doubt remembering how he'd ignored Scarlett that night on the mountain except to poke fun at the clothes she'd worn.

"John David Ramsay, do you have designs on my daughter?"

He'd started shaking his head when Tully screamed. Angela spun herself around, as did the mayor and Landis. John David took off for the back and then stopped when he remembered Chessie's warning. Tully screamed again. At the front, Angela and Landis stared stone-faced. I suppose Tully's curses from that morning were still fresh in their minds, because he kept wailing, begging for mercy and aid, but none came.

-4-

Tully Wiseman was used to being cold. He'd tell people that's why he drank so much, it was the only way he could stay warm stuck inside that refrigerated meat shop all hours of the day, carving up beef and getting himself all filthy and bloody so Landis could keep Kayann happy inside that fancy car. Truth be told, that room really was cold. Cold and stark and smelling of raw meat. You ask me if there's a wonder why Tully was always drunk, I'll tell you no.

His only respite was the steel door on the other side of the room that led to the loading dock. He'd walk out there a couple times an hour and stare out at a field full of weeds and mice, take a smoke and a nip. Took his lunch out there most times too. Landis had a little break room fixed in back, but the last thing Tully wanted was to sit and listen to Angela drone on about her TV stories.

He was just about to grab a smoke when Briar's gun went off. Tully ducked behind one of the steel tables spread about the room when the door leading out to the store opened. I expect he thought that was Landis coming in, having finally snapped under the weight of what his boy had done and wanting to explain his side of things with the end of a gun. As if whatever sob story that man could offer about Hays would even come close to what Tully's daughter, Daisy, had endured the past day. Tully already had his mouth cocked and loaded when he raised his head, even got "Don't you—" out before he realized the one who'd stepped inside the meat room wasn't Landis at all.

"Say, Hodge." Tully smiled.

Briar had tucked his gun back away. "Tully," he said. "Need a word."

"Sure, sure. Got all the time in the world for you, Briar. Been a busy day so far. Everybody's coming out to stock up." He laughed a little. "Almost like a snow's coming, ain't it? What's that racket out there?"

Briar didn't say. He walked on around Tully, past the tables and saws and slicers and all that raw meat, to the door leading to the dock. That left Tully looking square at Chessie. The skin on her face was flushed near as red as the hair on her head. Her eyes were wide and they did not move from him. That was about the time Tully realized he had a Hodge at each door, and he'd been caught in the middle.

"What brings you up, Chessie?" Asking casual like, no different than Tully would inquire of the weather.

Chessie nodded to Briar, who turned and opened the door behind him. Sunlight washed into the room. Briar looked out. He nodded and whispered, "Come on," as if that big man was trying to coax a pup, and Tully saw a shadow on the cement floor that grew and then ended when Scarlett Bickford stepped through.

Tully's face, which had taken on the color of cherries over the years from all that hard liquor, now turned milky white. His hands fumbled with the apron around him, smeared with streaks of browns and reds.

"You pay a visit to Scarlett yest'day, Tully?" Chessie asked. "And before you answer, you choose your words."

"Scarlett?" he asked. "Well, I . . . I don't recollect."

Chessie's eyes bored into him. Tully turned from hers only to meet Scarlett's. That girl looked scared. Angry and scared.

"I mean, I may have," he stammered. "Just to see how she was getting along. Tell her of my Daisy." And when he finally understood there was no other way through what he'd gotten into, Tully finally said, "Yes'm. I did visit."

"You strike her?"

Here, Tully wouldn't say. But his silence was more than enough for Chessie. She nodded again to Briar. What happened next was over before Scarlett could flinch. Briar was a mountain, but he was fast. Lightning fast, and he had an arm around Tully's head before Chessie could finish raising her chin. Tully's head slammed atop the metal table in front of him. The sound bounced off the walls, making Scarlett jump, and it was only when Tully stopped struggling that Chessie stepped over to him. She bent down close, making sure he saw her face.

"You got a nerve, Tully Wiseman," she said. "Coming to me for liquor and preying on my Christian sensibility. Then you use my jar to find the courage to go after a defenseless girl? What was in your mind?"

Tully was already crying. "It was Daisy," he was saying. "My Flower's sick. Please don't hurt me, Chessie."

Briar lifted Tully's head, slammed it down again.

"Which hand was it?" Chessie asked. "Which one'd you hit her with?"

"Chessie, please. I'm sor—"

"Which hand?" she asked again, this time to Scarlett.

The girl looked as pale as Tully. Her hand trembled as she drew out her pen and pad. She wrote *right.*

Briar reached down and brought up Tully's right arm, stretching it out onto the table. Tully struggled, but it was no use.

"I know your mind, Tully Wiseman," Chessie said. "I know the kind of people you run with in the shadows, and I know 'twas y'all behind what's happened to the kids here in town. You think I don't, you're even more stupid than I thought you was. But it stops. You hear me? It stops now. You get the word to the rest of your little Circle. You need proof to show how serious I am, you show them this."

Her hand found was what closest. Not the cleaver (and Tully'll spend the rest of his miserable life thankful at least for that), but the metal meat tenderizer he'd used that morning. A heavy thing, mottled on one end and tiny, dulled spikes on the other. She held it out to Scarlett.

"Go on," Chessie said. "Eye for an eye, Scarlett Bickford. That's how it is in the Holler."

Scarlett shook her head.

"You can and you will. You take all that hurt and rage and you let it out. Stand up or bow down, girl. Right now."

Friend, I won't even pretend to know what went through Scarlett's mind right then. She stood there shaking her head

No, making her will known even to the likes of Chessie Hodge, and then that *No* became *I shouldn't*, and that led to something like *Maybe* before Scarlett's head stopped moving at all. Was hurt inside that girl. Hurt over a momma she didn't have no more and a daddy who was intent upon fixing her with a future as bleak as her past. It was a rage over the Crow Holler witch. But it was more than that, friend. I know it was. There came a hurt as well. Bubbling up as it had when she'd run off at the mines and hurled those rocks and twigs at the night.

She strode forward. Tully now looked her way, begging her no, begging her pardon, screaming that he'd only been drunk and in sorrow for his child.

"Do it," Chessie said.

Scarlett held out her hand. Chessie went to hand that filthy meat tenderizer over. Her grin melted when Scarlett refused to take it. Instead, she placed her hand atop Tully's own. Shaking her head at Briar first, then at Chessie.

"Fool," Chessie whispered. "Just like your daddy. This the way you think you'll rid the town of what you wrought? Is it? Standing up for ones who'd sooner spit on you than help?"

Scarlett looked like she wanted to write something, but she wouldn't move her hand from Tully's.

"Fine, then," Chessie said.

It was the spiked end a that tenderizer she brought down, doing it in a flash. Scarlett managed to move her hand at the last instant. You ask me if Chessie knew it would happen that way, I don't know. All I know is she meant to teach Scarlett and Tully both a lesson.

The teeth on that tenderizer struck Tully in the back of his hand. His wail was a piercing agony so pure it sounded like death itself. Chessie swung it again, this time to the noise of bone breaking. Blood splattered the table, the side of Chessie's face, Briar's thick beard. Scarlett's arm. Tully screamed again, so deep and long that all the air was gone from his lungs. And then he could only whimper.

-5-

Back at the mines where Hays Foster had built his fire the past Saturday night, Bucky sat on the hood of his car and tried acting like a real lawman. He held his phone to his ear and listened to what the voice on the other end said. Saying little and nodding much, like this was something he should've done two days before.

Only a dozen miles lie between Crow Holler and the town of Mattingly, but it might as well be a thousand. It's a burden getting between there and here with those steep and winding roads between, and I guess that's why we in the Holler decided over time it'd be better to stick to ourselves. But our two towns being so close as the crow flies, the Commonwealth of Virginia long ago decided in all its wisdom to include us in Mattingly's jurisdiction when it come to matters of the law.

That put us under the eye of Mattingly's sheriff, Jake Barnett. I'll say I've had dealings with that man in the past, though indirectly. People in these parts respect him as much as we can an outsider. And I'll give Jake this—he understood what's good for the city folk up in Richmond usually ain't for the mountains. We take care of our own here and punish those who need it, and we need nobody to tell us how. Jake made a drive through the hill country onced a week or so just to keep appearances, but that was it. We never needed authority until Alvaretta.

Now Bucky knew Jake well enough, having served as constable for so long. And it seemed then was as good a time as any to reach out, hoping Jake could give some guidance. Shame of it was, old Jake didn't have much to give.

"You say how many girls are sick?"

"Near thirty," Bucky said. "That's my guess, anyway. Pretty much all the young ones in town. All girls, Jake. Not a boy yet among'm."

"What's your doctor say?"

"What any doctor would. But I don't think you believe that as much as me or anybody else up here does, Jake. I'm at the mines now. Those tracks Cordy found are real. Something's loose up here."

"Anybody else been to see Alvaretta?"

"No."

"Might have to be you then, Buck. Maybe somebody can reason with her."

Bucky chuckled. "You think she's one to reason with?"

"Want me to come up there?"

"No. I can handle this, Jake."

"You sure?"

Bucky didn't answer that—couldn't, I expect. He nodded into the phone and hung up. Put his face in his hands, wondering what to do next. The answer came when his phone chirped again.

Angela, saying Tully'd hurt himself. Mashed his own hand somehow, drunk old fool that he was, and broken it good. Things were too busy at the grocery for anyone there to take him to Doc Sullivan's, so would he? Bucky checked his watch and found it nearly two. He said sure, wasn't like he had anything to do that afternoon. She told him to come around to the loading dock in back. He never asked her why.

He tried the Fosters next to check on Cordy and Hays. Kayann answered. She said she hadn't heard anything about Tully and maybe she should go down to the grocery since they'd be shorthanded. Bucky laughed at that like he thought she was making a joke about Tully's injury. Then he said maybe so. Once he got to the store, though, Bucky must've thought Kayann had been exactly right. Landis would need help that day. He would need Kayann and more.

The mess outside Foster's was even bigger than what Bucky had found at the clinic the day before. Cars everywhere, trucks and clunkers and even some old farm tractors, all jammed into that lot. Bucky slowed to gawp at it all and caught sight of Briar's truck and John David's leaving off toward the farm. He pulled around back, weaving his way through traffic and waving to friends and neighbors who looked at him like he was a stranger.

Tully sat on an old stool propped against the dock's wall. He'd found some ice and a dirty rag to wrap his hand in and held his wrist gentle, the same as he'd held his Daisy all the night before. His face had gone from the pale of fright to a suffering gray.

Bucky got out and said, "Have mercy, Tully. What'd you do?"

"Slipped," he said. "Slipped is all." And I guess Tully was right about that, if he was talking about losing what little sense he had long enough to put his hands on Scarlett Bickford.

Bucky wanted to go inside and check on Angela, but Tully begged him no. All he wanted was to leave. Whole way to Doc's office, he kept saying how sorry he was for what'd happened to Cordelia. A shame, Tully told him, and when Bucky said he'd always thought Tully a good man despite his demons, Tully started to cry.

It was at the doctor's office where Bucky first heard of the grocery closing. Maris asked him. You could hear the doctor through the door of the exam room telling Tully he was worthless in one breath and feeling sorry for him in the next, asking how drunk a man had to be to mistake his own live hand for a slab of dead meat not once but again and again. Bucky said he'd heard no such thing about Landis closing up, but Maris told him people had been coming in saying it all day.

"You don't think Landis would do that?" she asked. "Shut his doors because some idiot decided to turn his fear of Alvaretta into a rage against Hays?"

"No," Bucky said. "Landis ain't like that. But I was just over there to pick Tully up, and you ain't never seen such a rush of people. He closes down, it'll be because he's run out of everything."

"Run out?" A shadow fell over Maris's face. "I never thought of that."

"Could happen, I guess. Grocery ain't so big that it could ever hold a lot. And since the trucks only come once a week or so . . ." Bucky shrugged. "Don't make a difference though, does it? We ain't in the South Pole, Maris. We can make do."

"That ain't the point, Bucky. The grocery ain't just the grocery. We don't just go there to get our milk and bread. We get our news there too. That's where we go to connect with each other. If the church is the soul of this town, the grocery is its heart. Close it for a day or a week or forever, Bucky, you take that heart away."

Tully walked out with his hand braced and bandaged. That would have to do until he could get up to the hospital for a proper cast. He promised the doc that would happen soon, but he never went. Tully was a no-count drunk who spent much of his time out in the woods with Raleigh Jennings and his merry band of racists, but he loved his child. Daisy was the world to that man, and seeing her suffer was enough to lay a crack in his otherwise stone heart. He wouldn't leave her, even if it meant a trip to Stanley to take care of his broken bones. To this day, you greet Tully and he'll offer his left hand instead of the misshapen claw on his right because half of him got ruined. Guess he turned out like Cordelia that way. Some would call that irony.

Bucky said he'd take Tully home. Maris wished them both well and promised she'd be praying. They were no more out the door than she told Danny to get his keys. She was gonna make a few calls first, then he had to take her to the store.

-6-

I guess now I come to it, friend. There's gonna be harder parts to this story, I don't doubt that and neither should you, but that don't mean I'm looking forward to saying what comes next. It ain't been easy, me sitting here with you. People catch me telling you all this—people like Bucky or John David or his momma, Belle, who I know's peeking at us through one a the church windows—they'd have a fit. They don't want nobody else to know, you see. Plenty already do, least down in Mattingly and all the other towns dotting these mountains, and that's why they stay away.

Everything that happened up until Bucky sat in that waiting room with Maris? All of it could've unfolded as it did, and things still mighta turned out different. But what I'll tell you now? That's what led to everything else, the stuff with Wilson and Medric and Bucky and all the rest, all of it falling like a line of dominoes some ignorant soul kicked over on accident.

People think they're free in life. Maybe they are for a while. But sooner or later all the choices you make narrow down to a single end, and that's the only end you can meet. After what would happen at the grocery that evening, was but one way it could go for everybody in Crow Holler.

Doc Sullivan took Maris to Foster's just like she'd asked. He said Landis wasn't gonna do anything more'n call for a grocery truck a little earlier than usual, but Maris thought otherwise. "You don't know this town like I do," she said. "Be just like that man to close a couple days and reopen with prices twice as high as they were." Well, Maris wasn't gonna fall for that.

Neither would the two friends Maris had called to say what was going on. Course, both Helen Pruitt and Belle Ramsay had close friends too. As did those friends. And even though all of them to a person swore on all that was holy and good not to go and start a panic, that was all a lie. No other way to put it, friend.

It was near four thirty by the time Bucky brought Tully back to his home. Tully's wife, Lorraine (a horrible woman, and if you'd spend a minute with her you'd know how right I am and why Tully drank so much), had pinned a note to the door. Three words were scrawled on the page—DAISY SLEEPING STORE!!! Bucky got some ice out of the freezer and a couple aspirin for Tully's hand. Tully thanked Bucky again and said how he'd always liked Scarlett Bickford just fine.

Angela got off at five. Bucky was late getting there, but that didn't matter. The lot at Foster's was so jammed that even people couldn't move around, let alone cars. Horns blowing, voices shouting and cussing. Customers ran out with bags pressed tight to their chests and sides, ready to pounce on any who dared steal what they'd bought honestly. The sun had fallen over the mountains by then. Even in springtime, evening comes to Crow Holler not much past four, casting all this hard part of the world into hours of dim dusk. Bucky parked nearer the Exxon than the grocery and started walking. Those who passed him never said a word. Their eyes were on the store instead, and how quick time could run out.

He found Raleigh Jennings, Joe Mitchell, and Homer Pruitt in a circle at the lot's edge. I don't believe Bucky had any intent to have a chat with the man who'd fired him just that morning, but Homer shouted, "What's going on here, Bucky?" and Bucky felt a need to answer.

"I don't know," he said. "Just came up here to get Angela."

Somebody shouted up near the doors. All up there was a tangle of arms and legs.

"Grocery's closing, Buck," Raleigh said. "That's the word."

"Grocery ain't closing. Where'd you get such a thing?"

"One I got it from said she got it from Angela."

"From Angela? No, Raleigh. That can't be right."

"Looks it to me," Homer said. "Helen come in earlier and said wasn't much left. Now she's back in there getting what she can."

Joe Mitchell spoke up: "You heard what happened to Tully, Buck?"

"I did. Took him to the doc's myself. Just got back from there."

"Who called you?"

"Angela." They all looked at each other. Bucky couldn't help but say to Homer, "Was my pleasure to give Tully aid, seeing as how I had the free time."

"Tully say how it happened?" Raleigh asked.

"No, just that he slipped. You know how he is when he's in a bottle."

"Wasn't a bottle did it," Raleigh told him. "Tully called me after it happened. I was gonna take him to the clinic myself until he said no. Told me to keep away. Said the grocery wasn't safe."

"What's that supposed to mean?"

Joe spat a brown streak of tobacco juice onto the lot. "Go ask your wife," he said.

"Guess I will."

Bucky went on toward the front of the store. People came out of the grocery with whatever they'd had the chance to grab. Not just food and drink, but tubes of toothpaste, boxes of detergent, cans of dog food, mops, buckets. Anything Landis had to sell had taken on a lusty sheen of need in the town's eyes. There came David and Belle trying to get inside and the mayor jogging from his truck. Everybody, friend. Everybody was there.

Bucky turned when he heard his name. John David Ramsay waved his arms and ran toward him.

"Get in there," he yelled. *"Go."*

"What you doing, John David?"

He grabbed Bucky's collar, pulling him along. "We got to get inside right now."

Bucky tried planting his feet. It didn't work. John David's wiry, but he's strong as an ox.

"Chessie heard there's a run on Foster's," he said. "My fault." He cursed. "This is all my fault."

The doors loomed. Bucky could see Angela at her register. Her hands were moving over the counter in a blur, but it wasn't fast enough. Her hair had gone limp and hung over her eyes. And those people. Lining the aisles and pressing in. The crowd outside was too much, but it was worse inside, and that's when Bucky finally understood what John David had been trying to say.

"Something's gonna happen."

John David let go when Bucky's feet started moving on their own. They ran side by side to the door. John David started tossing people aside, telling them to back away, make room for the constable. They squeezed through the doors at the same time. Angela looked up but couldn't say a word for all her stress and fear. Her face said enough. Fingers flying over the buttons, trying to shove groceries into bags or letting them pile up wherever the conveyor belt on the counter spit them, ignoring the pleas and threats of those in line demanding that she hurry.

Some didn't wait. Landis ran back and forth along the stretch of floor where the aisles began, begging people to be patient and get only what they needed. Those who avoided him—and there were many—ran straight for the doors with all their goods in tow. Kayann Foster demanded they turn and pay, screaming it in a panic. I don't reckon Kayann had been told no more in her whole life than she had in the few hours she spent at the front of the grocery that afternoon. But those who got by Kayann now had to deal with John David. Let me tell you, folk were a whole lot more afraid of him than her. Mayor, Belle, and the Reverend had made it through by then. They were shouting, too, telling people to calm down and be orderly. Bucky didn't know what to do and so joined in. Didn't take him long to get the hang of it.

They was all up front, see. Landis and Kayann, Bucky and Angela, Wilson and the Ramsays. They were all trying to get a handle on things from where they were. But not a one of them was toward the back, and that's where the trouble started. The shelves were all but bare by then, everything gone or spilled or broken. But the last of the milk was still up for grabs—a single gallon of 2 percent and a few quarts of skim. Ruth Mitchell had returned with her husband, Joe, as soon as she'd gotten word the grocery might not be open for long (so said Helen Pruitt, who'd gotten it from Maris, who'd gotten it from someone she said "would intimately know if such a thing were true"), grabbing all she could get whether her family needed it or not. Same could be said for Lorraine Wiseman, who'd not only gotten news of Tully's injury, but that Foster's was running out of food. They both reached for that gallon of milk the same time, Lorraine gripping the handle and Ruth the base.

Lorraine looked about ready to say that gallon was hers alone when somebody pushed past for one of the quarts of skim, running her straight into Ruth. Ruth pushed back (everybody always said Ruth Mitchell had a fire to her, Raleigh loved that in a woman), sending Lorraine into an empty stack of soda crates. Those crates tumbled right down onto Homer Pruitt, who'd come in looking for his Helen.

And friend, that's all it took.

Bucky never saw all that happen, but he saw the wave it started. It rolled toward him from the back of the store slow and gathering, a wall of shouts and screams and fists meeting flesh, and by the time it reached the front, that wave crested and tumbled upon them all.

Wilson tried to help but got caught in the throng. He didn't see who hit him. David and Belle were brave enough to keep shouting for calm but not so courageous that they dove into the crowd. John David, though? Guess that boy'd been trained to run toward trouble rather than away, because he got Wilson off the floor before they both got trampled. Landis hollered for everybody to leave when a few hours ago he'd been praying for them all to come in, while Kayann stood pale and motionless. Angela ran from her register screaming Bucky's name.

You think about it, that could've been Bucky's time to shine, the single moment when he rose above. But he eased away from all that pushing and punching instead, overcome by the sight of it all, and no one would've noticed had he not backed into the fire alarm stuck to the wall.

The Klaxon went off like the angel of the Lord blowing his trumpet. Landis screamed *Fire!* and all that did was trade one panic for another. Everybody ran—the ones inside trying to get out, and the ones stuck outside trying to get in—and they all met in a wall at the front doors. Someone picked up a newspaper rack and threw it through the window. Another window broke and then another. Those able crawled for safety over shards that sliced their hands and legs. The siren's wail shifted from loud to unbearable as Bucky clamored past bodies in search of Angela. He found her huddled and crying in the first aisle and grabbed her hand. They ran through Tully's shop and out to the dock, and friend, I don't think either of them started breathing again until they were halfway to the Foster home to get Cordelia.

Everyone else in and around Foster's gathered at the far end of the lot. No one went to their car or truck. Not a soul ran for home. I always thought that a queer thing. Even now, I don't understand it. All them people just standing there, staring back at what remained of Landis Foster's dream and legacy, their fight and anger gone. Those too stunned to cry laid their hands to the backs and heads of those who whimpered, holding them, trying to comfort, asking if any were hurt or still inside. Not a one of them paused to consider how it was that the kind and merciful people they were now could be so different from the violent and hateful people they'd been only minutes before. You ask me how that can be, I have no idea.

You can't figure folk.

-7-

It took awhile for everybody to scatter. When they did, it was with the slow, confused pace of a funeral procession, like they all could understand *how* such a thing had happened but not why. Most shuffled off with their heads hung in shame. Some managed to tell the ones nearest good-bye—ones they'd shoved and beaten and cursed over deodorant and cans of potted meat. A few even had the gall to tell Landis and Kayann they hoped things could be put back together before morning, they still had groceries to get.

Landis went inside long enough to turn off that infernal alarm. He came back in a dead run, looking over his shoulder like he expected another crowd to be chasing him. His chest heaved and his face was drowned in sweat, or tears; now that I think on it, it was probably some of both. What few muscles grew on his body were locked and flexing.

John David bent over Landis and told him to breathe deep,

let his blood settle. Landis kept saying, "It's gone, isn't it, my whole life?" and nobody said a word because they knew it was. Kayann still had her hands over her ears. She didn't pull them away, even when the horn stopped and Belle put her arms around her. Maybe Kayann didn't feel that. I don't think any of them could feel much at all.

The Reverend was still there, too, along with Raleigh and Wilson. Belle turned to David and said, "Naomi's at the house alone."

"No she isn't," John David said. He glanced up from Landis. "Briar picked her up a little bit ago."

The Reverend's eyes flared. "You sent your sister to Chessie?"

"I called Briar little bit ago. Said he'd take her out to the farm and get her settled. Chessie needed to know what happened."

"Chessie doesn't need to know anything, boy."

John David straightened his back and took three long steps, putting his chin inches from his daddy's nose. "You don't get to tell me what's wrong and right anymore," he said. "And don't you call me boy again."

You ask me, them two would've come to blows right then and there. It'd been building to that point for months. David thinking his boy had strayed from the Lord's path, John David thinking his daddy'd lived too long in the Holler to understand the world beyond lay colored in something other than black and white. But Briar's truck pulled into the lot right then, and that gave them both something other than each other to fret over.

Chessie didn't wait for her husband to walk around and open her door. She got out on her own this time, and in her expression lay both Kayann's shock and Landis's sorrow.

"Where's Naomi?" Belle asked.

"Set up at the cabin with good food and safety," Briar said. "She's a strong girl and she's fine, Belle Ramsay."

"What happened?" was all Chessie could say, and in a voice so soft and womanlike that John David had to look to see who'd spoke. "We's up here only this afternoon, and all was well enough."

Mayor said, "I got a call from Raleigh saying there's a run on the grocery. It was too late when I got here."

Chessie looked at the school's principal.

"Heard it from Ruth," Raleigh said. "Angela told her Landis was gonna shut the doors."

"Angela said no such thing," Landis snapped. "And shame on Ruth and you for thinking otherwise, Raleigh Jennings."

Briar studied the wrecked building. He rubbed his beard and reached into his back pocket for his pipe and tobacco. "Take forever to get this place back in order."

"What good is that?" Kayann asked. Her hands were gone from her ears, but her lips twitched like she could still hear that blaring horn. "They'll just come back and destroy it again. They're animals."

"They're our neighbors," the Reverend tried, though even he didn't sound much convinced that was the case anymore.

Wilson humphed. "In body, maybe. Not in deed." He looked to the building as well, now shadowed in evening. "It's like they were . . ."

"Cursed?" the Reverend asked.

Maybe Wilson had that word in mind. If he didn't, he looked too run-down to argue about it.

"This how it is, then?" Briar asked. "Witch lays a mark on us, so we eat our own? That what Alvaretta had in mind all along?"

No one had an answer for that, at least one that wouldn't come out sounding like a yes. Yes, that's how things were now. Yes, that's what it'd all come to. Crow Holler was unraveling, and whether what happened inside Foster's had been a part of Alvaretta's design or not, there was no denying things felt that way.

"Everybody's here," the mayor said. "Both council members; me; David, you and Belle know how important you are to this town; Chessie and Briar, y'all too."

Chessie offered a solemn nod. That'd been the closest Wilson had ever gotten to showing her a measure of respect.

"We ain't all gotten along in the past," he said, "but we all come up together. We're all family whether we like it or not, and Lord knows we love this town despite its hardships. This will grow beyond our strength to manage." Wilson pointed to the broken hulk of the grocery for anyone needing proof. "Our children are sick. People are scared. Scared for their own, scared of the witch. And since they can't go after Alvaretta, they'll come after us, as sure as the sun rises and the rain falls. They already went after our kids. Hays. They went after Cordelia. They attacked my Scarlett."

Raleigh said nothing.

"They've come after our children no less than the witch did, and with just as much evil in their hearts. And now they're coming for our livelihoods. It was Landis first. Who's to say it won't be Medric's next? Or the church, David."

"Never there," the Reverend said. "Holy Fire's God's house."

"But the man who speaks for God has a little girl who crossed Alvaretta Graves. How long you think it'll take for people to decide Naomi's as much to blame as Scarlett or Hays or Cordelia? How much time passes before all their praying comes to silence, and they figure maybe it's not Alvaretta who's got too much power but you who holds too little? How long before they come after you, Chessie? Briar? Everybody already knows John David was on the mountain too. He left Hays and three girls alone at the mines. How much a stretch is it to think those were your orders?"

Briar was already swelling up. "You'll watch yourself, Wilson."

"I speak true," the mayor said. "Chessie, you tell me I'm not."

The softness that had been in Chessie's face hardened to its usual stone. "What's in your mind, Wilson?" she asked.

"People need authority now. They need to know there's still rules and expectations. They need somebody to answer to. We all got our own lives and children to look after. I know I ain't been with Scarlett near as much in the last days as I should. We're running around and trying to get a handle on things, and all the while Alvaretta sits up on Campbell's Mountain, cackling at us."

"Ain't nothing to be done about that," Raleigh said.

"Yes, there is. We can appoint a sheriff."

"Town don't need a sheriff," Briar said. "Never has. We take care our own."

Kayann asked, "That what we're doing, Briar?" She waved into the lot. "Is this taking care of our own?"

"Who?" Chessie asked. She stared at Wilson. "You thought of that, Mayor? Tell me anybody dumb enough to put on a badge right now."

"Could call Mattingly," Belle said. "Get Sheriff Barnett up here."

Wilson shrugged. "Won't nobody heed Jake. He ain't of the Holler. They may listen to Bucky, though."

"Bucky?" Raleigh laughed. He looked at Wilson and saw the mayor's even stare, then laughed again anyway. "Now look here, Mayor. Bucky's fine for making sure nobody poaches deer outta season and no kids graffiti up the schools, but what good's he gonna do against the witch?"

"What good's anybody gonna do?" Chessie asked.

Wilson pointed at her and said, "Exactly. Bucky's wanted this a long while. He's been constable since most of us graduated, and he loves doing it. Don't know how many of y'all heard, but Homer let him go this morning. Bucky'll jump at the chance, if only so it'll provide for Angela and Cordy."

"Bucky ain't man enough," Raleigh said.

"He was man enough to take care of things in there," Wilson said, pointing at the store. "Seen him myself. Everything went to pot inside the grocery, Bucky pulled that fire alarm. He got everybody outta there before people could start killing each other."

"There'll be an election," David said. "That'll take weeks."

"Not if I call this an emergency situation," Wilson told him. "If this ain't one, I don't know what is. It'll be a council vote. Right here, right now."

And there they stood, friend. Each one looking at the other, no doubt shocked all over again that things had come to this.

"I vote yes," Wilson said.

Raleigh looked at Briar, who stuck his bottom lip out as if to say *Beats me*. Chessie looked over her shoulder to where her newest employee stood.

"You been awful quiet back there, John David. I'd hear your counsel."

"He doesn't have a say in this," the Reverend said. Belle's look shut him up quicker than Chessie's could.

"Don't think you want what wisdom I got, Chessie," John David said.

"I'd have it anyways."

"All right, then. I think you're all cowards."

Chessie grinned. She always did like that boy. Not a streak of fear left in him. That's what made John David a dangerous man, and what makes him one still.

"That ain't true," Wilson said. "This is what's best for all. Raleigh, I'll have your vote."

"Raleigh's vote is no," Chessie said. "You put Bucky in charge, somebody's gonna die. Bucky, most likely."

"I need it from him, Chessie. Raleigh's his own man."

But Raleigh wasn't his own man. Not anymore. His vote was Chessie's and had been ever since she'd gotten him back on the council, and though Raleigh hated her nearly as much as he hated Medric Johnston, he still said, "I vote no, Wilson."

"It's no for us," the Reverend said. "Me and Belle. Bucky's a good man, and I'll not let anyone accuse me of thinking different. But this is a fight that can't be won with badges and guns."

"Vote ain't yours, Reverend," Wilson told him. "It's on Landis now."

Landis looked up at the mention of his name. They were all staring at him, all except Kayann, who couldn't seem to see any farther than the tip of her nose. Some in Crow Holler thought Hays had inherited his momma's mind right along with her looks, and sooner or later one a them was gonna take a leap off the edge of reality. Kayann looked near that edge now.

"Landis," Wilson said. "I need your vote."

Landis looked at his wife. At the rest. At the store. You'd have to wonder if that man even knew what was going on.

"I don't care," he said.

For Wilson, that was good enough.

-8-

Angela looked at her family and asked the only question that had come to matter: "What do we do now?"

She'd posed the very same a million times before for a million different reasons (after the chores were done; once the shelves at the grocery had been stocked; in the minutes following her and Bucky's twice monthly attempts at lovemaking). But this time was different, as was the weight of feeling behind the words. This time Angela wasn't looking for their next item to check off the day's to-do list. She was trying to figure out how to pick up the pieces of their shattered lives.

The faith she'd meant to display over Bucky's sudden unemployment had barely lasted twelve hours, left somewhere on the littered floors of Foster's Grocery alongside toppled racks and smashed boxes of dishwasher detergent and powdered doughnuts. The Vests wouldn't've made it long without a steady paycheck from the dump, however puny that check had been. But now all indications were Angela wouldn't be getting paid anymore either. Foster's was gone, bills were due, and the cupboards all but bare, so *What do we do now?*

She paced in front of the window, cracking one knuckle and the next. Cordelia sat on the floor with her back propped against her daddy's knee. Her blank expression hadn't changed since they'd picked her up from the Fosters' house—Bucky and Angela rushing in, silent against Hays's questions, only to spout to Cordy everything that had happened on the way home. Poor Hays hadn't had a clue what had gone on up to his daddy's place of business.

Now Bucky leaned back in the recliner and tried to find something on the TV. He dipped his chin toward Cordelia and said, "Maybe we should just talk about this later, Angie. It's been a rough day. Lot's happened."

Family finances were never discussed in their daughter's presence, if for no other reason than Cordelia didn't need to know how far the money had to be stretched to cover things like a big-screen television. Besides, the odds of a calm discussion of the money becoming a loud argument about everything else seemed too great. But now Cordelia looked up and shook her head. She turned her hands up as if to wave, then opened and closed them, telling her parents to talk. They all had to talk. No use hiding the truth anymore.

Bucky was working on something inspiring to say when

the doorbell rang. Angela gave a yelp that Bucky shook off. He threw down the recliner's footrest and said, "Somebody gonna come up here and kill us, Angie, I doubt they'll ring the bell first." Even so, he made it a point to peek through the curtains before heading to the door. "Well," he said, "this is either something promising or something awful."

He opened the door to Briar Hodge's giant face. Behind him, the others crammed onto the trailer's small front porch—Chessie and Wilson, Raleigh, the Fosters and the Ramsays—minus their kids.

"Briar?" Bucky asked. "What y'all doing?"

Wilson stuck his head under Briar's arm. "Need a word, Buck. I know it's late, but mind if we come in?"

They filed in close, saying their hellos to Angela and Cordelia. Kayann paused when she reached Angela, and don't you know that woman actually hugged her? Did so with both arms, right there in Angela's own living room, and Angela was so shocked that she hugged Kayann back.

Angela said, "Let me get y'all some chairs."

"Won't be necessary," Wilson said. "This'll only take a minute. Got Scarlett and Naomi up at Landis's house with Hays, and we don't want to let them alone for long. It's been a hard day all around, and we could all use some rest." He looked at Bucky. "Seen what you did tonight at the store, Buck."

"What I . . . ?" Bucky dipped his head. Doing it quick, I expect, because he couldn't look at any of them. Not at the mayor, who was the best friend he'd ever had, not at his pastor or the two men on the council. Not at his own family. "Wilson, I don't know what happened there. I just got so overcome, like I couldn't think straight, and—"

"What you talking about, Bucky?" Chessie asked.

They all stared at him.

"I don't know," Bucky said. "What're y'all talking about?"

"The fire alarm," Wilson said. "I saw you hit it when everything got bad."

"Fire alarm?"

"You saved us tonight, Constable. Maybe saved us all. It's a dark time, I don't have to tell you that. You and Angie and Cordelia know it as well as any of us. We need the strong to stand and fight, good men with smarts and quick thinking. Folk need to feel safe again."

Bucky nodded through all this. Angela too.

"That's why the council met just a little bit ago, along with Chessie and Briar, the Reverend and Belle. We all voted in accord to come up here and ask if you'll do Crow Holler the honor of becoming its sheriff, effective immediately."

Angela gasped. *"Sheriff?"*

"We know what Homer Pruitt did to you," Wilson said. "Wasn't right what he did, so we want to help make up for it. Job will be a paid position, of course. We ain't settled on how much, but it'll be more than what you'd get working a dozer. Town funds will cover most, along with your insurance. Briar here said he'd contribute—"

Chessie threw in, "'Long as you leave us alone, Buck."

"—the rest," Wilson finished. "You'll be an important man, Bucky. Time like this, maybe the most important we got."

Angela couldn't say a thing. She'd gone just as slack in the face as Cordelia, who'd retreated to the very corner of the room alone and had found a sadness no one bothered to notice.

"We need you, Bucky," Wilson said. "Town's all here asking. Will you do this?"

And what could Bucky answer but yes, friend? Couldn't have been anything but that, because these were his friends and this was his town and it was just as the mayor had said—to be sheriff had always been Bucky's only dream and want. Yes, he told them, yes and yes again, and when Bucky shook their hands and waved as all those friends made their way back to their dark homes and frightened children, he never once wondered why none of them could look him in the eye.

VIII

Angela quits. Crow feathers.
Revival. The kids meet.

-1-

I wouldn't say Bucky was late rising for the first official day of
the rest of his life, but he wasn't early. Angela served him breakfast in a bed that had endured more rocks and squeaks in the
night than it had in quite a long while. Twiced a month may've
been good enough for a trash man, but I guess Angela thought
a *town sheriff* (that's how she kept saying those two words, hard
and almost awestruck) deserved to partake in the pleasures of
the flesh more often. She kissed Bucky on the cheek and neck.
Let her hands wander, invited him to do the same. When it was
all over, she laid out Bucky's best jeans and shirt for what was
to be a new start for them all.

The mayor called, wanting Bucky to meet him at the grocery so they could take stock of how much damage had been
done the night before. Wilson also asked if anybody there had
found a flyer either in the mailbox or left inside the screen door
that morning. No one had.

"Maybe I'll just come on up," Wilson said. "We could ride
over to the grocery together. Talk some things over."

Bucky said that'd be fine, Angela needed the car anyway.
She had a special errand down at the grocery that morning.
Bucky wasn't the only member of the Vest family who'd looked
forward to this day for a long while.

Cordelia was adamant she would go as well. Not only

would Hays be there, chances were good she'd see Naomi and Scarlett too. There'd been texts between the three of them since returning from the hospital, but nothing more. What Cordy had to discuss with her two best friends needed to be done face-to-face. She hadn't forgotten what Hays had told her the day before or the fear in his voice as he'd said it. And how could she, faced with even the possibility of such a thing? Of something following them home from the mountain? She hadn't told her daddy and would never tell her momma. I guess she feared that would only poison Hays to Angela even more, and she didn't want to put further strain on Bucky.

Besides, nothing had followed them from the witch's house. She would have seen something if it had, yes? Someone else would have seen it, Scarlett or Naomi. She would ask them and they would both say no, of course not, that was just Hays being Hays.

Wilson arrived in his T-bird not long after. Angela sent Bucky off with his own mug of coffee and waved good-bye from the front porch. Bucky grinned and waved back. Should've seen how that man smiled, like the whole scene was something straight out his dreams. And I guess it was. He was happy, his wife was happy. The only thing that dulled it was the sight of Cordelia peeking out from her bedroom window, looking at Bucky like he'd never come home again.

"Here," the mayor said. He took a crumpled piece of paper from his suit jacket. "Look at this."

Bucky took the page and held it out near the windshield, saying he hadn't brought his readers with him. He squinted as his lips moved in silence.

REVIVAL!!

ALL THIS WEEK NIGHTLY BEGINNING AT 7:00 P.M.

THE LORD CALLETH FROM THE DARKNESS

WILL YOU ANSWER?

"Found that in my paper box this morning. Found another taped to the door on the council building. Reverend's done put them up all over the place."

"Well, I don't see nothing wrong in Preacher calling a revival, Wilson. Maybe it'll do some good."

"Won't do no *good*, Bucky. I went to his house, and you know what he told me?"

Bucky said he didn't, though I imagine he could've guessed.

"Said Crow Holler needs a rededication of faith. A turning away of sins past and present. David means to purge the Holler of evil, Bucky. You know what that means? That man stood at the grocery last night and spoke long of battling the witch, now he turns around and tells me the fight's not on Campbell's Mountain, it's in the town itself."

The mayor drove on, shaking his head, telling Bucky over and over this was all so bad. Bucky sat there like he was trying to put together a puzzle without a picture to go by.

"Preacher didn't say nothing about revival when I went down to see him yesterday."

The mayor's foot slipped off the gas pedal. "You went to see David?"

"I needed prayer, Wilson." Which was true. In a way. "I got stuff going on you don't know about."

"He say anything about me?"

Plenty, Bucky looked to think. But he'd given his word to David Ramsay that he'd say nothing of it. In these parts, a man's word is about all he's got. "What would he say about you, Mayor?"

Wilson didn't answer. "Listen here, Bucky. I'm gonna be straight with you. A few people at the meeting last night didn't want to see you in this job."

"Like who?"

"Chessie and Briar, for one. Raleigh too."

Bucky cocked his head. "What's Raleigh got against me, Wilson? I ain't ever done a thing to him. Chessie and Briar, I can see. Them two—"

"Will be left alone," Wilson said. "That was a condition, Bucky, and you'll abide by it. Look here, all I'm trying to say is this won't be easy. Most in this town don't even want a mayor, much less an officer of the law. Don't matter if Alvaretta Graves is looming over us all or not. Now I stood up for you last night because I trust you. Always have, Buck, and you're about the only one.

"Raleigh, he's gonna do what Chessie wants. I don't think Landis is in much shape to be on the council at all right now, not after what happened to the grocery. And the Reverend . . ." Wilson shook his head slow. "He's gonna make this whole mess into some kind of crusade, Bucky. You mark my words, that man'll turn neighbor against neighbor just to satisfy his own conscience. What you need prayer for? This thing about Homer firing you?"

Bucky nodded, glad to change the subject.

"Well, we got that taken care of, didn't we?"

"Some of it," Bucky said. "There's other stuff I don't think you'll be able to fix, Wilson. Or me."

"Don't you worry about Cordy. All our girls are gonna be fine soon as we figure out a way to fix all this."

"Ain't just Cordy's face. It's Hays. She was upset when we picked her up last night. I mean, she'd have to be, you know, when we told her what all happened at the grocery. But there was more going on. I think it's that boy."

"Ain't a problem," the mayor said. "Cordy ain't got no ring on her finger. Best she get away from him. You know that."

"She might not got a ring," Bucky said, "but she's got something other."

"Like what?"

"Like a baby inside."

That nugget of news stole the mayor's tongue for a good long while. Other than the usual *How'd this happen?* and *Are y'all okay?* and *That boy did that to Scarlett, I'd gut him,* them two rode like strangers rest of the way into town. I don't guess Bucky minded. It meant the mayor wasn't asking him anything else about what the Reverend had said, and it meant Bucky wouldn't have to either lie or ask Wilson why the Reverend would think Alvaretta Graves had taken both John David and Wilson's dead wife.

-2-

I don't know how many hours of her life Angela had wasted pining for the day she'd be free of the grocery. Dreaming of marching up to Landis and Kayann (Kayann especially) to say she was done. Now and finally that day had come, which made it all the stranger that she looked so cold and distant driving along in the family's little car. But I guess Angela had built that day up so high that actually living it was bound to disappoint. Sure, she was quitting, and she was quitting because her husband was now an Important Man. But it had taken Alvaretta Graves and the evil she'd claimed from the mountain for Angela to gain what she had. It had taken Cordelia and all the other girls getting cursed and the man Angela once loved and maybe still did to lose his business. That's what I'd guess. And the way Angela stole a peek at Cordelia beside her would tell me I'm right. Because there wasn't motherly love or heartfelt sorrow in that long gaze at her daughter. It was more a kind of anger.

They pulled into the grocery only a little while after Bucky and the mayor. Angela spoke the very words her husband had only a few minutes before: "I didn't realize it was this bad."

Others had already arrived. Along with the mayor's T-bird, there was Briar's truck and the Ramsays' Jeep. Everybody was inside but Bucky, who'd taken it upon himself to go through the lot and pick up the refuse the crowd had left behind. You'd have to chuckle at the irony of it—Bucky getting fired from the dump and then handed the job of his dreams, only to spend his first day of it picking up trash.

Cordy went inside to find Scarlett and Naomi (and Hays, of course, though I'd be lying if I said he was first on that girl's mind right then). Angela lingered and helped Bucky bag up what they could.

"You sure you want to do this?" Bucky asked. "Cut ties here? Wilson ain't even said when I'm gonna get my first pay, much less how big it'll be."

"Wilson said it'll be more than the dump, plus insurance. You got reason to doubt him?"

Bucky looked at his wife like maybe he did. "Reverend's calling revival."

"I think revival's a fine idea," Angela said. "Town needs saving, Bucky. You and the Reverend both have parts to play. If this curse means anything, it's that we've all strayed from the right and good." She stroked his arm. "I know that means me too."

"That ain't how Wilson sees things. I think he come up here this morning looking for the preacher. Belle told us he's down at the church, getting things ready."

"Why's Wilson want words with the preacher?" Angela asked. Her whole face brightened. My, does that woman love her gossip. "What's he say?"

"Tell you later. Where'd Cordy go?"

"Inside."

"She act okay on the way?"

Angela shrugged. "I guess we both got a lot on our minds."

"I guess so," Bucky said. "You go on and do what you gotta."

She kissed his cheek and went inside, ignoring the little group of girls that had gathered near the door. Nor did Angela notice Hays's absence from the store that morning. Her mind held room enough for only one thing, friend. The only thing that mattered.

It was Belle Ramsay who told Angela where she could find Landis. The Reverend's wife tried to smile as she pointed back toward the dairy section, where most of the damage lay. Belle's top lip was sweating and her clothes were filthy from cleaning—a happy woman, doing the Lord's work.

Angela found Kayann trying to piece together the back corner of the store. Landis was with her. The sight of him was enough to give Angela pause—the bent posture, the pale skin, the faraway look to his eyes. Like he'd gone old in a single night. But this was to be Angela's day, her new start, so she picked her feet up again and kept walking. Not to Landis, though (she'd found she couldn't bear to wound that man, no matter how he'd once wounded her), but to Kayann. The woman's clothes weren't near as soiled as Belle's. Clean, pressed jeans and a bright orange top with the sleeves rolled to give the appearance of labor. Even Kayann's makeup was perfect. Angela hated her.

"Angela," she said. "You're late. There's a lot to be cleared away up front. And open or not, you need to wear your smock."

"I'm afraid you'll have to do that on your own," Angela said. "I quit, Kayann."

Kayann near dropped her broom and dustpan. "You what?"

"I'm quitting. I'm not working for you anymore."

Landis shuffled his body over, and Angela told him the same, though with a softer tone.

"You can't quit now," Kayann said. "Look around you, Angela. We have nothing left."

"I'm sorry," Angela said, which I suppose she was some, but not really. "I have other duties now."

"Is this about Bucky?" Landis asked.

"It is." She turned to Kayann. "My husband is now a man of importance, Kayann. He'll need me for support."

"You can't stay on at least until we get things back the way they were?" Landis asked. "We're already short Tully. Doc says he won't be able to work for maybe six weeks." Then, lower and mostly to himself, "If even he wants to come back, after what we let happen."

"I can't. My husband's gotta come first, Landis." It was almost an apology—Angela giving him permission to finally let her go.

"How much of this is because of your husband," Kayann asked, "and how much of it is because of mine?"

Angela whirled around. "What's that supposed to mean?"

"You know what it means. You're still in love with Landis. You always have been. This is revenge, pure and simple, your way of getting even because he chose *me*. Bucky's never meant anything to you, and I dare you to stand here and say otherwise."

Landis tried acting like he hadn't heard any of this, but there was no doubt he had. Everyone'd heard it, Kayann had all but shouted the words. Angela looked up to see Cordelia staring from the other side of the store. Bucky stood not ten feet away.

"I quit," she said again. "*I quit*, Kayann Foster, and I hate you."

"Alvaretta should've taken more than Cordelia's face. She should've taken *you*. That would've solved all of—"

"*I quit*," Angela screamed. "You are a vile and evil woman, Kayann Foster, and there is a hole in your black heart."

She stormed out, trying not to see Bucky's face (but doing so anyway, and oh, how his expression hurt her, to Angela's very bones), screaming for Cordelia to follow. She didn't wait when Cordy didn't come. Angela roared out of that little lot at the grocery and never once looked back, leaving everyone to stand and stare.

No, friend. I expect that weren't the way she'd dreamed it going at all.

-3-

It hadn't taken much effort for Hays to sneak away from the grocery that morning. One look at that place had been enough to let him know there would never be any putting it back together.

Took him all of ten minutes to walk the road down to Medric's. Spent another thirty waiting for Medric to get back from wherever he'd gone. His black car came down the road the opposite way sometime later and pulled straight into the back. Medric got out and slammed the door.

Technically, it was business hours. The laminated sign taped to the window said Mon–Sat, 9–1, and it was well after opening. But knocking seemed good after what Medric had found nailed to his door two days before, and knocking at the front seemed best.

It was a good thing Hays went that way. As he took the steps leading to the front door, Medric sat in the small kitchen in back, cleaning his shotgun.

Hays knocked and toed at one of the potted plants Medric kept in the porch planters in the warmer months. He looked through the little window to the side of the door and saw a dim room of empty caskets for sale. Then he saw Medric and the shotgun in his hand.

The knob jiggled and turned as the door cracked open. A tired baritone voice spoke. The past days had been unkind to Medric Johnston. In some ways, he suffered worse than the others. That old dead raccoon only played a small part of a larger danger, one that even now he felt charging up behind him. "What you doing here, Hays?"

"Come to see how you were. Come every day since what happened, but you ain't been here."

"Been taking care of business. Now you get on from here. Ain't safe. Sides, I don't think I wanna see you."

"I'm sorry," Hays said. "I only meant to sneak the key. Scarlett was the one who wanted to go up to the mines. None of us thought anything would happen."

"That's your problem," Medric said. He looked around to make sure no one was watching. "Y'all din't *think*. You know better, Hays. You know what kind can a worms you opened?"

"Can I just come in? Let me explain?"

Medric said, "Ain't nothing *to* explain. People after me now."

"They're after all of us. The grocery got tore up last night. People are getting sick."

"You don't think I know? Now you get on. Parlor ain't open for business. I'm shut to further notice."

The door went to close. Shotgun or not, Hays blocked it with his boot.

"Something followed me, Medric. I need help."

"What you mean something followed you? From Alvaretta's?"

He nodded, and in that nod was an agony I cannot describe. "It was in the shed, Medric. The *shed*. It's bad things in the shed. I've seen it around my house, following me. Glimpses. But I can feel it more. I don't know what to do."

"You pray, that's what you do. And stay outta sight." He said it again: "You know what can a worms you opened? You gonna get me killed, boy."

"Why?" Hays asked. "Everybody knows I took the key. You haven't done anything."

"Go," Medric said. "I ain't joking with you."

It didn't seem right. None of it did. I wouldn't say Medric was much loved by the town. Neither was Hays. I guess that's the sort of thing two people can share in common and make something of a friendship out of in spite of their differences in age and skin. Medric never had kids. Hays would say he'd never really had a daddy. They both just took to each other I guess, drawn by a fascination with death and things unseen. And in all the time they'd spent together, not once had Medric acted so strange. Not like he was scared, more that . . .

"Medric, you hiding something?"

"No. Now get on, Hays. I mean it." He racked his shotgun.

Hays nodded slow. "Okay. I'm sorry. Okay? I didn't mean for any of this to happen."

"Nobody did," Medric said. "But that don't matter now."

Hays backed off the porch then, shrugging like whether it mattered or not, he was still sorry. He glanced down long enough to clip one of the pots with the edge of his foot. Both the plant and the dirt inside went sprawling.

"Dang it," he said. "I'm sorry. I can clean—"

"Just get," Medric told him.

Hays got. He turned and stepped off that porch and kept his hands in his pockets, acting just as innocent as he could be. Medric cussed and stepped out the door to survey the mess. Hays turned then, slow and in stride—and saw something that sent a chill down his back. He fought the urge to run screaming. As it was, he only allowed himself to break into something like a trot. Medric saw his wide eyes and hollered, wanting Hays to come back.

No way was that boy ever going to do that. Not now.

Not after seeing all those crow feathers stuck to the bottoms of Medric's boots.

-4-

It was nearing supper when Bucky finally told Cordelia they had to get on home, and then only because Belle said they all had to get ready for revival. I don't think Bucky or Cordy much wanted to leave, even if the place they were leaving was the ruined wreck of Foster's Grocery. Going home meant facing Angela, you see, and having to deal with everything Kayann had said. In a week that had been full of uncomfortable conversations, Bucky didn't want another. Especially that one.

Sheriff or not, he still went home smelling of filth and sweat. They'd all pitched in that day, though by the end it was plain to everyone the grocery would be closed for a good long while. Cordy had spent much of her time as close to her daddy as she could get, fetching him drinks and a sandwich from the Exxon for lunch. About the only time she drifted away was when Hays sent a text. Cordy checked with Scarlett and Naomi. They'd gotten one too.

Bucky kept the window on the Celebrity down so Cordelia could breathe something like fresh air. The radio played Brad Paisley, pining on the pleasures of country life. Bucky turned it off.

"You okay?" Cordy asked.

"I guess."

"Ith Mom?"

"Hope so," Bucky said.

"You know thee loves you, wight?"

Bucky reached over and squeezed his daughter's knee. He smiled. "I know."

On and on that went, Cordy slurring her words and Bucky trying to understand them enough to answer right. But all them two did was pass the fifteen minutes between the grocery and their house the same as always, chitchatting away but saying nothing much at all.

It was like that for the other families too—the Fosters and Bickfords and Ramsays. On the surface, Alvaretta's curse had changed everything. But underneath, things weren't much different than they'd ever been. The parents still worried of their jobs and the bills past due, the kids still worried how popular they weren't and how ugly they looked, and nobody really said anything to anyone else of value. No one really said what they thought or felt. And in a way, I believe that was part of the witch's curse too. It reminded every family in Crow Holler just how thick the walls between them had grown.

Angela had her best I'm-sorry supper waiting on the table. Fried chicken and dumplings, Bucky's favorite. She spoke nothing of what had happened at the grocery at first, saying only that Reverend Ramsay had called to personally invite them to revival. Angela spoke that bit of news from behind the prettiest smile either Bucky or Cordelia had ever witnessed. Seemed as though Bucky's newfound prominence in Crow Holler had paid off already.

When the meal had descended into the same awkward silence Angela had sworn would be banished from the supper table, she felt she had no choice but to wade into murky waters and put Bucky at ease.

"You know Kayann, always so paranoid about everything. And really," she said, "you can't listen to a word that woman says after all that's happened. You'd likely be speaking nonsense, too, and nobody would much listen because they'd know it was just your hurt talking. Why, their whole lives have been upended. Everything they spent years building up, torn down in a night. It's a shame," Angela said, and yet there lay a grin upon her mouth and a lightness to her words.

There wasn't much argument when Cordelia said she'd rather stay home. Bucky tried saying things still might not be safe, but she countered by saying everyone in a dozen miles would be at church. Besides, she wasn't feeling well. Nothing to be worried about, she said, just tired from the day's work.

I think it was plain to most everyone in Crow Holler what David Ramsay and Mayor Bickford both had in mind for the night. It was solutions both men were after, and while one would speak of the Lord and the other of the community, each would stress the only way to bring Crow Holler back to the slow and dying town it had been would be for everybody to start helping each other.

For Angela, though, all business of witches and demons and evil came in a distant second to what the night truly meant. This was her time, and she was going to shine. She put on her favorite dress, a dark blue one that somehow made her look skinnier than she really was, and demanded Bucky put on his burying suit. When he came down the hallway with that big belly of his peeking out from his jacket, Angela looked to swoon.

They kissed Cordelia good-bye and told her to keep the doors locked. She promised she would and glanced at the clock on the TV stand. It was 6:27. Half an hour until revival, and an hour before Hays would arrive to take her to Harper's Field. Cordelia still had to text everyone else to make sure they were going. Had to get dressed, find more paper and a new pen in case Scarlett ran out. She needed her parents gone so bad that she didn't even give pause when she heard Angela ask Bucky if she looked fancy enough, and how she only wished she had that diamond bracelet to wear.

-5-

Friend, you ever have occasion to attend a proper country revival? I ain't talking about a quiet little gathering where the preacher talks on taking the country back for the Lord while your young'uns are off cutting out paper crosses and singing "Jesus Loves the Little Children." I mean *revival*—steepled church with its doors and windows wide to the world; everybody crowding inside, fanning themselves from the heat; bodies swaying as the piano grinds; voices singing of sin and blood; preacher's face streaked with sweat, Bible in hand as he paces, calling down the Spirit and shouting down the devil. You never been to one a those, I don't expect what I tell you next will make much sense. Don't make much sense to me neither, and that's why I stay away from church. There's no grace to a revival, only judgment, and maybe that's the point of the whole thing. If a man of God can't convince you to embrace heaven, I guess he figures scaring the hell out of you will accomplish the same thing.

Pretty much the whole town started making its way down to the Holy Fire after supper. Men and women and children alike, crowding into those pews and aisles. Didn't take long for folk to notice not a single one of the kids who'd gone to Alvaretta's was there. Even the Reverend's own daughter was missing, having told her daddy the shakes in her bones were just too horrible. Medric wasn't there neither. And though Maris Sullivan had shown up early with her Bible in hand, her husband the doctor had not. Just tired was what she told the Reverend, all those patients they'd seen over the week.

Didn't take long for things to get hopping. Reverend had set the whole first pew apart special. Belle sat there, along with the mayor and the Fosters. Raleigh Jennings showed up late, having first stopped at a place in the woods across town for a revival of his own with his men of the Circle. He squeezed between Kayann Foster and Briar Hodge, who whispered to Chessie that John David had the right idea in deciding to skip the circus show. Of course the Holler's new sheriff and his wife was there too. Not banished to the back where there was neither room nor air, but up front with the town's elite.

My, but it was a sight to see. There was sick girls come for healing and parents come for answers, everybody determined to find both and scared they'd leave with neither. There was a power inside church that night. You could feel it straight off—anticipation and desperation and fear and anger, all coming together to explode. Medric couldn't see much from the little side window of the funeral parlor across the street, but he could hear, and every note sung and word preached only filled him with more dread.

Reverend began with prayer like he always did, though this time he got down on his knees and bid everybody do the same, with mixed results. Lord or not, Chessie Hodge would never take such a position of submission without a measure of resistance and enough cussing to turn everybody in the front row red with embarrassment. It took Briar and Bucky both to get that woman back in her seat.

A silence settled in as David took the pulpit, broken only by the peeps and thrashings of the town's girls under the witch's curse. They sat apart from their families toward the back, huddled together like lepers, their only comfort the sufferings of one another. David looked at them and nodded in much the way Belle had seen him do with Naomi just the day before. Telling them all was well, the battle had already been won.

He spoke: "I feel the power of the Lord in this place tonight."

And all his flock said, "Amen."

"I will say I have not felt power these past days. I have searched for the Lord, friends. I have panted for Him as a deer pants for water. I have gone to Him as a broken man for the healing of my daughter, just as you have gone to Him for yours."

"Amen."

"And I know you've done so because we are a God-fearing

people. We are a community of the righteous. The chosen few who carry the banner of heaven into a dark and desolate place."

"Amen."

"We war against the powers and principalities, legions of doom and destruction, the dominion of eternal night, and we are seen. Never let it be forgotten, good people. We are seen. By heaven, oh yes, and upon us the angels gaze and rejoice, for we are the light of the world. And yet every man and woman of God who dares speak His truth to an unbelieving generation will catch the devil's eye as well. The Prince of Darkness will curse our light, for it reminds him of the beauty and truth he once possessed, and he will seek to snuff us out."

Softer: "Amen."

"And what is next when the devil finds us? Brothers and sisters, what shall we do? For a pale horse has come to Crow Holler, and its rider is death, and her name is the witch."

David looked to the mayor as he said this. His hands flexed open and closed as he paced the floor, like thunderbolts danced between his fingers.

"Long have we known she lurks, hiding in the bowels of the mountain as she consorts with the powers of darkness and mocks our way of life. We let Alvaretta be. We believed the truce between us and thought that the Christian way. Well, I ask you tonight, good people—is there truly peace where darkness can dwell? Can we say there is light when evil is allowed to gather and grow?"

Louder: "Amen."

"I say no. And I say I stand before you tonight as one accused no less than any of you. I know of Alvaretta Graves. I've seen her power. I know what she seeks. And I know I am not the only one."

Wilson's eyes narrowed.

"I stood idle even as the Lord charged me with protecting

Crow Holler. I did not seek out Alvaretta Graves and demand she turn from her wickedness or flee our town. And for that, I have failed you all."

There came no amen at that, friend, just the silence of a people shocked and stricken. And it was right about then pretty much everybody inside the Holy Fire started realizing this weren't like any revival they'd ever been to.

"Yes," David said, "I have failed you. I have not been a good pastor. At times, I have not been a good husband. And I'm sure you all know enough of my family to agree when I say I have not fulfilled my duties as a father. Only a few days ago, my Naomi went to a party with some of her friends. I won't name them; you know who they are. I'm sure you've all heard stories of what happened after. Most of them will be wrong. Where we can all agree is those children run across the witch—led there by . . ." He paused. "Something. Devil or demon, call it what you will. But I know my daughter, and I know she speaks the truth. They were cursed. Now that curse is ours. All of ours."

The Reverend stopped his laps back and forth on the raised stage. He looked out over all those faces staring back in nods and tears and want, and I think he realized what his flock needed wasn't the holy sword of God's Word or the threat of damnation, but the truth. Only that. He laid his Bible down and stepped forward to the small ledge in front of the pulpit, where he sat. And when David spoke next, it was no longer as one of authority. It was as one of them.

"What are we doing, good people? The witch comes for our children, and so we come at each other? We lay the burden of what has happened on the victims, but not ourselves? We destroy the property of those we love, people who share this same building with us every Sunday and pray and worship and give of their labor so that our lives may be sustained. Can we call such a thing of God?

"Brothers and sisters, I will tell you with joy that according to Maris Sullivan, there were no new instances of the curse brought into the clinic today. Praise the Lord for that."

"Praise Him," came the reply.

"But I tell you with a heavy heart that those who suffer from it suffer still. I have spoken with many of you these last days. I have prayed over your stricken children, and I will be the first to say it has had no good effect. They are still sick. They are still hurting.

"Look at our children back there," he said, pointing, "and tell me who it was did this. Was it anyone other than Alvaretta Graves? Should that not be where our rage is focused?"

Someone tried, "Amen," but David was already shaking his head.

"Should it be the creature Alvaretta summoned to draw our children her way?" he asked, and this time no one said a word. "No. If we want to know where to lay blame, let us look not to the witch or the darkness in which she dwells. Let us look to ourselves."

And now silence. One so deep and penetrating that it seemed a spirit in itself.

"Can we call Crow Holler a place of grace when we give safe harbor to one who has killed a man named Wally Cork and has ruined both crops and lives with her incantations?"

The Reverend now looked at Chessie and said, "No more than we can call ourselves children of the living God if our right hands dip into the poisons of this world even as our left hands reach heavenward in praise."

To Landis and Kayann: "Or seek the fruits of the earth rather than those of the Spirit."

To Angela: "Or seek the Lord's blessings while refusing to see how He's blessed us already."

And, finally, to Wilson: "Good people, can we ever hope to

overcome the poison of the witch's deeds if we do not confess the poison in our own? And I mean to confess, brothers and sisters. What has befallen us is what we deserve."

"That's enough," Wilson said.

Chessie and the Fosters seemed to agree. Angela, too, though she was so embarrassed by then she couldn't say it right out.

"You turn all that's happened around to *us*, Preacher?" Wilson said. "That ain't right, David."

"Isn't it?" The Reverend stood and lifted his voice to all. "What say you, people of Crow Holler? Could Alvaretta Graves gain power over us if we truly stood under the Lord's protection?"

Murmurs was all David got.

"And so who has failed us? That is the question we should seek, brothers and sisters, because that is the answer that will save us all."

The voices inside the church grew then, from murmurs to talk. A loud amen from the back, followed by another and another still. David Ramsay walked back behind his pulpit. He lifted his worn Bible high into the air, letting it catch a shaft of light from the ceiling.

"'If my people, which are called by my name, shall humble themselves, and pray, and seek my face, and"—shouting it now—"turn from their wicked ways; then I will hear from heaven, and will forgive their sin, and will heal their land.'"

And then a great wave of applause and amens, so many as to not be counted, rising up from the back and the front and the sides, David saying, "So sayeth the Lord," nodding, praising God, Belle standing to clap with tears falling from her eyes, girls caught in tremors and stutters and those whose tongues had been stolen crying out for their Savior, everyone shouting hallelujah except for those few in the front row—the mayor and the Fosters, the Hodges, and even Bucky himself—who'd come to church that night looking for hope but would leave knowing their pastor had damned them. And friend, Mayor Wilson Bickford wasn't about to let that happen.

-6-

"Doublespeak!" Wilson shouted from his pew, and then he stood and turned to all gathered behind him. All that clapping stopped then and stopped quick. "How's it a man of God can stand up here and speak out both sides of his mouth?"

The Reverend said, "I don't know what you mean, Wilson."

"Well then, that makes two of us, because I don't know what you mean either, Preacher. I hear Alvaretta's to blame, then I hear we're to blame. I hear we're battling the witch, I hear we're battling ourselves. It's the curse that's struck our girls, it's our sin. Well, you want to know what I think, David? I don't think you know at all what's going on."

"I know exactly what's going on," the Reverend said, "and you know I do. You of all people know, Wilson. Alvaretta has cursed us, but that curse was born in her hurt and her pain."

"It was born in the evil she embraced," Wilson shouted, and now that sanctuary went all but silent. "Nothing more. You say it was her *pain*? We *all* know pain. *Living* is pain, Reverend, and the bad of the world visits us all the same. Was the witch's choice to stay closed up on the mountain. Her choice to give in to hate. Not ours."

David said, "Mayor, this is my place to speak."

"You spoke enough. All you done here is stoke fires that were already fanning and flaming. I'm calling a meeting of the town."

"This is a church, Mayor. There's no place here for town business."

"You ain't ever said a word against mixing God and government before," Wilson said. "Why you starting now?"

The mayor stepped forward, right up onto the stage beside the preacher. He whispered, "You will burn us both with this nonsense, David," then eased the Reverend aside.

Sure weren't many people in the church right then who had a good understanding of what was going on. First had come a revival that hadn't really been a revival at all, now come a town meeting with what might end up being a fistfight between the preacher and the mayor. Say what you want about those few days back then, but they was exciting.

Wilson faced the crowd. "I've no silver tongue like David here, but I can speak plain truth. Heard a lot of people give a lot of opinions on what's happened these last days, and I'm here to say ain't a one of them right. Now I got respect for David Ramsay. We come up together. Played ball together. I call him a friend, but that don't mean I have to sit here silent as he bends circumstances to his own desires and calls it the will of the Lord.

"Is it the will of the Lord my own daughter's laid up at home because she's too scared to go out in public? That we go about at each other's throats casting blame? I ain't no preacher, but I don't think it is. David says look at all them poor girls back there. Well, I tell you the same. Go on, look at 'em. Now you all tell me what happened to any a them is your own fault. Any you poor children out there think you deserved to be struck down mute or no longer be the master of your own body?" He nodded. "I thought so. Yes, good people, I *knew* so. David Ramsay can blame us, but I say we're the victims here. And I say the only guilty one's named Alvaretta Graves."

Shouts now—*Yes* and *Amen* and *I'm with you, Mayor.* Wilson cocked his head toward David and winked, nearly sending the Reverend into a rage.

Raleigh Jennings stood then, hand raised. He said, "That's all well and good, Mayor, but I speak for most here when I say I want to know what it is you plan on doing about it."

Amens again. Lord a mercy, friend, you ain't never heard so many amens as was uttered in the Holy Fire that night.

"Reverend least has the beginnings of a plan. We ain't heard nothing from you."

"You ain't heard nothing from me because I been busy keeping this town together, Raleigh Jennings. But I'm glad you asked that question. It's a good one, and I got an answer. Come on up here, Buck."

Bucky flinched at the sound of his name. He looked down the pew, past the Fosters and the Hodges. He looked at Angela.

"Come on, Buck," Wilson said.

Bucky stood. When he took to the stage, he whispered, "Excuse me," to David and walked straight into Wilson's outstretched hand, feeling it grip his shoulder tight.

"I'm sure most of you all know by now," Wilson said, "but in case you don't, last night the council voted to elect a sheriff. This was not an easy decision on any of our parts. I know as well as anyone the pride every citizen of Crow Holler takes in tending to its own troubles and responsibilities. But these are dark times. Pastor Ramsay might've been wrong on some things, but he was right on that, and in dark times we need good men to stand up for service. Bucky Vest has always been such a man."

Angela clapped twice and hard, sitting up tall in her pew. She looked at Chessie on one side of her and Landis on the other, coaxing them to join. Neither did. Wilson nudged Bucky with his shoulder, prodding him to the pulpit. Bucky wouldn't dare—the mayor could stand there and talk all he wanted, but to Bucky Vest, that spot was for a preacher and nobody else—but he did find courage enough to speak.

"All y'all know me," he said. "You know my heart. I love this town and always will. It's home to me just as it is to you, and that's why I give my word right here in front of Jesus and everybody: I'll work hard to keep y'all safe."

Angela had her hands clasped in her lap. Her chest heaved in and out in big breaths. Her eyes had turned to wide moons. A hand went up in back, easy to see because it was wrapped in white tape and gauze. Wilson nodded to the man raising it.

Tully Wiseman stood and asked, "What you gonna do, Buck? You say you're gonna keep us safe, that's fine. Preacher says he's gonna keep us safe, mayor says he'll do the same, but I don't believe none of it. We're up agin more than we can bear here. Ain't just the witch we battle, it's others too. Some in this town are up to no good, and you know it."

Chessie leaned over and whispered into Briar's ear. I've no idea what she said, friend, but I can near guarantee that woman mentioned Tully himself was chief among the no-gooders.

"What you got planned to do, Bucky?" came another question from the other side of the room. "Or are you just somebody to carry out whatever Wilson wants?"

Bucky got out, "Now that ain't—" before others joined in, wanting to know how their girls was gonna get healed and when the grocery would be open and what was keeping Alvaretta from doing something like this again, and Wilson felt Bucky begin to shudder and shake and saw the way his throat hitched up against all those questions that wouldn't stop coming.

"Now wait," the mayor said. He held his free hand up and gripped Bucky harder with his other, pinning him in place. "Y'all just hold on now."

But they wouldn't wait, and they wouldn't hold on. People kept wanting to know what Bucky was going to do with a badge and fearing deep down that he wouldn't do anything at all, no one could. The crowd grew louder, hollering even as David demanded calm, and then Bucky shouted the worst thing he could.

"I'll go to Alvaretta."

Wilson's hand dropped as the crowd went silent. Even Chessie looked dumbfounded. Bucky's eyes started to glisten, probably because he'd just figured out what he said and realized he was a grown man standing on the stage at the Holy Fire where a promise couldn't never be broken instead of a boy on the school playground where backsies were allowed.

"I'll go to Alvaretta," he said again. There was a catch in his voice that was all fear, but that didn't matter. "The witch did this all. Hurt my little girl. People are suffering in Crow Holler. That's Alvaretta's fault. I got fired from the dump. That's Alvaretta's fault. Grocery's gone because of her, Doc's so tired he can't come to church because of her." He took a deep breath. "So I'll go have a word. I'll tell the witch what she's done and ask that she end it, and I'll ask that she send her demon back into the mines. I'll do it. That's my job."

-7-

Far from all the tumult at church, in a lonely spot four miles past what remained of his daddy's store, Hays Foster had built a fire. It was a good fire, not as large as the one he'd built at the mines but still fair sized. He looked at Cordelia on the other side of the flames as though he'd forgotten she was even there, then stood next to her because he was supposed to. Cordy wouldn't leave him now, not with the baby she hadn't told him about yet, and I have to wonder if she'd leave him even without the baby.

And Hays? Well, you could say that boy'd been stuck all his life. Now sure, what he'd been stuck with was what every other boy in the Holler would give his right eye to possess. Hays had the prettiest girl in town to snuggle with and a good-paying future waiting on him at the grocery (assuming his daddy ever got it fixed up again). He had it all really, everything that passed here for the American dream. But he wanted none of it. Wanted nothing of piddling away his life pondering what to put on the Tuesday special and how much to discount the day-olds, nothing of having to come home to a wife and (God forbid) children. He understood there was love on Cordelia's part, or at least some thin film of it, but he possessed nothing in the way of tenderness toward her. He liked Cordy, yes. Hays liked Scarlett and Naomi too. But he did not love them, and for no other reason than love made no sense.

"Had to be a big fire up on the mountain," he said. "Mines being so close and all. And Alvaretta. Even before y'all got there, I felt something. Like, watching me."

Yet there was nothing watching in Harper's Field that night, and none but the two of them for now. Cordy leaned a cedar branch against the side of the fire. Hays had used other wood already, a few sticks of pitchy pine to catch a spark and then some maple to get things going proper. Oak went on after, letting the flames burn long. Now the cedar. Hays liked cedar best. The flames were always even with cedarwood, with a color of wet gold and a sweet smell he found pleasant.

"The others coming?" he asked.

"Yeth."

"Good."

Cordy studied the fire. It cracked and hissed like a living thing. No, not *like*—living is what it was. Some sticks and pitch, a handful of bark, Hays's lighter. Take them all separate, you had nothing. Put them all together, and that nothing sparked a life. Not unlike the one in her belly.

She reached for his hand. "Hayth, I need to tell you thumthing."

"Later," he said. "Here they come."

The first splash of headlights swept across the field, followed by another. Scarlett's little bug bounced along the divots and rises and through all that blooming grass, followed by John David's truck.

"What's he doing here?" Hays asked. He turned and looked at her. "Did you tell him to come?"

"No," Cordy said. Not a lie, at least not exactly. She hadn't texted John David herself. She had, perhaps, suggested to Naomi that afternoon at the grocery maybe she should call her brother.

Both vehicles parked near the fire. Scarlett and Naomi got out, as did John David. They all met in a circle around that fire in the middle of Harper's Field, and nobody said a word. Just looking at each other. Wondering what had become of them and what would become of them still.

John David said, "Hey, Scarlett," making her flinch. "You look nice tonight."

Scarlett held the pad and pen in her hand but didn't write. She gave a soft nod instead.

"Thanks for coming," Hays said to them all. "I know it wasn't easy for some of you to get away."

"Everybody's at the revival," Naomi said. "Daddy said I had to go, but Momma told me to stay." Her head and right shoulder jerked at the same time. Scarlett tried not to make a face. "I think Momma had it in her head Daddy was gonna try to chase the devil out of me."

"Ain't the devil," John David said. "Naomi?" He waited until she looked his way. "This ain't the devil."

"They say the devil's everywhere in Crow Holler," Naomi

said. "You haven't been gone long enough from here to forget that, have you?"

"Naomi's right," Hays said. "Me and Cordelia felt something up at the mines even before we saw those tracks. Now I'm starting to feel it again. Like something's watching."

Scarlett scribbled down *You didn't feel anything* and held it to Cordelia.

"I did," Cordy said. "I didn't thay anyfing. I didn't want to woo-in your pahty."

"Doesn't matter," Naomi said. "Now. Now's all that matters."

Hays nodded. "Something's coming. Something else is going on here."

John David had stepped away from the fire, closer to the shadows. Watching. That man loves to watch. But what Hays said was enough to make him speak up. "How do you know something's coming?"

"Why are you here, John David? I didn't send you a text."

"Naomi invited me," he said. "Thought I'd tag along. Make sure y'all didn't do anything else stupid."

"None of us meant for this to happen, okay? Look"—he paced the fire as Cordy followed him—"it's up to us to stop this. Scarlett, your daddy thinks the best way is to just ride things out. We don't get riled up, the witch might get bored and go away. The Reverend thinks this is somehow up to him to fix, else he wouldn't have called revival. But that's"—he paced faster now, trying to reach for the right words—"that won't *work*."

John David's hands went open and closed in that funny way again, like he expected shooting to start. "Hays," he said, "why don't you take a deep breath here. Tell us what's going on."

"I went to Medric's yesterday. To tell him I was sorry, and because . . . because there's just stuff going on."

Cordelia looked away from Hays, toward Scarlett and Naomi.

"Medric was acting all freaked out," Hays said. "I thought it was just about that raccoon nailed to his door, but it wasn't. He said people were gonna come after him, started talking all kinds of crazy stuff. And he wasn't *there*. Medric wasn't home at first when I went to see him. Where'd he go? And then he came in later and parked out back, went inside all quick-like. He wouldn't open the door all the way to let me in. Like he was hiding something. So when I left I knocked over one of his flowerpots, thinking that would bring him out, you know, because Medric's always been a neat freak. So he did. He came outside and he didn't think I'd see, but I did. I *saw*, John David."

"Saw what?"

"His boots. They were covered in crow feathers."

Scarlett looked so shocked that I don't think that girl would've said anything even if she could. Cordy's mouth fell open.

"Oh my God," Naomi said.

"That doesn't mean anything," John David said. "You know how many crow feathers are in these mountains? Crying out loud, Hays. They call this *Crow* Holler. Now you stop this. All y'all. Somebody's gonna get hurt."

Scarlett wrote *Somebody already got hurt.*

"Listen to me," Hays said. "Please?" He took hold of Cordelia's hand.

And when Hays looked up at his friends, Scarlett saw a look she had never believed possible upon his face—a grimace of both fear and torture that made Hays seem full alive instead of the half dead he'd always acted.

"We used to have this shed in the backyard when I was a kid. I never liked it in there. It was dark and smelled like mold and dirt. Dad always kept his tools in there. Saws and blades, stuff like that. Momma never wanted me around there. I guess she thought I'd hurt myself or something. You know how she is."

Cordy glanced down—*Oh yeah, we* all *know how your momma is.*

"Dad never wanted me in there either. I don't know why. He'd go out there in the evenings and piddle around. I guess it was his way of winding down. He always told me to stay away from the shed because there was a monster in there that would eat little boys. Sometimes in the summer when the windows were open at night, I'd hear shuffling in there, like something trying to find a way out.

"Shed caught on fire this one Saturday afternoon. Dad was at work. By the time he got there, it was too late to save anything. Mom called the store, out of her mind, screaming for help. Wilson and Medric were there and they came running. Medric said it was maybe a pile of oily rags that got hot and sparked. Took the lawn mower and the tiller and all Dad's tools. Took the shed. But you know what? That fire took the monster too. I never heard anything out in the backyard again, and I listened. Every night, I listened."

Scarlett looked at Cordelia, who could only hold Hays's hand tighter. The boy looked about two breaths away from tears. It had never felt right to Scarlett that Cordelia had kept news of her baby from Hays. But right there, I don't think Scarlett felt that way anymore. Because Hays had been keeping a secret, too, and for far longer.

She wrote on her pad and held it up for him to see: *You burned your shed down.*

Hays dipped his chin. "Had to. Don't tell Mom and Dad, though. Scarlett? Don't. You neither, Naomi." He turned his head quick. "Cordy? They'll think I'm crazy. Do y'all think I'm crazy?"

Naomi whispered, "No," even as her head spasmed yes.

"Good," Hays said. "Because that's why I asked y'all here tonight. That's why you have to believe me. The monsters are back."

-8-

Didn't take long for the meeting to break up once Bucky announced he'd go to Campbell's Mountain. If the only reason he'd promised it was to restore a smidge of peace, it worked. All them people who were shouting at him before were shouting still, but now it was things like *I knew you were the man for the job, Buck* and *You'll go first thing in the morning, right?* and *Alvaretta gives you any trouble, you tell her I'll be up there next.* The first was true enough, the second meant to ensure Bucky wouldn't welch, and the last an utter and complete lie. Because if that week had taught any of us anything, it was you didn't step foot on the witch's land, no matter what.

David Ramsay even prayed for him. Laid his hands right on Bucky's shoulders and pleaded for a hedge of protection around our brave sheriff as he walked straight into hell. And as every head bowed, Bucky felt Wilson's hands upon him, too, and how shaky they were.

I'd say Angela was doing her share of praying just the same, along with a little *How could You curse me with such a stupid man?* thrown in. Most of that went away as soon as David said his amen, though. That's when everybody descended. Upon Bucky, sure, but upon Angela as well. Telling her how proud she must be to have such a brave and righteous husband, how they'd be there for her just as much as him, asking of Cordelia. Even Kayann Foster visited long enough to ensure whatever ill will stood between them could be set aside. Last time people paid that much attention to Angela Vest she'd been Angela Shavers, head cheerleader for Crow Holler. And let me tell you, that woman ate it all up and asked for seconds. Voices were raised in the parking lot as everybody filed out. Old Medric probably thought that was everybody finally coming for him after all those years of secrets and lies, but instead it was jubilation at the idea of all our nightmare put to an end. Even the stricken town girls looked something close to happy as they shook and stumbled for their parents' cars. Everyone looked happy, really, except for the man who was to restore what'd been taken from us all.

Soon as Bucky got Angela and himself in the Celebrity, he asked, "What'd I just do, Angie?"

"You said you'd take care of things," Angela said. "That's what you did. You said it was your job."

But she couldn't look at him. Angela waved once more before her own grin faded. In its place grew fear. For her husband, yes, but also for something greater.

Bucky went to start the car but found he couldn't. The mere act of turning the key seemed too great a task for him to undertake. He let the keys dangle and said, "I can't go up there. To see the witch? Angie, I can't do it."

"You got to now, Bucky. Look at all them people."

"I know."

"No, look at them."

He did. Weren't many left, but enough that Bucky could see their smiles. Wilson and David stood at the top step of the church, shaking hands. Chessie and Briar lingered a bit. They were over there talking to Tully Wiseman for some reason. Bucky watched as Chessie leaned in close and whispered something. She patted Tully a little too close to his bandaged hand, making him pull back. Across the way, one of Medric's curtains fluttered.

"What's been ailing all them people?" Angela whispered. "It's Alvaretta, sure, but it's something worse. It's *dread*, Bucky. People done lost their hope. That's why the grocery got tore up and why David called a service. But the Reverend didn't do anything to restore people's hope tonight, Bucky. You did. And that's a grand thing. That's maybe the grandest thing you can do."

"But I can't," he said. "It's a fool's errand, going up there."

"Cordelia went. All them kids. They faced down the witch. You're saying you can't summon more courage than what's in them?"

That one hurt, friend. You'd've seen Bucky, you could tell.

"Don't be like that, Angie. I'm coming to you for counsel."

"And I love you enough to give it, hard as that counsel may be." She laid a hand over his and squeezed. "You'll go, Bucky. First thing in the morning. Ain't no choice in the matter now, because you done told everybody you will. In church, no less. You make a promise like that in church, the Lord'll go with you. He'll have an army of angels standing on that mountain, wait and see."

"I don't know if I got that kind of faith."

"You do. It's buried, but you do. You *got* to, Bucky. Don't you understand that? You see the way all them people treated you in there? Like we was *somebody*. And what happens if you don't go now, Bucky? You go talk to Wilson in the morning and tell him you changed your mind, or you go to David, what happens then? Maybe Wilson takes away that shiny new badge you're wearing, that's what. We'll both be out of jobs, and all the good standing we just made inside that church'll be gone. They're looking to *you* now. Not the Reverend, not even the mayor. It's *you*."

"Guess that don't leave me much choice, does it?" he finally said. She squeezed his hand harder and smiled.

Chessie had finished telling Tully Wiseman that if he ever got fancy with his words about her in church again, he'd have to pick his nose with his elbows. Wilson left David at the top step with an agreement that everything concerning their past with Stu Graves would be set aside until Bucky returned from Campbell's Mountain. Medric settled back in his chair inside the funeral home, wondering what had gone on to make everybody leave so happy. He made sure both doors were locked and went upstairs. That night, he would sleep with his shotgun.

Angela leaned across the seat. "Let's go home." She kissed her husband deep and hard. Bucky felt her tongue meet his own as she guided his hand to her chest and her hot, quick breaths on his neck.

He'd be rewarded that night for honoring his word and his wife. But it was not love they made while Cordelia lay awake in the next room, thinking of Medric Johnston and Hays's monsters. It may have been love to Angela, or at least what passed for it. But for Bucky, that act was something far other. It was near a punishment, the way he treated her. It was heartache disguised in groping hands and the meeting of their flesh, and the rage on his face was only made worse by the look of ecstasy on her own.

I X

Bucky on the mountain. Alvaretta.
The demon. To the cemetery.

-1-

He left early that next morning, not wanting to risk poor feelings with Angela and wanting to avoid Cordelia, who would've begged her daddy to stay. Bucky left his phone behind as well. They'd be calling soon. Wilson for sure, but also plenty others, wanting to know if he was really going to Alvaretta's or if the night had brought on a measure of good sense. Bucky didn't want to talk to any of them. He'd made his bed. Weren't nothing left now but to lay down in it.

But there was one person he wanted to see before leaving the Holler, and Bucky was right in thinking Reverend Ramsay would be down to church. Him and Belle both with Naomi still twitching up at the altar, the three of them waiting for a miracle that wouldn't come. Reverend looked surprised to see Bucky there with his daddy's big pistol strapped to his side. I don't think that was because he thought Bucky would back out of what he'd promised. I'd say it was more simple shame. No way the Reverend would ever step foot on Graves land, friend. Not after what he did, and not for anything.

The four of them sat, Bucky in one pew, the Reverend, Belle, and Naomi in the next. They talked for a good while. Little things at first, like how Cordelia was and if Naomi was getting any better, and how everybody was going back down to the grocery that morning to help Landis and Kayann clean things up.

"You should come up there too, Bucky," Belle said. "When you're done and all. The Fosters would be happy to see you."

Bucky smiled at that. Not because the Fosters would be happy to see him, but because that was Belle's way of saying everything would turn out all right that morning. Bucky would head down to Alvaretta's, have a good word with her, and then come on back to town. Like he was to call on one of the church's homebounds rather than a woman with black in her soul and power in her words, and who may have called forth the devil himself from under the mountain.

"I'll see if I can do that, Belle," Bucky said. "That might be fine. You know, after."

David reached over the pew and gripped Bucky's shoulder. "You don't have to be afraid, Buck."

"Yes, he does," Naomi said.

Her brown hair had gone stringy and greased with oil. Dark half-moons that had rose beneath her eyes made her look far older than her years. Her shoulders jerked, pulling her head down. Alvaretta had done that with a single word.

"Naomi," David whispered, "don't you say such a thing."

"It's true. Don't go up there, Mr. Vest. The witch has something protecting her. Something even worse than she is."

"Gave my word, Naomi," Bucky said. "Stood right up there where your daddy stands every Sunday and said I'd go, so I got to. Some people go through their whole lives without a chance to do real good to the world. Maybe I can talk Alvaretta into releasing you girls and come to a peace."

"There's no peace with her, Constable. I mean, Sheriff. Does Cordelia know you're going?"

"She doesn't, and I'd appreciate it if you didn't let her know.

Keep that phone in your pocket until I get back, okay? There's no need to scare Cordy more'n she is already."

The Reverend promised for her.

"Maybe if you took along someone else," Belle said. She looked at her husband, who refused to look back.

"No," Bucky said. "I wouldn't want anybody doing that."

"I understand you going up there, Bucky," David said. "I respect you for it. But you be careful out there, and don't you tarry. Say your words and get out. And whatever you do, don't you mention Stu Graves."

"Why not?"

"Just don't. The answer to this ain't out in Alvaretta's holler, Bucky. Ain't in the mountain. Answer's here in town, with us. You heard my words last night."

"I did. They were some powerful. Was a good sermon, Reverend. Wish you hadn't spoken of Angela like that, though. She tries. You just don't know her like I do."

"We right this town and keep it from foundering, Bucky, we'll rid ourselves of this curse. I'll ask your help to do that."

"You'll have it," Bucky promised.

"Good. Now let's go to the Lord."

The four of them joined together and bowed heads. Bucky felt David's strong hand and Naomi's trembling one. The Reverend's deep voice filled the sanctuary as he spoke of dwelling in the shelter of the Most High and deliverance from the fowler's snare and the deadly pestilence. He spoke of angels guarding all of Bucky's ways, and an army to bear him up against the witch lest his foot strike a stone. There was faith in the Reverend's words that morning, friend. It was a belief so strong and of such great might that it seemed to brighten the pale sun, and yet Bucky looked to feel none the better when they all said amen. Maybe it was the way Naomi's fingers felt so small and scared in his hand. Like that was enough to remind Bucky that deep down, he was still nothing more than a scared little kid himself.

-2-

Bucky left the Ramsays to prepare for the night's revival in earnest. It was a good thing he did. As things turned out, David and Belle would need all the time they could to get things ready. The coming service would be the most attended hour of preaching Crow Holler ever had, and it was all thanks to what Bucky was about to find on Campbell's Mountain.

He made a slow walk to where he'd parked the Celebrity—or the Sheriff's Car, as Angela had come to call it—on the right-hand side of the church, just across from the funeral home. What stopped him from climbing inside and getting the whole thing over with wasn't anything having to do with Medric. (Though if Bucky had decided to knock at the back door and have a few words with our soon-to-be-departed caretaker of the dead, he maybe would've saved us all a mess of trouble.) No, what gave Bucky pause was the gray Dodge truck parked down the way and the man sitting inside it, waving him over.

Bucky looked back to the church to make sure no one saw. He certainly didn't need Belle and the Reverend's permission to talk to their boy, especially since John David had gone and gotten himself fallen away. But he kept close to the church just the same, even ducking under the windows as he passed, then sidled up to the passenger window.

"Morning to you, John David," he said. "What you doing out here so early?"

"Chessie asked me to come out, take a look at things."

"Anything in particular?"

John David pointed at the big house ahead.

"Why's Chessie got you out here looking at Medric?"

"Been some whisperings," John David said.

Bucky moved his head back and looked up the dirt street, where the funeral home stood. "Talked to Medric couple days ago," he said. "He was a mite jumpy. Can't blame him for that, though."

"No," John David said. "And I can't either. I don't expect anything to come of it, but you know Chessie. She likes to wet her finger and keep it in the air to know where the wind's blowing. She wanted somebody here, I said I'd do it."

"To keep an eye on Medric."

John David shrugged. Bucky nodded and stuck his head partway inside, keeping his voice low.

"They're doing okay, John David."

"Who is?"

"Your momma and daddy. Naomi. Chessie might think you're out here doing something else, but I know only reason you come is to check on your family. So I'll lay you at ease and say they're good, and you should just go on in there and see them. They miss you fierce, son. Your daddy especially. I mean, Naomi's . . . you know. But she's none worse. Wilson talked to Doc Sullivan yesterday afternoon. Doc says it'll all pass. I believe him."

John David smirked. "You believe him, then why you headed out to the mountain?"

"Because that's what people want me to do."

"People like who?" John David asked. "Wilson? My daddy?"

"You know well as I do, John David. Once you put on a uniform, you go by the will of something greater than you. Got to be willing to step where no one else will. That's your duty."

"Don't give me talk of duty." John David stared through the

windshield. "Don't you go up there, Bucky. You stay away from Alvaretta Graves."

"I can't do that, John David. You know I can't."

"I don't know nothing, and neither do you. These people you say you're serving? They're using you, Bucky. Can't you see that?"

"Nope," Bucky said. "They're depending on me."

"You think Wilson wanted a sheriff? Daddy, Chessie, Raleigh, they don't either. They really wanted law, they'd get Sheriff Barnett up here. All Wilson wants is a face he can put to the curse. Can't be Alvaretta, everybody's too scared of her. Can't be the kids, because Wilson knows that'll mean Scarlett. But he'll give you a badge and let everybody see it. That way what goes wrong from here on out will be square off the mayor's shoulders and straight on yours. That's all he cares about."

"That ain't true," Bucky said. "Wilson loves me like a brother."

"Then go over to his office, tell him you're staying in town today. Go up to the grocery and help Landis get things up and running again. Let people see you helping, Buck. Go out to where all those sick kids are and ask their mommas if there's anything you can get them or if they need a ride to the doc's. Something. Anything, so long as you leave that old woman alone."

"Why don't you want me going up to Alvaretta's, John David?"

"Because that's not your *job*," he said. "Your job's to protect the peace, Bucky. Going up there and confronting that woman sound like protecting the peace to you?"

"There's a kind of peace that only comes on the other side of a fight," Bucky said.

"You sound like my daddy."

"Your daddy's a good man."

John David chuckled. "My daddy's like everybody else. They don't mind using strong words because they ain't the ones who have to back those words up. They get people like you to do that, or me. You got a choice here." He pointed at the church. "Forget about what you promised everybody in there last night and do what's right. You stay in town and make sure nothing gets any worse. Get people back to living the way they're used to. That's when those kids will get better. You cast your eyes out to Campbell's Mountain like Wilson and Daddy, you're gonna miss the danger in front of you."

"You talk like you know a lot for a boy who's been gone from here," Bucky said.

"I know enough to say you don't got to be a great man to make things better, you just got to be a good one."

"That a fact?" Bucky asked. He leaned in closer. "You making a difference, John David? Huh? You a good man? That why you took up with Chessie and Briar and left your parents like that? What's the matter with you?"

"You wouldn't understand," John David said.

"No, I guess I wouldn't. Just like I guess you wouldn't understand that I got a job to do and a family to feed"—*and a wife to pacify*, Bucky didn't say—"so I guess I should get on it."

He tapped the truck's window and backed off. John David tried one more time.

"I seen you hit that fire alarm at the grocery. I know it was an accident, and I know you're too proud to say it. Daddy always said Alvaretta Graves was a danger. He said she holds a power over this town that could ruin us all. You go out there, you better know what you're getting into."

Bucky said, "I know exactly what I'm getting into."

He didn't.

-3-

In those days you'd be hard-pressed to find any who'd not seen their lives rent by ailing children or talk of demons and curses. There remained none untouched by a fear that Crow Holler had lost its moorings from the world. None but a single person anyways, because life had continued on unshaken for Alvaretta Graves.

That ain't to say her years spent in the bosom of Campbell's Mountain had yielded a bounty of peace and joy. Far from it. Is a dark place, that mountain. I know I've told you that, but you'd do well to hear it again. It's no home for a widowed woman to be sure, forced to spend your days defending your land against a wood determined to claim it inch by inch. Alvaretta had done that and more as time snuck away the good bits of her and left behind wearied muscles and arthritic bones. But she'd never lived those years without aid.

The witch had always enjoyed company at the mountain's edge. Plenty had come in the time since her Stu had been taken, ones Alvaretta knew to define and others beyond her knowledge. The man from town, he came as well. Not often and never nearer than the porch (for that was the warning Alvaretta always gave him—"Step closer, stranger, and you'll meet your end") to leave the town's bounty. FOSTER'S GROCERY was writ on each of those bags, YOUR HOMETOWN VALUE under it. Alvaretta would scoop them up after the man left, hoard them inside the cabin for barren winters or when the garden crop failed. That had sometimes happened back before Stu was taken—hours and days spent with the hoe and scythe, sweat upon the brow of his hat and seeping into the deep creases in his face, only to find the crop ruined by hail or heat. But that had not happened since Alvaretta had found the power.

Her eyes were dimming now. No longer could she stand

atop her porch and count the crows that settled on the far hill. Her hip ached with the approach of each harvest, and she found herself accustomed to fevers and a numbness in her toes. Once, on a cold February night the winter past, Alvaretta had woke with a rage in her belly that felt to boil her very blood. The outhouse proved too distant; all she could manage was to reach one of the cast iron pots in her small kitchen. She'd cried out as she squatted and then cursed the blood she voided.

She was dying. That knowledge had come near a surprise, given all she had done and was able to do. Alvaretta Graves may have believed she had power over life and death, but not her own.

Her view from the cabin's front window was narrow, yet it gave a good enough view of the lane and the crows that swayed in the trees. Alvaretta rubbed the smooth bone that hung from a leather cord around her neck—a gift from the one in the back room. The air was hot from the hardtack baking in the wood oven, though she would not open the front door to let in the air. Not yet.

Because something was near.

That Alvaretta knew this should come as no surprise, given what you've heard of her. Campbell's Mountain may have belonged to no one in the eyes of the world, but to all in Crow Holler it was the witch's. No twig snapped and no sparrow fell between the cabin and the mines that Alvaretta Graves did not see or hear. There are worlds beyond this world, friend, of that you should have no doubt, but there are worlds inside this one, too, hidden to all but some. Alvaretta Graves could read the stars and clouds. She could feel the soft beating of the trees and the secret breaths on the wind as she could her own heart and lungs, and all of those things now whispered for her to stand ready.

Behind her, a voice spoke. Alvaretta did not understand the words but said, "I feel it."

She had not felt the trespassers at first. They'd snuck over the far hill and into the trees before Alvaretta had known they were there, trapping her in the shed. She had not felt them, but she had felt the sting of the Bickford whore's hand against her face. Even now, Alvaretta could taste the blood that oozed from the cut on her mouth. She took it as a warning of how fragile things lay and how easy all she had obtained could be taken from her again. She would not need that warning again.

The car that crested the hill along the lane was one Alvaretta had never seen, as was the man who drove it. He eased to a stop far enough from the cabin that he could turn in a hurry if need be. She smiled at the sight. The thing behind her smiled too.

A fat man got out. He was alone but for the big gun in the big holster slung under his big belly. Looking at the dead crows hanging from the trees, looking at the shed, the edge of the garden, the truck. Backing off as Alvaretta's children crept out from the woods, barking and growling as they gathered. The man's hand went low to his pistol.

The witch smiled again. "You'll stay," she said. "Don't you dare come out and don't you be heard. I'll not have you disobeying me again."

She walked past the one with her and past the shotgun propped against the crude kitchen table. The fat man jerked at the sound of the cabin door opening. Alvaretta held on to the knob, pulling until the door disappeared back on its hinges before stepping from the darkness. The wind gathered about the bottom of her plain dress and played at the fringes of her long, graying hair. She licked the blood that stained the corner of her mouth and moved onto the porch. Looking down at Bucky. Eyeing him like prey.

-4-

Within the comfortable bounds of the town's streets Bucky could talk about duty all he wanted to with the likes of John David Ramsay, but all notion of obligation fell away the moment he saw the witch step onto the porch. One look at that old and leaning cabin had been enough to fill his face with dread, and one glance at that old broken truck was enough to make him question the idiocy of his errand. It was Medric who'd told Bucky and the rest that Alvaretta was more story than fact, but I'm telling you all it'd take was seeing the swaying bones of all them dead crows and the dogs circling Bucky now—dogs with missing ears and mangled eyes but who seemed to think and move as of one mind—for anybody to know how wrong our undertaker had been. That whole stretch of land, not just the cabin but the open space that held the garden and the shed, too, looked dimmer somehow than everything else. It was like Bucky had left Crow Holler in one world and had somehow slipped into another.

"Who you?" the witch asked.

One of the dogs slunk close enough to lash out a paw that grazed the leg of Bucky's pants. He kicked the animal away by instinct, making it yelp.

"Alvaretta," he said. "Missus Graves. Ma'am. I'd be obliged if you'd corral your animals."

"Children," she said. "Not animals. I tend to them as they to me, stranger, and I'll have your leg if you try an kick another."

Bucky cleared his throat. "My apologies."

"Who you?" she asked again.

"Name's Bucky Vest." He leaned the left side of his chest out, showing the star above his uniform pocket. "I'm sheriff in Crow Holler."

"Ain't no law to Crow Holler but my own."

"Oh yes'm, there is. Just came on the job. Used to work the dozer down to the dump?" Bucky chuckled like that was funny and clenched his hands, hoping that would calm the tremble in his fingers. "Probably buried plenty of your trash over the years."

"Burn my own waste," Alvaretta said. "Do my own buryin', too, so you best get on."

"I'm afraid I can't do that, ma'am. I'm here on law business."

She studied him. Alvaretta may have been weak in body but she was strong in mind, and her stare was such that it caused pain.

"I don't see the face behind your eyes, Bucky Vest. Who's your pa?"

Bucky said quiet, "Don't have one. My daddy died in service when I was a boy."

"I have no quarrel with you then."

"Well, I appreciate that."

He might've smiled again, Bucky was always grinning whenever the nerves and fears in him got stirred. But then his ears caught the sound of movement behind the cracked door of the cabin, the rustling of a foot.

"You got anybody in there with you, Ms. Graves?"

Alvaretta eased the door shut and took the first step off the porch. She was eighty pounds of leathered skin and sagging bones, yet woman enough to back Bucky away.

"Din't hear nothing," she said.

"You armed?"

"Why? I need iron here, Sheriff?"

"No, but you can stay up on the porch if you don't mind. I only got questions. There was some trouble up here few days back."

She pointed a bony finger at the ground near Bucky's feet.

Singed into the dirt and patches of crabgrass were the odd horseshoe prints Cordelia and the rest had followed. They led to the front of the cabin, then on past the truck to the shed. And there was another thing as well, something those kids had missed. Tire tracks, not more than days old. Not from Stu's truck, neither. The looks of that rusted hulk, it hadn't run since the night he'd died.

"Had a demon come by," Alvaretta said. "Weren't the first. Won't be the last."

"You had words with this demon? You give it aid?"

The witch didn't say. "Othern's came after. Trespassers."

"Yes, ma'am, I know. One of them was my little girl. Friends and her was up to the mines. She had a bracelet? Says you're in possession of it now."

"It's mine by rights. Payment for what they did."

"Trespassin' ain't cause enough to keep it, ma'am." Bucky looked at the tire marks again. "Anybody been up here to see you, Alvaretta?"

"No one dares the mountain," she said. "And the bauble's payment enough for beatin' on me."

Alvaretta turned her face, showing the dried blood and gash on her lip. Bucky gaped at the sight. Cordelia hadn't said anything about laying hands on the witch. None of them had.

"They do that to you?"

"Bickford's whore."

The boards inside the cabin creaked again.

"How you know the mayor's name, Alvaretta?"

"I know them all and I know what they hide, Bucky Vest. You'll not do well to think otherwise. I got eyes," she said. "They see far."

"What you got inside there, Alvaretta?"

"None but the spirits. Now you get on afore you rile them."

"I can't do that, ma'am. My girl and her friends've taken

sick. Much of the town too. They say the demon you succor levied a curse."

Alvaretta's mouth widened to a slow smile. It was an awful thing, like a snake readying to taste the air. The dogs—her children—crept close once more.

"We'd ask you to lift it," Bucky said. "Don't none of us want trouble."

"Then you shoulda stayed 'way from here."

She turned for the door. Bucky stepped forward and thumbed the snap on his holster. When he spoke, there was a tremor to his words: "Can't let you do that, ma'am. We demand satisfaction."

"Satisfaction?"

Her back was to him. The wind gathered in the witch's hair once more, fluttering it to the side like a line of thin gray clouds. It had gone cold on the mountain all of a sudden. Cold and dark.

"You speak to me of satisfaction, Bucky-Vest-with-no-pa? I who have been denied the very thing you now seek? Let your children suffer, they will not suffer as me. Not until they're laid in the ground will you suffer as me."

"I know where you lay the blame for your man's death," Bucky said, "but none of us had a hand in it. He was drinkin' and you know he was." He spoke fast, the words coming so slick that Bucky couldn't stop them, and not once did he look to remember the Reverend's plea not to mention the very thing he just had. "Blame Stu for his weakness or blame the Lord for His ways, but you cain't blame us."

"Get out."

"I won't do that."

"*Get out.*"

Alvaretta turned. The blood on her face, once dried and crusted, now flowed in a slender streak that fell in tiny drops from her narrow chin. She stretched out her hands from her sides and lifted her head to the breeze. Dogs scattered as the witch's voice rose in a language Bucky could not comprehend. He fumbled for his gun as Alvaretta leveled her eyes to his.

"Get out get out and curse ye Bucky Vest, curse ye and all of Crow Holler. Curse ye by the hands of darkness and death."

Bucky pulled his pistol and squeezed the trigger, squeezed it again, and yet the barrel was silent, itself damned by Alvaretta's words. She took the steps down, slurring English with devil-speak in a voice deeper than her old lungs could make, and through the crack in the cabin's door came three fingers of a soiled hand. Bucky saw them, saw the witch stepping off the porch and into the yard, and all his ruptured mind could think to say was, "Momma, the bad man's here."

He squeezed the pistol as hard as he could. Still the bullets would not fly. Bucky tilted the gun to the side and saw the safety was switched on. He thumbed it to fire and aimed at Alvaretta's chest. She did not waver and strode for him, looking taller now, stronger, looking like something Other with a wide grin of one who smelled his fear, and then Bucky let his pistol fall when the door in front of him began to open.

"Get out," she yelled again.

Bucky ran. He took the lane as fast as the car would let him, caring neither for the four bald tires nor the one wheezing engine, wanting only to get away. Alvaretta kept shouting, cursing him and cursing them all, calling down heaven and summoning up hell. Bucky looked into the mirror and screamed as the cabin's door swung open and what was inside began to step out.

He was to the main road before he discovered he'd left his gun behind, and halfway to Crow Holler when he realized he was sitting in his own urine.

-5-

Say what you will of Bucky's success in stating the town's demands to the Crow Holler witch, at least he'd gone prepared. He'd been smart enough to bring along an extra change of clothes just in case he'd have to go crawling and sneaking about in Alvaretta's woods. The pair of old jeans he'd snuck out that morning were wrinkled plenty, but wrinkled beat pee-stained any old day. He pulled off the road at a spot about five miles from town and slipped into the woods to change. You'd pity that man if you'd seen him, trying to unbuckle his belt and pry off his boots, unrolling those clean pants as the breeze fell against his naked legs like a cold finger. His head turned at every rustle of the leaves, thinking Alvaretta was there.

He didn't know where to go or who to tell first about the terrible things he'd learned at the Graves homeplace, so he ended up calling everybody to come down to the church and bring the kids with them. That's all Bucky said, and not a word more. He left his pair of soiled pants underneath a dead tree in the woods. Far as I know, they lie there still.

It took all of five seconds for everybody to get down to the Holy Fire. David and Belle were there already, along with Naomi. Wilson left the council building to fetch Scarlett. On the way, he picked up Angela, Cordy, and Hays. The Fosters were up to the grocery, trying to salvage what life they could. Wilson called to Chessie's. Raleigh, he showed up at the church too. I've no idea how he found out about Bucky's call. Bout the only one wasn't there was John David, though I'll tell you he was close.

Poor Cordelia had no clue what was going on and pitched a fit when Naomi told her where Bucky had gone. For all her faults, Angela looked the most worried of all. She put an arm around Cordy and said not to worry. Bucky'd called, that meant he'd gotten away. I don't know if that made anybody feel better about things.

So they all sat in the sanctuary, worrying and praying for the next twenty minutes when only fifteen were needed, because by then Bucky was standing outside the door trying to figure out how to tell them what he must. Every head spun when those front doors opened. Cordelia jumped from her seat beside Angela and wrapped her daddy in a hug. Fear and rage and worry swirled in the part of her face that still carried feeling.

"What happened, Buck?" Wilson asked. "You see her?"

Bucky kept walking. He led Cordy back to her seat and took the stage, though not behind the pulpit.

"You see her, Bucky?" Landis asked. "Alvaretta gonna make things right again?"

Looking out at them, the kids especially. Seeing Cordelia's ashen face and Scarlett's silent one. Seeing Naomi twitch. Seeing Hays, who hadn't been able to stand against Alvaretta either. Bucky didn't blame that boy anymore. He no longer condemned Hays Foster at all.

"I saw her," he said, and they all leaned forward.

"You spoke with her?" Belle asked.

"I did. She won't break the curse."

Chessie, who was always one to read her Bible but never one to read it well, let loose a single word from her foul mouth, making the Reverend cringe.

"What'd she say?" Wilson asked. "You tell us everything, Bucky."

Bucky looked at his feet and nodded, then took a slow breath.

"It's awful up there. Like . . . I don't know. Like everything got trapped in time. I saw Stu's truck. Can you believe that, Wilson? Wally Cork dropped that truck off twenty years ago and it ain't moved since, and then Wally died. Everybody says Alvaretta willed him dead. I'll say I never really believed that, not deep down. But I do now. I could feel Wally there, Reverend. Like he'd been trapped too."

The preacher's face went a sickly green.

"There's crows strung up in her trees. Dead ones. And all kinds of wild dogs Alvaretta calls her children."

Naomi nodded slow, either remembering or suffering under her curse. Cordy hugged herself like she'd gone cold. Hays put an arm around her, though I don't think he much cared to.

"It's all true, what the kids told us," Bucky said. "Every word of it and more, and I'm so sorry y'all got stuck there over some stupid piece of jewelry."

Cordelia sniffed back a tear.

"Alvaretta come out on the steps. I told her who I was and stated my business. She's still got the bracelet. I didn't see it, but she said it was hers. Payment for what was done."

"What was done?" Raleigh asked.

Bucky took another breath. "Seems Scarlett struck her."

Wilson's jaw fell open. He turned to Scarlett, pleading: "You struck Alvaretta?"

"She was defending her friends," Chessie said. "Nothing more, Wilson."

"You knew?" he asked Chessie, and then, to his daughter, "You told Chessie of this but not your own *daddy*?"

Scarlett started shaking. It was a strange sight, looking like she was about to split herself in half. Chessie got to shouting at Wilson and Wilson got to shouting back, and all that did was draw in the rest to one side or the other until Bucky raised his hands and screamed at them all to shut up and remember they was in a church.

"We ain't got time to sit here arguing," he said. "There's other stuff I got to say. Kids was right about more than birds and dogs. I saw those tracks they followed, and I'll say they're from no beast. I saw other tracks, too, and that's one thing we got to be concerned about. They was from tires."

"Tires?" Briar asked.

Bucky nodded. "Stu's truck ain't been run in years, from the look of it. That leaves only one thing it can be. Somebody's been out there. I think someone from town's been aiding the witch."

Hays looked at Cordelia, who looked at Scarlett and Naomi. You can bet only one name filled their minds.

"That's not possible," Belle said. "Nobody would do that, Bucky."

"I can only tell you what I saw, Belle. Tracks went clear up close to the porch, like whoever it was dropped off something. Makes sense. We always thought Alvaretta just got by on her own grit and meanness, and maybe she did for years. Some do, least that's the stories we've heard. Backwoods folk who leave off everything and aren't seen again. But an old woman like that couldn't get by for long without help."

"Alvaretta's got a spy," Raleigh said. The words came out slow, like even he couldn't believe one of his neighbors could do such a thing.

Nor could the Reverend. "We have to find out who it is," he said. "Maybe then we can put a stop to this."

"That ain't all," Bucky said. "That ain't even the worst. What I got to say next, I don't even know how to put to words."

Chessie spoke in a soft and kindly way that looked to chill Bucky to the bone. "You go on, Sheriff. Was a good thing you did, going out there. You just take your time and say it plain."

"Alvaretta said it'd only be when bodies are buried that we'd suffer as she. We're cursed by the hands of darkness and death. There's no stopping it."

Angela started to cry then. Belle too.

"She called forth the thing she's keeping. It was inside her cabin. I didn't see all of it and I thank the Lord for that, else I'd of given up my ghost right there. But I seen enough. I seen a hand and a boot. They was filthy and covered with earth."

"Did it speak?" Naomi asked.

"No, and it didn't have to, child. I know what the witch has conjured. Not demon and not man, but some of both." Bucky shook his head again, too afraid to speak it but more afraid to not. "It's Stu Graves. Alvaretta's done raised her husband."

-6-

You take a man telling something like that, saying a witch had used her dark magic to breathe life into dusty old bones and saying it all in church? Well, I expect that man would be met with howls and whoops and then escorted to the nearest padded room. But that didn't happen with Bucky, friend. Only silence greeted him.

Some like Naomi and her momma, Belle, looked ready to jump up and run as far from the Holler as they could get. But all of them looked to be thinking the same—that such a thing was possible. Even Bucky, who believed the spirits had been gone from Crow Holler ever since his kin chased off the Indians. Even Hays, who'd never believed in anything beyond his monsters.

Wilson said outright, "That ain't possible," though I believe that was because he was too afraid to consider otherwise. "Stu's been in the ground since we was kids. Once you're gone, you're gone. This ain't Bible times."

He looked at the others, people who were not just friends now but friends on the night Stu Graves ran his truck off the road. The Reverend couldn't meet his eyes.

"You sure on this, Bucky?" Briar asked.

Bucky didn't say right off. Not because he wasn't sure, but because Briar's voice sounded so strange and scared.

"I'm sure, Briar."

Raleigh shook his head slow. My, but that man'd have a story to tell all his secret friends that night. "She always said Stu wouldn't rest until he got justice."

"Shut up, Raleigh," Wilson said. "You're scaring the kids."

Briar stood up. "We can put this to rest right now. Ain't but a minute over to the cemetery. We get Medric's key to the storage garage, run the tractor up there."

"You want to dig Stu up?" Angela asked. She wasn't as shocked by the idea as she was excited. Don't get me wrong, friend, that woman was scared. But this promised to be something straight out of her stories on the TV.

"Don't know how else to settle things," Briar said. "We gotta know either way. Right?"

They all looked at the mayor, who fiddled with his hands.

"We'll do it," Bucky finally said. "I'll knock on Medric's door, tell him what we need."

The meeting broke. Briar and the mayor left for the big garage out back of the council building. Hays slipped out, following Bucky across the street. The rest tried their best to saunter the half mile to the town cemetery without drawing too much attention. That's the cemetery down there, past the Exxon. Can't see it too good because it's on the other side of them trees, but it's there. Full too. Wasn't on the day Wilson and David led all a them down there to make sure Stu was still in the ground, but it is now.

Bucky slowed down so Hays could catch up. "What you doing out here, Hays?"

"It'll be easier if I come too," he said. "I know him. Medric's my friend. Or was."

They stepped onto the curb. "Gonna need to sit down and have a good long talk with you once this is all over," Bucky said. "Gonna have to do the same with your parents."

"About what?"

"Your future with my daughter." He held up a finger when Hays opened his mouth. "Let's just leave it there. I'm a little worked up as it is right now. Don't got the time to have you spoutin' off at the mouth."

It took Bucky five minutes' worth of knocking to get Medric to finally answer the door, then another three to convince him there was no trouble. Medric listened and pronounced Bucky a liar, because it sure sounded like trouble to him.

"You think I'd ever desecrate the resting so you can satisfy your fears?" he asked. "No way, Buck. Keys are inside. Inside's where they stay."

Hays kept a fair distance back, remembering Medric's shotgun. I don't think he cared much to listen in on Bucky's conversation as much as he wanted to study Medric, the way he acted and talked. What Hays came away with was that man was guilty. For what, he didn't know, but it was surely something.

Only thing that changed Medric's mind was Bucky saying there really wasn't a choice in the matter. It had been a town decision, what they were going to do, and not going along with it would only make everybody more suspicious of our undertaker than they already were. That's what Bucky said—"People been telling me something's going on with you, Medric"—and even if it all had to do with that raccoon nailed on his door, it was high time our undertaker started acting like he was part of the town.

"We're all scared," Bucky told him. "Not just you, Medric. Fear ain't got a color, and sometimes it makes people do awful things."

No way Medric thought Bucky right about fear and color—deep down, he'd always thought Bucky as simple as they come—but the sheriff been right about something. There wasn't a choice. He shut the door to get the keys, refusing to let them inside.

Hays took that opportunity to tell Bucky everything about his visit to the funeral home. The part about Medric being gone most of a day and coming home with crow feathers stuck to his boots was what got Bucky nervous. He went over to Medric's car and checked the tires. The tread was nothing close to what he'd seen at Alvaretta's.

"That doesn't mean anything, Sheriff," Hays said. "He's still acting weird."

"Witch has got us all, Hays. Everybody's acting weird."

Medric came back out jangling the keys to the garage, the tractor inside, and the cemetery. He made a crack about being thankful Hays hadn't stolen that chain along with the chain that held the key to the gate and said, "Let's get this over with."

Hays ran the keys back up to the mayor and Briar. The sight of that old John Deere rolling down the road brought everybody close running to see what was going on. Angela was more than willing to fill them in.

At the gates, Medric bucked one last time. "What you all want is an abomination," he said.

Briar smiled. "Medric, I reckon those keys in your hand will open the lock whether you're conscious or not, so you better shut your mouth and free that gate."

Medric snapped off the locks and swung the gate open. He turned to everybody waiting and said, "Damn you all."

Briar maneuvered the tractor through the rows, stopping at the plain stone marker where Stu Graves had been laid to rest. The people crowded in when he started to dig. By then, more folk had come. Shovels were brought up. Men stood close as women drew back.

Wilson started praying right about the time Briar hit the

top of the coffin. Bucky, Medric, and Landis crawled down into the hole to pop the sides and pry away the top.

I guess I don't need to say much more on that, friend. You look smart enough to know what come next. Everybody'd known for years Alvaretta had power, and that power held root in a rage over who had been taken from her. She'd told Bucky it was darkness and death that stalked Crow Holler, and she had not lied. No doubt remained of that, nor could there be doubt that both of those things had taken the form of one person. The casket lay empty, friend. As empty as their hope.

-7-

Well, didn't take long before every soul in town heard of the empty casket that'd been dug up at the cemetery. Wilson could plead with everybody the rest of the day and all that night to keep quiet on it, wouldn't a done any good. And could you blame Angela and Landis and the rest, telling everyone they could that the demon who'd cursed them all was none other than Stu Graves raised up from the dead? News like that's got to be spread.

All the kids hung back from the cemetery gates and had themselves another meeting. Just like before, Hays led the whole thing. I'll leave it to you to decide how that boy came to take Scarlett's place as leader of their little group. I myself don't know, other than Hays was the only one among them who seemed to understand what was going on. Didn't much matter to Cordelia or Naomi if those ideas were truth or lies, neither. You get into the kind of spot them kids was in, even a false answer sounds like a good one.

Hays told them about Bucky checking Medric's tires and how the treads didn't match up. "And I don't care if they don't," he said, "Medric's still hiding something. He didn't want to dig that grave up, and I don't buy it was because of some undertakers' ethics. He knew nothing would be in there."

"If it wasn't Medric at Alvaretta's," Naomi asked, "then who was it? Does that mean there's more than one person helping her?"

"Vat's cazy," Cordy said.

Hays said, "It's Medric. I know it is."

Scarlett started writing: *Did Bucky say what the tire marks looked like?*

"No, just that they weren't Medric's."

You seem awful sure of yourself its Medric

They all read that, friend. Every single one. It was like that page on Scarlett's little pad was a magnet, and all those kids' eyes were made of lead.

"What are you trying to say, Scarlett?" Hays asked.

She turned the paper around and started scrawling. Fast, like it wasn't Scarlett writing at all. Like something had taken her over. And maybe it had, friend. But I won't put that one down to Alvaretta and her demon. I'll say it was just Scarlett's pent-up fear of losing the best friend she'd ever known to a boy she'd never really liked.

Big, looping words, *You didn't do anything to help us, you just stood there and let it happen*, that pen pressing onto the page so hard the paper began to tear and shred. *Your a freak everybody knows it even Cordy and now you're talking about freaking monsters????* And then, in a final flourish, *Did Bucky see your tires??*

"Thtop it," Cordy said. "Hayth ithn't *helping* her."

Naomi was saying they couldn't start fighting, but it was too late. Fighting they were, friend, and loud enough to get Bucky's and Medric's attention. Briar and Chessie had hung around long enough to get Stu Graves's casket back in the ground (there'd been some discussion on that, whether it'd do any good reburying an empty box, but Bucky had figured they might as well), but now it was just the sheriff and the under-taker left to tamp down the dirt.

"Things is gonna get bad, Buck."

"Things is already bad, Medric."

"Then they'll get worse."

Bucky hollered at the kids, said they should all get home or at least lower their voices, this was a place of the dead. He looked back down to his shovel and spoke low, so only Medric could hear.

"You'd tell me if something was going on, wouldn't you, Medric? I mean, we always been friends. You get in a bind, you'd tell me, right?"

"Ain't nothing going on you need to mind, Buck." Medric shoveled another scoop of dirt and mashed it with his boot. Bucky didn't see any crow feathers stuck to it. "Will say I'm scared of what's next, though."

"Me too," Bucky said.

X

David sees a shadow. Stu comes to town.
A death in the Holler.

-1-

Reverend Ramsay made it back to church alone that Thursday morning, leaving the cemetery much the same as Medric had left the hospital the night the witch's curse struck. I'll say he didn't walk so much as run. He spent the rest of that afternoon locked inside the small office off the sanctuary. Prayer and fasting is what he'd tell you, but I'll say that man was too plain scared to come out.

He nearly screamed when a knock came awhile later—Belle, wanting to know if her husband was okay. David lied and answered he felt fine, all things considered. Belle said she, Landis, and a few others were going to bring chairs over from the council building. Word's getting out, she called through the door. They'd need all the seating they could get for that night's revival. The Reverend tried saying that sounded fine while keeping a tight grip on the panic that had overcome him. It all came out in a jerky, "Okay," then he dared not open his mouth again. He watched the bottoms of Belle's tennis shoes in the long crack at the door's bottom until she finally left.

The old leather Bible that Belle had gifted him upon his ordination lay open on the desk. The brown cover had been worn to a silky tan, supple and faded from years of handling. Of providing comfort. The pages inside were underlined and noted, dates scribbled in the margins like signposts marking the dark times in David Ramsay's past when a verse or passage had served as an oasis. He could've search through those then, looked back on all those times the Lord had comforted and guided him through the valley of the shadow of death. But the Reverend didn't. That Bible lay in front of him, but he didn't see it. His eyes kept to the crack at the bottom of his office door instead, to that thin strip of bluish-yellow air marking the boundary between himself and the world of witches and monsters outside.

We would look to him now. That's what Reverend Ramsay was thinking. The town would turn not to the mayor or the sheriff, but to him. That's how it had gone on plenty of times in the past—Crow Holler was once a peaceable place, friend, but that don't mean it was never calamitous—and in those times the Reverend had led them both and well. But this valley was different. Darker. And now that he and the town had set upon it, David Ramsay felt his faith begin to waver.

Stu.

It had been a single night those many years ago. Not even that, really. A single hour of that single night and a single moment of that hour. And though the Reverend had somehow justified everything that had happened after by saying it hadn't been *him* too drunk to drive or not *him* who had done it, and the only thing he could be guilty of was trying to protect his friend, he now understood the frailty of that logic. Because he had done enough harm that night. A lifetime's worth.

It was a power beyond his reckoning that could empty a grave of death. It was a power far greater that could breathe into that grave not life, but vengeance. Bucky said someone in town had turned traitor to neighbor and kin alike. That meant Alvaretta Graves had claimed both the living and the dead as her acolytes—an ally the Reverend thought could be most anyone, and a murdered husband. The only question left for David was the same one I expect we all must ask at some point: Did he believe?

Mayhap he hadn't before, friend, back when the Reverend was no reverend yet, slumped over his desk at the university or the little table in him and Belle's apartment with a wailing John David nearby wanting his bottle or his diaper changed. And maybe he hadn't when the family returned to Crow Holler to stake their claim on the souls of this town—John David now out of those diapers and Naomi growing in Belle's womb. Alvaretta's memory (Stu's memory, to be more specific) still burned inside and always would, which was why even someone with as much faith as David Ramsay would X the windshield when his travels took him by the Graves place. But is there not a bit of night in even the brightest life? Is there not still a sinner's heart beating inside every saint? Yes. Yes, friend. Such was what that man had told himself all these years, all in order to put that single moment of that single hour in that single night behind him. And so did he believe that Alvaretta's fury still burned bright enough to bring forth what darkness she could from the mountain? Could she indeed summon an evil that would consume them all?

David Ramsay believed yes. He always had, deep down. Not simply because Alvaretta Graves had power, but because the Holler had none. Ours was a cursed place. Maybe always had been. Not because of the mines or the mountain, not even because of the witch, but because the people themselves had lived unclean. Reverend had told Bucky as much, days ago. It held truer now. Crow Holler needed the Lord, friend, and yet the Lord would never come to a place such as this. Not as long as those who called upon Him did so through lying lips and blackened hearts.

Outside, he heard the wooden doors of the church open and shut.

Sitting there behind a desk that had spawned sermons aplenty, our Reverend believed. Oh friend, he truly did. Not only because of his own sin, but because he had seen Stu Graves's empty plot with his own eyes and now saw the bottoms of two dirt-crusted boots in the crack at the bottom of his office door. They did not move from their place, those boots, only sank into the dark blue carpet as bits of dirt and mud fell from the sides. The Reverend found he could not swallow.

A soft rap on the wood.

He called in a weak voice from behind his desk, "Who's there?" And when no voice returned, "Leave this place in the name of the Lord."

I know the preacher wondered if it was Stu Graves or Alvaretta's helper that knocked at his door—the hand of death or that of darkness. He couldn't know for sure without turning that knob, and that knob would never be turned. The town had let evil in, but David Ramsay would not. No, he would not ever. And so he remained there shaking behind that worn leather Bible, knowing not what sought him that lonely afternoon. Neither did the Reverend know what bade those two muddy boots to finally turn and leave, his prayers or his tears.

-2-

The only thing the mayor wanted to get clear with Scarlett was she couldn't be out of his sight now, not until everything was done. No more going alone, no more spending time with her friends. Scarlett didn't look to care much for that idea, as I'm sure you'd guess. She even went so far as to take out her little pen and scribble *Prisoner* on her pad. Wilson didn't care a whit what she wrote, that was the way things had to be.

"You were at the cemetery. That grave is *empty*. Don't you understand?"

She didn't. Any of it.

They were at the house by then. Wilson had locked all the doors and drawn the blinds. He peered out at the empty road from their living room window, watching the day begin to wane.

"This is what it comes to," he muttered. "Spending the rest of my days hiding. She said she wouldn't rest. Nobody believed her. Wally died. Crops failed. Business left town. Nobody believed her. I didn't. Not even when your momma's cancer came."

He snapped the blinds shut and looked at his daughter. Her brow had wrinkled.

"Never mind. You should go get dressed for church. I'll have to be there tonight. That means you're going too. We still don't know who it was that hurt you the other day, and I'm thinking it's whoever's thrown in with Alvaretta. They'll come for us first, Scarlett. Stu or the other. Alvaretta's gonna send them here."

He was ready for Scarlett's protest, but not her tears. They came slow like a spring shower, drop by drop, curling around her plump cheeks. Then came a torrent that seemed to pour from the girl's very soul. She buckled and collapsed onto the wood floor, her mouth crying out *I don't understand* though she produced no sound.

Wilson told her it would all be okay even if he knew by then it wouldn't, because that's what good daddies tell their kids. They would figure a way through this. Faith and honesty, Wilson said, that's what they needed. Scarlett nodded against his chest.

They sat holding each other and rocking away their fears on that cold living room floor, seeking and (I believe) finding faith enough to believe they'd be together always. But I guess the honesty part came harder for them both. Scarlett never wrote it was Tully Wiseman who'd attacked her, not in the name of the witch but for his ailing little girl. And Wilson never once said the reason Stu Graves would come for them first was because Wilson had been the one who killed him.

<h2 style="text-align:center">-3-</h2>

I'd say word of Stu Graves's return from the hell to which he'd surely gone would've gotten out without Angela Vest's help, but it would've been a whole lot slower. She hit the phone as soon as she got over the shock of seeing that empty casket and called everybody she knew on the drive home. When the battery on her cellular finally winked away and died, she set that right down and picked the phone in her trailer right up. There was much to discuss all that afternoon and early evening.

Yet even with all the excitement down to the cemetery, all everybody wanted to gab about was the one among us (or the two, if you hold to what Hays Foster said) who had taken up with the witch. I know that might seem strange, but it ain't really. Not to say there weren't nobody scared to death of what the witch had conjured from the grave or what her plans for Stu were. They was terrified, and you're about to find out just how much when I tell you what went on at revival that night. But see, we all had the benefit of knowing *what* the demon was now. Didn't make a difference if it was Alvaretta's husband back from the dead or some fire-breathing hound from hell, once a thing's got a name, it ain't so horrible anymore. If a thing's got a name, you can kill it.

But the one helping Alvaretta? That was still a mystery to be solved. And since nobody knew for sure who it was, it could be anybody. And friend, there is where Angela and her friends sank their teeth.

So far that afternoon, Angela had spoken with Belle Ramsay and Maris Sullivan, as well as Lorraine Wiseman, Tully's wife. Lorraine had brought up the fact that Medric had been acting awful strange of late, even before the kids had their party up on the mountain. She had it on good authority (that authority being Tully, which made Angela question just how good it was) that Medric had taken to sneaking away from town over the years, heading to parts unknown before slinking back to the funeral parlor. He was always a funny sort of man, dealing in death like he did. And who do you think was the one who put Stu in the ground to begin with? Yessir, Lorraine said, that would be Medric Johnston. She remembered when Stu died, said her momma and daddy both had seen him inside that casket. Said they'd both spoke for years how mad Alvaretta'd been over having to put her husband in the ground with all the townfolk, too, and how Alvaretta and Medric sure did talk a lot in the days after.

Belle didn't think it was Medric and said she found it hard to believe anyone in Crow Holler would dare even step foot on Alvaretta's front porch, much less agree to her bidding. She did, however, confess to Angela that Naomi had grown worried of the way Hays had been acting. Angela perked her ears but said nothing directly to that, as Bucky and Cordy both were sitting just across the kitchen table and staring at her. Belle said she was sure it was nothing, teenage years were hard on every boy, but maybe Cordy should make a little gap between her and her boyfriend for a while. Some space, Belle said, "for the Holy Spirit to dwell in." Angela asked if the Reverend might have any ideas as to who it could be. No, David didn't know either. He'd been shut up in his office all day readying his spirit for revival, so Belle promised she'd ask her husband later. Yes, she'd make sure to call and let Angela know what he said. How's Cordelia? Naomi's the same. Doc Sullivan said he'd call to check on her but hasn't yet. Isn't it strange how no one's seen him about? He hasn't even been to revival. Maris came alone last night.

According to Maris, that was because her husband was tired. She tried her best to get out of Angela the name of the person who'd dare accuse our doctor of such a thing, but Angela had never been one to reveal her sources. Maris said if anybody would take up with the witch, it'd be those Klansmen that was around. Hate-filled people, she said. Angela said there hadn't been Klan in Crow Holler for years. Maris said she knew better. She had it on good authority Chessie Hodge was the leader of them all.

By evening time Angela'd tangled and untangled the phone cord around her finger so much all the spring had gone out of it. She'd write down a name someone gave her on a scrap of paper and slide it over to Bucky. He'd hold it up and look at Cordelia, who looked sadder and sadder every time. He asked Cordy if she wanted to go out on the porch with him. She was at the door before Bucky could even get the words out.

They sat overlooking the big hole in the ground where Angela's roses used to grow. Tire marks still dotted the yard; one look was all Bucky needed to know they were different from the ones he'd seen at Alvaretta's. Had he taken a closer look at the rubber on Joe Mitchell's Toyota when he'd been in the Exxon a couple days before, Bucky would've known who to charge for wrecking his yard. As it was, he could only stare and think.

"Vy is Momma thpreading rumerth?" Cordy asked.

"She ain't the only one, case you weren't listening. Just her way. Your momma can't help it. People always compare themselves to others. I guess it helps us know where we stand with everybody else. Problem is, every time we compare who we are to how we think someone else is, we always come up short. Somebody's always better looking or richer or liked better. But when we gossip?" He shook his head. "That's different. That's the only way we can compare ourselves to somebody else and come out looking better than they are."

"Who do you compare yourthelf to?"

"Nobody. Least, nobody better than me. One man, maybe. He was the worst man I ever knew."

That was the most Bucky had ever said about the bad man from his childhood, and I could almost swear he hadn't meant to say any of it. But I guess he thought he'd turned down that road now and so might as well drive it.

Bucky wasn't the only person in Crow Holler burdened by the past that day. Wilson and David suffered from it too. What set Bucky apart from them, though, was he decided to do something about it.

-4-

"I was just a kid when your Granddaddy Vest died," Bucky said. "He went in the army cause there weren't no work here. Wasn't so bad. It was a steady check, and that meant just as much back then as it does now. Anyway, the plan was me and your grandma was gonna move up to Fort Eustis because that's where he got stationed, but then he got killed in that training thing.

"It was a bad time for your granny. She had me to care for and no money coming in but what the government gave her, which weren't enough to last. What helped was she started taking in boarders for the upstairs bedroom. You know that house, Cordy, up a ways from Harper's Field.

"Anyway, most the people we rented to was passersby from one place to another. I won't call them vagrants, but I don't have another name for them. They'd come off the train in Mattingly and find their way up here, looking for what odd jobs they could get. I'd say they were all okay men except for one. Called hisself Tom. I don't know if that was his name or not."

Bucky looked out across the waning evening. It had been evening when the bad man came too.

"He stayed near a week. Worked a couple days up at the grocery for Landis's daddy, sweeping the lot and taking the trash and whatnot. What money he got for pay went to the bottle. Folk could drink in Crow Holler back then. Time come for Momma to collect the rent, Tom couldn't pay. He wouldn't leave when Momma said he had to and said maybe they could work something out. I was too young to know what that meant. Guess you're old enough, though."

He couldn't look at her—a good thing, because Cordelia couldn't look at him either.

"She finally chased him off, but Momma knew Tom'd be back. I hoped he wouldn't because she said he was a bad man. Next night, we was eating supper when he busted in the door. You could smell the liquor on his breath the minute he come in. I hollered out, 'Momma, the bad man's here,' and she screams to me to run and get help. I got pushed down before I could get past him. Sent me sprawling. All I could do was crawl under the couch.

"Momma was screaming. Tom started shouting, 'I'm gonna start tearing stuff up woman if you don't give me what I want.' I looked out and saw him bend her over the table and start tearing at her dress, and then I just shut my eyes. But I heard it all. Heard Momma crying and heard plates falling off the table, food and drink and the apple pie she'd made for dessert. I laid there under that couch and bit my lip until it bled because I was so scared, but I heard it all. Sometimes I still do."

Inside, the phone rang again. Bucky wiped at his face.

"Momma did her best to set it all aside. She told me after that the only thing she cared about was I was safe. Tom, he did what he did and then went on. Nobody ever saw him again. Sometimes I wonder what came of him. I hope he died hard. I hope he screamed as he went to the grave. Lord help me, I do.

"She was a strong woman, your granny. You remember when she passed. Whole town turned out. Pastor Ramsay said she lived a good long life, but that ain't how I saw it. To me, my momma died the day she got bent over that table and raped with me listening underneath that sofa. That's the day I said I was gonna be a policeman. It's all I ever wanted to do, Cordy. Always thought constable was the closest I'd get. I know that ain't much, constabling. But it's all the town ever had to give me and so I took it, and I think they're all thankful I did. Because I kept them safe, you see? I made sure of it. Now, here I am. Sheriff Bucky Vest."

"I dun't want you to be theriff."

He winked at her, spilling a tear. "I know. I got to be, though. There's bad men in the world like that Tom, and there's bad women like Alvaretta Graves, and there's got to be people who stand between them and good people like you. But all this?" He held up the papers in his hand. "I can't do all this, Cordy. Keep watch on Medric, who's my own friend? Hays, whose baby is inside you? And the doc? Lord help us, Danny Sullivan don't even know who Alvaretta *is*. But now I got a town full of people scared to death. I don't know what happened to get Stu out of the ground. I don't even know what it is Alvaretta wants. But I know something's coming. I can feel it, and I just don't know what I'm gonna do when it gets here. I ain't even got a gun no more. Alvaretta scared me so bad I dropped it and ran. My daddy's gun, Cordelia. What's people gonna say?"

"I wun't tell anyone."

"That ain't gonna make things better."

"Vu need thumone to help."

"Ain't gonna be nobody to help me, Cordelia."

And there wasn't. Bucky was all alone in this, and he knew that. Wasn't nobody to tell him what he should do, just a crowd who wanted him to keep them all safe. Wasn't nobody who could give things to him straight—

He sat up. "Come on. I gotta get you and your momma down to revival, then I got to go somewhere."

"Vere you going?"

"Someplace I ain't supposed to know about. Because you're right. I need help."

-5-

Wasn't no revival up on Campbell's Mountain that evening, but I guess you could say there was a service. Alvaretta Graves had never been one to love the Lord. Living was wood and stone and cold wind, it was work and sweat and suffering. Wasn't no place for God in such a world as that, though maybe there was room enough for faith. Everybody's got to believe in something, friend. Alvaretta? She believed in hate, and she believed in stoking the fire of that rage nightly.

Out back of her tiny little cabin lay a worn path that led to the edge of the woods. Alvaretta walked that path now. Her ears were tuned to what news the wind brought and the howls and yelps of her gathering children. The footsteps behind her grew closer. She looked to the ground, where a shadow like the mountain itself grew beside her own.

"You'll stay here with the children," she said. "Me first, then you after. Watch the trees."

The shadow stopped as Alvaretta's own continued on. Playful barks called out from behind her, tiny bays like near words mixing with the grunts and not-words of what played with them. And though the years had not given themselves over to happiness, Alvaretta's mouth broke into a small grin. That smile was short-lived, though. The cut on her lip left by the Bickford whore made her wince, turning the grin to a scowl. No matter. This was no place for tittering.

She reached the edge of the woods and cleared away the roots that had taken hold there, brushing aside the fallen leaves and scurrying a spider. Only then did Alvaretta stand and bow. What she fell into was not prayer—never let what she did be called a prayer, friend—but more a silent conversation that took place in a troubled spirit. Twice now, town people had come. First children and then the sheriff, though if that man Bucky Vest was truly the law now, Alvaretta believed she had nothing to worry herself over. He'd been as scared as the Bickford whore when he scampered off, and for good reason. Had he remained, he would have died. There'd have been no choice, because he would have seen what she had hidden inside. Her secret.

Her love.

"Keep them away," she whispered. "Do my bidding now, as I did yours."

She was still then, listening to that cold mountain breeze with that same troubled look, and when she had heard enough, there was only one thing to say.

"Then get me ready."

-6-

It didn't make much sense to Angela why Bucky wasn't planning to stay long at revival that night. Law business was what he told her, nothing more. He'd drop her and Cordy off and be back in time for the benediction. None of it would work out that way, though. That was plain enough as soon as Bucky got to town and saw all the guns.

Everybody had them. Rifles and shotguns, pistols, even some black powders. Briar alone had brought with him enough barrel iron to invade a small country. Reverend Ramsay and Belle stood on the church steps between the people and the front doors, telling everybody they'd have to leave all that outside. Well, nobody wanted a part in that. Preacher had already gotten into a shouting match with Raleigh Jennings, David saying the house of the Lord was no place for weapons of mass destruction, Raleigh answering he wasn't going nowhere unarmed so long as a dead man and an agent of the devil was on the loose.

Now Chessie got involved, saying something about one of the Lord's disciples cutting off some slave's ear, and unless David wanted to end up the same he'd better let them on in. Ruth Mitchell, who'd come to worship with her husband (Joe had shut up the Exxon special that night), their ailing daughter Chelsea, and the 12-gauge that hung over their fireplace, started up about how David owned more guns than anybody in the whole blamed town. Ain't no reason to get skittish over anyone else having one, Ruth said, unless maybe the preacher was the one Alvaretta had enchanted.

Boy oh boy, did that ever start a ruckus. Wilson and Landis tried calming things down. They didn't get very far. Bucky started in, too, shouting about how this was exactly what Alvaretta wanted. Belle then hollered the same. That's what got everybody quiet. Belle Ramsay was about the only person left in Crow Holler liked by all.

Well, you can imagine how hard it is to humble thyself in the sight of the Lord with all them guns and shouting. That's what David Ramsay found out that night. He and Belle managed to

get everybody inside without a single bullet flying, Belle sooth-
ing people with that smile of hers, David shaking everybody's
hand and saying there were no hard feelings even if there was.
He barely registered Angela's quick words and the slips of paper
she'd placed in his hand before taking her pew. Everybody sang
and prayed like always, but there was no heart in it. No . . .
community, I guess. I don't know if that's what Alvaretta had in
mind, killing the town from the inside. If so, that plan worked
something fine. You think of standing in one a those pews and
trying to sing your praises, all the while wondering if the person behind you's the one been sneaking out to hear the witch's
counsel. Imagine bumping your neighbor's hand by accident
and feeling the notion that the skin you just touched had maybe
caressed Alvaretta Graves.

Only one person there that night looked to give himself
over to the spirit of the occasion, and that was the one person you'd never think. But by then Hays Foster felt he had
no other place left to turn but heaven. His friends—if they'd
ever been his friends—had abandoned him. His parents were
more worried of their precious store than their only child.
Scarlett and Naomi had all but accused him of being the one
who'd fallen in league with Alvaretta, calling him a coward
in the process. Well, didn't nobody else do anything either
that Sunday morning, did they? Scarlett, sure, but look what
she got for her trouble. Only Cordelia had come to his rescue.
Even then, that defense hadn't felt particularly spirited. Hays
had taken it as Cordy's way of telling him *You might not love
me like I love you, but I'm all you got.* Maybe that was true. But
even if it was, that didn't change the most important issue
in Hays's mind right then: Cordelia couldn't save him from
the monsters. How could she, when she didn't even believe
in them?

Pastor Ramsay preached on the darkness that chased every

living soul and the devil that crouched at every door. I know as he spoke those words he thought of whatever had crouched at his own door that afternoon. I know, just as I know Hays thought of the shed that once stood in the Fosters' backyard.

When the time came for healing and acceptance of the Lord, it was Hays who stood up. Bucky was checking his watch, trying to figure where Chessie's load of moonshine would be by then, and thus John David. He glanced up to the shocked looks on Landis and Kayann's faces and the Reverend's hands upon Hays's shoulders, and what our sheriff and all who had gathered witnessed next could only be described as a boy reborn. The preacher prayed and the people lifted their voices to the night, overcome by the Spirit descending into that place. Hays stood overcome, too, friend, so full of the Lord that he began shaking worse than even Naomi, and what poured forth from his lips was not the dark speech of Alvaretta's demon, but words of wonder and praise and second chances that brought tears to Cordelia's eyes.

"The Lord calleth from the darkness," David Ramsay proclaimed. "Hays Foster has answered."

It was air Hays walked on as he returned to the waiting arms of his girlfriend and parents, and it was air Briar Hodge decided he needed right then. Too much religion, I guess, or maybe Briar needed to make sure his guns were safe in the bed of his truck. Whichever it was, he got up from Chessie's side and made for the back, past where Raleigh sat. He pushed on those double doors and breathed in deep. The air outside had cooled, the sun gone in favor of a moon that glowed dull and pale. What small light remained covered the buildings and trees like a thin blanket, turning the world dim yellow. He managed the first step when he saw what had been left in the street. What came next is something even I have a hard time believing.

Briar Hodge, Briar the Bear, the baddest man you'll ever find in these mountains, began to scream.

He turned and ran back through the tiny foyer, his big boots shaking the wood floor. When Briar reached the first set of pews, he bellowed the words again.

"Stu. Stu Graves is here."

-7-

They poured out, friend. You just let that sink in. Wasn't a safe place in all of Crow Holler that night but under that steeple, and yet they went out. Not just David and Wilson and Landis and Bucky. Chessie, Angela, and Belle too. All the kids. Everybody.

What lay beyond the doors wasn't Stu Graves, but you could say it was close. The hoofprints looked to have been seared into the dirt, same as they'd appeared all the way from the mines to Alvaretta's doorstep. Only now they stretched in a long and meandering line down the middle of the road that cut through town, stopping in front of the church before meandering left to the council building. There the tracks turned in a wide arc around back of the church, skirting Medric's funeral home, then moved off south to where many of the townspeople lived. Hundreds of tracks. Thousands. Like it hadn't been a single dead man that had come for them, but an army.

"Find them," someone called. "Find them" echoed. They rushed for their guns before fear could take them and fanned out, every man and woman according to their own will. Landis led a group toward the grocery, Briar another toward the council building. Joe and Ruth Mitchell went with him. David mustered men to follow the trail toward the far houses. Wilson grabbed Scarlett, Cordelia, and Naomi and pushed them back inside, warning them not to leave. Angela, Belle, and Kayann joined them, along with many more of the women and children.

Bucky pulled Chessie aside and said, "I need a gun."

"Where's yours?" she asked.

"I left it. Give me a gun, Chessie."

"You're the blessed sheriff, Bucky, and you're asking me for a gun?"

"*Give me a gun,*" he screamed.

He settled for the double barrel she threw at him and ran for the funeral home. This time Bucky didn't have to knock. Medric answered with his finger on the trigger of his shotgun. Bucky shoved the barrel aside with his own.

"I don't know what's going on with you, Medric, and I don't care, but you come help me or somebody's gonna die out there."

Medric shook his head. Terror flashed in his eyes. "What if it's me dies out there?"

"You see those?" Bucky pointed to the tracks. "They come right to your door, Medric. You see what left them?"

"I didn't see nothing, Buck. You hear me?"

"Neither did anybody else. But people see that Stu Graves passed here and you're nowhere to be found, they'll like to come in here guns blazing. You want to be part of this town, it's now."

I don't think Medric much wanted to be a part of anything (and for good reason), but he did as Bucky said. They both ran into the street toward the council building. Shots rang out. Bucky couldn't tell from where. From the direction of the grocery. Somebody screamed, *"He's here."* Over at the council building, people shouted the same. Raleigh ran that way. Joe Mitchell, Tully Wiseman, and Homer Pruitt went with him. All of them carried pistols and rifles both.

Bucky broke into a sprint. He turned to yell for Medric, but Medric was gone.

-8-

Reverend Ramsay gripped the revolver in his hand and tried to keep in the center of the six men around him. You call that cowardice if you want, I won't say a word against you. But you should remember that not a few hours before, our preacher heard a knock made by a shadow standing on the other side of his door. Stu Graves was coming back for everybody, friend, but the ones who'd killed him were first in line, and no amount of prayer and service to the Lord would ever be enough to wipe the stain of that sin away. God forgives. David had preached that particular sermon many times in his long past, and for each one he'd made sure to add that God might forgive seventy times seven, but that don't mean you get off scot-free. You might get heaven eventually, but that don't mean you won't have to walk through hell on earth first.

It was hell enough down that dark road past the church where no lamps led and only a pale moon shone. Those other men with him felt it too. The footprints were burned into the dirt and led straight on, but that didn't mean Stu Graves was ahead of them. He could've just as easy doubled back and be sitting right now in the thick brush to the side of the road. Waiting.

The circle around the preacher got tighter with every step away from the church. David's lips moved. Whether it was the Twenty-Third Psalm or a plea for Alvaretta's forgiveness, I don't know. Nothing but a long stretch of black ahead. The houses lay farther down, a mile or so on. In between lay nothing but the same scrub and trees that make up much of Crow Holler. Have a look yourself, if you want. Tell me you'd want to be walking down that road at night with a demon loosed.

David was about to suggest they all turn back and at least get a few trucks when something moved in the bushes. His eyes went there before his gun. Rising up from a clump of weeds and grass came a black shape. He blinked, found it gone, then saw it again when he blinked again. Bigger now, and moving for him.

The warning he shouted came not in words but in a piercing shriek that could be heard all the way back to town. David fired his gun, barely missing the side of the man's head closest to him, and then they all fired. The night exploded to booms and shouts. Round after round, pummeling the trees and grass, grown men screaming like children. And there was David's voice high above them all, yelling to kill it, kill Stu.

-9-

Landis made it halfway to the grocery when he heard a man shout that something had just run into the store. He thought he'd seen it too. Something on two legs but not human at all, at least not anymore.

They slowed when they reached the lot, guns forward. Landis shook so bad there was no way he could get off a straight shot. With a shotgun, though, that didn't matter. One pull on the trigger would send a spray of buckshot wide enough to hit anything close. Problem was, Landis had never pulled a trigger in his life. I know that seems a stretch, seeing as how that man was born and raised here in the mountains, but it's the truth. You get to be a big businessman, you leave the hunting and shooting to the lower classes.

But this time was different. This time it was his grocery being threatened, Landis Foster's livelihood, and there weren't no way in the world he was gonna let Alvaretta Graves snatch away what not even the town had been able to destroy.

The tracks led straight inside. Landis led the four men with him in a slow creep toward windows still broken and jagged. All looked still and dark inside but for the two red eyes on the steps to his office. Landis yelped, jerked the shotgun in that direction, and fired the first gun of his insignificant little life.

The twin barrels erupted in flame and the kick, which Landis hadn't counted on at all, knocked him backwards. The gun's roar drew the others, some of whom were screaming it was Stu, they could see him, don't let him get away.

-10-

Medric might have thought it best to be seen helping things, but that didn't mean he possessed a mind to try. What he wanted more than anything was to get away from the crazy white people and back inside the funeral home where it was safe. He'd lost Bucky somewhere between the house and the council building. No way he could know whether that had been an accident or something the "sheriff" (he'd tried saying that word to himself and never could leave off those quote marks around it) had done on purpose. I do believe Medric thought Bucky had left him to die. Because Bucky knew, you see. He might not've known everything, but he knew enough to think Medric had something to do with the witch.

And it wasn't fair. If Medric could've taken all the anger and pain inside him and given it words, those three are what he would've chose. It wasn't fair, him suffering and being singled out. What he'd done was out of a sense of right. He alone had done what the Lord would want. And that alone now made him a target.

He saw Briar and Chessie and Raleigh Jennings gathered with a group of people along the far side of the council building. Medric had gone too far to turn back, but the wide space behind the building looked empty enough for him to hide until things calmed down. He lowered his shotgun and broke into as much a trot as his old body would allow, making for the closest corner and the trees beyond. Whether by grace or plain dumb luck, he made it without anybody seeing. Medric laid his head against the cold brick of the wall and shut his eyes.

When he opened them, something stood not three feet away.

There was no time to ponder, no time to scream. All Medric saw was that dark shadow coming for him, and all he thought was Stu Graves. Stu coming back for him, even if Medric Johnston had been the only man in Crow Holler to show Alvaretta respect. The figure stopped. It did not speak, did not move, and that hesitation was all Medric needed. He raised the barrel and fired, sending the figure backward into the dirt and leaves with a humph that came out sounding not like a demon's cry at all.

-11-

Hays Foster spent his first moments as a member of the Lord's elect just as afraid as he'd spent all his years as a heathen. Landis had run off to his precious grocery, Kayann screaming back inside the church, and each of them must've thought Hays had gone with the other. Not even Cordelia remained with him in the parking lot. Chessie had been handing out nearly every gun imaginable from the bed of Briar's truck, tossing them to those who'd been fool enough to not bring their own, but she'd never given one to Hays. He'd tried, but Chessie had just smirked when she saw him standing there with his hand out, and what she'd said was it'd be best if Hays got back inside the church with the rest of the women.

He saw Bucky running past with a man who might've been Medric, heading toward the council building where everybody was shouting. Hays couldn't tell if it was his friend for sure. Shots rang out from the road and the grocery and the council building. It was full dark by then, and not even the moon or stars could bring enough light to put him at ease. He fumbled for the lighter in his pocket, flipped the top, and spun the wheel just as Medric passed by again, running back toward the funeral home.

And that's when Hays Foster knew that the Lord may have claimed his soul, but Alvaretta Graves had claimed his sanity. He'd been cursed beyond anything Cordelia endured, or Scarlett or Naomi. Their sufferings lay in the frailness of their bodies, and yet they'd still found comfort in their blindness to what circled them all. That was true for him no longer. The witch would have all of Crow Holler drown in darkness, but she would have Hays Foster bear witness to the truth.

He'd been right about it all. The demon, the monsters, the ones in league with the witch. Because you see, it wasn't Medric Johnston that Hays had seen by the light of that flame, running back to the funeral home. At least not the Medric that Hays had always known. Oh no, friend. What raced past him had Medric's puffy belly and Medric's skinny legs, but it wore a demon's face.

-12-

Someone screamed. Bucky didn't know who it was because so many guns were going off, but he knew the voice was one of terror and pain because it was the voice his momma had made while the bad man Tom hurt her on the dining room table. He ran harder and racked Chessie's shotgun.

He saw Briar waving, calling for help, and now Chessie come from around the back of the council building, waving too. People were still shooting up at the grocery and the Exxon. More gunfire echoed from the road where David had taken his men. But whatever fight there'd been around Wilson's office was done, and everything there had gone quiet.

Briar and Chessie ran back around the council building. Bucky followed and raised his gun, then stopped when he rounded the corner and saw everyone gathered in that small patch of trees. It wasn't Stu Graves who laid there. Pains me to say that. Pains me more to tell you it was one of the Holler's own. Joe Mitchell and Raleigh were bent over the body of Joe's wife, both men crying. Ruth Mitchell's face held the same look of frozen horror that Angela had seen Nikki-whoever wearing on the TV back when the world made sense. Only this time it was real.

I think even Bucky could've handled seeing one of those hoofprints seared into her chest better than he did seeing the scattershot that had been her end. Those dozen tiny holes in her body meant it wasn't no curse that had killed Ruth Mitchell. Nor had it been the ghost of Stu Graves. It had been one of our own.

-13-

It wasn't that Danny Sullivan had no religion, nor even that he found fault with the chorus of amens and hallelujahs that got passed around the Holy Fire every Sunday like candy. He simply thought the whole thing hypocritical. You have to figure Danny seen the people of Crow Holler at their worst, walking into his little office with their aches and pains, needing pills for their depressions and pills for their lovemaking, hearing the women talk about their men beating on them and the men talk about all the times they want to pick up a gun and end their sorry lives, only to see them all standing up in the pews a few days later, praising the Lord for His goodness. Danny knew the sins of this town even more than David Ramsay did.

When Maris said she was going to revival, Danny said fine. She had kin in Wilson and Scarlett, a history in the Holler, and that was something Danny didn't share but was grateful his wife could possess. But he wouldn't be going to church that week. It was the hypocrisy, yes, but it was also his belief that religion turns to something else when paired with fear and hate. By then, plenty of both had taken up residence in town.

He was sitting in front of the TV watching a rerun of *The Twilight Zone* when the gunfire started. He didn't hear it at first, or thought it was young'uns shooting off some firecrackers.

It'd been a long week. There'd been no new cases of what Danny had taken to calling Teenaged-Gotta-Fit-In-Disorder (privately, of course, and to Maris alone), but none of the girls were getting better either. The sickness had stopped spreading. That was good news worth spreading, but then all everybody wanted to talk about was Alvaretta Graves and, now, her dead husband, Stu. It was a mess, that's what Danny'd said to Maris. A sorry mess.

More shots. Not firecrackers.

He muted the TV and got up, wincing at the crick in his back, and flipped on the porch light before stepping outside. The sounds were coming from town. The first thing he thought was the only word he mumbled—

"Maris."

He'd turned to go back inside for the car keys when he saw them—horseshoe marks burned into the ground. Coming straight off the road and up his gravel drive. Right to the porch, where they turned and went back.

Danny Sullivan let out a whimper. He ran a shaky hand through his white hair. There were other houses down that way, Wilson's and the Fosters', but they were all at revival. That was good, because the doctor had begun to panic.

"No," he said. "No, no, nonono. Why did you do this, Alvaretta?"

Gunfire again. And now voices, coming from up the road.

Maris would have to wait. Danny hated the thought, but she couldn't find what had crept up to their door and neither could anyone else. He ran inside not for the keys to the car but the keys to the small garden shed in the backyard. A rake was all he could find. That would have to do. Danny only hoped he could cover the tracks before anyone saw.

XI

John David arrested. Cold.
A new deputy. Alvaretta prepares.

-1-

By eleven that night, the only person who didn't know Alvaretta Graves had loosed her demon was creeping along an old service road that wound its way through miles of trees and river bottoms between the Holler and the little burg of Camden. Wasn't much of a run for John David that night. Half the bed of his truck had been empty when Chessie sent him off; he'd had to be careful the whole way down from the mountains to keep the jars from jostling. Wasn't even worth the gas money, taking that small a load out. Then again, John David knew it wasn't a run Chessie wanted. No, all that woman had in mind was getting him away. Away from the Holler. Away from his daddy. Just away. Which I guess speaks a lot on why John David had taken up with the Hodges after he come back from the war. Chessie and Briar might not've been what you'd call one of Christendom's bright lights, but she understood that boy. She understood that boy better'n anybody.

He drove without headlights, as Briar had always instructed. It was as dangerous as it was pointless (in all John David's trips back and forth to Camden, not once had he seen another living soul on that old service road), but he enjoyed being part of the night, blending into all that darkness. It gave him time to think.

Chessie had called that afternoon to say they'd dug up Stu Graves. It'd been a crazy notion to John David that Chessie and the rest of the town (not to mention Medric) had agreed to do something like that. Crazier still that Stu's coffin had been empty. I wouldn't say John David believed all the stories of the witch, at least not right off. I wouldn't say he thought Alvaretta had even raised up her husband. But all the news of the day had done one thing, and that was to further convince John David of what he'd come to know as true—every time you say the world can't get darker, it finds a deeper shade of black.

I expect that was the thought on his mind when he slammed the brakes halfway to town and flipped the headlights on. Up ahead, just at the outer edges of his sight, something had walked across the road. Not a deer (unless there was a deer in these mountains who'd learned to walk on two legs). Not a man, neither. He crept forward and took his hand off the gear-shift, reaching for the sawed-off on the passenger's seat.

Nothing. Nothing there.

Just the moon more than likely, nearly full and easing in and out of a bank of low clouds over the mountains. That didn't explain why John David's knee was twitching, though, or why the hand still on the steering wheel had begun to flex. He put the gear back into drive and switched off the lights. With no jars to worry of breaking in back, he stood the engine up to thirty and kept an eye on the rearview. Up ahead, the road curved and rolled over a small hill that led on into the Holler. And on the other side of that curve, a pair of headlights flashed on.

He rounded the turn, and there John David stopped. A heavy man stood basked in shadow between the headlights, waiting. A shotgun rested on his right hip. The barrel pointed high and out.

The man hollered, "Take what you got and put it through the back window."

John David reached onto the seat beside him and eased the shotgun through the little square of open glass behind him. It clunked into the bed. The pistol tucked under the driver's seat stayed put.

"That it?" the man yelled.

"All I got."

"You promise?"

John David wrinkled his forehead at such a question. Almost like it'd come from a child. "Pinky swear," he called.

The man moved away slow and easy, like he expected an ambush. John David strained to see who it was. He didn't recognize the face until Bucky stuck his head through the window.

"Say, John David."

I don't know whether John David wanted to laugh or reach under the seat and shoot Bucky where he stood for scaring him so bad. "What you doing out here, Sheriff?"

"About to ask you the same thing. How's things in Camden?"

"Didn't go to Camden."

"Sure you did. Camden's the only place this old road goes. What? You think all of Chessie's secrets are hers?"

John David cocked his head. "What you doing with Chessie's shotgun, Bucky?"

"That don't matter right now. John David, I'm placing you under arrest."

He tried grinning. "You serious? What's the charge?"

"I'll think of something," Bucky said.

"You can't do that. Chessie's got an agreement."

"With the mayor, not with me. Things has happened in the Holler. I expect Chessie and Briar are both plenty busy at the moment."

"Heard about y'all's little trip to the cemetery."

"And what we found?"

John David nodded.

"Well, more's happened since you been out . . . riding around. Stu came to town, John David. During revival. Left his mark all over the place, and it's the same tracks Cordy and her friends found. There was a fight. Ruth Mitchell got shot. She's gone."

John David leaned back into the seat. "Ruth's dead?"

"She is, and ain't nobody gonna know who did it. People's shooting at anything that moved, saying Stu was everywhere. So come on, you're under arrest."

"Bucky, none of this makes sense."

"You'll follow me. I'll give you that mercy rather than taking you in the car. Stinks in there anyway. But you get a notion to take off, you'll have more than me to answer to. I'm tired, John David. I'm tired, and I'm scared. So don't give me no trouble. Please."

John David could only look at him. "Where we going?"

"Jail, I guess."

"Bucky, we ain't got no jail."

The sheriff tapped on the door. He turned and started walking back to the Celebrity.

"I'll think of something," he said.

-2-

Wasn't a doubt in anybody's mind Stu Graves walked through town that night. Never mind how impossible it seemed, or how he'd managed to grow horse feet in death when regular feet was all he'd had in life. When all you got is the impossible, that's what you believe. Then was this: There were too many hoofprints covering the area between the grocery and the church and on to Doc Sullivan's house. Too many for only one demon to make, anyway. That meant either Stu'd been walking around the Holler a good long while as everybody sought the Lord inside the church, or he'd brought some friends along from the grave. You can bet Bucky thought it was that second one, else he wouldn't have left family and friends to go after John David.

But such things didn't matter to those still in town. What mattered was Stu had been *seen*. Not just by Landis and the Reverend but by others as well, and they'd all swear to it on a Bible. After all the shooting was done and the demon (or demons—I'll leave that for you to decide, friend) was gone, people found some of those tracks led straight to the cemetery. Right to Stu Graves's empty plot. I know that myself, and I'll tell you it bothered Reverend Ramsay something awful. It was almost like Stu'd been dragged back to this world against his own will, and now he was pining for the death he once had. Reverend told Belle later he couldn't shake the feeling that by raising Stu up, Alvaretta had cursed her husband right along with everybody else.

I'll tell you another feeling nobody could shake that night—the only reason Stu disappeared agin was because he'd accomplished what Alvaretta wanted. Someone had died. The first shot in the war between the witch and the Holler had been fired, and the bullet had struck one of our own.

Joe Mitchell managed to wrestle the body of his dead wife away from Raleigh long enough to carry her from behind the council building to the church steps. He slumped down and held her like one of Alvaretta's dogs would bring a dead animal for her pleasure. His wailing brought everybody back from searching and all those people out from the Holy Fire. Angela made it out the door first, Cordelia right behind her. Belle shoved her way back inside to find little Chelsea Mitchell and make sure the girl wouldn't be scarred for life by seeing her dead momma. She found Chelsea with Naomi, the two of them herking and jerking together in embrace as Scarlett stood guard over them. Wasn't much Christianizing went on that night, friend, but I'll admit what little there was came straight from those women. Belle, Scarlett, and Naomi sat with Chelsea for near an hour that night. They took turns holding the child until Joe could find courage enough to deliver the sad news.

Mayor screamed for Bucky, but of course Bucky'd already gone. The Reverend kept asking Chessie and Briar if they'd seen who'd fired the shot, but there was no way to tell. Everybody with a gun had pulled the trigger at least once that night. Chessie understood right off that had been Alvaretta's plan.

"Stu was a distraction," she said. "Nothing more. He come so Alvaretta's spy could do her bidding in secret."

Joe cried out, "Ruthie never hurt nobody." He shook his wife, begged her to wake. Ruth's right arm fell free of his grasp. It dangled lifeless and swung like a pendulum off his right leg. "Why'd the witch want her dead?"

Landis Foster bent his head to hide the tears he shed. He whispered, "Because she never hurt nobody."

Kayann came down the steps around Joe, calling for Landis and Hays. She went to her husband and held him as Angela looked on. Landis let his shotgun fall to the ground, and there it would stay. He would pick up a gun only once more in his life. That would come the next night under the blood moon, when he went with the others to kill the witch.

Mayor Bickford charged up the steps as Cordelia charged down, she looking for Hays, him looking for Scarlett. Wilson kept his gun raised, and I'll tell you why. He was about the only one there who had the thought that one of them in the crowd was a killer. Ruth hadn't been murdered, because she was innocent, though the mayor saying that outright would risk exposing his greatest and most secret sin. No, *he* was the one Alvaretta had sought. That's why those hoofprints were scattered about the council building more than anywhere else. Poor Ruth had just been in the wrong place at the wrong time.

Chessie told the Reverend to tend to the dead. He said

something about getting Medric, but of course Medric was nowhere around neither. That all became moot when Joe Mitchell said dead or not, no black man was ever gonna touch his wife. Maris said she'd arrange for the body to be taken to the clinic instead.

Hays heard Cordelia calling to him as best she could. He felt her hand on his arm, watched as her lips moved to form something like *Vhat hoppen?* The Zippo in his hand burned so hot that it had begun to singe the skin. One image consumed his mind—Medric Johnston running away from where Ruth had been killed. Medric's demon face. That shotgun in his hand. I think a part of that boy had known a long while Medric was giving aid to the witch. It only made sense, the way he'd changed since Hays and his friends had spent that night on the mountain. How he'd been sneaking out. How he'd protested the unburying.

"I loved her."

Hays and Cordelia both flinched at the sound. He remained still but she spun, banging her hand against the side of the truck behind her. Raleigh Jennings stood mere feet away. His cheeks were streaked with tears, his hair a wild mess. The hem of his white dress shirt had come loose of his pants and gone drenched with blood. The gun in his hand shook.

"You thcared uth, Printhipal Jenningth," Cordy said.

Raleigh spoke again, "I loved her," like she and Hays weren't even there. Hays looked up and saw the pain in the man's eyes.

Angela called for Cordelia from the church steps. She looked there to see her momma alongside Scarlett and the mayor. They had to go, Angela said. Now.

"Come with me," she told Hays.

"I have to go," he said. "I have to get away, Cordy. It's not safe here anymore."

He turned, searching for his mother and father. Cordelia

watched her boyfriend go. She turned to the spot where Raleigh had stood, but he had gone. Left to wander back behind the council building, to mourn the loss of his last good thing.

-3-

John David had never been incarcerated, but it didn't take him long to find life as a convict wasn't so hard if your prison was Bucky's trailer. Not that it wasn't awkward at first. Wilson arrived not long after Bucky did with Scarlett in tow, looking for our fair sheriff so he could find out why Bucky had run off when the town needed him most. Angela and the mayor both near fainted when Bucky brought him inside, Angela more from anger at how Bucky'd left her and Cordelia at the church, the mayor out of fear of how mad Chessie would be at the breaking of their agreement. But once all that wore off, things were near fine. Angela brought out a plate of biscuits and sausage gravy left over from supper, along with a glass of her mint tea. As good as all that looked, John David couldn't touch any of it. He could only sit there in a sad sort of silence as the mayor and Angela recounted all that had happened in the last hours. When they were both done, Bucky informed John David of his rights (which, I'll add, was delivered with neither hesitation nor error; Bucky'd been waiting just about all his life for the chance to tell somebody that).

"You figure a charge yet?" the mayor asked.

"Driving around at night with your lights off. It's a serious one, Wilson. Risk of life and limb, reckless driving, maybe even intent to cause bodily harm. You're looking at hard time, John David."

"I weren't so scared of Stu," Wilson said, "I'd fire you right now, Bucky."

There was John David's phone call, of course. Bucky said that would be to his momma and daddy and nobody else. When John David said that wasn't going to happen, Bucky had Angela call the Ramsays in his stead. The call down to the Hodge farm came next, followed by a final one to the Fosters. That was all the talking Angela Vest did on the phone that night. Oh, you can bet that line rang plenty of times. Didn't matter if the clock had already struck the other side of today, people wanted their news. But Angela never picked up once. Ruth Mitchell might've stood in the grocery only a few days before proclaiming this was all Angela's fault, but nobody deserved to die that way. I guess for Angela, things had gotten way more real that night and a lot less like the TV.

"I expect they'll be here soon," Bucky said. "Chessie, Briar. Your folks. Meantime, I think I might just sit here with Wilson and cry some over all I seen tonight. You go on out on the back porch, John David. Give us a little bit. Me and the mayor got some things to talk over."

John David sighed (his night just kept getting better and better) and got up from the table. He tried once more—"You think you're scared of Alvaretta, you wait until Chessie gets here"—and then pushed on the little door off the kitchen. The moon that would burn red over Crow Holler the next night now glowed almost white, hanging up in the stars as a near perfect circle. It cast its light down upon what passed for the Vests' backyard and the porch itself, along with the two girls sitting in the lawn chairs by the steps.

For what must've seemed to John David an eternity, he stood part inside and part out, unsure what to do. Cordelia made that decision for him. She got up from beside Scarlett and moved to the door, putting a hand to John David's shoulder and whispering, "You got to get thith thtraight" before walking inside. Scarlett only stared at him. He took Cordelia's chair and sat.

"Hey, Scarlett. How's things going?"

She hadn't brought her pad or pen and so only shrugged a little.

"I know I was rude the other night. Up at the mines. I didn't know you'd done all that for me. If somebody'd said something . . ."

Well, if somebody had said something, nothing at all woulda changed. I don't think John David really understood that until he'd started to speak the words. He woulda told Scarlett back then the very thing he was to tell her now.

"Look, Scarlett. You're a sweet girl and I've always thought that, but I'm not the guy for you. Maybe before, back when I was younger. Things are just different now. With me, they're different. That night we had at Hays's party, that was great, you know? That was fun. But I didn't ever mean it to be more than that—one night. I'm sorry you thought otherwise."

Scarlett turned away.

"I just wanted to . . . feel . . . ," he said, "something. Anything. I don't . . . you wouldn't understand, Scarlett. And even if you could, I couldn't say it." He looked off into the trees and then to the stars. "My dad used to tell me there's hot people and cold people and people in the middle. The hot ones were the best. They knew what life was about, you know? They had answers and faith. Passion. The cold ones, they were bad. They were the ones who'd gotten so turned around and lost in life that they couldn't love or feel anything at all anymore. Daddy said that was their choice, though, and they'd burn for it. 'The punishment for the frozen of soul is eternal fire, because that's the only way they'll feel anything.'

"But you know who Daddy says is the worst of all? The ones that ain't either. Not hot, not cold. Not a thing. Those get judged the worst, because they don't care either way. That was me before I left. I don't know how I got that way. I just did. I was so scared that I ran away and went to war. You want to know what I found over there, Scarlett? At the end of the world?"

Scarlett didn't nod. She didn't shake her head, neither.

"I found there was lots of guys like me. Ain't that something? I mean, I guess there's plenty who sign up looking for glory. Wanting to serve their country. Whatever. But most of them are just looking for a place to belong. People trying to feel something. I saw some awful things I won't ever forget. People who make Alvaretta Graves look like a child at play.

"I killed people. Lot of us did. We were on patrol one evening and came up on an ambush. Just . . . stuff exploding everywhere, people screaming, shooting and getting shot. Just . . . I *hear* it, you know? Even now I do. I went through eight clips in my rifle, just *bapbapbap*, you know? Just shooting at everything. And I hit this guy. Tore his face clean off. And when it was over and we were going over the bodies for intel, I kicked him over—we all did that, you never knew when they'd booby-trap themselves—I saw it was just a kid. Couldn'a been more'n eleven, twelve. A *kid*, Scarlett. And I *killed* him." John David shook his head. "I didn't kill anybody over there for my country. I never thought I was protecting all of y'all back here. I did it to stay alive and keep the guys with me alive, and you know what? The people I killed, they were just trying to do the same. This world, it's just so . . . messed up. Just an asylum full of crazy people who do crazy things for no reason at all. I went from lukewarm to solid cold over there in all that sand, and I realized Daddy was wrong. Cold's worse, Scarlett. Cold is hell. Daddy preaches that it's fire but it ain't, it's ice. It's the coldest ice there is. That's what I carry, and that's why I took up with Chessie and Briar when I got back. Why I don't talk to my folks anymore. Because there's bad in me, and I can't get it out. That's what you can't know and why you can't be thinking of me the way you have."

The two of them sat in silence. John David said he was sorry one more time, then got up to leave. Scarlett reached out and grabbed the hem of his T-shirt. She stood and met his eyes with her own, and with one hand she eased up the long sleeve covering her arm, holding her scars close to John David's face. Letting him see. She needed no paper, no pen.

John David understood:

I can't get the bad out either.

She came closer. John David did not back away. He did not move when he felt Scarlett's breath and the closeness of her body. He did not even move when she raised up to her tiptoes and kissed him softly on the cheek.

-4-

Wasn't long before the first vehicle turned up the drive, and all you had to do was listen to the sound of that big engine to know it was the Hodges. Bucky'd hoped Chessie and Briar wouldn't get there first. Then again, I don't think he would've been happy to see the Reverend and Belle either. Either way, he couldn't help but flinch at the sound of the truck doors being shut. Slammed, I should say, and so hard it was a wonder the windows in those doors held. I expect that was when Bucky started to think his grand plan might not be so grand at all.

"Sounds like they're pretty mad," he told Angela.

"You guess?" She eased the curtain aside, peeking out. "You fool enough to arrest John David, Chessie ain't gonna throw a party for you. And you do it on a night like this one we had? I swear, Bucky, sometimes you're just so *stupid*."

Bucky ignored that. Stupid or not, he was doing what he could the best way he knew. "They got guns?"

"No."

Briar's fist hit the door. Angela fluttered the curtain, removing all notion of stealth. The back door squeaked open and shut. Scarlett came in with her head low and her cheeks flushed. John David looked much the same. The mayor ignored it.

"This ain't gonna work, Buck," he said.

"It will, Wilson," Bucky told him. "John David, you stand right there. This all goes south, you remember the kindness we've showed you."

Bucky took hold of the knob and inhaled deep, then opened the door to Chessie's face.

"We had an agreement," she said. No *Hello*, no *May I come in?* Straight to business, that was Chessie Hodge. She and Briar pushed Bucky aside and walked into the Vests' living room like it was their own. "Only reason I supported Wilson's fool idea of appointing a sheriff was he promised the family business would be left alone. Now here I stand, wasting my time because our new lawman's as drunk on power as our mayor, when we should all be in town trying to figure out what hell's coming next. What were you thinking, Bucky?"

"I had to, Chessie."

"Had to, you say? No. *No*, Bucky. What you had to be doing was trying to get a town that's done lost its mind to quit shootin' at each other long enough to shoot at whatever demon Alvaretta's sent us. Come on, John David."

"Stand right there, John David," Bucky said. "Ain't everybody here yet."

Chessie gritted her teeth. "Don't you test me, Sheriff."

Bucky put his hands out. "I'm not trying to, Chessie. But he's got to wait. Reverend and Belle are coming. Raleigh's nowhere to be found, but Angela got hold of Landis."

"What you got the council coming for?" Briar asked.

"Because it's time we get a handle on things. I think I got an idea, and after I talked to Wilson, he agreed."

Agree or not, the mayor only sat there silent. His eyes had gone red, his cheeks puffy and wet. Scarlett had moved beside him, and yet he didn't seem to know she was there at all. Now sure, there was a rage to that man by then at the thought of losing his grip on the town he loved. You can bet there was a hurt inside him as well. But you ask me, what Wilson most looked was scared, and not of Chessie Hodge.

The Ramsays were next to arrive, Naomi in tow. She and Belle went to John David as soon as they saw him there. Belle stood a good three inches shorter than her son and a good fifty pounds lighter, yet her embrace looked to cover every inch of his body. He held her and held Naomi as the muscles in his right arm bulged from trying to calm the tremors in his sister's body. I think it was that sight alone that kept the Reverend from strangling near everybody there—Chessie and Briar for ruining his boy, Bucky for daring to arrest him, and the mayor for starting this whole mess all those years ago. Not to mention John David himself, for being such an all-around disappointment to the good Ramsay name.

He glared at Bucky. "This why you ran off and left us all there? To go arrest my son?"

Chessie's ears perked up at that, as did everyone else's.

"Wasn't nothing more I could do in town, Reverend," Bucky said. "Ruth was dead, all the shooting had stopped. Stu'd gone."

"So you decide to harass John David?" Belle asked.

Briar spoke up: "Who told you where he'd be, Bucky?" to which Bucky responded by waving his hand and saying he'd been in the Holler long enough to know where every road went and what every road was used for. He looked around for the Fosters.

"Where's Landis?"

"Not coming," Belle said. "He won't leave the grocery. Said he saw Stu there himself. Landis is scared he'll come back."

"Well, we can go ahead and do this anyway. You got a vote,

and Raleigh will go along with whatever Chessie says. Reverend, you can speak for Landis."

"What are we speaking on?" Belle asked.

"Charges, first," Bucky said. "I got John David for improper use of a vehicle and trafficking illegal goods, namely oxy and shine."

Briar puffed up. "Weren't no oxy in that load, Buck, and he done dropped the shine off fore you pulled him over."

"So you're saying there was shine, Briar? Okay, then."

Chessie turned and slapped her husband across the face. Bucky couldn't help but grin. It was the first time he'd ever outsmarted a proper criminal.

"Charges stand, then," he said. "Bail's next. I don't know who's supposed to set that."

The Reverend didn't either. Nor did Wilson. Far as they knew, nothing like that had ever come up in Crow Holler.

"Figured as much," Bucky said. "Guess that responsibility falls to me then, since there ain't no judge and I'm sheriff. I'd say a million ought to ensure John David stays in town long enough to face trial."

Chessie snorted. "A million dollars? You lost your mind, Bucky."

"Probably so. Better make it two million then, just to be safe. You got that much stuffed in your mattress to get John David out of custody, Chessie? Preacher, you think you can take up that much in a special collection during tomorrow's revival?" Bucky didn't wait for an answer. "No? Well then, that's a shame. Guess that means John David's remanded to my custody. That sound good with you, John David?"

Wasn't nobody who could say anything; it had all happened too fast. A tired grin crept over John David's face. Didn't nobody else understand what was happening, but I think he did. You gotta watch that boy. He ain't stupid, I'll give him that.

"You can't do this, Bucky," he said.

"Can and will. But I'll tell you what. You can go on back with Chessie and Briar if you want, though I'd rather you try and make peace with your proper family. It'd look good at trial. Come the morning, though, John David'll have to be in my care. He'll be my responsibility until it's time for his trial. That means I'll have to keep him close, even if it pains me. You'll have to be with me wherever I go and no matter what I do, even if it's on official business. Can't have you running off."

Chessie started to grin.

"Thing is," Bucky said, "the days might get some dangerous now, especially with what all happened tonight. I guess you might as well bring a gun along, John David, when I'm out conducting business. And just in case people want to go and try to take a pop at you for being among the town's felonious element, I reckon it'd be best if you carried a badge too. For your own protection, of course. Still got my constable one. Guess you can borrow that."

"What are you saying?" the Reverend asked. "You want John David to be constable?"

"Didn't say that," Bucky said. "You hear me say that, John David?"

"Nosir," John David managed. "But I won't do it. Told you already, I'm done fighting."

"Fighting's never done. Told you already too." He turned to them all. "Look, y'all want me to be sheriff, okay. That's all I ever wanted, and I don't care why it was you finally let me now. Fact is, I said yes, and it was my word I gave. I mean to do the best I'm able, but I can't do it alone. This has gotten too big. Someone died tonight. Somebody we all knew. It'll get worse if we don't do something to get our town back, and John David's the man I need. Man I want. But since it'll mean a badge and gun, I guess I'd like the town's approval so there's no questioning after. Wilson, he's already agreed."

The Reverend shot forward, putting a finger into the mayor's face. "You mean to sacrifice my son? Haven't I done enough for you, Wilson?"

"Wasn't just *me*, Reverend," Wilson said, and though everybody there thought that meant our mayor hadn't decided to draft John David alone, I can tell you it didn't. "We all gotta stand now."

Bucky nodded and turned to the Hodges. "Chessie, I know your vote's Raleigh's. You understand now why I had to do this?"

"Don't mean I got to like it."

"No, it don't. You and Briar'll have to tend the family business alone for now, but that's a small price to pay in the long run. Whatever it was come through town tonight and however many, it'll be back for us all. Don't think you're immune, and don't think the witch fears you."

Scarlett had kept quiet this whole while, letting the adults have their say and tasting the salt off John David's face on her lips. But now she moved away from Wilson to Chessie's side and took her hand. Chessie bent down. No words passed between the two of them. Plenty was said nonetheless.

Chessie lifted her head and said, "John David, you'll stay at Bucky's side. He'll keep you safe, and you'll do the same for him."

"Thank you, Chessie," Bucky said.

He turned to the Reverend next. David's blessing would be the hardest, and that's why Bucky had saved him for last. Belle never gave her husband the opportunity to say no.

"You do with him what you think's best, Sheriff," she said. She kissed her son on the very cheek Cordelia had earlier. "But you keep him safe."

John David said, "Don't guess I got a say in this?"

"Nope," Bucky told him. "Why you think I arrested you?"

-5-

Strange to say, the only peaceful spot in all of Crow Holler that night was the little cabin on Campbell's Mountain. Alvaretta had kept the lanterns lit inside and put still more out, where they glowed soft against all that hard darkness. She preferred the black but her companion did not, though there was light enough through the windows that he had come out onto the porch to join her.

He handed her the prize he'd found. She took the bit of bone and closed her fingers around it without looking, mumbled a thank you neither one of them quite heard. Alvaretta had no time for such things. Her eyes were to the sky.

"On the morrow," she said. "That's when they'll come. And come they will. For me, and for you."

She looked beside her, listening to what may have been growling. Or laughter. Alvaretta didn't know, though she'd long thought the two sounded near enough the same. Somewhere out in the trees, her children barked.

"Let'm starve tonight," she said. "Get the children nice and hungry. They'll feast come the blood moon." She looked at the one beside her. "I smell it on the air. There's a cold wind blowing, and it'll sink to bone. The mountain speaks. We got work. I know what to do."

This time there was no confusion on her face about what she heard.

Laughter.

XII

Alvaretta's spy. Scarlett warns.
No escape. The arrests. Chessie surrenders.

-1-

My, would you look at that sun. Near gone already and not yet suppertime. That's the thing about the Holler, friend. Easiest place in the world to let a day slip right by, and here I've sat jabbering all this while. Well, I'm almost done. One more day's all I got to tell you about, that night of the blood moon, and it won't take long. I'll make sure to have you down the road and gone by dark. That's when they come, you know. Whole mess of them, and if they ever took a shine to finally come for me, all I got to defend myself with is this old cane. It's a sad thing, friend. This was once a safe place for an old man like me, but it ain't no more. Holler's full of them now. But say here, don't you worry. You'll be back in civilization before you know it. And my, won't you have a tale to tell. Ha!

I expect everyone shut themselves up in their houses the night before with Ruth Mitchell on their minds, and how it wasn't the demon who'd gotten her but one of our own. Reverend tossed and turned that whole night, thinking on devil's footprints right outside his church doors. He near woke Belle more than once with a mind to finally confess everything about Stu Graves. Near, I said. David never did. It's pride that leads people to their sinning, that's what I always thought, and it's pride still that makes them hang on to the memory of what they done.

Pastor Ramsay preached that confession was balm for the soul. No doubt he'd flirted with that idea early on, when Naomi had first been struck by the witch. But now it was like he'd grown accustomed to even the twitches and sufferings his daughter endured, so much that he could no longer remember a time without them. David had grown numb, you see. I think we all had. Cordelia could walk down the street in the days leading up to the demon's coming to town and not even turn a head, because we'd got used to her face looking so sickly. Nobody paid much attention to the grocery looking the way it did, all busted up and emptied, because most still had their cupboards full. The schools were closed, but it felt like they'd always been.

What I'm trying to tell you is life found its own rhythm again. Even in Alvaretta's shadow, we could see things as normal. We got used to sick children and looking over our shoulders. Go ahead and call that a good thing. Say it's the triumph of the human will or a model of adaptation, I'll call you crazy. Anybody who can get used to something like that ain't fit to call themselves human. They're animals, nothing more, and that's what Reverend Ramsay decided. Bucky sat up all night trying to figure out what he was gonna do, Wilson and Hays and John David the same, but our Reverend had already made up his mind. It wasn't no longer his job to rid the town of sin. His was to rid it of sinners.

The sun had yet to rise over the mountains on that last morning when John David reported for work at Bucky's door and the pastor knocked at Wilson's. I guess it all come down to father and son that day, though neither knew it.

Angela had coffee ready, as did Scarlett. John David told Bucky they should spend their first (and only, as it would happen) day as partners calming people's fears and poking around for anything on Ruth's killer. It'd been an accident is what John David said. Had to be, Ruth being shot like that. Somebody got spooked, and now whoever'd done it was too scared to come forward. Bucky thought on that as Cordelia waited by the window for Hays. She'd texted him earlier, saying she had to talk about things. She told her parents they were going up to the grocery to help clean things up. Course, that was a lie.

At the mayor's kitchen table across town, the Reverend told Wilson that Ruth's death hadn't been an accident at all. It was vengeance, nothing more, and it could've just as easy been either of them who ended up dead on the church steps. My, but that was an argument. David saying all this had to stop and the mayor asking how, each of them blaming the other for the mess everybody'd found themselves in, and you can bet Scarlett heard most of it even if the mayor had sent her to her room. About the only thing Crow Holler's most important citizens agreed upon was just that—they were needed now, more than ever, and so their secret had to stand. And they agreed on this one other thing: More people would die unless they did something. Alvaretta would see to it. What they needed, the Reverend said, was an end. What they needed was Alvaretta's spy. Get him, and you'll get the witch.

Wilson said that all sounded well and good, but didn't nobody know who Alvaretta's spy was. That's when David reached into his pocket and pulled out the slips of paper Angela had given him before revival the night before.

"Maybe not," he said, "but I know where to start."

-2-

By the time they got to the council building that morning, John David had almost convinced Bucky his view of things was right. Granted, that sounded a whole lot more appealing to the sheriff than the alternative. Sure, it could've been an accident. People were shooting at everything that moved the night before. Who's to say Ruth Mitchell wasn't just in the wrong place at the wrong time? But there was one problem with all that: it didn't explain all them footprints. Try as he could, John David didn't have an answer to that.

Bucky pulled on the doors to the council building and found them locked. He knocked until he saw Scarlett looking out from the window in Wilson's office. She met them out front and then locked the door behind them. The piece of paper on her pad was already filled out, like she'd expected them:

Daddy says nobody else can come in until you find out who killed Ruth.

"Your daddy scared?" John David asked.

She flipped the page over to reveal more words. Bucky smiled. Scarlett was a bright one.

He said Stu is coming for us next. Something's wrong with him. I don't know what. The Reverend and him had a fight this morning. He's as scared as Daddy is.

"I'll go talk to him," Bucky said. "John David's got an idea on what happened last night. Makes some sense."

Scarlett led them down the hall to the mayor's office. She stopped at the closed door and raised a finger like she was telling them to either be quiet or be careful.

Bucky knocked and opened the door. John David followed him inside. The shades were drawn tight, all the lights off. You could barely see Wilson's shape in the chair behind the desk. A pistol rested on the blotter.

"What you doing sitting in the dark, Wilson?" Bucky asked.

The mayor spoke, but only to his daughter: "Scarlett, why don't you go check the doors one more time. I gotta have a talk with our sheriff and constable."

Scarlett went out but didn't bother checking the locks. She leaned against the wall and kept her ear close to the door, listening.

"Took everything I had to come in this place today," Wilson said. "But I'm here. Town needs me. Especially after Ruth."

"About that," Bucky said. His foot got to jumping up and down, nervous. "John David thinks . . . Wilson, can I turn on some lights? I can barely see you."

"Leave them off."

Bucky rolled his eyes. "Okay. John David thinks what happened to Ruth was an accident."

"You see them tracks all over town, John David?"

"I did," John David said. "But that's got nothing to do with what happened to Ruth, unless whatever made them prints can pull a trigger."

"You forget Alvaretta has aid."

"I haven't. But why shoot Ruth? She was just a kid when Stu died."

"Ruth wasn't the target. I was."

Bucky's foot stilled. "You, Wilson? Why'd Alvaretta want you?"

"That don't matter, Buck. You don't need to know that. But I need to know something. I need to know why you're keeping things from me." He slid the papers the Reverend had given him across the desk. "You got a list of suspects you don't bother to let me know about? I gotta get it from David, who got it handed to him by Angela?"

Bucky stared at the names. "They ain't suspects, Wilson. That's just gossip."

"Gossip's all we got, and it's as good a place to start as any. Reverend agrees, even though he said Belle liked to pitch a fit over it. I need y'all to go bring these people in for questioning."

John David picked up the papers and read off the names. "Hays? Medric? The doc? Chessie? Wilson, we've known these people our whole life."

"Maybe," Wilson said. "Or maybe we just thought we did. Never did like Hays Foster. That boy's about two fries short of an order, and we all know it. I know how things are with him and Cordelia, Bucky. How she . . . is. But I need him down here. We all know Medric's hiding something too. He's acted funny ever since he come up to the hospital. And don't nobody know where he was last night."

"He was with me," Bucky said. "He was out there looking for Stu with me."

"I need him to answer some questions. The doc too."

John David started laughing. "He's your brother-in-law, Wilson. You can't think he'd have anything to do with this."

"He's also the only one determined to convince everybody ain't nothing wrong with our girls but some loose wiring in their heads, and that's a lie. Danny Sullivan never cared to fit in with this town, never bothered to learn our ways. He don't even come to church half the time."

"I don't either," John David said. "You gonna question me too?"

"I do got a couple for you, as a matter of fact. You know anything of Chessie's involvement with the Circle?"

Bucky looked like he'd just been punched. "The Circle? Wilson, ain't been Klan round here since before we was born."

Wilson didn't take his eyes off John David. "Well?"

"You're out of your mind," John David said.

"No, I think I'm thinking more clear than I have in a long while, son. Chessie's been trying to take this town over for her own use for years, and the only person between her and what she wants is me. Why not use Alvaretta? Why not get help from the one person who'd love to see us all burn? And why not fix everything up nice and pretty so Bucky'd have no other choice but ask you to be our new constable?"

John David shook his head. "I'm not doing this."

"You will, or I'll call down to Mattingly and get Sheriff Barnett up here. I'll make sure you get locked away for so long you'll forget what the sun looks like. One call's all I need, boy. I'll tell him I saw you put two barrels into Ruth Mitchell's chest myself. I don't care what your momma'll say, and I don't care about Chessie Hodge none either. This here's bigger than you. Bigger than all of us."

"You wouldn't do that, Wilson," Bucky said.

"You think I won't? I made you the law here, Buck. I can take that away. Time's come to make the hard choices, and that's what I'm doing." He pointed to the papers in John David's hand. "I want them people in here today. I'll extend charity enough that it'll be you two who brings them in instead of a lynch mob, but I don't trust them. I'm getting Raleigh to set up roadblocks in case one of them gets word and decides to run. Either way, they'll all stand in church tonight and give an account. It's time we get some answers."

-3-

Scarlett listened till she'd heard her father's list of suspects, then she walked as fast and quiet as she could away from the mayor's shut door, taking the phone from her pocket. She might've no longer been master of her tongue, but her fingers were still her own.

I don't know if that girl even suspected what had gone wrong inside her father. More likely, she thought what had overcome the mayor was nothing short of a furtherance of the very curse she herself was responsible for unleashing on our town. That being the case, Scarlett shouldered the burden of trying to make things right again. And that wouldn't start with allowing Bucky and John David to bring in Medric and Chessie and even Hays, whom Scarlett had never liked. No, it would start another way.

She'd already lost so much, and if her daddy didn't stop what he meant to do, Scarlett would lose the little she had left. It had been a hard thing, losing her momma. It was hard still. Not just on Scarlett and not just on Wilson, but on them both together. Tonya Bickford had always been the soft middle between her equally hard husband and daughter, keeping them from scraping against each other and sparking a fire. There had been a time not long after she died that Scarlett had prayed God would bring her momma back and take her daddy instead. But Scarlett loved him, she truly did, and she'd never once set out to undo something her daddy had done. Not ever, until now.

Because the evil didn't lay in town, like her daddy and the Reverend believed. The evil lay on the mountain. It lay with the witch.

Scarlett reached the glass door her father had warned her to keep locked and scrolled through her phone for the numbers she needed. She paused on Medric's (thinking, no doubt, of all those crow feathers Hays had seen stuck to the undertaker's boots) and then pressed his name as well. To her, it must've felt the same as shielding Tully Wiseman's bare hand with her own.

The text she sent contained only four words:

GET OUT THEIR COMING!!!

-4-

I don't know how it was that Hays and Cordelia found themselves in bed together that morning, other than what I already

told you: Hays didn't have nobody left, and Cordy was hoping
to fill up on what small bit of love remained in him before telling him of their child.

As it happened, there had been no act. Them two only laid
against each other, and that seemed enough for them both. I
think it was a way for Hays to feel close to somebody and a way
for Cordelia to hang on to a thread of something that once might
have felt Supposed to Be but had increasingly become a Never
Would. Hays had changed. Everyone had, really—another ten-
tacle of Alvaretta's curse. It was as though the whole of Crow
Holler had discovered things long buried somewhere inside
them. Some, like her father, had found a kind of strength there.
Others, like her momma, had uncovered a kind of darkness.
And a few, like Hays, had seemed to find both and neither.

No talk of love or the future passed between them, nor did
Hays tell Cordy of the way he'd seen Medric's face the night
before. To tell her of that would be to place them both in danger. Cordelia would no doubt tell Bucky, and Bucky would go
after Medric to the sheriff's own end. No, Hays would have to
take care of Medric himself. He would have to find another
way, because Medric was a monster and the monsters had to
die.

Cordy's stomach pressed into his side. He flinched when he
felt a tear settle on his neck.

"I need to tell you thumthing, Hayth. About uth."

"What about us?"

Another tear. "I'm pwegnant."

Hays spun in the bed, knocking Cordelia in the stomach
with his knee. She made a clogged little *oomph!* sound that
looked to scare them both equally. Both of her eyes were stained
with tears. He saw a thin runner of snot leaking out from the
nostril she couldn't feel.

"You're *what?*" he said.

That only made Cordelia cry harder.

"You can't be pregnant. Cordy? Are you sure?"

She nodded.

"No," he said. "No, don't you tell me that. How could you do that to me?"

Cordelia shrank back, pulling the covers up. "How cud . . . ?"

"Does anybody know? Do your parents know?"

"Yeth."

The blood drained from Hays's face. "This can't be happening." He shook his head. "This can't be happening, Cordelia. No. Nonononono. This can't be happening."

"Hayth—"

Sitting up now, his legs tight against his chest and his hands to his knees, rocking slow like he'd fallen into some kind of trance, repeating those same words over and over—*Nonononono.*

But yesyesyesyesyes, friend.

I do believe that boy had settled on the idea that in a week full of bad moments, this one was worst. There'd be no escaping Hays's future now, that other curse he'd always kept in his head of produce prices and Tuesday specials. Coming home to a wife and a kid. Picking the grocery over the family, just like his own father had done.

Nonononono.

"Hayth, I'm thorry."

Sorry! Sorry, friend! Well, that would just fix everything now, wouldn't it? Yessir, that would set it all back to square one, all the way to that night in the back of the Camaro, when the very same *Please* and *I want to* that had once come out of Angela's mouth had come out of her daughter's. But instead of that, it would now be *We shouldn't* and *Let's wait* all because Cordelia was *Sorry.*

"This is it," Hays said. "This is my end."

But it wasn't, friend. Not yet. Because right then, his cell phone chirped.

Hays reached for it even as Cordelia told him no, they had to talk about this, what was going to happen next. He didn't hear her as he read what Scarlett had sent him. He didn't hear anything. The world had fallen away.

He scrambled from the bed, reaching for his jeans and shirt, reaching for his shoes as a knot of panic inside Cordelia began to grow and harden like the baby in her womb.

"I got to get out," he said.

"Vhat?"

"I have to get out," he said again. "They're almost here. Scarlett found out. I don't know how, but she did."

He scrambled for his keys as Cordelia began to scream, wanting to know what was happening, wanting to talk about the baby, Hays screaming back *The baby, the baby, I wish that baby was dead*. He left her in a ball on the bed but found care enough to beg Cordy to go home. Go find Bucky. Tell them they were coming—the monsters. They were coming for us all.

-5-

Hays wasn't the only one who had it in his mind to get out the Holler right then. By the time he'd found the keys to the Camaro and backed it out of the garage, Medric had already gone from the funeral home.

He'd taken nothing but the clothes he wore. He'd watched Bucky and John David walk into the council building that morning, seen the way they'd stood there staring at the funeral home. And then came Scarlett's text. They'd come for him first, and for no other reason than the color of Medric's skin and the goodness of his heart.

The only reason he'd slipped past Bucky at all was John David had tried talking sense to Wilson. Now Medric barreled past the very spot you're parked now, friend, and he had the fear of the devil in his eyes.

Flying now, bringing his old car up to fifty on the potted dirt road that runs on down past where the Reverend had seen Stu Graves, blowing by the clinic in a blur. Aiming for the edge of town and freedom—freedom finally—from all he'd done. Looking on past the blue mountains that rose around him on all sides. Thinking of Richmond. That's where he'd go. He had kin there, and they wouldn't know what he'd done. He could start over. Do anything besides tend to the dead.

And he almost made it, friend. But as he rounded the last turn and neared the flat spot where Bucky had caught John David the night before, he saw ahead the two trucks set up in the road not a mile on. Four men, all armed. Medric couldn't tell their faces, but he didn't need to. The only thing he could do was stop before they saw him and make a slow drive back to town.

-6-

He got as far as the town line. That's where Hays found Raleigh Jennings waiting with a shotgun and a box full of shells, standing in front of the Cadillac he'd parked sideways in the road. Raleigh'd known it was Hays long before Hays even seen him. It was the Camaro, you see. That car sounded like nothing else in town.

Wilson had called early that morning after his meeting with the pastor. Told Raleigh to get some men together and block

Crow Holler off, and then he read off a list of people to watch for especially. Troublemakers all, that's what Raleigh said as he wrote down those names. Wilson agreed, then asked Raleigh if that was something he could handle. Raleigh said it would be no problem, he knew just the men to call for help.

The rest of the Circle were now scattered along the other roads leading to either Mattingly or the deep woods. Good men who knew how to protect a town.

Hays didn't slow.

Raleigh tried waving. When that didn't work, he racked his shotgun and leveled it at the windshield. That would be the boy's only warning. Twenty more yards, he'd get a face full of buckshot.

Hays hit the brakes, nearly losing the Camaro's back end in the process. He fishtailed on the dirt and nearly went sideways before finally gaining control, stopping in a cloud of dust barely beyond the scatter-gun's reach.

Raleigh stepped forward to close the gap and yelled, "Out the car."

Hays opened the Camaro's door. He eased out with his hands high. What little color that boy kept in his face was gone. His arms shook like they each weighed more than the world.

"Always thought there was something wrong with you," Raleigh said. "Now I guess I know for sure. Where you running off to, Hays?"

"You have to let me pass, Principal Jennings. You gotta let me go. They're coming."

"Who is?"

"Them."

"Well, the mayor says nobody comes in or out. He'd like to have a few words with you."

"Don't take me back to town," Hays said. His voice cracked. "They'll kill me."

Raleigh smiled. "You don't get in my car right now, boy, I'll kill you first."

"You can't."

"Can't?" Raleigh said. "You ain't in no position at all to tell me what I *can't*. Playtime's over. Order's gotta come back to this Holler, and I'm the one to do it. Time to put things right, and that means taking you back to town. You think of a reason why I can't do that, you better let me know now."

Hays had one.

"I know who killed Ruth."

-7-

No one was home at the funeral parlor, or at least no one answered the door. John David said they couldn't go in without a warrant. Bucky told him that was a good point but not to go getting a big head about it, because all that was just an easy excuse to go against Wilson's orders.

"Whose side you on here, anyways?" Bucky asked.

"Side where everybody lives."

They tried the grocery next. Hays wasn't there and neither was Cordelia, but Landis and Kayann were. They didn't know where their boy was. Kayann asked what was going on, and that's when Bucky told them the mayor and the Reverend wanted Hays at church that night for questioning. John David tried answering when Landis asked what sort of questioning that might be, but Bucky held up a hand and shushed him. Concerning the witch, our sheriff said, and then he said Wilson had a list of people, one of which happened to be their boy, who'd been seen or heard doing some awful strange things in the days since the Curse.

Well, I guess you can imagine what happened next. Didn't

matter Bucky was still carrying Chessie's old shotgun or that John David was there and had seen war. Landis said he'd sooner die than see his son brought up to some kangaroo court over something he didn't do. Bucky tried saying it wouldn't be a court at all, it'd be in the church and only a couple questions, but he never got that out because Kayann started throwing things at him. Boxes, busted bottles, half a head of lettuce that had somehow gone unclaimed during the run on the grocery and had since rotted, anything she could reach. Bucky had one hand over his face and the other trying to hang on to his gun, yelling for Kayann to stop before he ran her in on a charge of assaulting an officer of the law. Landis started screaming that Stu Graves had been there the night before, right there next to his *office*, and if Bucky and John David should be looking for anybody, it was what Alvaretta had raised up. Took John David every bit of muscle he had to drag the sheriff out of there. He told Bucky maybe he should do the talking next time.

Neither of them was too fired up about going to Chessie's, so Bucky decided to try the clinic next. They were nearly there when Angela called. Cordelia had walked all the way home from Hays's house. She'd cried herself into such a fit that it took Angela near half an hour to understand what had happened. Somehow (Cordy wouldn't say exactly, though Angela said she believed Kayann had gotten word to her son), Hays had found out he was wanted. He'd gone, and Cordy didn't know to where.

Bucky hung up and repeated all that to John David, who just sat there staring out the window. Bucky said aloud what he knew his new constable was thinking: "I don't see a good end to any of this."

It was quiet at the Sullivans' place. Nothing at all in the lot and no patients lined up outside, as that part of Alvaretta's curse seemed to have ended so a worse one could begin. Danny's car wasn't in its spot, but the sign on the door said *Open*.

Before they got out of the car, John David said, "You let me try this one, Bucky."

"Well, I got to do something, John David. I'm the sheriff, you're just the constable."

"Be my backup, then. Stand there and look pretty. And keep that scatter-gun down. Makes me nervous."

Bucky looked through the windshield, watching the door. "You want a pistol? Got one in the backseat. It's a beater, but it shoots straight."

John David opened the door. "I don't like guns."

Bucky followed. He let the shotgun lay in the seat but reached back for that old pistol anyway, tucking it in his belt at the back. John David could say all he wanted about keeping things calm; after hearing what Angela had said about Hays, Bucky didn't have a good feeling about whatever would come next.

Maris stepped out onto the cement porch as they got out. She put a hand to her forehead to shield her eyes from the sun and parted her lips into a grin.

"Angela told me you went and got yourself some help, Buck," she said. "Where's your badge, John David?"

John David smiled. "Didn't think I'd need one to come visit the doctor, Maris."

"That what y'all are doing? Visiting? Because I just got off the phone with Belle, and she's gone half mad because the Reverend's got it in his head to round up half the town and set'm up in front of the church tonight. You two wouldn't know anything about that now, would you?"

John David let that be. "Doc around?"

"No, and I don't know where he went. What's your business with him?"

"Just need a word."

She nodded and grinned again. "Buck, you want to add anything to this conversation?"

Bucky shrugged. "I'm just standing here to look pretty."

"Maris," John David said, "truth is me and Bucky don't want to be out here at all. Mayor's orders, though, and Bucky's just loyal enough to say Wilson's orders are what we gotta carry out. Everybody in town's scared, sure you know that. Scared of the witch, scared of Stu. But they're scared of whoever it is that's been visiting Alvaretta most of all, because we don't know who that is."

"What's that got to do with Danny?" she asked.

"Well, somehow his name's come up. Just people talking. But there's been some question of why he ain't been out to church all week and why he's the only one seems to think whatever's wrong with my sister and the others is something other than the witch. What we'd like Danny to do is come down to the church tonight, talk to everybody. Just put folks at ease. So if you know where he's gone, we'd be obliged if you'd tell us."

"I only got a quarter tank in the car, Maris," Bucky said. "I can't be running all over town looking for anybody. I ain't got paid yet."

"I don't know where Danny went, if you got to know. And shame on y'all. Wilson's my own brother."

"I know," Bucky said, "and I'm sorry, Maris. Like John David told you, we don't really want to be out here."

"Well then, you go tell Wilson if he wants Danny, he can come out here and get him on his own instead of sending his flunkies."

"We ain't flunkies, Maris," Bucky said. "We're the law."

"Law was better when we didn't have any, and I ain't the only one to think so."

John David looked about ready to remind Bucky he was

just supposed to be looking pretty when they all saw Danny Sullivan's car leading a cloud of dust up the road. The doctor pulled in with a grin and popped the door open with, "Morning, gentlemen. What brings you out? Not more trouble, I hope."

"Trouble enough," Maris said.

John David asked, "Where you been this morning, Danny?"

"Oh, just about. Had to check on some patients. Congratulations on your new employment, by the way. I'd dare say it's more honest work than what Chessie can offer."

"Not by much," John David said, "and not by choice. These patients you seen. Anybody we know?"

"I expect so. Why?"

"Because Wilson thinks you're Alvaretta's spy," Maris said.

The doctor stood there like Maris had spoken in some kind of foreign language. He chortled and said, "That's absurd."

Bucky kicked a rock at his feet and watched it go tumbling. I don't expect this was how he'd thought being a policeman would work, too much worrying and having to do things you didn't think should be done at all. Danny went on about how Wilson had never liked him and all the power had finally rotted his brother-in-law's brain, and Bucky kept looking at that rock that had come to a stop right behind the doctor's tire, right in the groove of one of the treads, and wasn't that tread a funny-looking one? Didn't it look familiar somehow—

Wasn't it—?

He reached for the pistol he'd stuck in the back of his pants, this time remembering to free the safety. Maris screamed as Bucky's trembling hands tried steadying the barrel. Danny Sullivan backed away with his hands held high. John David came forward with his hands the same, asking Bucky what in the holy hell he was doing.

"It's you," Bucky said. "Doc? It's you, ain't it?" The barrel went from Danny's chest to his head, to his leg, back to his chest. He was scared, sure enough (and wouldn't you be, friend?), but it was more than that. I think Bucky couldn't find his aim because his eyes had started to tear up.

John David stopped at that question. He looked at Danny now.

"Doc?" Bucky asked. He took a deep breath and steadied the pistol. "You been going out to Alvaretta's house?"

Faced with that, Danny Sullivan had no choice but to answer the truth.

-8-

Bucky shook so hard he had to lower the pistol before his finger jerked and he killed the doctor right there. It got awful quiet in that little parking lot. For a while, nobody even breathed. Doc still had his hands raised and Bucky looked about to puke. John David's eyes had gone from warm to cold. And Maris? Well, Maris couldn't believe what she'd just heard.

"Danny?" she asked. "What you saying?"

"It was me. I did it."

Then it got quiet all over again, all except Maris, who started saying No much like Hays had awhile earlier, over and over again. Bucky said she couldn't ride with them into town because she'd have to bring Danny's car as evidence. John David collected himself enough to suggest Danny going out to Alvaretta's wasn't a crime. Bucky said aiding the woman who'd both sickened his little girl and raised up the dead sure did sound like a crime to him. Maris looked to protest but didn't. No way that woman believed her husband of near fifty years had anything to do with Alvaretta Graves. And yet all of what Danny had just admitted had put a hole in Maris's heart, and out of it leaked every bit of moxie she held.

John David came up behind the doctor. He said, "Go on and put your hands down, Danny," and helped him toward the sheriff's car. Gravel crunched from up the road. Maris made her way to Bucky, wanting to plead with him, but Bucky's attention had settled more on the car driving past. Didn't nobody in town drive a black car but Medric, him saying it went with his funeral duties. Bucky saw the grill come into view through the trees, then the hood, and then there was Medric behind the wheel, staring straight into Bucky's eyes. The car went on past before it stopped and backed up. Medric swung into the lot behind Danny's car. He got out and raised his arms.

"Buck," he said. "I need help."

"Medric, me and John David been looking for you all morning."

"I know it. Want to turn myself in."

Bucky wrinkled his nose. "Well, I appreciate the offer, Medric, but there's no need now. Doc here just confessed, so I guess we don't need you."

"Don't know what Doc's got to do with things," Medric said, "but I'm the man you need. You just keep me safe, Bucky. I'll let you take me in, but you and John David can't let nobody get me."

"He's the one you want," Maris said. She winced as she did. It was like a part of her realized this was a chance to get her husband back, but not before another part said she'd have to sacrifice Medric to do it and still another said that didn't matter right now. "You let Danny go, John David. Turn him loose now."

John David wouldn't, not yet. "Why you the man we need, Medric?" he asked.

"Because it was me," Medric told them. "I did it. I helped the witch."

-9-

In the end, Bucky decided the only thing he could do was go on and arrest them all.

They left the clinic in a line of three cars—Bucky in the lead with Doc Sullivan in the backseat, followed by Maris in their car and John David driving Medric's. John David had said he shouldn't drive Medric's car, specially with Medric so scared he wasn't going anywhere. Bucky said no, that's the way things had to be done now.

The former Marine-slash-criminal and current constable did as Bucky said. I'm guessing John David thought he'd take that time to have a word with Medric, try to figure out what the world the man had done. It didn't work. Medric sat in the backseat and uttered not a word the whole way to town. Ended up, John David just said he'd be praying. Strange thing for him to say; most in the Holler thought going to the Lord was something that boy'd long given up. But I guess in times like that, praying's about all you can do.

They all pulled into town that way, looking like some sad parade that drew folk not to cheer and clap, but condemn. I don't know how word got out of what Wilson and the Reverend had sent Bucky to do. My guess falls to Angela and the way that woman always slobbered for a bit of attention, and I suppose that's right. Cordelia had been so shaken by Hays that Angela had called Belle Ramsay for prayer. Belle, believing there was no better place to seek the Lord than an uncomfortable church pew, ran right out to haul them both back to town. They arrived just as Bucky and the rest entered town, and now Angela stood front and center at the doors of the council building along with about thirty others. Scarlett come running out when she seen John David in Medric's car. Wilson even dared peek out of his office to watch it all. Belle come down the steps from the church with a worried look on her face. The Reverend followed right behind and nearly tripped.

Bucky got out and told Danny it'd be best if he just stayed in the backseat a minute. He turned to tell Maris the same, but she was already out of her car and running toward Wilson with hell itself in her eyes. Screaming at her brother, telling Wilson he should be ashamed. Believe you me, Wilson was. Fear can do that to you.

What got Maris calm enough to set aside the murder in her heart was the Reverend. He told Maris they'd straighten it all out soon as they talked to Danny, and then he had Scarlett take her on inside. John David brought Medric up. I'd say close to thirty people stood by then, wanting to know what was happening. John David saw no need to cement the idea that Medric had done something wrong. Keeping his back to the man they'd brought in gave the impression Medric could just turn around and walk off if he wanted.

Bucky motioned for the doctor, who got out of the car slow. That crowd pressed in. Angela had in the last minutes managed to squeeze through everybody and stood close enough to smell Danny's sweat as he passed. He went inside to where Maris waited. Medric trailed behind like a lost puppy.

Wilson asked John David, "Medric say anything to you on the way over?"

"No. But he knows something. Bucky says Hays took off."

"Took off after he broke my girl's heart," Angela shouted.

Kayann Foster shouted back, "You wait right there, Angela. Hays is guilty of nothing, and you know it."

Angela spun around. "Don't you give me that. Everybody in this town knows that boy's half crazy, and they know you're the one who turned him that way." Saying it with venom in her words. "Bout time you get knocked down a notch, Kayann Foster. That boy got my Cordelia *pregnant*."

Bucky winced as everybody's jaw dropped. Doc Sullivan bent his head.

"Pregnant?" Landis asked.

"Stop it," the Reverend said. "Both of you. Landis, if you know where Hays is—"

"I don't know," Landis said. "Can't you people see that? I don't know where he is. And even if I did, I wouldn't tell you. He's my son."

"Son or not, he needs to be found. We just want to talk to him, Landis. That's all."

"He couldn't've left town," Bucky said. "Raleigh's got everything blocked."

"Raleigh took the roadblock off," Wilson said. "Called me a little bit ago. Said nobody's seen nothing all day, and he was just wasting time he could be spending looking for whoever killed Ruth."

"Do you think Medric did it?" Angela asked. "Or Danny? They've already confessed to being spies."

"They confessed?" Kayann asked. "See? Hays is innocent."

Wilson said, "Right now, nobody's innocent. There's two, there could be more. Bucky, you and John David find Hays. But the first thing you need to do is go out to the Hodge place and bring Chessie back."

Now believe me when I say that was something Bucky had no mind to do at all, and neither did John David. They'd sooner go to Alvaretta's and drag her to town than try the same with Chessie Hodge. If Hays had found out people were coming, surely Chessie had found out first. So it wasn't with no small measure of gratitude they heard a rumbling come from the other direction just then, and seen Briar's truck making a slow crawl up the road. He stopped in the middle of the street in front of the council building and got out to open the passenger door. Chessie parted the gathered like Moses through the Red Sea, that red hair of hers wild and her jaw set hard. She walked up to Wilson and offered no fear at all.

"Heard you were looking for me," she said. "Well, here I am."

XIII

The Circle. Confessions.
Wilson tells his secret. Hays makes a plan.

-1-

Hays could see nothing with the rag tied over his eyes. He gauged that Raleigh had driven nearly twenty minutes, putting them somewhere on the other side of town. They'd been walking at least twenty minutes more. Walking in the woods. He could tell because of the leaves crunching under his feet and the fresh smell of the pines and the way Raleigh kept steering him to the right or left, dodging trees.

The boy showed no fear. There'd been plenty of that back at the roadblock, and I don't think Hays cared much anymore that he hadn't acted brave. I think he would've messed himself on purpose if he'd thought that would've gotten that gun pointed somewhere else other than at him. It'd been some quick thinking, him putting two and two together to figure Raleigh would want the murderer of the woman he'd loved more than he'd want Hays. Then again, maybe it was all the Lord's doing. Hays probably thought that instead, him being born again now.

Either way, didn't take but a few seconds for Hays to go from Raleigh's catch of the day to Raleigh's best friend. He told the principal all about the curse of Alvaretta Graves, and how he'd seen Bucky and Medric running from the funeral home toward the council building the night before and then Medric running back alone a short time later. Hays told him Medric was a demon, and he swore to that truth upon his very salvation.

Raleigh had taken all that in with surprising ease, like he'd suspected something of that about Medric Johnston for a long while. And then he'd asked Hays a curious thing—"How would you like to become part of a secret group of men, son? People like-minded as you and me in battling the demons of this world."

It was yes from Hays. It was *Praise God, yes.*

Then came the drive and now the long walk through the woods, which was done in silence but for the occasional question of, "Are you sure it was Medric, son?" and "You ain't gonna tell nobody this, are you?" Hays nodded or shook his head from behind the rag, depending on the answer. Raleigh guided him on.

His eyes were covered, but Hays still had his ears and nose. He heard nothing of the forest itself, only their soft steps over the dirt and leaves, but it didn't take long for him to catch a whiff of smoke and feel a comforting fire warm his skin. Raleigh stopped him. He said don't move and don't take off your blindfold, then backed away. Hays turned a bit to one side and then another, like he could feel the presence of others around him.

"You all know this boy," Raleigh said. "Mayor gave me Hays Foster's name this morning from a list of those suspected of aiding the witch. This boy's here because I say he's innocent. He knows who killed Ruth, and that's why Wilson Bickford wants him. I accuse Wilson Bickford of being in league with the witch, because power craves power.

"Hays Foster says it was Medric Johnston killed Ruth. Says he seen Medric running back to his funeral shop alone after the shots was fired, and Medric wore a demon's face. I accuse Medric Johnston of being in league with the witch, because of the hate in his heart for those unlike hisself.

"The time has come for the good in Crow Holler to beat back the bad. Hays Foster, will you stand with us?"

Hays said, "I will."

"Will you swear to the Almighty Yahweh that you will keep the secrets you see this day and never divulge them?"

"I will."

"Will you swear to the blood of your kin to wage holy war on the lesser beasts and those who seek destruction upon our way of life?"

"I will."

"Then Hays Foster, I say take off your mask."

Hays did it slow so as not to rile them. His right hand gripped the bottom of the rag around his eyes and lifted it off. He winced. The first fingers of evening had drifted over the woods, but there was light enough from the lowering sun and the wide circle of torches he stood in to make him shield his eyes. Gathered at the circle's edges, fifteen cloaked and hooded men watched in silence.

Raleigh spoke: "Welcome to the Brotherhood of the Circle."

The men removed their hoods one by one, nodding to Hays as they did. The fire now felt hotter somehow, and farther reaching. Hays began rubbing the thighs of his jeans with his hands, looking ahead and to his sides and the back, watching them close in. Raleigh said, "Greet brother Hays," and Hays saw their hands outstretched not to shake his own but to grab him. He barreled past the two in his way before they could reach him, screaming as he sought the safety of the thick woods. The men took after him and then stopped when Raleigh called them back, saying there was no time, the boy had given them what they needed.

Hays kept running and did not look back, too fearful of what he might see chasing him. He'd been a fool all along and had nearly paid for it with his life, though I expect his mind paused enough to appreciate the irony. In the end, he knew it had been Alvaretta's curse that had saved him. That was the only way he could've seen the demon faces under all those masks.

-2-

John David went to talk to Medric, and Scarlett to tend to Chessie, but Wilson wanted to speak to his brother-in-law first. Danny was the important one.

He let Maris stay. That wasn't out of any love he had for his sister (of which there was plenty, don't get me wrong), but because Wilson had decided Alvaretta's plan to destroy his family would end there. He wanted Maris to hear it herself. He needed her to know.

Bucky wanted to do the questioning. Wilson said fine. Wouldn't look good to Maris if he did it himself, and why not let our sheriff enjoy this moment? He'd earned it. So much, in fact, that Wilson decided making that man sheriff had been one of the wisest things he'd ever done. He got the Reverend to join them, too, wanting both a witness to whatever Doc would say and someone to keep Maris calm should things get out of hand. I doubt even Bucky thought they would. The look on the doctor's face when they all walked into the little meeting room could only be described as defeat. Danny was ready to talk.

Maris went to the other side of the small table in the middle of the room where her husband sat and hugged him tight. She kissed his forehead and asked if he needed anything. Danny said all he needed was her forgiveness for all this trouble. Wilson, the Reverend, and Bucky took the other chairs. As he always did, David opened with prayer for a wisdom I believe all who gathered there never had.

"Danny," Bucky said, "just to start things out here, I want you to know it's the truth we're after. That's all I want from you, okay? Now for the mayor's and the Reverend's benefit, I want to ask you again: you been up to Alvaretta's?"

"I have," Danny said.

"And was it your tire marks I seen up at her cabin on the mountain?"

"I'm guessing so."

"Danny . . ."

"Well, I don't *know*, Bucky." It was about as close as Bucky had ever seen Doc to getting mad. "I wasn't there with you when you saw them. But the last time was the day before the kids went up to the mines. So, yeah, I guess. Those were my tire tracks you saw."

Bucky nodded and took a deep breath, moving on. "Did you kill Ruth Mitchell?"

"Bucky," Maris said.

"I gotta ask, Maris."

"No," Danny said. "I most certainly did not kill Ruth, nor would I even ponder such a horrible thing."

"How long you been going up to Alvaretta's?"

"I don't know. Years."

"Years?" Wilson asked, and Maris nearly did the same.

"Started not long after Maris and I moved back to Crow Hollow," Danny said. "I was trying to build a practice. I had to gain people's trust. Wilson, David, most of the people around here never even saw a doctor before I came. They'd get a cold or the flu, they were more likely to bury a mockingbird feather under a full moon than seek professional medical help."

"Don't make fun of us, Danny," the Reverend said.

Danny waved him off. "I'm sorry. I didn't mean that the way it sounded. But I wasn't trusted. Maris had grown up here, she had you for a brother, Wilson, but I was just the doctor from Away. It took awhile for people to come around, so I decided I'd go to them. Knock on their doors and introduce myself, ask if everyone's okay and if there was anything I could do. You remember that, Maris. How it was."

Maris nodded.

"Well, I got to know almost everyone that way. And people told me it was okay to go about people's houses, but I'd better keep a distance from Alvaretta Graves. I had no idea who she was."

"I remember you asking me," Maris said.

"I did, and you told me I never had to worry about Alvaretta Graves because she never came off the mountain. But can't you see that was cause enough for me to worry? An old woman up there, living all alone? For all we knew, she could be up there dead."

"Be a blessing if she was," Wilson told him.

"I tried putting it out of my mind, I swear I did. Then one day I was by there going to see a patient, and I saw that turn to her lane. I took it. I didn't even give myself time to ask what in the world I was doing, because I knew it was the right thing. I'm a doctor, don't you understand that? It's my job to care for people, no matter who they are."

"All them crows hanging from the trees didn't turn you back?" Bucky asked.

"I didn't see any crows," Danny said. "They didn't start showing up until years later. I guess by then, the loneliness had got her."

"Loneliness," the Reverend said. "You really think that's what it was now? After all she's done?"

"I don't think she's done anything."

Bucky said, "Your niece would say otherwise, Danny. So would my Cordelia. Now you best get back to your story, before one of us loses our temper."

The doctor apologized again. And so as the Hodges waited in another meeting room down the hall and John David sat down in front of Medric next door, Danny Sullivan recounted to our preacher and mayor and sheriff (as well as his own wife) how he'd nearly befriended the witch of Crow Holler. How that first time he'd barely got out of his car before Alvaretta chased him off with a shotgun and a mouth fouler than any he'd ever heard. How he'd gone back the next week with a sack of groceries from Foster's that he left in the yard without a word. How he'd come again the week after that with more and had finally gotten the chance to introduce himself. And that's how it'd gone since. Not weekly now, more once every month or two, always with what provisions he thought she'd need and occasionally some medicine she'd requested the time before—aspirin and, once, a bottle of cough syrup. Danny had never gotten closer than five feet to the front porch. That's where he'd park, just long enough to retrieve the groceries from the trunk and set them on the first step under Alvaretta's watchful glare.

"You ever see anybody else with her?" Bucky asked.

"No. Never. But I always got the sense she's protecting something. She always kept herself between me and the door, like she was afraid I'd try and go inside. And those crows. Some of them are hung up higher than she can reach."

"Maybe Medric did it," the Reverend said.

"Alvaretta never mentioned Medric to me. She never really talked at all, just accepted what I gave her."

"She never tried turning you against us?" Wilson said. "Never mentioned what'd happened to Stu?"

"No. I swear she didn't."

"You see?" Maris asked. "Danny didn't do anything."

"Danny did plenty," Wilson said, "and you know it. Taking groceries to the witch is aiding the witch, and that's something we don't do, Maris. She keeps to the mountain, we keep to town. That's how it's been and how it was supposed to stay."

"Well then, Danny wasn't the only one to break that truce. Case you forgot, the girls did too."

"I didn't do anything," Danny said. "Wilson, I know we

haven't always gotten along. And David, I know we've had our disagreements over religion and church and whatever else. But Bucky, I've known you over half your life and you've known me. You know I'd never do anything to hurt this town or anyone in it. Not willingly. All I did was try to give aid to an old woman."

"Ignorance is no excuse," the Reverend said. "You always turned your nose up at us, Danny. Not so much in words, but in how you acted. You think us backward for our ways and never once considered our ways are for your own good."

"What are you gonna do?" Maris asked. "My husband might be guilty of idiocy, but he didn't break a law, Buck."

Bucky knew that was right. "I don't think Danny's guilty," he said.

Reverend shook his head. "Maybe not of having a direct hand in what's been going on, but Danny's sure guilty of pride. He'll stand before church tonight and confess what he did, right along with whatever Medric's telling John David and whatever Chessie'll say next. There has to be an atonement," he said. "The man's gotta learn humility."

-3-

It was awful quiet in that little room next door to where Bucky and the rest argued. Medric had asked for some water. John David had done him one better and brought coffee from the pot in the mayor's office. It sat between them in a Styrofoam cup, barely sipped. The steam rose up in thin clouds.

"Medric," John David said, "I ain't ever questioned anybody on anything. Bucky just told me to come in here and try to talk to you, so that's what I'm gonna do. All the mayor and my daddy got in mind is to get you and the doc and Chessie in front of the church tonight. Ain't gonna be no violence. They just want . . . well, I don't know what they want. I guess they think having somebody to blame will make everybody else feel better. But you need to talk to me. I'm here to help you, and Bucky is too. But you got to tell me what's going on now, and what you meant when you said you helped Alvaretta."

Medric didn't say nothing for a long while, just watched the steam rise up from his coffee through a pair of saddened eyes. John David allowed the silence. He'd said all he needed to, and wasn't about to speak another word. Medric flicked the cup. Picked it up and took a sip. Then he let out a tired sigh.

"Thought I got out these mountains, I'd be okay." He grinned as though he found the notion funny. "I come up to the town line, there sits some men. Couldn't see who they was because I was still a far ways off. Seen their guns, though. I knew they was looking for me. Circle always has been, I guess. Just biding their time, waiting for a good enough excuse."

"Ain't no Circle, Medric," John David said. "Those were just people Wilson got up for some stupid reason. Klan's been gone from here for years."

He raised his eyebrows. "Chessie think so?"

"Chessie lives by a lot of facts that ain't so, but that's not one. I'd appreciate it if you didn't tell her I said that, though."

"More's gone on since you left here, John David. Holler's dying. People need a reason why that's other than themselfs. Gonna be me. Not just cause I'm colored, neither. For what I did."

"And what'd you do?"

You'd think what Medric said next would've had a harder time coming out than it did, friend. I mean, something like that? Well, it'd get that man in more trouble than he was already in. Whole lot more. But as it was, those four words slipped out of his mouth like they'd been greased. Guess it just felt good, finally having that weight off his soul.

"I took that body," he said.

"What body?"

"Stu's."

John David blinked. He could've heard Medric say just about anything and taken it all in stride. Wasn't much that could shock that boy, not after all John David had been through. But that did, friend. That shocked John David something plenty and stole whatever words he'd been ready to say. He reached down for Medric's cup of coffee and took a long sip himself. Wishing, probably, that he'd spiked it with some of Chessie's moonshine first.

Anguish burned across Medric's face. "I didn't have no choice," he said. "I thought I's doing right by it, John David. Town said Stu had to be buried here. Some stupid law the council or Wilson's daddy come up with, I don't know. And I didn't care. All that woman wanted was to bury her husband's bones on their *farm*. You know? The land he tended to and sweated over. She was heartbroken over it, raging against us all. So I buried him in the day and then dug him back up that night. Couldn't take the casket because it was too heavy for me to handle alone. Just wrapped him good and stowed him in the trunk. Alvaretta met me on the porch. Was all I could do to keep my wits. Was hell in her eyes, John David. Like a fire burning."

"I don't believe this. You robbed a *grave*, Medric."

He pleaded now: "Tell me what you would've done, John David. That woman was *hurting*. Getting ready to spend the rest of her sad life all alone up there on the mountain? And people were already talking. You weren't here, so you wouldn't know. Even back then, people thought she was a witch. They were *scared*. I thought it'd be the end of things, delivering him back to her. But it wasn't. I didn't know she'd raise him up, John David. I swear I didn't. Stu Graves come to town looking for me. Bucky all but told me so. And then Bucky dragged us both outside, trying to make me feel guilty enough to help, and then I don't know. I don't know what happened. I didn't mean to. You got to believe me, John David. I didn't *mean it.*"

"Didn't mean to do what?"

Medric shook his head.

"Medric? What else did you do?"

But Medric wouldn't say. Funny how something so horrible as digging up Stu Graves had come out of that man so easy and something so tragic as shooting Ruth Mitchell wouldn't. That had been an accident, there was no doubt about it in Medric's mind and not in mine either, friend. But how could he say that now? Who would even believe him? And would it even matter in the end?

"Went to your daddy yesterday," Medric said. "After I dug up that casket. I wanted to tell him everything. He wouldn't even open up his office door for me. Don't matter what else I did now. I done enough. They'll string me up, John David. Don't you doubt it." And then in a final statement that turned to prophecy, Medric said, "I won't last the day."

-4-

While Bucky took care of the doc and John David tried to console Medric, the Hodges were left to Scarlett. She made them as comfortable as she could (Briar needed nothing, though Chessie asked for some of that coffee she smelled) and wrote down that she was sorry.

"I appreciate that text you sent, young lady," Chessie said. "And I won't forget it. But it was time to come on in. I won't spend the rest of my life hearing me an Briar is what's wrong with this town. We did our best to do what good we could. People say that was all done in a bad way, let'm. Like I told you before, people can't change the minds of others. But I mean to have an end to this either way, and that end comes now. I gotta stand up in church to do it, I will."

Down at the end of the hall, someone tried pulling on the locked doors of the council building. Scarlett let Chessie and Briar have a moment alone and walked down to see who it was. Turned out, it could've been any of a hundred people, because that's what looked like the crowd outside had become. That parade of cars coming into town from the clinic along with Angela's wagging tongue had brought everybody in from the surrounding area. All of them wanted to know the same thing—which of the people locked up inside had helped the witch bring ruin upon us all.

Scarlett ran back down the hall and knocked at the door where her daddy sat listening to Danny Sullivan, writing as she waited. Wilson and Bucky stepped outside.

If somebody doesn't go outside soon, they'll try to get in here.

"We're almost done," Wilson said. "Bucky, why don't you get the Reverend out here."

Bucky did as he was told, though with a troubled look. The mayor knocked at the door to the next room. Scarlett could hear Medric sobbing on the other side. John David came out of one room looking twice as bad as Bucky had going in the other. He didn't even bother to smile at Scarlett, only nodded his head a little. Still, her heart looked to soar. She had been seen.

Reverend Ramsay and Bucky came back out, and everybody shared what they knew. Wilson went first, telling John David and Scarlett everything the doc had said. John David went next, saying how Medric had dug up Stu Graves, and not anytime in the recent past. Maybe even the very day Stu'd been put in the ground. Had to say it twice, as a matter of fact, because didn't nobody else believe it. I don't think John David could quite fathom what Medric did himself.

"Why would Medric do such a thing?" Wilson asked.

John David rubbed the scruff on his face. "He says he just felt sorry for Alvaretta. Thought a man should have the right to be laid to rest on the same land he lived on. He didn't think Alvaretta was going to . . ." He trailed off there, not knowing how to finish that sentence. ". . . do whatever she did."

"The arrogance of that man," the Reverend said. "Thinking he alone knew what was right. Did he say if he reburied Stu somewhere on Campbell's Mountain?"

John David shook his head. "He didn't. Said he ain't been out to Alvaretta's since."

"Doc has," Wilson said. "Medric say anything about killing Ruth?"

"No," John David said. "Swore to me he didn't know who'd done it. I believe him. He's a broken man, Wilson. Any chance Danny was the one?"

"Bucky doesn't think so," the preacher said. "I'm inclined to agree. Which means Ruth's killer is still out there."

"Maybe Stu Graves really did do it," Wilson said. "She was felled with a shotgun. Danny said the first time he went out to the mountain, Alvaretta chased him off with one."

"Maybe Alvaretta did it herself," the preacher said. "Come to town to lead Stu here."

Wilson didn't much like the sound of that. "Whatever the case, we got a crowd of angry people outside. I'm gonna need you to go out there, Reverend. Calm them down. I don't care what you say or how you say it. Tell them this'll all be put to rest at the church this evening."

Scarlett flipped a page and wrote *Chessie's waiting.*

"Chessie Hodge has done more to harm this town than anybody but the witch herself," the Reverend said, staring at his son. "She may not have had anything to do with Alvaretta Graves coming for us, but Chessie weakened the walls around

Crow Holler enough to let her. She'll stand up in church along with the rest, if only so she can finally be brought down."

He walked off for the front doors before either John David or Scarlett could say a word about it. John David went back inside with Medric. Wilson waited until the door was closed before asking Bucky, "You watch him all morning?"

"Sure, Wilson."

"John David never wandered off for a minute?"

"No. Why?"

"Because we're still missing somebody. There's one other person helping Alvaretta."

"How you figure that?" Bucky asked.

"It took hours for y'all to do what shouldn't've taken one. Hays is gone, Bucky. Medric was running—you told me so. And Chessie turned herself in. How'd she know to do that if she wasn't supposed to know you were coming for her? Somebody tipped her off. I think that somebody was your new constable."

"No," Bucky said. "No way. John David wouldn't do that."

"Wouldn't? How you know that, Buck? The boy was *living* with Chessie and Briar. He was up there on the mountain with Scarlett and Cordelia."

Scarlett opened her mouth to speak and then remembered she couldn't anymore.

Wilson waved her off. He said to Bucky, "I want John David took in."

Scarlett's mouth fell open. She started scrawling.

"What?" Bucky asked. "No, Wilson. This is all gone too far now. You can't—"

"I can, Sheriff. I'm the mayor, and I know the Reverend will agree when he hears what I got to say."

"I won't do it."

"You won't?" Wilson took a step toward Bucky. "You *won't*? Listen here, you fat tub of nothing, I *made* you what you are.

You've had my pity your whole life, and that pity's what got you everything from the wife you bed to the badge in your pocket. Now when it comes time to finally do something to justify your sorry life, you say you *won't?*"

Bucky looked as though someone had shot him. He could barely summon a single word: "Wilson . . ."

"Shut up. You'll do what I say. You'll do it or I'll—"

And that's when Scarlett held up her pad.

-5-

I told them Bucky was coming

That's what Scarlett had written on the page. In a morning full of confessions that rocked the fragile world that Wilson Bickford had long given his blood and sweat to build, that one cut the deepest. All you needed to know that was the look on his face.

"You did what?" he whispered.

Scarlett wrote: *It's wrong what you did!!!*

"Bucky, go on back in with Danny and Maris."

Our sheriff stayed put. He was staring at what Scarlett had written with a kind of marvel.

"Bucky?" Wilson asked. "Please."

There was an apology inside that last word, one plain for everyone there. But Bucky didn't look to accept it. The mayor's words had stung him, and that pain still smarted. They'd been friends for years—best friends, Bucky often said. And yet now he looked to think maybe that had all been on his part, not Wilson's. He turned and put his hand on the knob of the door leading back inside that little conference room. Before he turned it, Bucky said, "Scarlett, you come find me if you got to."

Scarlett winced as the mayor took her arm and led her to

his office. He shut the door and told her to sit, then peeked through the blinds to the Reverend and the crowd outside. David Ramsay looked busy giving one of his mini-sermons. Sure did look like he was ginning everybody up a whole lot more than he was calming them down. He turned to find Scarlett slumped into one of the chairs in front of the desk, knees drawn to her chin. She didn't look as mournful as she did tired.

"All my life," he said, "all I ever did was try and protect you. I couldn't protect your momma in the end. I'm big in this town, Scarlett, but cancer's bigger. I wanted to keep you safe. I wanted to give you a future. And after all I've done for you, you stab me in the back. You take off up to Campbell's Mountain thinking that would impress some . . . *boy*. Cross the witch. And now, just when I think I found a way to set things right, you go and give aid to the very people who sought to destroy all me and your granddaddy built. You put us all in more jeopardy this morning with that damn phone of yours than you ever could traipsing around the mines. She wants me *dead*, Scarlett. Me and everybody I love. And she's coming for the preacher too."

Scarlett picked up her pen. Wilson told her to put it down. She didn't and set to writing—a W, an H. Part of the Y that came next. Stop it, Wilson told her, and when Scarlett would not, he reached across the desk and took her pen away. Silencing her. Making his little girl unseen again. And whether Scarlett believed just then that was the way her daddy had always wanted her or if her rage and hurt had reached its limits, she picked up her pad and flung it at her father. It hit the side of his face with a *whump* and fell atop the desk, leaving Wilson stunned.

Why? she mouthed, screaming it though only air came out. *Why?* as she reached for what she could—a tape dispenser, a stapler, the picture of her dead momma—and flung them at her father's head and chest. *Why?* as he told her to stop, *Why?* as he tried pinning her arms but couldn't, *Why?*—

"Because we killed Stu Graves," Wilson shouted, and then disbelief engulfed him. For a moment it looked as though his admission had brought a new level of Alvaretta's curse upon his daughter. Not only had Scarlett been struck mute, her body slackened like one side of Cordelia's face. But it was not witchery that had overcome her, it was shock.

Wilson sat. He put his elbows atop the desk and leaned forward, letting his fingers massage the ridge of his nose.

He said it again, softer. "We killed Stu Graves. Me and David. We killed him, Lord help us we did. We'd all gotten together a week before the state game. David came down from college with Belle and John David, who weren't no taller than a weed. Landis was there with Angela. They were still together then, at least for a few months more. Me and David cut out a little early and went driving around. Just hanging out the way we used to before he left. We both got drunk. Me because that's just what I did back then, and I guess David just wanted to blow off some steam from all that right living he'd been doing. We were coming back on the Ridge Road.

"I was driving. We got to playing this game where we took all the turns in the opposite lane. I know it's stupid. Even then, I knew it. The first few times was fine. It was late, and we both knew there wasn't anybody around. But that last time we took the turn, there was Stu Graves coming right at us. I managed to swerve the same time as he did, but I had a whole 'nother lane. Stu didn't. He went off the road and into that tree.

"I didn't know what to do. David was screaming and so was I, and he wanted me to keep going but I knew I couldn't. I couldn't just leave him there, Scarlett. What if he was okay? What if he was still alive? Stu'd go straight to my daddy and tell him what we done, that's what. It'd cost me everything, all the future I'd planned. David too. You think they'd let him back in that Bible college after he'd gotten drunk like that? So

I threw my car into reverse and went back. We got out, and Stu was . . ." Wilson shook his head. "He was all mangled up. It was the awfulest thing I ever seen before or since.

"I wanted to go for help, but David starts going crazy, saying we'd get sent to jail or worse. We had to make it look like an accident. So we took all the jars we had and put them in Stu's truck. Made it look like he'd been drinking. We swore to each other we'd never tell a word to anybody. Me and David'd carry that secret to the grave. But Alvaretta knew. I don't know how, Scarlett, but she knew it was no accident that killed her husband. She swore vengeance at the funeral, and then Medric and Danny gave her everything she needed to get it. One gave her back Stu's body to raise up, and the other kept her living long enough to do it. So you have to leave. Don't you understand? The only reason Alvaretta let you live in the first place is so you could spread what she gave you to the whole town when you and the rest got back here."

Scarlett didn't need to write down what she thought. Wilson saw it plain.

"I'm trying to save this town. I will not let those people go, Scarlett. Your uncle and Medric and Chessie carry as much blame for what's happened as you or me."

Scarlett shook her head.

"You stand with me, Scarlett, or you will stand against me. Let there be no mistake in that. My duty is to Crow Holler first. David and me have given our lives to this town. We done a whole lot more good than bad, and I won't have anybody, anybody, try to take that away."

I don't know if Wilson truly meant that. Maybe he was just trying to scare his daughter into seeing his side of things. But it wasn't the old Scarlett Bickford he was talking to, remember. This was the new Scarlett, the one risen up from all of what the witch and everybody else had done to her. The one whose mother'd been snatched away and the one the whole town (and even her own father) called guilty for bringing all this on. So I guess it weren't much surprising what she did.

She got up from that chair and went out the door, leaving it open for Wilson to see. Chessie and Briar sat in the room across the hall. Scarlett opened that door and walked in, taking a seat at Chessie's side. Her decision had been made. Not for her daddy. Against him.

Wilson Bickford sat alone in his office and wept. I suppose he could've made other choices in the hours after and changed things, both for himself and everybody else. Never did, though. People never change who they are. You might like to think they do, friend, because thinking so gives you a kind of hope that maybe you can change your own self, but it's a lie. Nosir, people never change. And that is how Alvaretta Graves would end Wilson's life. She hadn't gotten her vengeance yet, but it was coming. In white hoods and a dead man's face, it was coming.

-6-

Was a time when John David Ramsay would sit in church and be transfixed by his daddy's power to sway people. The lowly and the downtrodden; the sick and the dying; those who longed for heaven and those who feared hell; men and women and children. They'd all seek refuge inside the Holy Fire from a hard and fallen world, and then they'd walk out with their heads high and their spirits renewed to face that hard and fallen world once more. Make no mistake on what I tell you, nothing carries the might of words. Give me a sword or a gun, give me the power of death. Those things can only strike flesh and bone, friend. They can change neither nation nor world. But give me words and I may rule, for by them I reach the heart and the mind. John David understood that. He bore witness to it every day of his childhood under his father's roof. He felt that power even now.

He'd left Medric with Bucky and now stood outside the council building, arms folded in front of his chest as he listened to his father speak to the crowd. Watching the Reverend stir them up, give them reason for hope. Telling them of the three inside who had helped cast the pall that had fallen over the town. Saying the service that night would be a cleansing of all their sin and a welcoming of the Holy Spirit of God to drive the witch away from Crow Holler forever. And all that while John David kept his arms tight around himself, like he was cold still, wanting to feel the warmth of his father's fire and yet not daring his own heart and mind to venture too close, and when the crowd had had their fill and began drifting away in peace, only the two of them remained.

You would think a man so gifted in speech would have plenty to say to his own son, yet the Reverend could only stand there and look. John David kept his back to the wall of the council building. He said, "Forgot how good your tongue worked."

"You'd be reminded if you ever came to church. I'm sure Chessie would allow it. Her and Briar come themselves."

"Chessie leaves my soul up to me," John David said, settling things.

"Your momma misses you, son. Naomi too."

"And what of my father?"

Here, the Reverend looked away. Only for a moment, just enough time for him to say, "Sometimes I think your father misses you more than they do." He looked back. "What happened to you over there, John David?"

"I don't know. Nothing. Everything. Sometimes I think whatever happened, happened here. It wilted in Crow Holler, then finally died and fell away over there. And I guess I'm just trying to get back what I lost."

"I can help you," the preacher said.

"I don't think anything can help me. Time. Maybe that."

"Time only lasts so long, John David. This week's taught us all that. The days are dark and the burden is heavy."

"Don't try to witness to me, Daddy."

"It's my job."

"No. It isn't. Your job is to comfort these people, not whip them into a frenzy."

"We are soldiers, John David. We fight the good fight. Part of that is calling evil what it is and rooting it out."

"That what you're doing in this service tonight? Rooting it out?"

"That's exactly what I'm doing," the Reverend said. "This town was pure, maybe the witch would've never come. All that stands between the shadow and the light are men willing to take up and fight. There's a peace that only comes with war. You should know that."

"All I know is the people who say such things are never the ones who have to take up and do the fighting. They leave that to the common folk. Maybe you suffer and bleed, you'd think otherwise."

"Don't you challenge me," the Reverend said.

"And don't you pretend to think I don't know what I'm saying, because I do. You call other people evil, fine. But know when you do, those people are calling you the same."

He eased away from the wall and made for the door. The preacher watched his son go and said, "Was a good thing Bucky did, making you constable and getting you away from Chessie Hodge."

"You'd take the time to understand Chessie, you might think different."

"I know her heart," the Reverend said, "that's all I need. She's dealt with the devil just as much as the witch has, and it's led just as much to our ruin."

"That a fact?" John David asked.

"It is."

John David opened the door. "Sometimes I think the same's true of you."

-7-

Most kids around here grow up with the wild. They suckle as much from nature's breast as they do their momma's, fishing the mountain streams and hunting along its ridges, whiling away the summer days in fields of sage and honeysuckle. But Hays had no such memories to comfort him. Kayann Foster grumbled even of the dirt roads that sullied her car and the summer flies that latched to her clothing; the mere mention of what dirt and crawlies lived in the woods made her shudder. And Landis? He would happily speak to the pleasures of taking inventory at the grocery, but that man remained ignorant of the bliss to be found in the Holler's lonely places. So I guess you can imagine Hays thought he'd never get out of them woods alive, and how what was chasing him had little to do with it.

I don't know how long he ran. I know there was no method to it and no particular direction, because there was no way for him to tell where lay the safety of town. He simply ran as Scarlett had the night John David had not seen her—away.

He'd had no idea the witch's reach had extended so far into Crow Holler. That Medric was one of Alvaretta's demons couldn't be understood. Hays cared much for that man but his parents never had, said they couldn't respect anyone who made his life by peddling death. But there was no denying Medric's heart now. And the men with Raleigh, that Circle he spoke of? All of them had worn demon faces beneath their hoods. And friend, that only begged the question of how many more of them were in town. How many neighbors and friends? How many monsters, waiting for the witch's command to kill them all? You think about it like that, maybe being alone in the wilderness wasn't such a bad thing. In fact, I'd say Hays Foster was about the safest person in all of Crow Holler right then. He kept pushing his way through the trees, turning to look for who may be chasing him, trying without success to find a signal on his phone. No one followed him. Raleigh and his merry band were already on their way to town, intending to dispense a final stroke of justice.

The sprint that had carried Hays away from the Circle slowed to something well short of a fast walk. His breaths were labored and deep, his legs unable to keep moving. He finally collapsed against a fallen walnut tree and tilted his face to wisps of clouds colored red and orange by the setting sun. There, Hays Foster waited for death to call him. No doubt the Dark Angel would have, friend. I'd say that specter was there even then, waiting as it waited for all in Crow Holler. And yet Hays then did something wholly unexpected as he kept his eyes to the broken places of sky beyond the tall trees around him. He began to pray.

So far as I know, it was only the second time in that boy's life he'd lifted his voice heavenward, the first coming the night before at Reverend Ramsay's altar. His words weren't flowery like the Reverend's, nor filled with grief as was Angela's or Cordelia's on the times they'd offered them. Five words in all, but then I guess you could say they were the five that most mattered:

"Tell me what to do."

There came no answer. No Spirit descending from the

sky as a dove, no burning bush, no stone tablets writ by the Almighty's hand. Only emptiness filled that boy. Only emptiness ever had.

Somewhere close, a twig snapped. Hays sank beneath the log. He saw nothing in the trees but a fluttering leaf.

A sound again. Not someone stepping over a branch. More like a scrape. Wood over stone.

Hays rolled to his side and jumped up in one motion. This time he ran even faster than he'd fled from Raleigh's demons, certain they'd followed or—worse—that Stu Graves had found him. Evening fell upon the woods, blending the trees into one, but Hays refused to slow. He bounced off some and ran into others. Each blow stole what small amount of strength of him remained.

He looked near to surrendering again when he saw the clearing ahead and tumbled through the last of the trees. A cabin and barn rested in the middle, along with a struggling garden out back. Hays uttered a cry as he stopped, and I think that was because his mind had twisted things so far as to think he'd arrived once more at Alvaretta's. But this was not the Graves homeplace. The house was larger and the barn newer, and the truck parked between them was not Stu's, but the rusting Chevy that Briar Hodge sometimes drove.

"Chessie?" he screamed. "Mr. Hodge?" Running for the porch, looking over his shoulder, where there was nothing now but forest. "John David?"

Hays banged on the door. No one answered. He ran to the barn and rolled open the big doors. No one. Yet here, his panic went quiet.

Lined against the barn's far wall were crates filled with jars glimmering with the clear liquid of Briar Hodge's famous moonshine. Gallons of it, packed neatly and with care. Waiting not for delivery, but for Hays himself.

Tell me what to do, he'd prayed back at that fallen tree. The answer had not come, not there and then. It had instead waited for Hays to pick himself up and go looking for it, and in that I do believe that boy found the only lesson of the spirit he'd ever receive. He knew what to do now. There were monsters in Crow Holler, and that was a sorry thing. But no one but him could see the monsters, and that was worse. Everyone Hays knew in his life, his parents and his friends, Cordelia and their baby, were at the mercy of the witch. The only one who could make things right was Hays, because he was the only one who had been cursed with the truth.

He ran back to Briar's truck and found the keys in the ignition—yet another small miracle to prove this was all the Lord's doing. The revving engine broke the forest's silence. Hays backed up to the doors and left the engine running. He headed to town twenty minutes later with all but two cases of Briar's moonshine jostling in the truck's bed.

XIV

The service. The Circle arrives. Monsters.
Blood flows in the Holler. Burn it all.
Stu comes for Wilson.

-1-

You can believe it was standing room only at the Holy Fire
that night; not even all the chairs brought over from the council building were enough. People piled into the pews and the
aisles, into the choir loft above the sanctuary, even behind the
pulpit. Any place big enough to put a body, Reverend Ramsay
put one there. Wilson helped, along with the other deacons. All
but the head one, of course. Everybody wanted to know where
Raleigh'd run off to. That man hadn't missed a service since
Eugenia left.

Most everybody came: Belle and Naomi had sought refuge
in the church most of that day. Bucky walked over from the
council building and met Angela and Cordelia at the steps. The
mayor came along by himself. Scarlett followed later, though
only in body. Her spirit seemed to lay elsewhere. She had spent
quite a long time with Chessie and Briar, along with a new pad
and pen. Every piece of that paper had been used up by the
time Chessie had all she needed. Both Foster parents arrived
late, though I expect the only reason they showed up was to
make sure Bucky hadn't found Hays, who was nowhere around.
They went on and sat down anyway. Kayann understood their
absence would only make Hays look more guilty in the eyes of
Crow Holler.

The front row had been blocked off for those that mattered. Wilson sat on the end with Scarlett, though I suppose she'd tell you she wasn't sitting with her daddy near as much as she was sitting with Briar. On Briar's other side sat Maris Sullivan. Bucky sat with her and Cordelia. He tried to tell Maris he agreed Danny was innocent, but Maris had gone quiet. And wouldn't you know it, John David stood against the wall next to the side door, attending church for the first time since leaving for the war. He held his arms crossed like he always did. Much like Scarlett, he'd come more for the Hodges than for his own family.

Angela sashayed about in that red dress she liked so much. She shook what people's hands she could reach and waved to the ones she couldn't, flashing her best smile. This was Angela's big moment, and no way would she let that moment pass without sopping up every bit of pleasure in it. Bucky had brought in the witch's spies, you see. To Angela's mind, that meant she'd had just as much a hand in it as Bucky. "I believed in Bucky when nobody else did," is what she told everybody. She finished her lap around the sanctuary and waved at those in the choir loft, then took her place between Bucky and Cordelia.

On the stage to the side of the pulpit sat three metal chairs. That's where Medric, Danny, and Chessie waited for judgment. Seeing those three would remind you of one a them pictures they show in school of man's evolution. Medric leaned so far forward in his chair that he looked like a ball. His elbows rested on his thighs and his eyes were to the floor. Danny Sullivan fared little better. The day had worn on him such that it looked a migraine had broken out in him. He too was hunched, though less so than Medric. His hand moved over his eyes and forehead, massaging them. Every once in a while he'd glance to Maris and mouth *I'm sorry* over and over. Only Chessie remained tall—back straight, eyes forward, hands in her lap—as calm and sure as she would be sitting on her porch at home.

David Ramsay came through the side door at seven o'clock exactly, just as the full moon rose over Crow Holler. He carried his Bible in one hand. The other gripped a large metal bowl with a plain white towel inside, and a pitcher of water he'd prayed over from the fountain in the hallway. A hum fell over the crowd as he walked up the stage. Never once did the Reverend look at the three accused. He laid the bowl and pitcher at Chessie's feet and turned to the people.

"And all God's people said . . ."

"Amen," came the chorus.

"Amen," he whispered back. "Brothers and sisters, we've spent each night here under heavy burden, seeking the hand of the Lord to guide us through what the darkness has wrought. We've prayed together, sung together, lifted up our hearts as one for God's favor. And yet that favor has not come."

He turned a little and looked at Chessie. She kept her eyes to Briar.

"Long did I pray, asking the Father why still we suffer. That answer came when our Sheriff Vest brought news that the witch has aid in her doings, aid that came not from the evil of hell, but the evil inside the human heart. It has been determined by myself and Mayor Bickford that the three who sit behind me have colluded to bring about the rot that has overtaken Crow Holler. I will give evidence of their deeds. I will tell you how it was that Medric Johnston came to deliver the body of Stu Graves to Alvaretta so she might raise him up for her vengeance."

A gasp came from the congregation, making Medric shrink more.

"I will tell you how our very own doctor offered aid to Alvaretta by procuring her food and medicine that kept her body strong so that she might weaken us all."

"No," Maris said from the front, "No, I will not have this," but she was shouted down by those behind her.

"I will tell you how Chessie Hodge brought the Lord's wrath upon us—partaking in the devil's schemes by peddling her filth and cleansing her own conscience by corrupting us all with her gains. I will tell you all of this, brothers and sisters, though it pains me. Yes, it pains me." David grimaced. I don't know if that was for show or if he truly did feel that hurt. "The Word says pride goeth before a fall. Well, we have all fallen. We writhe and moan in the dirt when we should soar with the angels. It is humility we lack, not faith. Meekness rather than love. That is why the witch holds power. Alvaretta Graves is our judgment, and the demon she's called forth is our sentence. And yet, still we may turn. 'If my people, which are called by my name, shall humble themselves, and pray, and seek my face, and turn from their wicked ways; then will I hear from heaven, and will forgive their sin, and will heal their land.'"

"Amen," they all sang, and Amen again.

"Tonight, friends, we turn. Tonight, those responsible for the curse upon us all will humble themselves." David turned and pointed to what lay at Chessie's feet. "Tonight these three will confess their prideful ways, and their penance will be to wash the feet of all gathered."

Friend, the silence that greeted David at those words could only be one of shock, nothing else. Chessie glared at the Reverend, but he did not turn. In the front pew, Cordelia's cell phone buzzed. She blushed and squeezed her purse.

"Let us go to the Word," David said. "Thirteenth chapter of John, verses three through eleven."

Cordy unzipped her purse as quiet as she could. Not even Angela's hard stare could stop her. She reached for her phone and hit the button to read the text. It was Hays:

MEET ME AT THE FIELD COME ALONE THEY'RE EVERYWHERE

"'Jesus,'" David began, "'knowing that the Father had given all things into his hands, and that he was come from God, and went to God; he riseth from supper, and laid aside his garments; and took a towel, and girded himself. After that he poureth water into a bason, and began to wash the disciples' feet, and to wipe them with the towel wherewith he was girded.'"

Cordelia stared at her screen.

MEET ME AT THE FIELD

Hays wanting her.

Needing her.

"'Then cometh he to Simon Peter: and Peter saith unto him, Lord, dost thou wash my feet? Jesus answered and said unto him, What I do thou knowest not now; but thou shalt know hereafter. Peter saith unto him, Thou shalt never wash my feet.'"

COME ALONE

But could she? Could Cordelia do such a thing for a boy who was no longer the person she'd shared herself with? The boy who had been bruised somehow, the one who had once said he loved her but now said things like *It isn't safe anymore. Nowhere's safe*, because *they're everywhere*? You would think such an answer would require a measure of deliberation, but I'll tell you Cordelia did no such thing. Of course she would. She had to go, friend, and for the very reason girls her age did most anything—for love.

She let the screen drop long enough for Angela to see. Their eyes met, a daughter's pleading and a mother's fear. Bucky couldn't come. He would have to stay here, make sure Medric and the rest got what they deserved, and so the two of them rose together and walked toward the doors. Bucky watched them go. Kayann watched them too. She did not look at Landis as she rose to follow them out.

David said, "'Jesus answered him, If I wash thee not, thou hast no part with me. Simon Peter saith unto him, Lord, not my feet only, but also my hands and my head. Jesus saith to him, He that is washed needeth not save to wash his feet, but is clean every whit: and ye are clean, but not all. For he knew who would betray him; therefore said he, Ye are not all clean.'"

And that was the last thing Cordelia heard as she and Angela stepped out beneath a bright and full moon. Kayann remained farther back, picking her way through a tangle of arms and legs and ugly glares. The last thing she heard was David asking for witnesses to the evil deeds of the three gathered upon the stage. The last she saw was Chessie Hodge stand.

-2-

He stood in the middle of the field where a fire burned and the moon had already taken on a strange glow. Hays believed that high color a sign. Whether of the Lord or the witch, he did not know. I expect he had come to see them as one and the same.

He'd waited longer than it should've taken for Cordelia to get there. That had been more the fault of their two mommas wasting time on the church steps, arguing this was all Hays's fault and this was all Cordelia's, arguing about the past and the now and the future and the little child that connected all three. In the end Angela couldn't well refuse Kayann's insistence to come along. Hays was her boy, after all. Made for a pile of silence in Kayann's fancy car, you can believe that. None of them said a word when they passed Raleigh Jennings and the four trucks with him, late for service and headed toward town.

Hays flicked his lighter one last time when he saw Cordelia walking out of the scrub of pines and spruces at the edge of the field. It had been a risk, texting her. It had been a bigger one asking her to meet him. He had no way of knowing how far Alvaretta's reach had grown through town, or how deep her evil had spread. But as Hays watched Cordy moving towards him, I do believe he felt thankful. I wouldn't say he loved Cordelia, least not the way Cordelia loved him. But really, what does that matter in the end? What child that age knows what love is? I'm an old man, friend; I've no idea myself. Sometimes I wonder if anybody does. But I think Hays had come to see the baby inside her as the only pure thing left in Crow Holler and the only person untouched by Alvaretta Graves.

He stepped away from the fire and craned his neck, wanting to make sure Cordy was still herself. "You came," he said.

She smiled and kept the flames between them. "Vere have you been, Hayth?"

"I'm sorry. I left you, and I'm sorry. Scarlett was right. They were coming for me."

"Whooth 'they'?"

"The monsters. Alvaretta's monsters. They're everywhere, Cordy. I've seen them. Medric's one."

"Medwic?" she asked. "How do you know about him?"

"How do—" he started, then closed his mouth. "How do *you* know about Medric?"

"Daddy bwought him in eawier, wif Chethie and Doc Thullivan. They're in church now. They helped the witch."

Hays smiled for maybe the first time all week. "That's good," he said. "But there's more of them, Cordy. They're everywhere. I tried getting out of town, but Raleigh got me. He took me in the woods with a bunch of men in hoods."

She took a step around the fire, closer to him. "Vut men in hoods?"

"The monsters. They were after me, but I'm safe now. We have to leave. You and me and the baby, we have to go."

Another step. Cordelia stopped close enough to touch him. Reach out and grab him. She winced at the heat of the flames. As she did, a piece of her forehead peeled away. It broke free of her skin and floated before the fire's current lifted it above her head, where it burned like an ember before winking away.

Hays stumbled back. "What's wrong with you?"

"Nuffing." She came forward again as the tip of her chin bubbled and popped, revealing a patch of mottled black skin beneath.

"You're one of them," he said. "Cordelia?"

"Thtop, Hayth. Let me help you. We'll make it okay. Juft tell me you wuv me."

Her right cheek slipped free of her face, followed by an ear and a lock of her thick hair. Cordelia stood by the flames and had no idea her mask was falling away.

"Tell me you wuv me, Hayth," she said, begging to hear those words. "Tell me you'll be wiff me alwayth, no matter vut."

"Get away."

He stumbled back as Cordelia moved away from the fire's heat, and at the far edge of the field came the others. Angela screamed his name. And there came Kayann, there came Hays's own mother, hollering for her boy and saying she loved him, and all Hays could think of was how horrible it would be once they all reached the fire and their masks burned away, too, and how that sight would snatch what remained of his sanity.

"Vey're here to help you," the thing that had once been Cordelia said, but Hays wanted no such aid. He tore for the woods where he'd hidden Briar's old truck, and he did not turn to the calls begging him to turn back and join them.

You'll ask me, friend, if that's what Hays had truly seen—
that piece of hell beneath Cordelia's pretty face and all them
faces at the Circle. I'll tell you I don't know. Like I said, I don't
know the whole of the story I'm telling you, but I can guess on
the parts I don't. My guess as far as Hays Foster is concerned
is that *he* thought that's what he saw, and that's the only thing
that matters because it's the only thing that explains what he
did next. He'd been inside the Circle's ring of fire when he'd
seen the true faces of Raleigh's men. Medric Johnston had
crossed by the lighter's flame when Hays had seen the undertaker's truth. That's what Hays had thought as he loaded up
all that moonshine into the back of that truck. Now fire had
exposed Cordy, too, and I guess that settled things. There was
only one way for Hays to expose the rest of Alvaretta's demons
that had overtaken Crow Holler, and that would be to burn
the town.

Burn it all.

-3-

"I'll speak," Chessie said. She kicked the chair she'd sat in away.
The tumble sounded like thunder. "I'll tell you what I know."

The Reverend said, "Chessie, you stand accused. The time
for you to speak is done."

"My time to speak is whenever I get the urge, David Ramsay.
You got the nerve to shut me up, come over here and try."

The Reverend looked at Wilson, who rose from his pew.
It'd be tricky, getting Chessie to shut her mouth without Briar
throwing the whole church into a riot, but I think that's what
Wilson had decided to do.

And yet as he turned to speak to the congregation—tell
them what a fool Chessie was for thinking she could do all that

sinning all those years and not have it all come back on them all in spades—his eyes went to the crowd huddled in the choir loft. Someone there stood. The figure was basked in shadow, moving from the back row up toward the front of the balcony with a slow ease that seemed impossible given how they'd all been packed in.

"You'll sit," the Reverend told Chessie.

Wilson watched as the figure passed Helen Pruitt, then Helen's stricken child Maddie. On past the others, moving not around them but almost *through* them, easing its way to the wood railing that overlooked the sanctuary.

"I'll speak and I'll be heard," Chessie said. "Stu Graves did not die by his own hand. He was murdered. And I know by whose hand."

Doc Sullivan looked to have forgotten his migraine. Even Medric raised his head some.

Now not only standing but leaning over the rail, not so the figure could get a better look, but so the mayor could see clear the man who had haunted him since that night so long ago. Stu Graves curled a hand of skinless fingers over that railing and stared through two black holes where his eyes had rotted away. His face was little more than a thin layer of gray and mottled skin stretched taut over bone. A scream built in Wilson's throat, one that threatened to escape not simply because the man he had killed had come back to return the favor, but because no one else seemed aware of the danger around them.

Wilson did not hear Chessie say she would bear witness against him and the Reverend both. His mind was overcome by Stu's empty stare and Maddie Pruitt's sudden look of shock over what Chessie had just said. He didn't hear Chessie announce that Scarlett had told her all that Wilson had confessed only a short time ago, or the screaming the Reverend had started next, the *No* and *That's not true*. Wilson did not feel Scarlett's hand upon him or see the scrap of paper with *I'm so sorry Daddy I love you* that she waved in his eyes. He did not even hear the congregation's gasp when Chessie said our mayor and preacher had killed Stu Graves along the Ridge Road that night. All of these things were unimportant to Mayor Wilson Bickford just then, inconsequential. Stu smiled through two rows of black and needled teeth. A worm fell from his mouth. It tumbled down from the choir loft and landed unseen and unnoticed atop Landis Foster's head, where it stretched and flopped as though dumped into water.

Three things happened then. That whole church started hollering. Stu Graves disappeared from his place beside Maddie Pruitt. And Wilson Bickford fainted dead away.

The Reverend shouted for Bucky to take Chessie out of there. Bucky remained in his seat, too stunned to move. Then the preacher tried to do it himself, even with Briar standing in front of him. He didn't get far. John David grabbed Scarlett from behind, getting her to safety, but there was no place to go. The crowd had rose up, shouting and cursing and wanting to know if it was true. There's not a doubt in my mind, friend, that our preacher and our mayor would've been torn apart right there. But that's when the front doors of the church flew open and the fire poured in.

-4-

The staff had been fashioned from a stout limb of oak, wrapped on one end with an old shop rag doused with a few cents of the Exxon's finest 87 octane, and the only reason it didn't strike anyone was they'd all moved to the front when Wilson fell. It tumbled end over end down the center aisle and landed with a clang against one of the metal chairs. Next came a soft *whoomp*

as the fire took hold. It bloomed like a flower in the thick carpet. Doc Sullivan had already left his place on the stage to
tend to Wilson. He paused now as the flames took hold and
screamed *Fire*.

Bodies collided as people scrambled to get out of the way.
John David left Scarlett to care for her unconscious daddy. He
charged through the crowd, ripping off his shirt to beat the
flames. Bucky ran to join him. Reverend Ramsay stood behind
the pulpit with a look of confusion, like he couldn't figure how
there could be a fire because it hadn't been printed up in the
bulletin.

John David grabbed the torch and ran it to the stage, where
he shoved it inside the pitcher of water beside Chessie. The fire
let out an angry hiss as it died. People clamored to the foyer.
John David saw them and shouted, "No. Wait. Everybody wait."

Didn't make no difference he said that, weren't nobody
going to listen. All everybody wanted was get out of there and
into open space. They all charged to the doors, and there's
where they stopped. Not a one of them dared a step more. A
silence fell over the room.

Briar rose to see what was outside. Chessie called his name
and then shook her head, telling him to stay put. She sat back
down in her chair on the stage and stared at the empty seat
between herself and Medric. Doc stood with Maris in the
middle of the sanctuary near where the torch had hit, asking if
anyone was hurt. Briar nodded to his wife and returned to the
front pew.

Wilson's eyes fluttered open to see Scarlett bent over him.
There was agony and shame in his face. He kept muttering
something about Stu. Belle and Naomi stood like islands in the
middle of the church, not sure what to do. John David looked
at his father and asked the one question his momma and little
sister were afraid to ask.

"It true, what Chessie said?"

The Reverend didn't answer.

"You're coming with me," John David said. "I ain't letting you out of my sight." He walked up the center aisle past Belle and Naomi, leaving his father to follow like a lost puppy. John David met Bucky halfway up the aisle, where a black spot had been left in the floor. "Come on," he said. "Town needs us."

By then the Holy Fire had turned from a place of worship to a place of fear. The whole church smelled of sulfur and sweat. I don't believe Bucky wanted to follow John David out there at all. I think he'd got the feeling that whatever waited outside was something horrible beyond his reckoning—Stu Graves, maybe, or Alvaretta herself. But Angela and Cordelia were somewhere out there, too, and maybe they were both in danger, and that's what made Bucky take that slow trip to the doors in the end. He caught up with John David and skipped his feet to get in front of him and the Reverend.

"Excuse me," he whispered as he moved aside those in his way. "Pardon me, let me through please, watch your foot," until he reached the open doors and stepped out.

Fifteen men were gathered in a circle around the church, all done up in white robes and hoods. Each man held a gun in one hand and a flaming torch in the other. Across the street beside the church, a wooden cross burned in front of the funeral home. More men stood there, guarding the fire like it was a holy thing.

"What's this?" Bucky asked.

"Judgment," one of the hooded men said. He stepped out from his place in the circle and made himself the center.

John David stepped forward. He said, "Mask can hide your face, but it don't hide your voice. Take that thing off and talk like a man, Raleigh Jennings."

"Raleigh?" the Reverend asked. It was his first word as a fallen man whose sin lay exposed to the world. Gone was David

Ramsay's confident manner. He spoke for God no more, only himself, and that voice sounded as frail as a child's. "Raleigh, that you?"

The man carried a gun but no torch, at least no longer. The one he'd come with had been thrown through the church doors only minutes before. He used his free hand to pull the hood up from his face, bringing a cry from the people who could see.

Bucky took a step down, like that much distance closer would prove the man he saw wasn't Raleigh, but someone who looked just like him. "Raleigh, what you doing?"

"What needs done. I want Medric, Bucky. You get him out here right now."

"Why?"

"Because he killed my wife," another man said. And since saying it dispensed with all question of who that man was, Joe Mitchell took his hood off as well. "Medric shot my Ruth. He left me a widower and my Chelsea and Little Joe without a momma."

"How you know that?" Bucky asked.

"Hays Foster told us," Raleigh said. "The boy witnessed it himself."

A voice somewhere inside the church said, "Hays?" Landis pushed his way out onto the steps. "You've seen Hays, Raleigh?"

"Seen him this morning, running from Wilson."

"From Wilson?" Bucky asked.

"Mayor knows the truth. I'll need him out here too, Bucky. There'll be no judgment. Judgment's past. Landis? You hear me? You want to see your boy again, you bring'm both to me. You don't, we got gas spread whole way around the church. I'll light it, and I won't think twice."

"You wouldn't dare," the Reverend said. "Raleigh, this is the house of God."

"It's a haven for the guilty and the dead," Raleigh told him.

"Your life worth less than a murderer's, Preacher? Do you count yourself a poorer soul than a liar who wants nothing more than keep an iron grip on this town?"

A few inside the foyer decided they'd had enough of church for one night. They tried coming past John David and Bucky down the steps. Raleigh's men leveled their guns, stopping them.

"Anybody tries to leave before I get Medric and Wilson," Raleigh said, "they die first. Your call, Buck."

David said, "Raleigh, you can't—"

"I can. I will."

Bucky leaned toward John David. "What do I do?"

"They're armed, Buck. We're not. Raleigh's not kidding."

"I know that. What do I do? You ain't got a gun?"

"Don't like guns."

"Time's up," Raleigh said. He motioned for one of the men closest to the church, who lowered the torch in his hand.

"Wait," the Reverend said. "Raleigh, just . . . *wait*. I'll bring them out."

"You can't do that, David," Bucky said. He looked around for someone to say the same. No one did.

"I'll bring them out," the preacher said again.

-5-

If there remained a single blessing in what David Ramsay did next, it was that hardly anybody remained at the front of the church. Belle, Naomi, Scarlett, Briar, Wilson, Medric, and Chessie. That's all. Everybody else had crowded at the doors, trying to figure out how they were going to get out of church that night without ending up in glory. And yet I imagine it felt a hard thing, what David had to do. Yessir, a hard thing indeed.

He come back down the aisle with all but Medric and Wilson

watching. You could see the Reverend's lips moving—trying to remember how to pray, I guess, wondering if such a man as he would even warrant the Lord's attention. All those years up there behind that pulpit telling folk how they should live, when all the time he'd been a liar to his family and his town and to his own self especially. Stu's blood had never been on Wilson alone. It had stained David Ramsay plenty too. And so there he was, forced to make the impossible decision of saving one man or saving them all. Up the stage he went, and I have no doubt every step felt harder than the next. Medric looked up with sad eyes, but the Reverend didn't stop. David walked right on past him instead and knelt in front of Chessie.

"You have to do something."

"What say?" Chessie asked.

"Raleigh's out there with a bunch of men. They're armed. He wants Medric and Wilson, and if he don't get them, they're going to burn the church."

Briar started to rise. He met Chessie's stare and sat again. Wilson took hold of the arm Scarlett had placed around his neck and stood on two feet made of sand. The place where Stu had looked down from the loft now stood empty.

"Medric," the Reverend said, "Raleigh's telling us you were the one who shot Ruth. That true?"

I would imagine that man's back hurt something fierce by then, having been bent over for such a long while. Medric rubbed his hands over his eyes and gave a heavy sigh full of tears. "Didn't mean to do it," he said. "I swear I didn't, David. I thought she was Stu come to get me."

"What's he want me for?" Wilson asked.

Reverend said, "Says you have to pay for your sins." And then to Chessie, "Bucky needs help out there. *My son* needs help out there."

Chessie looked at him. "You come to me, Preacher, when

times call for a hard hand? You ask a Hodge for aid when you say we ruined this town?"

"I will not turn Medric and Wilson over to them. Raleigh'll kill them both. He'll kill more if anybody gets in his way."

"And what of you, David Ramsay? Will you kill again as you killed Stu Graves?"

"That was a long time ago," David whispered. "I've suffered and made amends."

"Ha! Amends. You've made amends to nobody, David Ramsay. You preach, that's all you do. You use your words and call that faith. You call me hell bound and yourself a saint. What you need is what you say I lack. Humility."

"Time's running out, Chessie."

"It'll wait."

"No, it won't," Medric said. "Can't let y'all suffer on my account. I'm tired, Reverend. Chessie, I'm just tired. Of everything. If it's you or me, it'll be me."

He stood and made for the center aisle. No one stopped him, nor did Scarlett move when her daddy followed behind.

David watched them and turned back to Chessie. "I don't care if you hate me, Chessie. Just don't punish those two men because of me."

Chessie moved the bowl and pitcher beside her chair to in front of it, between her and the preacher. Out came the torch John David had shoved inside. Chessie laid it on the towel and began, "'If I then, your Lord and Master, have washed your feet; ye also ought to wash one another's feet. For I have given you an example, that ye should do as I have done to you.'" She removed her boots and socks, setting them aside. "'Verily, verily, I say unto you, The servant is not greater than his lord; neither he that is sent greater than he that sent him.'" And then that woman smiled. "'If ye know these things, happy are ye if ye do them.'"

You ask me if David Ramsay bent to his knees and dipped Chessie's feet in that water. Ask me if he put his hands to that calloused skin, brown with dirt and sticky with sweat, and cleaned the bunions that pocked Chessie's heels and the long nails at the ends of her toes. Ask me if the one everyone considered the holiest man in Crow Holler washed the feet of the one considered the town's most sinful woman outside of Alvaretta Graves herself. I'll tell you yes, friend.

I've heard tell it's a humbling thing, a foot washing service. Never been to one myself. Those who have say it borders a holy thing, though it's hard to endure. Not for the one doing the washing, though. The one being washed. I suppose that makes some sense. You being so grown, friend, imagine this—imagine washing your momma's feet. You get that picture? Ain't too bad really, is it? Now imagine your momma washing yours. That's what I'm talking about. Humbling. But you know what? It was the other way around up there on the stage of the Holy Fire that night. Chessie Hodge looked to be enjoying her time just fine, even if the world outside stood ready to burn. But David Ramsay? Friend, that man sobbed through it all.

-6-

It's hard to say what Medric thought as he walked to those doors. What's in a man's mind when he knows he's about to cast off from this world? I may know some of that, if I'm honest, friend. Way things are in the Holler now, I may know indeed. But I've no idea when it comes to Medric Johnston. All I know is Wilson trailed behind whispering this was the end of things, and Medric never said a word otherwise.

The crowd parted like them two'd caught a disease spread by simple nearness. Medric stepped out first. He took in the contempt on Raleigh's face and the hurting rage on Joe Mitchell's, but he could dwell on neither of them long. That burning cross in front of the funeral home held all his attention, and how those flames licked the porch's roof. How those cloaked and hooded men raised their pistols and rifles. How those torches burned in the night under that full moon. It was hate Medric felt, that much is sure. But it wasn't so much the hate he felt himself as it was the hate directed at him.

"You stay right here, Medric," Bucky said. "Don't you move."

"I appreciate that, Bucky, I truly do. But Raleigh means business this time, and we all know it."

"More of us than them," John David said.

"Not with them guns."

Raleigh lifted his chin. "Get on down here, Medric. Wilson, you too."

"Don't do this, Raleigh," Wilson said. "It's the witch we have to fight, not each other."

"You brought the witch. You and Medric and your girl."

Medric took the first step down.

Bucky tried stopping him. "This ain't the way."

"It is, Buck. It's the only way. Raleigh's right. I shot Ruth. Didn't mean to, but that don't matter. I go out there to him, I die. I go back inside, I still die, along with everybody else. I can't do that. You told me we a town. I never believed it, but I guess I do now. So you go on now and let me go. It's what I deserve for killing Ruth and giving Alvaretta what she wanted. Maybe y'all can get out of here and be safe. You do that? You keep everybody safe now."

He walked off then, down the steps slow and one at a time, in no hurry to meet his end. John David said they had to do something, but I think he had as many ideas as Bucky, and by that I mean zero.

"Wilson," Raleigh said. "Come on."

You could smell the gas spread around the church. All it'd take was one of them fifteen men to drop a torch, they'd all be burned alive. Wilson must've known that, because he went on down the steps too and didn't even listen to Bucky's pleading. Medric reached the parking lot first. He waited for Wilson, then they both made their way to Raleigh. Raleigh stepped away like the men in front of him carried a stench.

The pistol in his hand twitched and had started rising up when a voice shouted, "You'll want to hold off on that, Raleigh Jennings."

Raleigh looked up to see Chessie Hodge pushing her way through the crowd. Briar came along behind and then the preacher, looking like he'd just been squashed like a bug.

Scarlett came out last. She saw what was happening and tried to run down the steps for her daddy. Bucky and John David stopped her.

"I love you, Scarlett," Wilson said.

Scarlett shook her head—*Please no.*

"You turn'm loose, Raleigh," Chessie said. She came down those steps like she owned them, Briar too, and neither did not so much as flinch at the guns pointed at them. "You turn'm loose or you face my wrath."

"I'm not your lackey anymore, Chessie," Raleigh said. "You don't get to order me around. I don't see iron in your hand." He raised his voice and added, "Can't carry guns in the Lord's house, and I appreciate you making that rule, David," then lowered and said to Chessie, "That makes you just a plain old woman." He looked at Medric. "You said your prayer yet?"

"Don't you do this, Raleigh," Briar said.

Medric shook his head.

Raleigh smiled. "Good."

Folk will tell you the last thing Medric Johnston ever saw was the barrel of Raleigh's gun pointed at his nose. I'd go further and say the last thing Medric ever saw was the one thing that proved everything he ever thought true of this world. They'd come after him first, he'd told Bucky. And Medric had been right. He heard the trigger pull. By the time the shot rang out, the bullet had already gone in one side of his head and out the other. Medric fell backward onto the lot of the Holy Fire as Chessie and John David cried out. He landed with his arms stretched out at his sides, looking like the cross burning just across the way.

-7-

I told you Briar Hodge was quick on his feet for a man his size. As that night proved, Chessie could move even faster. Too bad it was all for naught.

She'd planted her fist into the side of Raleigh's head before Medric's body could even settle on the pavement. Raleigh spun around with a confused look in his eyes. Chessie hit him again, in the jaw this time and with all her knuckles, and did not flinch at the barrel rising for her. By then Briar had arrived, more bear than man.

John David jumped from the steps and hit the first Circle man he met, knocking him out and snatching his torch in one motion. He screamed for everyone to get out of the church. The rest of the Circle froze as if the world had suddenly gone cockeyed. I wonder just how many of the men under those hoods truly thought Raleigh would commit murder. You ask me, wasn't a doubt at all he would. Ruth Mitchell may have been Joe's wife and may have spent time with Raleigh just so she could feed her family, but aside from Eugenia, Ruthie'd been the only woman Raleigh had ever almost loved.

But once the Circle saw what John David did to one of their

own, they sprang to action. Bucky would later call it a miracle that none of them got it in their heads to light the church or shoot their guns. I guess by then the holy war had come and went. Now was about self-preservation alone. A few turned and ran, their white robes and hoods turning yellow and then orange in the moonlight. More than one, though, chose to fight it out. They jumped on Chessie and Briar, jumped on John David, and that brought Bucky down off the steps to do what he could. Wasn't peacemaking on that man's mind, friend, not that night. Bucky pushed and shoved and punched right along with the rest of them, and so did Landis and Doc Sullivan and Maris, even Belle Ramsay. And our preacher. Oh yes, you can believe Reverend Ramsay scuffled along with the rest. He went not after Raleigh, but the five men who'd set upon his son. Reverend wrestled four of them away and then grabbed the last just as John David landed a blow. The front of the man's hood flew up, revealing Homer Pruitt's face.

Wilson had somehow been left alone in the fight. Scarlett searched for him from her spot near the steps and tried running when she spotted him. Doc Sullivan grabbed her and told her to stay, he'd get the mayor. But Joe Mitchell spotted Wilson first. He got close and raised the pistol in his hand, then fell by Briar's fist.

"Fight or go, Wilson," the big man screamed.

The mayor looked for a place to hide. Doc Sullivan had lost him in the crowd, as had Scarlett. The only one who noticed Wilson at all was the hooded man who'd yet to move from his place in the Circle. He carried no gun, only a torch held close to his hood, and Wilson watched with horror as a fleshless hand raised that hood up, revealing Stu Graves's face. Now the demon walked, coming for Wilson as bodies crashed around it, pulling from beneath its cloak a long rope tied in a noose.

Wilson ran. He looked toward the church steps and saw

Scarlett. Their eyes met. He could not go there. He could not lead Stu to his little girl. He pushed through the edge of the fight to open space and ran for the council building instead.

Raleigh had slipped away from Chessie. She looked but couldn't find him for the blood in her eye. Someone grabbed her from behind, an arm wrapped in Circle man's cloth that ended at a bandaged wrist. Chessie bit down on Tully Wiseman's broken hand, making him squeal. Bucky saw Chessie struggling and wrenched Tully away. The grocery's former butcher scampered off into the throng. Chessie went after him, hollering for Briar and Bucky to follow. Briar did. Bucky never got the chance. He turned to see Raleigh standing not ten feet away. The man's face had gone blue and black with bruises. He raised a bloodied hand and pointed the pistol to Bucky's head.

I asked what lay in a man's mind when he knew he was about to die. I don't know about Medric, friend, but I know what Bucky Vest thought. He thought that all he'd done had not been enough to save his town, that Cordelia and Angela would have to live out the rest of their lives without him, scraping to get by however best they could. But worse would be them knowing that Bucky had failed in his calling, and that was a weight too heavy for him to bear. He could not lift his gun to counter Raleigh. Bucky could not do a thing. He closed his eyes and flinched at the pistol's report, waiting for his body to ignite in pain and his soul to break free of this cold and lonely world.

I swear Bucky felt that bullet go through him. He opened his eyes and felt his chest and stomach, but no part of him had gone missing. Ten feet away Raleigh lay sprawled on his back. Two holes no more than half an inch apart had been put into the center of his chest. John David kept the pistol in his hand pointed to where Raleigh had stood. Raleigh Jennings died with his eyes open to the moon and the empty sky above it. I expect his final thought was he hoped the Lord weren't black.

The sound of the gun scattered what was left of the Brotherhood of the Circle, sending them in every direction. A few of the Circle were never identified. Whole lot of them were. You can bet Chessie Hodge promised to see they all got what they deserved.

Men were running toward the funeral home, where the fire from the cross had spread to the porch and one side. Within the hour, the only remnant left of Medric Johnston's existence in this world would burn to the ground. Belle and Naomi ran for Bucky, along with the Hodges and the Reverend. Landis joined them. John David dropped the gun in his hand. Bucky looked at him and nodded thanks.

The Reverend hollered for more people at the funeral home. Buckets, water, anything they could find. Scarlett asked where her daddy had gone. Chessie sent Briar with her to look. People were breathless, wounded and scared, and yet an eerie calm had settled over the church—the peace after the war.

"Is it over?" Belle asked.

Chessie looked down the way and grumbled, "Think we're about to find out."

From the road that led to Harper's Field came a single headlight. Kayann's Mercedes looked to slow at the edge of town, then gained speed. She parked at the edge of the lot and let everyone spill out. Angela and Kayann ran to where Landis and Bucky had gathered. Cordelia flung herself into her father's arms.

"Hays," Kayann said. "Landis, I saw Hays."

"Where?"

"At Harper's Field. He ran off. Something's wrong with him, Landis. Bucky, you have to find our son before something awful happens."

"We'll find him. John David, you get up to the field, see if he's hiding up there. I'll take Landis and head—"

And that's all Bucky got out, because that's when Mitchell's Exxon exploded and they all learned things weren't over at all.

-8-

He barred the door and heard the clack of the lock swinging home, and yet Wilson knew that wouldn't be enough. No one had followed him to the council building—living or dead—but no way could he allow himself to remain so exposed. He pulled on the door to make sure it wouldn't budge and turned down the long hallway to his office. His key wouldn't work. He fumbled with the ring, making sure it was his office key in his hand and not the one to the T-bird or the house. Tried again. Fingered the lock to make sure it hadn't been tampered with. No, the key wouldn't work.

Wilson cursed. The word echoed down the hall. Outside came the muffled sounds of shouting and fighting—outside was Scarlett—and a part of Wilson must've struggled against the idea that he should be out there with her, fighting for his town. But Crow Holler was Wilson's town no longer. Oh sure, in the eyes of the law it remained his, at least for a little while more. But even if Crow Holler survived the night and Alvaretta and her demon were put down, nothing would ever be the same for Wilson Bickford. There remained Stu's death to answer for. It would be manslaughter at the least, plus whatever other charges of cover-up the district attorney felt a need to tack on. There would be a trial and there would be jail. There would be ruination. Wilson stood to lose everything, but all of that must've paled to losing Scarlett. And I do believe Wilson thought he'd lost her. What else could he think, seeing his own daughter abandon him along with his town? What else could Wilson believe after Scarlett had betrayed his secret to Chessie Hodge?

A sound at the doors out front. Someone pulling the handle, wanting in.

Wilson managed to still his shaking hands enough to plunge the key into the lock. He turned the knob and raced inside, barely missing the desk corner with his knee, and looked through the drawn blinds. No one stood at the doors, but he had a grand view of everybody knocking the snot out of everybody else over in the Holy Fire's parking lot. He heard the gunshot that killed Raleigh Jennings and dropped to the floor. Wilson crawled to the small closet in the corner and eased inside. Stu wouldn't find him. Alvaretta Graves wouldn't win. And do you know why, friend? Because Wilson Bickford was a *survivor.* Always had been.

I guess Wilson would've stayed in there until the Rapture were it not for the Exxon blowing up. Hays had stacked so many crates of moonshine around the pump and inside that store that when everything blew, the shock wave near shattered the windows. Wilson scampered out and raised his head enough to see. The fireball bloomed taller than anything he'd ever seen in his life—yellow and orange and red, rising like a monster to consume them all. From down the hall came the sound of a boot scuffling along the floor.

Wilson ducked again and crawled to the other side of the desk, past the two visitor chairs to the hallway's edge. He went to shut the door and then thought better. He'd been quiet. No way anybody'd know where he'd hidden unless he made a racket like shutting a door. He got down on his belly and peered down the hall.

Nothing looked back at him but the darkness, fuzzy outlines of the other doors and the coatrack at the end of the hall, the watercooler, a wooden table with a lamp on top that didn't work. And then from the darkness grew a moving shadow dressed in white, a hooded man with a hand of bone.

"Leave me alone," he cried. "Do you hear me? I didn't mean to, I didn't mean it didn'tmeanit *go away*."

He crawled back inside and slammed the door, but Wilson knew the futility of it. He did, friend. His town lay burning and his daughter had gone and Wilson had been left alone with no one but the man he'd killed, and even now he could hear Stu's boots stepping down the hallway. Growing closer.

I'll leave it to you to decide if Stu Graves truly met Wilson that night. I'll let you settle on whether what he saw was a demon born of hell or one born of guilt and pain collapsing in on the secret he'd held on to for so long. But I'll tell you this, and you take it as truth—to Wilson, that was Stu and nothing else. And I think that's why he decided what he had to do. Wilson had been the only one Alvaretta had wanted all along. He reached for a pen and a piece of paper from his desk and began writing as the knob on the door began to turn.

-9-

Four crates around the pump, another six inside the store, then the dozen or so jars Hays poured in a wavy line for a fuse to connect them all. He'd briefly considered adding a few more crates against the propane tank out back, but then decided no. Ten felt plenty. He didn't have to think about how to arrange it all. You understand? That kind of destruction didn't need to unfold in Hays's mind as much as it simply needed *uncovering*. Like that mental picture had always been there in some fashion, ever since he'd been a little boy. It was that easy.

He could see the demons thrashing about at the church from his spot between the Exxon and the grocery, whipping themselves into a frenzy. Hell. That's what Hays Foster gazed upon that night. Everyone he knew in the world, all he may not have loved but certainly did like, thrown to madness. He'd stood with the lighter in his hand, flicking the top open and closed as neighbor turned against neighbor. And what I like to imagine went through his mind was it truly had been a curse that had befallen his world, one beyond even the witch's doing. This evil lay deeper and held more power. He saw not the end of everything but how everything would end, if not that night then upon some night long distant. A night much like that one, in fact, when the mass of humankind would extinguish itself not with bombs and drones but clubs and rocks, completing some twisted circle first begun in the dim past. What he saw was hopelessness. There's no other word, friend. That night, Hays Foster had a front row seat on the folly of man.

He flicked the lighter open once more and spun the wheel, sparking the flint. The flame held steady as Hays bent to touch the lighter to the path. Fire traveled in shimmers of pale blue that forked off inside the store and to the pump. There came next a short instant of nothing. And then came everything.

The pump detonated with the light of a hundred suns, taking with it Joe Mitchell's truck and the front of the store. What remained became engulfed by the moonshine's endless burn. The shock wave threw Hays backward hard onto the road, sprawling him. He lifted his head to revelation.

A pillar of fire stretched to the heavens, blocking the moon in reds and oranges in what Hays must have thought was what Moses had seen to lead his people to the Promised Land. That column did not rise straight but tilted behind where Hays lay, toward the grocery. Pointing the way.

He scrambled for Briar's truck as the first of the demons ran toward the fire. Things would have to be quick now. Hays had barely managed to unload the last of the moonshine when the others reached the lot. There were not many. Some had run off, no doubt to wreak their havoc across the countryside. Others made it no further than the burning Exxon, too afraid to continue. And yet the small group of monsters that had pressed on to put an end to Hays Foster possessed the numbers to do just that. He counted thirteen—that unholy number—and even now, their leader shouted Hays's name.

There was little opportunity to arrange things as before. Hays stacked what he could against and beneath the grocery's weakest points, starting in back and working his way forward. For the rest, he had time enough to shatter jars wherever he could.

He had reached the front of the store when the demon stepped through the broken windows. Hays saw it coming and unscrewed the last two jars in his hand, popping the lids so they hissed. He poured the moonshine over his head and body and spun the lighter's wheel.

A voice spoke. "Hays?"

The demon stood just at the doors, dressed as Bucky but not Bucky at all. Its eyes were jaundiced and narrow, his face red, angled in rotting flesh and sores. It smiled rows upon rows of brown, jagged teeth.

"Hays? What are you doing?"

It tried stepping closer. Hays held the lighter to himself. The air inside the grocery had turned thick, sweet from the moonshine's smell.

"You want to put that flame out, son?" the monster said. "It's scaring me a little. Your momma and daddy's outside. Cordelia too. Naomi. Everybody's out there, Hays. They want to make sure you're okay."

"They're not them anymore," Hays said. "You're not you."

"I'm just Bucky. Things is a little mixed up right now is all. It's the witch, Hays. Alvaretta did this."

"Alvaretta saved me. She meant it for loss, but it was gain. I can see all of you now. What you are."

"We're the people you've always known, Hays." Closer. "The people who care what happens here. Now you come on before your momma and daddy can't take waiting anymore and decide to come in here too. I told them I didn't want that. It was too dangerous. But we ain't in no danger here, are we?"

Hays backed away toward the far aisle. The metal of the lighter grew hot in his hand. "You take one more step, I'll burn this whole place down."

"Let it burn, I don't care. Kayann don't. Your daddy. You're what they care for, Hays. Cordy's outside. She's worried. We're all worried."

"She's pregnant," Hays said.

"I know. We'll talk about that later. It'll be fine."

"Won't be a later. Everything's gone."

"Everything's not gone yet."

The monster had pushed him all the way into the aisle now, where the frozen food had once been kept. The fire outside lent the color of dawn to the wreckage around them.

"Come out with me, Hays. We can fix this. I can help you."

He shook his head. "It's too late. The witch already has you. She's made you like her demon."

"That's not true, son." It reached out. "I look just the same. Just like you."

"Get away from me. I mean it."

Hays turned his head to measure the next step and screamed. Another demon had snuck in beside him, hemming Hays in on two sides. Its hand held fire. Hays shrunk away as the monster did the same, its shadowy body trembling. The fire at the Exxon reached the propane tank, bringing a sound of thunder and a flash of light that turned the inside of the grocery from night to noon. Bucky ducked in reflex, but both Hays and the other demon remained still and standing. And in that brief moment, the light allowed Hays to see the demon's body beside him thicken and clear from shadow to a body closed in jeans and a T-shirt. Its face—warped with deep canyons of sores with a hooked nose—looked out from beneath a mop of black hair, and Hays saw there had been nothing beside him at all but his own reflection in a freezer door.

"*No*," he cried.

The lighter fell from his hand. Bucky grabbed Hays by the arm and pulled as the flames caught fuel, spreading like a wave along the floor. They ran hunched together, Hays screaming *No* and *No* again as his mind fractured. Heat singed his hair and clothing. His legs gave way. Bucky picked him up and carried him as the fire spread to either side. The building moaned as it strained and began to give way.

John David, the Reverend, and Landis screamed for them to hurry. Bucky cleared the grocery as the last of the windows blew outward, showering them all in glass and flame. Kayann came running, along with Belle. Naomi struggled to hold Cordelia back. Landis and the others reached safety just as the grocery's roof collapsed upon itself. Sparks and embers lit the sky like fireworks. Chessie and Briar stood guard over Hays as his parents set upon him with more hugs and kisses than that boy had received in all the years before. Angela and Cordelia tended to a shaken Bucky as Crow Holler burned.

The noise from the grocery and the Exxon was too great for anyone to hear Doc Sullivan's shouting. He came up the road running, arms waving, calling to them all. Chessie turned her head and stood as the doctor neared. Briar and then John David too. Tears stained the doctor's face, and he cared not who saw them. His chest heaved from the long run and the grief that engulfed him.

"Everybody come," he said. "Wilson's dead."

-10-

Of Wilson Bickford, friend, I will speak but not dwell. To say too much would cheapen his life and cast a shadow over all he'd done for this town. In him beat the very heart of the Holler. He lived for this people and this land. In the end, he died for them as well. That's why I can neither risk saying too little of what Scarlett and Doc Sullivan found when they walked into the council building searching for her daddy. Saying too little of Wilson's death wouldn't go far enough to describing the pain of it, and how Wilson's final act led to Alvaretta's undoing. So I will say what happened, and nothing more.

It was nearing nine o'clock that night when the Circle arrived at the church, right when the moon began to disappear. By the time Bucky rescued Hays from madness, nearly half the moon lay in shadow. It remained shrouded still when Bucky, the Reverend, and John David found Scarlett slumped under her daddy's body. In her despair, she hadn't even loosed Wilson from the lamp cord stretched between his neck and the light fixture in the high ceiling. A toppled chair lay nearby, along with a piece of paper. Scarlett wrapped herself around one of Wilson's dangling legs, kissing the knee as she begged *Forgive me* through her tears and *Please come back*, mouthing it all in silence. John David and the Reverend went to her. Bucky could not bear the sight and so settled his eyes on the paper instead. He picked it up and studied the three words Wilson left behind.

Doc Sullivan and Briar tended to the body, wrapping Wilson

in the curtain from his office before placing him in the back of Belle Ramsay's Jeep. They would take the remains to the clinic, where Ruth Mitchell already lay. Briar stopped long enough to lay Medric's and Raleigh's bodies in the bed of his truck. The funeral home was gone by then, as was the Exxon and most of the grocery. Crow Holler lay in a fog of smoke and ash. No one called Mattingly or Camden. By the time fire trucks could get up the mountain, wouldn't nothing be left anyway.

I don't know what made John David speak some time later, whether he tried to find some blessing in the midst of all that destruction or he merely wished it so, but he looked at the others and said, "There may come a peace now."

They were all huddled in front of the council building—Chessie, the Vests, the Reverend and Belle. Landis remained with them, though Kayann had taken Hays inside the church with Cordelia and Naomi. Chessie stood away from the rest, cradling Scarlett as though the girl was her own. Of the six there, only Angela had survived the night without wounds.

"Don't get what you're saying, John David," Landis said.

"Alvaretta got what she wanted. Town's gone, or at least the town we knew. The man who killed Stu"—he glanced at Scarlett, who hadn't seemed to hear—"is gone. She hears of this, maybe she'll live with the balance and let us do the same."

Belle said, "One of the men who killed Stu is gone," leaving the Reverend to dip his head.

Bucky stood with his back to them all, looking out to where smoke from the funeral home rose over the church. He said, "There won't come a peace. Not ever."

"Don't say that, Bucky," Angela said.

Bucky reached into his pocket and unfolded the paper. He showed them all the three words written in the mayor's hand:

Stu was here

"Found this with Wilson," Bucky said. "I won't ever believe

he could do something so horrible as kill himself. Stu Graves did it, or what part of Stu that Alvaretta rose up. So there will come no peace, John David. Not until Alvaretta sees justice and Stu's put back down and kept there. We don't do that, all this will happen again. Sometime, somehow, Alvaretta will be back for more. Light and dark can't mix, just like the Reverend said."

"What are you saying, Buck?" the Reverend asked.

"I'm saying time's come to end this, one way or the other. We're going to the mountain. John David and me." He looked at his constable. "If you've a mind, that is. You're released from my care, John David. Consider your time served. You want to stay here, I've no ill will."

John David shook his head. "You go up there, Bucky—"

"Wilson's my friend."

The Reverend looked at him. "We all got friends, Buck."

"I don't."

"You do," John David said. "I'll go."

"Briar and me as well," Chessie said. "You'll need people who know how to shoot, Buck. No tellin' what the witch's got waiting up there. I'll get John David to drive me to the clinic. I expect Doc will need to come, too, assumin' you can trust him. He knows the lay of that land, and he's got skills we'll need."

David Ramsay kept silent. I don't reckon anybody figured on him going along. Why would he, knowing Alvaretta would seek his death right along with Wilson's? And yet it was not his own self the Reverend considered right then, but his boy. John David had gone off to war and come back a shadow of the man he'd been. Now he'd be off to fight another, and what would be left of him then?

He said, "I'll meet the witch before she meets me. I will not live in fear."

Chessie and John David left then, saying they would all meet at the end of Alvaretta's lane. Landis and the Reverend walked to the church to tell their families. Angela pulled Bucky aside and gripped his arm.

"You kill her, Bucky," she said. "Not Chessie or Briar or John David. Make sure it's you."

And then Angela smiled in a way that made Bucky tremble. He would return to Campbell's Mountain, face the witch and her demon once more, and yet Angela held less for her husband than for the boasting she could make that her husband had felled the witch. Angela kissed his cheek and walked toward the church, saying she wanted to look in on Cordelia and Hays. The Reverend and Landis followed to say their good-byes. Bucky stood alone, wanting to follow Angela but knowing he could not. He would not say good-bye to his daughter. He would wait until it was over, and then tell Cordelia hello. She would understand. She would have to.

He turned around to see Scarlett standing alone. She reached into a pocket and pulled out her little pad and a pen and held what she wrote to the pale moonlight.

Don't go

"I have to. I'm tired of all this suffering, Scarlett. Yours, your daddy's. Everybody's. Witch hurt my Cordelia. Stole this town from us. Alvaretta's got nothing left to hurt me with. She's already done all she can."

She'll kill you

"She can't," Bucky said, "because I'm not saying bye to Cordelia."

He walked to Scarlett and gave her the very sort of hug she would never again receive from a father. Then Bucky took the pen from her hand and scribbled something just beneath *She'll kill you.*

"But just in case, you call this number if we don't come back."

X V

Blood moon. Scarlett calls Jake.
To the mountain. The battle. Alvaretta's end.

-1-

Bucky escorted Scarlett over to the church. He had his arm around her the whole way, kept telling her how bad he felt and sorry he was. She shuddered against him, silent but for her stumbling steps. They'd all descended upon Scarlett, you know. Once Bucky and John David had found her and everybody else had run down from the grocery, all they wanted to do was wrap Scarlett in their arms and tell her how sorry they were. It's a horrible thing if you think about it. Scarlett Bickford was finally being seen, and she had her dead daddy to thank for it.

"He did it for you," Bucky said. "Don't you ever forget that. He thought that was the only way to rid us of Alvaretta Graves. Your daddy died trying to take away the sins of this town."

But that made her grieve all the more.

He walked her up the steps, meaning to leave her there, but the sight of Scarlett's torment wouldn't allow Bucky that benefit. And there was this too: Chances were good Stu Graves had made it back to Campbell's Mountain by then, but that didn't mean things in Crow Holler were safe. There were demons other than Alvaretta's loose that night, monsters of flesh and blood rather than spirit, and maybe not all of them had scurried home to hide their robes and hoods.

"You need to go on inside," Bucky said. "Angela and Belle will care for you. Time I go on and try to set things right, Scarlett. Okay?"

A line of townfolk with pails and hoses worked to keep the fire at the funeral home from spreading. After a final hug, Bucky eased open the church doors just enough to let Scarlett through. It was enough for him to see Angela talking to Cordelia near the altar. A glimpse of his family, all Bucky would allow, because to dwell on the two of them standing there in embrace seemed to Bucky a token of doom that would spill over them all in the next hours. He stepped away in silence and took the steps back down, making that slow walk to a car that would drive him into what remained of his future.

He pulled away and cast one final look at the church. Cordelia stood at the top of the steps beside Scarlett. The flames from the funeral parlor lit upon her face, and Bucky could see his daughter's anguish. They exchanged a small wave. It was the same one that they'd shared so many times before, when Bucky left for his work at the dump or Cordy left with Scarlett and Naomi for a Friday night football game at the high school. A flick of his fingers; a twist of her hand; an unspoken promise between them that said *I'm leaving, but only for a bit.*

But neither Bucky nor Cordelia thought that was true. Not this time, friend. Didn't matter who Bucky took with him to face the witch one final time. Didn't matter it was two hardened criminals and a father bent on revenge, a doctor, a holy man. Didn't matter it was a man who'd seen the worst of war and so had lost the best of himself. None of them would return. Those leaving from the Holler to Campbell's Mountain maybe had might and faith and the Lord on their side, but Alvaretta's might was greater. All you'd need to understand that was to look out from where Cordelia and Scarlett stood at the top of those steps, seen those burning buildings, and heard the shouts of men and women scrambling to save what couldn't be saved. You would've known Alvaretta's power then. You would've felt that hopelessness.

Cordelia watched Bucky's taillights fade in the distance. She turned her face to the sky. Sun and moon and earth fell into perfect line, leaving what looked like a bloody lantern hanging over the night, and all she could do was turn and walk back inside.

Scarlett let her go. She could hear the wailing inside the church. Belle and Naomi by the sound of it, reacting to where the Reverend had told them he would go. Cordelia cracked the door enough to see inside. The preacher stood in the middle of a family hug. Naomi begged him not to go with such feeling that it made her tremors even worse. She looked like a spring wound too tight and ready to pop. Scarlett could have told her friend that no amount of begging would work. It hadn't with Bucky, it wouldn't with David Ramsay. I don't doubt begging wouldn't've changed the mind of Landis Foster, neither. Kayann didn't even try to talk him into staying, though that may have been because she was too busy keeping her son still and quiet in his pew. Hays kept speaking of how they were all monsters underneath and so was he, and I guess the only thing that kept somebody from telling him to shut up was he'd fallen to whispering it. Kayann had never looked so stricken.

Landis walked out without even a good-bye and passed Scarlett as if she were a ghost. Bucky might've thought he'd almost lost his family since the witch lashed out, but friend, I'm here to say Landis Foster truly had lost his. He'd lost his wife and son all on the same night, and all that remained for him was the pound of flesh he would extract from Alvaretta Graves. The Reverend followed. His eyes were low to the ground as though in prayer, though Scarlett knew better. It was not the Lord that David Ramsay had given his soul over to, it was his own judgment.

The church doors closed. Scarlett turned on the steps. The dirt streets were crowded with people running from the funeral home to the Exxon, from the Exxon to the grocery. Scarlett raised her arms and began waving, trying to get someone's attention. She stood in the middle of absolute chaos, friend, and yet that girl had never felt so alone. The witch had taken Cordelia's beauty because beauty was all Cordy believed she had. She'd taken Naomi's control over her own body because that's what Naomi coveted. Alvaretta had given Hays what he most feared—the ability to see the monsters of this world. But I believe Scarlett understood then that the witch had stolen her voice for a different reason than she'd stolen from all the others. Alvaretta had silenced her for the simple reason that Scarlett had never found the strength to speak up and make herself known. The witch had simply taken what Scarlett had never used anyway. For that, I suppose you could say that girl had always been cursed, and by her own power.

She gripped the pad of paper with one hand and pulled her cell phone out with the other. The numbers were easy to read in the glow of all that firelight. Scarlett punched them one by one, slowing herself to dial right and summon the strength to speak. She held the phone to her ear as more men raced past. Someone screamed that the funeral home was about to cave in.

The line rang.

Scarlett could barely breathe, much less produce a sound.

Two rings. Three. Then the sound of Jake Barnett's tired voice: "Hello?"

"Hhhhhha." She squeezed her eyes shut and bore down on her throat and chest.

"Hello?"

"Hhhhhha."

"Who's this?"

"Hhhhelp," Scarlett whispered. And then she began to cry.

-2-

They all met at the end of Alvaretta's lane—Bucky and John David, Chessie and Briar, the Reverend, Doc Sullivan, and Landis—each as quiet as they could be inside that cut in the trees. Briar lowered the tailgate on his truck and pushed back the thick blanket he'd laid inside.

"Pick what you want," he said. "Just make sure you can handle what you take. Plenty of ammo for it all."

The Hodges began loading shells into their shotguns. Doc refused to carry anything but his own good intentions, saying he'd come to make sure nobody was killed rather than do the killing. Chessie looked at him and shook her head. She grabbed two pistols from the blanket and handed them to John David.

"Don't like guns," he said.

"Maybe, but they sure got a fondness for you."

The Reverend reached for the guns instead. He took them from Chessie's hands and loaded the clips with the steady movements of a professional, pulling back the slides to chamber the first rounds. "My son doesn't have to carry if that's his wish," he said. "Don't you worry about things, Chessie. I'll be with him."

John David looked to protest. But then he met the Reverend's eyes, and what lay there was not the patronizing gaze of a man who'd come to believe his son a disgrace, but a look of near equality. Whether John David had risen to his father's level in the last hours or the Reverend had sunk to his son's, I don't know. But to this day, I believe that was as close to an apology as the preacher had ever given.

Landis went next. He reached for the biggest gun Briar had brought, a full-on assault rifle like the ones John David had used in the war. Chessie slapped his hand away and handed him another scatter-gun.

"You're too worked up, Landis," she said. "We all are, but

you most. You take something like that down there, you're apt to kill us all before Alvaretta gets the chance."

Bucky took the machine gun instead, along with four extra magazines. When Chessie told Bucky maybe he should leave that alone, Bucky told her an automatic rifle was about as illegal as a thing could be and so he had to confiscate it for about an hour. He assured her he'd have no problem handling such a weapon. John David had to show him how to load it.

Everything ready and nothing more to do, the eight of them gathered in a circle for the Reverend's blessing. Even John David dipped his head. He knew things would turn bad. I reckon they all did.

Bucky said, "I don't want all of us rolling up on there at once and scaring her. We'll have to walk it. Quiet and slow until we get there, then we take her by surprise. And we take the witch alive. I need y'all to understand that. You're all acting deputies here, not a lynch mob. Landis? You hear me? Whatever that woman's conjured we'll send back to hell, but Alvaretta lives to face trial."

The group set off then, aiming for the middle of the narrow lane and wary of the woods to either side, where the darkness looked thicker and even alive. Over their heads the blood moon stood, and you can bet each of them glanced skyward to behold the terribleness of how that looked. To this day, you'll hear folk in Crow Holler speak of the blood moon, and how it'd been a warning for Bucky and the rest to stay away. But it was past late for that. Too many had suffered and died and too many more would if things was left as they were. Wasn't no going back. Not for Bucky or the Reverend, not for Chessie or Landis. Not even for John David. They'd come this far; they'd see the rest through.

The lane began to rise over the hill when they heard the

first scurry in the trees. Landis wheeled his pistol in that direction. He would've fired if John David hadn't pushed him at the last moment. It was a good thing he did. Not only would Landis have let everybody inside of five miles know exactly where they were, he'd've also shot Danny Sullivan square in the face.

"Dogs," Bucky whispered.

Briar nodded. "Heard'm a ways back. They get to wailing, Alvaretta's gonna know."

"Let's get on, then," Chessie said. "More time we stand out here, harder this'll be."

John David hesitated. "It's too late. She knows already."

He pointed on up the hill, where the top carried a glow that resembled the moon but wasn't that exactly—more fire than blood. Bucky led the rest of the way. He had John David to one side and the preacher on the other and felt safe enough, especially with the Hodges at his back. Landis and the doc traveled in the middle. Everyone strung out shoulder to shoulder when they reached the crest of the hill.

Below, stretched out in a half circle at the edge of Alvaretta's yard, burned thirteen torches. The fire lit all that stretch of wood so that nothing could remain hidden in the darkness. Even the solid black shapes of crows hanging off the trees could be seen. The cabin glowed with lantern light and a fire in the hearth. And the witch herself, standing at the open door upon her front porch, with a shotgun in her hands and a pistol tucked in an old brown belt she'd cinched around her vanishing waist. Waiting for them, daring Bucky to cross the wide space between the torches and the cabin, because that would be Alvaretta's killing field.

"Think our element of surprise is gone," John David said. He looked at the Reverend. "Better go on and give me one of those pistols."

-3-

No need for them to hide now, friend. Everybody knew what cards they held, except for whatever ace was up Alvaretta's sleeve inside her cabin. They were out of the witch's range, but that didn't stop Briar and Landis from raising their guns as the group descended the hill. The trees came alive. Alvaretta's dogs clamored, and those dead birds set to swaying in wind that never stills on that ridgetop. It looked like the forest itself had joined the fight on the witch's side. A mongrel mutt eased its way from the trees and growled deep and long at Chessie. She tried kicking it away. Her foot missed but sent the creature back into the darkness.

Alvaretta remained quiet on the porch, some sixty feet away. No farther than pitcher to catcher is how the Reverend described it later, and then he said he'd never been so close to the devil. Her shotgun was nearly as long as she was tall, and yet the witch's arms did not shake from the weight. She kept her legs spread just past shoulder width and her head still. Angela's bracelet glimmered on her wrist.

Bucky stopped them at the torches. He took a step toward the witch and yelled, "Alvaretta Graves, this is the sheriff. Throw down your arms."

Alvaretta did just the opposite. She brought the shotgun up and the barrel toward Bucky's chest. Bucky returned the favor. All you heard was clicks—everyone at Bucky's left and right, kicking off the safeties on their guns.

"Told you not to come back," the witch hollered. "Knew you would. 'Tis a blood moon this night. Blood calls for blood, always has. Turn tail, Sheriff Bucky Vest. Leave this mountain. I'll warn you onced and only."

"I won't leave without what I come for," Bucky said. "I know who you hide, Alvaretta. You go on and bring him out."

"He's mine. You won't have him."

"I can and I will, and I'll do the same with you. Your time's over now. Too many's been hurt."

Alvaretta racked her gun. She stared at Danny. "You come with them, man from town? Was it you betrayed me?"

"This doesn't have to end badly, Ms. Graves," the doctor hollered. "You cooperate, it'll turn out best."

"Shoulda kilt you when I had the chance. Shoulda kilt you all."

"You'll answer for what you did," Landis screamed. "You ruined my boy."

"Cain't roon what's already spoilt," Alvaretta said. "That's what ye are—spoilt. Rot of the earth. Now turn and get on or feel my power, it makes no difference."

The Reverend slid in behind Briar, as far from Alvaretta's eyes as he could manage. Yet now he came forth into the torch-light with his gun tucked in his belt and his two arms high, and the witch saw him and knew him. She spat at the ground and swung the barrel to the preacher's face. John David lurched forward in front of his father. He leveled the pistol at Alvaretta and shouted *No*.

"I see your face, David Ramsay," she said. "I'll have your heart. You took mine. You and Wilson Bickford, the night you took Stu. Bring Wilson to me, the rest can go."

"You've *taken* Wilson," Bucky said. "Wilson was my *friend*. Now bring him out here."

"He's mine."

"Bring him out."

She whistled low against the breeze in a tune none of them had neither heard nor believed could exist. The shadows beyond the firelight began to harden and move. One by one, Alvaretta's beasts crept from the trees. They came around the side of the cabin to where the porch stood and from the edge of the shed into the open. They came behind Bucky and the rest, turning

Briar and Chessie both. Heads low to the ground, hackles as straight and hard as razors, teeth bared such that you could see the slobber dripping from their maws.

"You'll not leave this place," she said.

Landis tried backing off but found the way blocked by what looked like a retriever mixed with coyote. One eye had been gouged away, but the other saw him clear. The dog barked hard, making Landis jump and Alvaretta cackle. Landis turned to where she stood and saw a shadow move beyond a drawn curtain in one of the front windows.

What Landis did next, he did for his boy.

-4-

Bucky saw that shadow, too, and how big it looked against the window. He watched Landis's face go stiff and felt his own slacken at the understanding of what was about to happen. And it was the worst thing that could happen, friend. They were armed, sure. And with John David and both Hodges, they were as capable as any posse you'd find in Crow Holler. But no amount of bullets and right could change the fact they were trapped by light in a wide open space with Alvaretta occupying the high ground, and they were surrounded by thirty wild and angry dogs.

But none of that played a part in Landis Foster's thinking. Only thing that man heard was the witch's taunts, and all he seen was her demon standing in the window. He saw his shot and took it, and there's no way you or I can blame him for that.

Alvaretta must've seen his finger settling down on the trigger, because right then she screamed and raised to fire. Landis emptied half his gun into that window, sending glass onto the porch and the dogs below. The spray knocked the witch's aim off just enough to send her shot wide into the trees. The shadow inside took off. Briar chased it with shots of his own while Chessie and the Reverend took aim at Alvaretta. She swung her shotgun their way and pulled. Fire leaped from the barrel.

"Eat," she cried to her children. *"Eat."*

Dogs pounced from all sides. Chessie got the first two, though she needed four shots and there were six more of the beasts right behind. Briar shot as fast as he could, as did the Reverend. Yet the more Alvaretta's holler erupted to gunfire, the hungrier her beasts became. Bucky aimed that army rifle to one animal and then another, yet his finger froze on the trigger. John David shot two. The third snuck behind and leaped, barking as it did. He spun too late. John David's world became nothing more than a black mouth with white fangs before the dog's head exploded in a shower of blood. The monster fell limp to the ground. Reverend Ramsay stood with his gun pointed not a foot from his son's head. He'd tell Belle later was a miracle he hit that dog and not John David, so bad his hand shook.

The dogs had backed them into a tight knot, and there is where Alvaretta aimed. She emptied her shotgun and cared not if she hit human or animal. Briar returned fire and missed. Landis ran for the porch. Whether to get away from the dogs or to rush the witch, I can't say. All I can tell you is Alvaretta saw his approach and grinned as she leveled her gun. Bucky ran for Landis, pushing him aside as the gun boomed. Buckshot lit his shoulder and part of his face afire. Bucky cried out and took a single step to his right when he heard the sharp sound of metal springing and the crunching sound of bone. The world went all bright colors and searing pain. Bucky wailed as the jaws of the bear trap Alvaretta had hidden in the scrub and grass devoured his leg. Four dogs set upon him. Landis shot one, John David and Chessie the others.

The witch threw her scatter-gun down and yanked the pistol from her belt. As soon as Bucky saw that long barrel in the blood moon's eerie glow, he knew that gun was his own. He had no time to call a warning. Alvaretta took aim at the only person she truly wanted to kill that night and pulled the trigger. The gun's kick would've knocked her off her feet were it not that it slammed her backward into the wall. A shot like cannon fire boomed over the holler. The Reverend's head snapped backward. He spun and fell at Briar's feet, clutching the bullet hole through his shoulder. Briar fought off the advancing dogs as the doc tried to stanch the wound.

John David yelled, "We have to get out of here," but there was nowhere to go. Twenty or so of Alvaretta's children remained, and while half of those had retreated, the other half pressed in to cut off any escape. The Reverend couldn't be moved, nor could Bucky until his leg could be freed. Strange as it is to say, the only safe place on Campbell's Mountain was inside Alvaretta's cabin. Bucky must've figured this. Either that, or some part of him he'd always hoped existed but was always afraid to know awoke. I expect it was just as John David told Cordelia about war—you don't think of good and evil in battle, you think only of your friends.

He raised his body and wrenched free the anchor chain from where Alvaretta had stuck it into the hard ground. Blood poured from the holes the steel teeth had carved between his ankle and knee. He staggered, lifting the rifle as he dragged all forty pounds of that trap toward the cabin, deaf and blind to the screams and barks around him.

-5-

For the first time in memory, Alvaretta Graves gave herself over not to the hate that had fueled the evening years of her life, but to the fear that had draped those years in shadow. The man stumbling for her had a rage-filled look in his eyes. Something had come upon him, a devilry Alvaretta could not comprehend. The bumbling fat man who had days before turned tail off the mountain with his own waste staining his pants now came forth like one who could not die. Like one eternal.

Most of her children lay dead or wounded. Others had scampered. A few, the hungriest, remained, and yet they could only fight off some of the intruders. This one—the Bucky Vest—would not be stopped by them. And so that fell to her.

All those years on the mountain, all that life she'd scraped and bled for, only to have this man try to take it away? Try to take her secret? Rape her hope as the man who'd called himself Wally had tried to rape her body after her Stu had been killed? No. *No*, she thought. The scrap of land upon which she'd made her stand may have been poisoned and unholy, but it and all it contained was hers and hers alone, and she would protect it even unto death.

She turned her face to the curtained window long enough to see the shadow inside. In that small glance, Alvaretta Graves poured what small bit of love still remained hidden inside her. One step to the porch. The clatter of the bear trap being dragged closer pulled her back to all that mattered now. Her children howled in pain and death as gunshots rang out, and yet time itself now slowed for the witch just as it had for Bucky. She leveled the pistol (*his* pistol, and my, how sweet that was) at the sheriff's head and moved down the steps firing, shooting and shooting again, no longer able to see or keep the gun raised as her elderly body began to fail. One boot landed upon the ground. The other stepped into a puddle of blood and fur. The crippled man (Alvaretta could no longer remember his name) stumbled over the trap that bit into his leg. He fell with a cry of pain that went unnoticed by those who had come with him to kill and steal. Going to him now, her eyes searching the grass and leaves for the other hidden traps. And when Alvaretta looked to Bucky once more, she saw not him but the barrel he pointed at her.

The pistol felt like an anvil in her hand. She tried to raise it but found she could not. Alvaretta could do nothing but gape in a kind of wonder at the flash of orange and yellow light that flowered from that dark tube.

In that brief and final moment, I believe the witch knew she would die protecting what she most loved. That peace came unbidden, yet it came.

-6-

Jake Barnett kept the blue light flashing and parked at the edge of the torches. He eased out and met the distant sound of baying dogs and the coppery smell of blood.

Chessie greeted him. Her cheeks were bruised and cut by then. Doc Sullivan had fashioned a crude bandage around the flab of her left bicep that had already soaked through with blood. He'd shaken his head as he cinched it, telling Chessie there was no way around the rabies shots she would have to get. She talked a long while with the sheriff, explaining as best she could all that had happened and why Jake wouldn't be arresting her that night. Then she turned and faded into the darkness. Looking for Briar, I suppose, who had set off to hunt the last of Alvaretta's hell hounds.

Jake watched her go and eased his way through the ring of torches toward the porch. He spotted two bear traps hidden in the leaves and stepped wide of the body, offering it only a glancing look. The bedsheet Doc Sullivan had found and draped over the body was worn so thin you could see the flesh he'd meant to cover. A single gnarled hand jutted out, exposing a thin wrist and the diamond bracelet clasped around it. Dozens of rusty blotches littered the body.

Bucky didn't see him, nor did he look to feel the bow in the boards as Jake took the steps. Two men sat slumped at a wooden table inside. Both were bleeding and silent.

"Hey, Buck."

"Jake."

It was barely a whisper, that word, and yet enough to tremble the fat that hung from Bucky's chin. His uniform had been rendered filthy despite its newness, as was the star on his chest. He ran a hand down the machine gun draped across his lap.

Jake sat, wincing at Bucky's mangled knee. Doc had done all he could with that, wrapping it tight. Said Bucky would have to get to a hospital soon or else risk losing that leg from the knee down, but Bucky had refused to go.

"You okay?" Jake asked.

"See her hand, Jake?"

Jake looked out into the yard. "I do."

"I think it moved a minute ago."

"Don't think so, Bucky. She's gone."

"Scarlett call you?"

"She did."

He smiled a little. "She tell you the witch come for her? For us all?"

"I talked to Chessie coming in. She told me most everything. Who got her, Buck? I need to know who it was."

Bucky looked over his shoulder to the men at Alvaretta's table. "Gonna have to get them outta here soon," Bucky said. "Take too long for the ambulance to get up here and then to Stanley. Belle and Maris, they'll take 'em. I expect Kayann'll want to stay with Hays. Chessie's gonna have to get that arm looked at. That dog took a chunk—"

"Bucky? I need to know what's inside there."

"I don't know, Jake." He breathed deep, let it out slow. "Something. Once Alvaretta fell, her dogs scattered. Briar tended to the Reverend while Danny tried to get that bear trap off me. After that, we all went after Stu. John David and Chessie took these steps hard. Had to. If any of us would've slowed even a little, we mighta found out we were too scared to go on. Chessie started firing soon as she hit the door, just in case he was still by that window. Tore the whole place up. But he wasn't there.

"We got to looking around. There's a door off from where we found her bedroom. Wasn't no lock on it—I mean, why would the witch need to lock anything, you know? We heard something in there and crouched down. John David busted in. That's where we found him. He's still in there. Guess he's gonna need help as much as Landis and the preacher."

John David came around the side of the house. His gun rested in a shaky hand, but that calmness still covered his face. He took the steps up and nodded to Jake, who nodded back. To Bucky, he said, "All clear."

"I'm gonna have to take Jake inside," Bucky said. "Let him see. You sit out here, John David? Keep an eye on Alvaretta for me?"

"How's Daddy?"

"Doc says he'll be okay. Bullet went through."

"Then I'll sit here."

Jake helped Bucky stand and then supported him as he limped inside. When they reached the door, John David said, "Buck? I ain't cold no more."

Bucky turned to look at him. And even though he had no idea what John David meant by that and would only when Scarlett told him later of their talk on the back porch some nights before, he said, "That's fine, John David. I'm glad you ain't cold."

The inside of that cabin was tiny. Barely big enough for one, but I reckon that's all the space Alvaretta ever needed. Jake spoke with Landis and David long enough to ask what they needed. Neither man answered. Shock, you see. Not just from what the night had brought, but from what they'd found in the after. Bucky took him to the far wall where Danny Sullivan waited by the shut door. He told Bucky again he'd have to call an ambulance. Bucky said wait and introduced Jake.

"Anything?" Bucky asked.

The doctor shook his head. "Not for a while now. Best thing, Sheriff Barnett, is to go slow and quiet. I don't know what's in his mind."

Jake thumbed the button on his holster as Bucky eased the door open.

That room was probably no bigger'n the closet you keep your clothes in, friend. One plain bed without a sheet, one little table, nothing more. A lantern's flame gave enough light to step inside. Jake stepped in and said, "Lord have mercy."

The walls were covered with the same markings Cordelia and her friends had found that first day, pictures and symbols that looked as some ancient language. More crows hung from string tied around nails hammered into the ceiling—five of them, Jake counted. On the table beside the lantern sat three pieces of chalk and a small pile of feathers.

Bucky staggered in behind. His head leaned to the left as he peered at the dark space on the other side of the bed. He held his rifle tight and said, "Come out of there. Do it slow, and we won't harm you."

Jake grabbed for his pistol as the demon raised a dirt-crusted hand atop the mattress. Another hand, this just as stained and leathered, came up beside it. The bed creaked as the thing behind it pushed itself up, revealing first a tangled mop of black hair; two wide and unblinking eyes; the patchwork of an unkempt beard; thin, weakened arms; a pair of overalls, faded and worn to the thickness of paper. He stood slow and kept his hands close to his chest.

"Who is this, Bucky?" Jake asked. "What's your name, son? Can you tell me that?"

"He can't understand you, Sheriff," Danny said. "I've tried. He can speak so far as I can tell, but there's something . . . wrong. Some sort of deficiency."

The boy—if I can call it that—looked near John David's age. Younger or older, I couldn't tell you.

"I think he's hers," Bucky whispered. "I think that's Alvaretta's boy. She must've been in the family way when Stu died. Nobody ever knew it." He shook his head and said again, "Nobody ever knew it."

Jake took his hand away from his gun and tried stepping forward. The boy lashed out a fist and backed against the wall. He looked as wild as Alvaretta's dogs.

"Those markings," Bucky said, "the crows. They wasn't Alvaretta's dark magic, it was just her boy . . . I don't know. Playing, I guess. Trying to make sense of his world. Alvaretta said we couldn't have him. We were talking about Stu, but she thought we'd come for her boy. Jake, she thought we were gonna do to him what Wilson and David did to her husband." He heaved a breath that caught on tears. "She was only protecting her child."

Jake looked at the doctor. "You didn't know?"

"Never saw him. I never brought anything here for a child, Sheriff. I give my word on that."

"You ever talk to her? Tell her of Wilson and David?"

"We spoke, but never too much," Danny said. "I had no idea of what Wilson and David had done until tonight."

"Then how did Alvaretta know they killed Stu? How'd she know their kids?"

"I don't know."

"She had power," Bucky said. "Maybe not the power we thought she had, but I don't know how else. Danny didn't tell her, that don't mean nobody did. She told me a demon come by, and it hadn't been the first."

The boy pushed away from the wall and made a shooing motion with his hands.

"Any missing person reports you remember from twenty years or so ago, Buck?"

Bucky shook his head. "Ain't nobody missing, Jake. Ain't nothing here. Just this cabin and a shed that's burned down, bunch of footprints outside nobody can figure. And a grave in the woods out back. Briar found it. There's a cross carved there. Says only *Stuart*."

XVI

The demon

There's where I'll leave things, friend. I'd say more, but we ain't got the time. It's getting dark out, and you best be leaving. Wasn't long back the night was safe for me and mine. Things keep as they are, the day won't be much better.

Way I heard it, there wasn't a sadder sight to see than Jake and the doc taking Alvaretta's boy away from the only place he'd ever known. He had no idea what they were doing to him. Kept screaming the same nonsense word over and over that everybody there took as *Momma*, even if nobody knew for sure. At least John David had the presence of mind to move Alvaretta's body before the boy saw it. No telling what would've happened then.

Didn't matter if Crow Holler wanted any outside law or not, they surely got plenty of it that night. Not just Jake, but all the staties he could muster out of Stanley too. They descended upon that little cabin on the mountain if for no other reason than to see what happened for themselves. A car arrived past midnight to take the last remnant of the Graves family away. Bucky let him take the dead crow he clutched in his hand.

I heard they put the boy in the hospital for a good while. They cleaned him up and got him fed, but he never said no more than nonsense. Doctors never did get a name. About eight months back, he run off. He was up to the nervous hospital in Stanley by then. I don't know how he did that, but I know he broke one guard's nose and another's kneecap before he disappeared on the other side of that fence. Nobody ever did find him, and nobody knows where he's gone. But I'll say there's a light on at night out at that old cabin again, and on a cold day you can see smoke rising from the chimney. Could be anybody in there, I guess. Don't nobody go up there to make sure. Bucky says he better not catch anybody on the mountain, and he means it.

Speaking of Bucky, he was among the little group of Chessie, Landis, and the Reverend who rode away from the mountain inside an ambulance. Bucky was also the only one handcuffed. That's how he wanted it. He told Jake what he'd done turned was wrong—killing an old woman who was just trying to protect her son. Ol' Jake didn't see things that way, and not just because Briar and Landis looked ready to put a bullet in him when he took those cuffs out. But Jake went on and did what Bucky wanted, if only so he'd get on to the hospital and see to that mangled leg.

By then everyone else had arrived—Angela and Cordelia, Naomi and Belle, Maris. Only Kayann remained behind to look after both Hays and a grieving Scarlett. Cordelia got to hug her daddy again. That alone let Bucky leave with a smile on his face, because it meant the trouble really was over. Angela, she was smiling too. She wears that smile still. And don't you think that woman doesn't take every opportunity to remind us all Bucky was the one to put down the witch, because she does. Guess that means Angela's somebody now. More power to her's what I say.

That's how the night of the blood moon ended, friend. But that's not how *everything* ended. That's what I been trying to tell you. What's gone on here is still happening, and it's worse. Bucky killed Alvaretta, that's all I know. Then things were fine for a while, and then . . . I don't know where it all went wrong after that. If it started when Doc and Maris Sullivan left this holler never to return, or when Bucky was let off on self-defense for shooting the witch, or when John David got elected sheriff. I don't know. Some things you can't see coming, even when they're right on top of you.

Now look there. Doors on the church just opened up. I . . .

. . . just sit here a minute. Maybe . . .

That's the Reverend on the steps there.

We have to . . . yeah, we gotta get going. I don't think . . . wait, there's Belle. Naomi too. You see the way she's standing? Still as can be. Naomi, she got fixed somehow. They all did, all but Cordelia anyways. Few weeks after Alvaretta fell, that . . . that *curse* . . . just, I don't know. Left. And let me tell you, that weren't supposed to be.

Here they come. Have mercy, friend, they're here. Just you sit still, I don't think they'll see us right off. Long as they don't see us, we'll be okay. Most the cars come down from the grocery way now. Not many live out where the doc and Maris did anymore, that's all deserted.

Just . . . yeah, that's good. They're all parking over to the other side of the church. You thank your stars you parked here and not closer.

There's Bucky and Angela, getting out over near the steps. They gave up the Celebrity—sheriff's car, remember?—and now they drive that beat-up old Chevy. Angela's got to drive. They saved Bucky's leg I guess, though I don't know how much saving there can be when you got to spend the rest of your life getting around with a cane and a measure of sweat. Limps something awful. Homer Pruitt gave him a new job up to the dump, working the scales. Chessie didn't give Homer a choice in the matter. It was either hire Bucky back or eat that hood and robe John David found stuffed under the Pruitts' sofa the day after the Circle arrived at the church. There comes

Cordelia out the backseat, carrying her little boy. Little Bucky, she calls him. You can say Danny Sullivan was right in his belief that the only curse in Crow Holler lived in them girls' minds. *Mass delusion*, he called it. Maybe that's true. All the girls in town did get healed up all about the same time. Still, I don't guess some sort of mass delusion explains Cordelia's face though, does it? Nosir, I don't think it explains what happened to her at all.

There come the Fosters. Most of them, leastways. Landis and Kayann still got Hays up in the same nervous hospital Alvaretta's boy took off from. He's seen the baby, but I don't know where that'll lead. You ask me, I'm glad that boy's gone.

Chessie and Briar are here. Have mercy, friend, I wish I wouldn't see them tonight. And John David, coming out the council building in his jeans and shirt with that badge on, Scarlett coming out with him, talking his ever-loving ear off. I hear them two are an item now. I hear he ain't cold no more. He ain't cold, and that means trouble. Don't you doubt it, friend. Trouble's in that man's heart.

It wasn't supposed to be this way. You understand?

Come on while they're all busy getting inside. Let's get you out that chair and walk you to your car. Road right there'll take you back to Mattingly. Plenty folk around there'll help you get where you need to go. I wouldn't tell anybody you been up here, though. People's funny that way.

Just help me along some, hand me my cane. Can't get around without it these days. Fancy thing, ain't it? That piece of wood on the end? Won't find nothing like that round here, friend, on that I can guarantee. You'd think it wouldn't grip a thing, but it does. That's it. Come on, then. Oh, these old bones creak. Nothing worse than having yourself wrapped up in such a frail body, but that's what it's come—

Say, what you doing all the way back there? Come on,

friend, I ain't kidding. Wrong people catch us out here, there's gonna be . . .

Oh.

Now wait, wait just a second, you just hang on. Nothing's gonna happen here, so there ain't no need to get all excited. Okay? Plenty things in this old dark world sound like my cane smacking the gravel. Don't mean a thing, hear? Don't mean *noth*—

That . . . no . . . those ain't what you think. Ain't none of this what you *think*.

Okay, sure. It's true. There, I said it. It's true, friend.

But so what if it is? You think of that? So what if this here cane sounds like wood over stone every time I hobble? So what if these old boots don't make a mark in the dirt like yours and I leave a hoof where you leave a shoe, what's that mean in the end? I ain't treated you nothing but good ever since you come up here. I sat here with you and told you all I could. Ain't never once laid a hand to you. Ain't never said a word untoward. I just needed someone to *talk* to. Can't you understand that? And before you go an put the blame to me for all you've heard this day, you remember one thing well: all I did was pick up a gold bracelet I found on the ground and leave it on a doorknob. I didn't do a thing but take a *walk*. That and nothing more. I strolled through Campbell's Mountain on a Saturday night and took another through town the night Ruth Mitchell died, and that's all I did because that's all I had *to do*.

That a crime? I ain't broke no law.

I didn't have to lift a finger to gain this town. Everybody says a devil walked in Crow Holler, but nobody cares to admit they did the devil's work. You call me a demon, fine. That's what I am, and I won't deny it. I am filth and evil and darkness. I am your nightmare. I am the storm that rolls over you and the shadow upon your horizon. I am the creature of hate and violence, but no more than you.

No more than you.

Hays Foster was right. They locked him up and called him crazy, but he was right. There's a monster inside you all, and it's a worse one than I could ever be.

You know how long I been wandering? Ages. Ages. One corner of this sorry world to the next. I endured history before history was made, if you got to know. I watched kingdoms rise and fall that you and no one ever heard of and seen wonders and horrors you can't fathom. Only thing I wanted was a place to settle. To be left alone. And I thought the Holler was just the spot. A people tired and rotting and weary of the world. A people without a will and who would turn upon one another with the slightest nudge. That's what happened. People kept to themselves. That old church went ruined from neglect like it was *supposed* to. And now look at them. They were broken, friend. Not by my hand but by their own.

But then it all went wrong. I don't know how. I don't understand. All I know is every night now they all walk inside that church and hold each other's hands and talk and pray and then . . . and then they . . .

sing.

They *sing*. How can they sing?

Reverend says the time is near for them to take back this town. John David. Chessie. Briar. Don't matter who it is, they all say the *same*. They're one now, can't you see that? Don't you care? They're one now and they say they're coming for *me*, and I'm tired of hiding. I'm so tired. I'm done hiding. I been chased and I been cast out, but I ain't never been afraid. Not until now. Oh yes, I fear them. Told you that at the start, and I'll tell you at the end. I fear what they've become. But that don't matter. You hear me? That don't matter none, friend. Holler's my home now, and I won't leave easy. So let them come. Let Bucky bring his steel and Chessie her iron. Let John David and his daddy try to cast me down.

They want a fight, I'll give them one.

Discussion Questions

1. Early in the story the narrator makes an almost incidental aside that the problem with Christians is that "they see the devil everywhere." Do you agree with this sentiment? Why or why not? Why do some in today's culture see religion as harmful if its theology states the presence of something that personifies evil?

2. Scarlett suggests prayer while she and Cordelia are huddled in the bathroom waiting for the results of Cordy's pregnancy test. The result is positive, a sign that God has answered their prayer the same as He has seemingly answered every prayer that comes out of the Hollow—Sorry. How does this play into the ambivalence toward God displayed by many of the characters? How does this reasoning affect the story as a whole?

3. Given the identity of the narrator as revealed in the final chapter, did you feel any sympathy for him? Did you feel sympathy before discovering what he is?

4. Is Hays right in his belief that there is a monster hidden inside us all?

5. How did Wilson and the town council use Bucky's desire to be sheriff as a means to their own ends?

6. From the beginning of the town's troubles, much of the

focus seems to be on who to hold responsible rather than how best to overcome the curse. Whether God or fate or others, is there a comfort to be found in having someone to blame for our misfortunes?

7. Until the final confrontation at Alvaretta's cabin, opinion is split on how best to return the town to some semblance of normalcy. Wilson simply wants to ignore the curse, hoping it will go away. Reverend Ramsay wants to treat the curse as a spiritual matter alone. Chessie wants to use fists and iron. Which of these would you have preferred if you lived in the Hollow?

8. What was the true nature of the illness that swept through the town's young girls?

9. Who, or what, was Alvaretta Graves? A bitter and paranoid old woman, or something more?

Acknowledgments

I am fortunate enough to have a close group of people around me who are blessed with not only expertise in all things literary but also a tremendous amount of patience to deal with a dumb hick like me. Amanda Bostic, Elizabeth Hudson, Jodi Hughes, and Daisy Hutton—every writer should be so blessed to have you alongside. My agent, Claudia Cross—thanks for letting me bend your ear. Kathy Richards, for allowing me to remain an analog guy in a digital world. And most especially my wife and children, who fill my notebooks with not only strong ideas but hearts and I-love-yous too.

You all make me a much better man than I am.

About the Author

Photograph by Joanne Coffey

Billy Coffey's critically acclaimed books combine rural Southern charm with a vision far beyond the ordinary. He is a regular contributor to several publications, where he writes about faith and life. Billy lives with his wife and two children in Virginia's Blue Ridge Mountains.

Visit him at www.billycoffey.com.
Facebook: billycoffeywriter
Twitter: @billycoffey